# SPIRES *of* STONE

OTHER BOOKS AND AUDIO BOOKS
BY ANNETTE LYON:

*Lost Without You*

*At the Water's Edge*

*House on the Hill*

*At the Journey's End*

# SPIRES of STONE

*A Novel*

Annette Lyon

Covenant Communications, Inc.

Cover image: *City Creek* © Al Rounds. For print information go to www.alrounds.com; *Rebecca's Place in Time* and *The Secret* © William Whitaker. For print information go to www.williamwhitaker.com



Published by Covenant Communications, Inc.
American Fork, Utah



Printed in Canada
First Printing: September 2007

11 10 09 08 07    10 9 8 7 6 5 4 3 2 1

ISBN 978-1-59811-448-5

# ACKNOWLEDGEMENTS

As always, I have to thank my husband and children for their constant support. The longer I write, the more they put up with! My critique group, who I've been with for nearly eight years, continues to be invaluable in both their friendship and evaluations. I also appreciate the association I have with the writers who are part of LDStorymakers for their warmth, friendship, and eagerness to help one another. They help take the solitary nature out of writing as they celebrate one another's successes and find ways to strengthen and improve the LDS writing community.

With my fifth novel being published, I am intensely grateful for being a part of the Covenant family. I feel blessed to work with people who are not only extremely talented but who have embraced me and my writing so warmly. I must express gratitude to the people at Covenant who have helped me and inspired me with their enthusiasm for what I do: Kathy Jenkins, Angela Eschler, Barry Evans, Robby Nichols, and Melissa Dalton. By lending their support and their talents, they have helped me succeed and have made me better than I could be on my own. The graphic designers who have worked on my book covers are some of the most talented you could find anywhere. I love how they've wrapped my "babies" in such beautiful packaging. Thank you all.

While I relied on a large number of resources for this book, I have to acknowledge one of the greatest: the thesis of Wallace Alan Raynor, written about the Salt Lake Temple for Brigham Young University. His research was thorough and fascinating, and I am grateful to have found it. Raynor wrote his thesis at a time when some people who had memories of the temple construction were still living. His interviews with these people—and with some of their posterity—are priceless. Much of the information about the Salt Lake Temple in this novel comes from his work.

Of course, I must nod to the Bard himself for inspiring this book. If he were still alive, I'd thank him for writing one of my favorite stories of all time.

I hope my version does it justice, even though it has some major differences. Fans of the original will note many similarities—especially in the early chapters—but fewer as the book progresses; such delinquency is inevitable when characters come to life and decide on their own how they're going to behave.

Finally, since I wouldn't be where I am without my loyal readers, I couldn't resist including a greeting of sorts to them in this book. While *Spires of Stone* takes place earlier than my previous novels, the setting is one where one of my prior—and, judging by reader feedback, one of my most beloved—characters would have lived in childhood. As a hello and thank-you for their support, I included one scene where that character makes a brief appearance. So when you see ten-year-old Abe running through Salt Lake City, consider it a hello from me!

To the gals who shared my love of the 1993 film version of this story—over and over and over . . .

We've also shared much more through the years, like *way* too many cheese fries, frightening amounts of chocolate, and therapeutic late-night talks. We are women who have, for more years than any of us would like to admit—and with tongue firmly planted in cheek—called ourselves, "The Babes."

And J. J.-Woman, that most definitely includes you.

#  PROLOGUE 

New York City, August 1867

Phillip carefully settled the last of his new photography supplies in the trunks, closed the lids, then secured the latches. He had spent a lot of money—and considerable credit—on the items inside them, plus a few days learning how to use the supplies. It wouldn't be long before he would have his own photography business in downtown Salt Lake City. He already had the newspaper advertisement planned in his mind.

Smoothing his hand along the edge of one trunk, he stood and looked around the empty room that he and his brothers had rented at the inn. They had packed for home and would soon be leaving their mission after twenty-nine months. It didn't feel as if they'd been there that long. Yet in some ways, it seemed a lifetime ago that they'd first arrived. Phillip really didn't want to return to the pre-mission world. Here was purpose and peace. Here he was an elder, nothing more—and even better, nothing less.

He figured his brothers were downstairs getting a bite of supper before they left, so he grabbed his coat and hat to join them. Halfway down the hall another door stood open, and Phillip slowed his step, waiting for it to close so he could continue along the narrow passageway.

A young couple stood close together, and even though the door partially blocked his view of them, Phillip flushed slightly at their intimacy and looked to the floor briefly as he waited for them.

"You will come back soon, won't you?" the woman said, and Phillip suddenly looked up at the sound.

The man kissed her, then answered in a quiet voice, "Of course, Cybil. How could you think otherwise?"

*Cybil?* Phillip's jaw dropped. *The man isn't . . . no, it couldn't be . . .* He had answered so quietly that Phillip couldn't be certain by his voice, and yet . . .

He leaned to get a better look. Could it be his brother Claude, kissing the girl they had just baptized?

"You know I love you," she said. "And after what we've done, you *will* come back? You promise?"

"Shhh . . ." the man said. "Everything will be all right. You can trust me."

At the side of the door, Cybil's blond curls bobbed as she nodded. Phillip's heart hammered in his chest. Between the woman's hair and the man's voice, Phillip no longer had any doubts about the couple's identity. What had they "done"? Phillip's stomach sank as he suspected the answer.

"You don't need to worry about anything," Claude said. He leaned in and kissed her again.

She threw her arms around him and held him tight. "Oh, Claude. Don't go! I can't bear it. I just can't."

He held her for a moment, then gently peeled her arms off him. "I must go. For a while." He kissed the tips of her fingers and smiled at her, then gently eased her back into the room, reaching in and withdrawing his hat from inside as he did so. He blew her a final kiss and closed the door.

Claude set his hat on his head, sighed, and, to Phillip's chagrin, said under his breath, "Glad that's taken care of." He strode purposefully down the hall, whistling as he went, not seeing his brother behind him.

Phillip stood there, stunned, watching him retreat. "Claude?" His brother's heel hit the floor and froze in place.

Claude turned around. Their eyes locked for a moment, Phillip's in confusion and disgust, Claude's in panic. "That's not what it looked like," he said, his hands moving nervously about. "I swear."

Suddenly two men came barreling up the stairs behind Claude—Cybil's brothers. Now, it was Claude's turn to appear shocked. "Hello, Thomas, George," he said, nodding to each of them in turn. "I was just about to come find you to say good-bye."

By the look on Claude's face, he'd had no plans to do any such thing. Thomas, a blond man whose arm was the size of Claude's leg, looked down at him and declared, "I thought you were sticking around to marry my little sister."

"Yes, well, I can't quite do that right now, you see," Claude said, his face so hot he looked as if he might melt into the floor like a crock of butter.

George took a step closer, inching Claude closer to the wall. "You are going to make a lady out of my sister."

Everything the two brothers said to Claude only confirmed Phillip's suspicions. Of course, it was likely no one besides Claude and Cybil knew for sure what had happened between them, but . . . Cybil must have said something her brothers had latched onto.

Squirming under the men's gaze, Claude glanced at their thick hands. Phillip wondered what damage they could do if Thomas and George decided to beat Claude. Two Mormon farm boys would be no match. And Phillip wasn't sure he wanted to defend his brother anyway, though he knew he'd be pulled into the fray.

"You see, gentlemen," Claude stammered, "I have to report to the Church authorities. After that I might be able to return. We could discuss wedding plans then." He tried to smile broadly, but his charms only affected ladies, not harbor workers who'd seen their share of conniving rats over the years.

George pulled his arm back, ready to strike. Claude ducked low, quickly crawling under Thomas's outstretched arm and scrambling down the inn stairs. Phillip swung over the banister and jumped halfway down the stairs in a single leap. Thomas and George let out a bellow and hurled their collective bulk down the stairs after them.

The chase continued to the main floor, where Phillip spied their brother Ben eating at a table. Claude raced across the room, shoving people out of the way and crying, "Ben, Ben!" His brother looked up at the ruckus, confused and startled.

"What's going on?"

Before anyone could explain, Thomas picked up Claude by the scruff of his shirt and turned him around. He punched his face, sending him flying across the room and onto a table—right in Ben's dinner.

Ben jumped to his feet and returned the punch, landing his fist on Thomas's nose. In spite of the man's impressive size, his eyes rolled back and he collapsed to the ground. The room fell silent for just a moment before George cried out, "You don't hit my brother like that, and my sister's going to get what she's entitled to!"

Ben tilted his head in confusion. He leaned toward Phillip, who now stood a few feet away, breathing heavily. "Could you explain what's happening?"

A chorus of shouts went up as men throughout the inn began hitting one another. A few men started for Ben and Phillip. "Tell you later," Phillip said. He nodded toward Claude. "Let's get him—and us—out of here."

In a single motion, Ben hefted Claude's limp form over his shoulder, then shoved one man and punched another in defense so they could get out of the room. They managed to sneak out of the inn, leaving a brawl behind them. They raced down the street as fast as they could while carrying Claude, constantly checking to see if George or Thomas had come after them. Fortunately, Thomas must have remained unconscious, and George must have gotten stuck in the row at the inn, because no one followed.

Ben found a quiet bar a few blocks away. "Let's catch our breath here," he said, slipping inside. "No one will think to find Mormon elders here."

Phillip found a long table in a dark corner. The innkeeper gave them a funny look when he noticed Claude, but gave them permission to lay him out on the table flanked with two long benches.

"Maybe we can pay someone to fetch our luggage so we can still make the seven o'clock train tonight," Ben said, taking a watch out of his pocket.

"I hope so, but it better be someone careful," Phillip answered, thinking of his photography supplies—the glass panes, bottles of fluid, lenses, his tripod. "Definitely no one who's been drinking."

"Agreed."

A few minutes later Claude moaned as Ben washed off a slight cut in his eyebrow. Ben pulled back toward Claude's feet and motioned for Phillip to join him at that end of the table. "What on earth happened in there?" he whispered.

Phillip swallowed hard. He glanced over at Claude, then back at Ben, remembering Claude's words: *It wasn't what it looked like. I swear.*

Technically, Phillip didn't know what had happened. But he could wager a decent guess. He knew what Thomas and George thought had happened. He knew what Cybil wanted from Claude. And he knew that Claude had no intention of coming back to New York.

"Cybil wants to marry Claude." Phillip didn't feel as if he could say more than that, at least not until he sorted things out with Claude. His brother needed to come clean about some things, but it wasn't Phillip's job to tell his secrets—or his sins.

"Should have guessed as much," Ben said.

"Oh?"

"Haven't I taught you well enough?" Ben said with a shake of his head.

"Oh, of course." Phillip laughed. He sat up straight and recited as if he were a pupil, "Most problems in the world boil down to womankind."

With his feet propped on the benches across from him, Ben leaned against the wall, folded his arms, and pulled his hat over his eyes. "Very good, Phillip. You *have* been listening."

Phillip gave his brother's feet a kick, knocking them off the bench. For their entire mission, Ben had been "preaching" such nonsense to his brothers, and it had all started with getting his heart broken by a girl shortly before they left. "You don't really believe that, do you?"

"With all my body, mind, and soul," Ben said, putting his heels back up and giving Phillip a bit of a shove with one boot. "If it weren't for Cybil, we'd be headed west right now. Instead, we're stuck here. Claude's got a black eye, and who knows what kind of damages we'll have to pay the inn. Nope, you can't convince me that women are anything but trouble." Ben closed his eyes again and appeared to be dozing off.

*But it wasn't Cybil who caused the trouble,* Phillip wanted to say. *It was our ornery brother.*

# CHAPTER 1

Salt Lake City, Utah

"They're back!"

Bethany looked up to see her sister Hannah yelling, boots kicking up dust as she ran toward Bethany and the road. Bethany's hat flopped into her eyes as she reached for another onion. She pushed the brim out of the way, yanked the onion from the ground, and tossed it into the basket just as Hannah skidded to a stop beside her.

"*Who* is back?" Bethany asked, standing and beating at her canvas work apron, which had layers of garden dirt on it. Soil also covered her work gloves and arms. Chances were good that it was smeared across her nose, cheeks, and chin, too.

Breathless, Hannah put a hand on her older sister's shoulder to steady herself. For a second Bethany's stomach flipped over itself with worry, but then Hannah broke into a grin. "They're back."

"Yes, you said that already," Bethany said, pulling away from her sister and hefting the full bushel of onions they would be storing in the cellar. She started walking toward the house. "So *who* is back? And from where?"

Still breathing heavily, Hannah stepped backward to keep her face to Bethany's. She jabbed a thumb over her shoulder in the direction of the street. "Look for yourself. They're right behind me."

A glance over Hannah's shoulder revealed three men striding toward the house, side by side. One was nearly a head taller than the others, and even at this distance—a good fifty feet or so—Bethany recognized him.

Benjamin Adams. For over two years she had managed to keep him out of her thoughts. She hadn't counted on his mission back East ending quite yet—if ever. But she supposed it was about time he came back. At the sight of him, a knot formed in her stomach, and she clutched the bushel of onions to her chest. Her lips pressed into a tight line, and her heart pounded with—what?

Anxiety? Yes.

Anticipation? Hardly.

Anger? Absolutely.

Would his mission have softened him, or would the two of them still exchange verbal barbs each time they met? She had never known Ben to be mean or rude to anyone—except her. And she wasn't proud to admit that, when provoked, she could rise to his level of sarcasm just as quickly as he could.

Hannah twirled away and raced to meet the men. Even though Ben was flanked by two others, Bethany could focus only on him. She knew without looking who the others were—Ben's brothers, Phillip on one side and Claude on the other. But her eyes refused to look at either of them, instead seeing only Ben's even gait and broad shoulders, his hat worn slightly askew—and, as he drew closer, the strawberry blond cowlick he had always tried to tame. The cowlick that, in years past, *she* had tried to tame . . .

Her stomach tightened as she waited. What would she say to him and how would she say it?

Hannah's voice broke into her thoughts. "It's *so* good to see you all!" Hannah exclaimed, her face flushed with excitement. But Claude was the only one she was looking at. "I was telling Bethany just the other day that it must be nearly time for you three to come home, wasn't I, Bethany?"

Hannah had said no such thing, but Bethany managed to swallow hard and nod stiffly from where she stood a few feet behind. Her eyes met Ben's. *What is he thinking right now?* He wore that familiar smirk on his face, the one she couldn't get out of her head, the one that could drive a woman mad. She tried to imagine what snide remark was about to come out of his mouth. If only she could get her feet to move, she could escape into the house. The fact that they remained planted on the ground infuriated her.

"I'm so glad you came to visit," Hannah went on, leading them toward Bethany and the house.

"We did promise your father a report," Claude answered with a smile as he followed.

"Yes, you did," Hannah said. Bethany thought she detected a hint of disappointment in Hannah's eyes that Claude had mentioned only their father. Hannah stopped by Bethany so that the men and her sister could exchange greetings.

Ben, still staring at Bethany, cocked his head to one side and opened his mouth to speak. Some foolish put-down, no doubt. She wasn't about to let him score at her expense.

After what he did to her, Bethany had convinced herself that regardless of how valiantly he had served his mission, regardless of how well respected he was in the city, Ben was still the devil incarnate. She would never allow him to weasel himself back into her heart only to break it again.

Refusing to let his presence paralyze her any longer, she thought of a witty greeting and stepped forward to close the gap between them.

But before she managed to utter a word, her foot caught on her dirt-covered hem. For one horrified moment, all she could do was see the inevitable outcome. In a rush, she tripped, the bushel of onions spilling onto the ground with her landing in a heap on top of them. Humiliation burned her face, and she closed her eyes as she got to her hands and knees, dreading having to stand and face Ben's jeers. She didn't have long to wait.

"Still as graceful as a pig, I see."

So the rules of their little game hadn't changed after these two years. What would the people he had preached to have thought of his greeting? She shoved a strand of hair behind her ear and stood, nearly toppling again when her foot landed on a couple of onions, which rolled away. Swiping at her apron and trying hard to keep her chin aloft, she said, "At least I don't have the manners of a pig." She cleared her throat and adjusted her skirt, painfully aware of what a horrid sight she was at the moment.

If only their reunion had been at a dance. Then she would have worn her new organdy dress, with her hair in tight curls. She could have watched Ben squirm by the wall as she glided across the floor on the arm of one dance partner after another. She could toss insults over her shoulder as she walked past him to the refreshment table, and refuse him when he asked her to dance—surely he wouldn't be able to resist asking her.

The corner of Ben's mouth lifted, as if he knew she had won a point in whatever game it was they were playing. With added confidence, Bethany went on before he could answer.

Gesturing at the spilled onions, she said, "A gentleman would not make jokes around a lady, and he certainly wouldn't stand idly by when she was in need of aid."

Ben innocently looked side to side, peered behind Hannah, and finally turned in a circle before saying, "I don't see any lady here. Except dear Hannah, of course." He wrinkled his nose. "I suppose I could be wrong. The stench of your work might be clouding my judgment."

*"Judgment?"* Bethany spat back. "You've never *had* good judgment since the day you were born."

Ben took a step closer and looked down his nose. Bethany stood defiantly several inches below. "That would explain certain elements of the past." He stepped to the side, leaving her paralyzed, eyes stinging. She couldn't quite convince herself that it was because of the onions.

He held out his hand to Hannah. "My, how you've grown while we were away. You were just a girl when we left."

Hannah's eyes darted uneasily from Bethany to Ben, uncomfortable with the exchange and unsure how to respond. She finally smiled and took Ben's hand—and Ben's compliment. "I'm eighteen now."

"Just as I said. A *lady.*" He shot a look at Bethany.

Insides roiling, Bethany turned to Claude and Phillip. "So, *gentlemen,*"—this with a pointed glare at Ben—"come inside and tell us about your mission. Father's in the parlor. I'm sure he'll be pleased as punch to see you again."

She gave a curtsy, avoiding Ben's eyes so she wouldn't scream or try yanking out that cowlick, and turned on her heel. She banged the door shut behind her, leaving the bushel and the mess behind. The family could go without onions this winter for all she cared; she wouldn't give Ben the satisfaction of seeing her crawl in the dirt to gather them.

* * *

An hour and a half later, when the men left the Hansen home, Claude had a lopsided smile on his face and seemed to be walking several inches above the ground. Ben caught the faraway look in his brother's eyes.

"What's the matter? Did Bethany's bread pudding not agree with your stomach?"

"I thought everything was delicious," Phillip answered. "Sure beats our sad attempts. Hannah's pie crust was almost celestial."

The truth was, all of the food the Hansen sisters served—especially Bethany's bread pudding—had been excellent, but Ben wasn't about to admit it. After being away from the falderal of womankind for over two years—and making sure he taught Claude everything he knew about so-called "love"—he hoped his brother had learned a few things. Unfortunately, Claude's starry eyes said just the opposite. Ben had hoped they had left such nonsense behind them when they left Cybil in New York. Apparently not.

"So what's wrong, then?" Ben asked with an elbow jab to Claude's ribs.

They turned onto the street, and Claude slowly shook his head as if in a dream. "Have you ever seen *anything* so beautiful?"

Ben looked around them, at the sky, and even inside his jacket. "Nope. Sorry. Don't see anything beautiful at all. Do you, Phillip? I know Claude thinks *he's* beautiful, but that's old news."

Phillip laughed and shook his head, but he didn't answer. Over the years the three of them had gone through the same dance enough times that they could all predict with relative accuracy what was about to happen. Ben wished Phillip wouldn't keep staying out of the ring. The anti-female side of the fence could use a few more members.

Phillip looked more uneasy at the joke than Ben would have thought he would, and he made a mental note to ask what was troubling him. But Claude's cheeks were bright red, and Ben knew he had hit a target; Claude did think he was handsomer than most. "I didn't mean me," Claude insisted.

"Maybe not this time," Ben murmured, a smile twitching his mouth. Phillip couldn't hold back a chuckle. Throughout their mission, Claude had spent more time grooming in front of the mirror than he would like to admit.

Turning around, Claude pointed to where they could just make out the fence of the Hansens' property. "Back there." He sighed. "Hannah used to be just a sweet girl. I know we were all good pals before, and I liked her well enough, but now—" He shook his head, turned back to the road, and plunged his hands into his jacket pockets. "Now, she's a beautiful woman."

"Oh, please." Ben yanked Claude's arm to keep him moving. "I saw no such thing back there, and I'm years away from needing spectacles."

"Little brother," Claude said to Phillip, stopping in the road and ignoring Ben. "*You* think Hannah's pretty, don't you?"

Phillip looked from one older brother to the other. "In a word, yes." He raised his hands in defense. "But this isn't a firestorm I want to get myself into. I'm going to talk to Mrs. Brecken about letting her attic for my shop. Either of you want to come along?"

"I'll be right there," Claude said. "*After* I try to knock some sense into our older brother."

Phillip seemed about to say something else, but instead he closed his mouth, shook his head, then walked around a corner toward State Street, leaving Ben and Claude to fight it out.

Ben watched his brother, curious. Something seemed to be eating at Phillip. Shaking off the thought, he turned to Claude. "First of all," Ben said, pointing a finger at Claude, "as far as I'm concerned, women-folk are a distracting and, unfortunately, necessary vice."

"Yes, yes," Claude said, looking at the sky dramatically. "We all know that it's your greatest aspiration to convert as many men to gray-haired bachelorhood as possible—in spite of the fact that it's contrary to every gospel principle."

"Precisely." Ben refused to acknowledge the sardonic edge to his brother's voice. But quietly, he sighed. It wasn't easy trying to run from marriage, especially since he was twenty-five. Ben hated to admit that it wasn't so much the idea of marriage he was running from as much as marrying someone he didn't really love, and that was now his only option. There was only one person who had ever held his heart—then broken it—and there would never be another. If he ever succumbed to the pressure to get married, it would be for practical reasons only. Having a woman around to do the cooking and laundry would be a pleasant convenience. "Let's pretend for a moment that I paid the *slightest* attention to Hannah."

"I'm pretending," Claude said dryly, eyeing his brother sideways as they walked. "So?"

"So it's obvious to any bystander that Hannah doesn't hold a candle to Bethany."

Claude's brow furrowed and, after a moment, his lips curved. "I don't believe it! You still have feelings for—"

Stomach suddenly knotting, Ben's step came up short. Claude of all people should know better than to bring that up. He pushed his face inches away from Claude's. "Say one more word and I'll yank out your tongue."

Claude backed down. "Whoa. Sorry," he said, raising his hands in surrender.

Ben shook off the anger, suddenly feeling a twinge of guilt for snarling at his brother like that. Not exactly the behavior of someone who had just returned from proselyting. *Neither was your behavior back at the Hansens',* he reminded himself. But that was different. With Bethany, it was a game of one-upmanship. That didn't count.

Claude turned to keep walking, and when he spoke again, it was in a softer tone, one free of debate. "I felt something when I saw Hannah today."

"Like I said, it was probably indigestion." Ben tried to act casual again, as if nothing had happened. All this woman talk made him uncomfortable. Things were much simpler when being with his brothers consisted of little besides preaching and baptizing.

Claude stopped in the road again. He closed his eyes and took a deep breath. "Ben, I respect your desire to remain a bachelor, whatever your reasons. But nothing you say is going to change the fact that I really like Hannah." He looked up at his brother, who was a few inches taller. "Please don't make light of that," he finished, then pulled the brim of his hat down and strode away.

Ben watched him go, feeling guilt worming its way into his mind. He glanced over his shoulder, but the Hansen property was no longer visible. Thinking back to the moment they had walked up the lane, he was painfully aware that his pulse had picked up its pace at seeing Bethany—covered in dirt and tripping on onions. A soft smile crept onto his face that he couldn't stop. She was still so beautiful.

At the memory, he coughed and walked faster, deliberately changing the direction of his thoughts from how she looked to what she had been doing. It was pretty funny to see her stumble like that—and a tiny bit satisfying.

*Nothing more,* he assured himself.

As he turned to go home, he muttered to himself, "Gotta be more careful, buddy, or one of them females might sneak her way through your defenses, and you'll end up a poor sap like Claude."

# CHAPTER 2

When Phillip reached Mrs. Brecken's general store, he went inside and retrieved a sign from the window which read, "Space to Let." Looking around the room, he searched for Mrs. Brecken, who had owned this store for as long as he could remember, and found her stacking feed bags in the back corner. As he approached her, she paused to catch her breath and count the bags. She shook her head as if she'd lost track, then added them up again, pointing to each bag as she went.

"Twenty-nine," she muttered, then—turning around to jot the number down—nearly bumped into Phillip. "Oh, heavens. You startled me. Can I help you with something?"

Since her face bore no recognition, Phillip realized he needed to reintroduce himself. "Sister—Mrs. Brecken, I'm Phillip Adams. Remember me?"

He held out his hand in greeting, but the plump woman just eyed it and wiped a strand of damp, gray hair from her face. "Back from your mission then?" He nodded. "Your brothers back too, or are you home early?"

Phillip's brow creased; she seemed to be implying something, and he had a feeling he knew what it was but prayed he was wrong. Mrs. Brecken was one of the handful of people who knew his family's history back to Nauvoo. Phillip couldn't understand how such people could blame him for something that happened before he was born. "No, it's all three of us—Ben and Claude, too. I noticed this sign in your window." He held it out.

"Yes . . ." She looked down her nose at it.

"I'd like to let the space," Phillip said, bracing himself. Mrs. Brecken was one of the few old-timers who still held his questionable birth against him.

"For what?" she asked warily.

"For a photography studio. I bought all the supplies back East and took lessons before we returned. It'll take a few weeks to get set up, but I believe I'll be able to have a successful business, and my customers will bring you more business, too."

She didn't answer right away, instead narrowing her eyes as if scrutinizing him. Just as he had the urge to blurt out that he really was a good person, she continued. "Hmm. I don't know. I've had a few other offers from people who—well, who I know better."

Phillip was tempted to remind her that she knew his family well—which was certainly true as far as it went. But since the circumstances that led to the shop owner's prejudice lay in the difference between Phillip's birth and that of his older brothers, that wouldn't do much in convincing her to give him the space.

The side door opened, jingling a handful of bells attached to the top. Claude entered and looked around. Spying Phillip in the back, he raised a hand and came to join them. "Do you already have everything arranged, then?"

"I . . ." Phillip hesitated, looking askance at Mrs. Brecken. "We haven't come to an agreement."

"Mrs. Brecken, it's so good to see you," Claude said, putting out his hand.

The elderly lady shook it and smiled. "Good to see you, too, Claude. You're a bit taller than I saw you last, I think. Unless I'm shrinking in my old age."

"Well, you're as pretty as ever," Claude said, flashing a broad smile.

Phillip pressed his eyes closed. That was the same smile Claude had used on a hundred other women—including Cybil. Until recently, Phillip hadn't thought anything of it. Now, it made his hackles rise; it was a sign of manipulation, and he wasn't sure he wanted that smile connected to his business.

Mrs. Brecken swatted his arm and blushed. "Oh, you young men."

Claude stepped a little closer to Mrs. Brecken. "So is Phillip going to rent your attic then?"

She glanced uncomfortably at Phillip. "Well, I haven't quite decided yet . . ."

Leaning in even closer, Claude almost whispered, "He's got great ideas for his photography, plus all the latest methods and equipment. He'll easily be able to pay you rent—and everyone who clamors to get one of his photographs will have to come through your door to do that. You'll get more customers, more sales. It's the best thing you can do for your store. What do you say?"

He touched her arm gently. She glanced at it, back up at Claude, then smiled. "More sales and customers, eh?" Mrs. Brecken chewed the inside of one cheek and eyed Phillip again. "You think you can do what your brother here says you can?"

"I'm sure of it." Phillip wanted to say more—or at least point out that he had just made all the same arguments—but he had a feeling that it would be best to keep quiet. Claude had a way with women *and* didn't have the supposedly dirty past Phillip did. His half brother was untainted, or so everyone thought. Phillip realized he'd expected this reaction from Mrs. Brecken—she'd never treated him as well as she had his brothers, even when they were boys. It was something he just had to accept.

With a curt nod, Mrs. Brecken snatched the sign away from Phillip and said, "Very well. I expect the rent paid by the first of the month. No exceptions."

"Agreed."

"You can start moving your things in right away. We'll count this month as partial rent, since we're already halfway through. I'll draw up the papers in the morning."

"Thank you, Mrs. Brecken," Phillip said, getting excited now. "You won't regret this."

She nodded without another word and went back to work. He hadn't even seen the attic except from the outside. He knew it had three windows along one side—critical for the light he'd need. But at that moment, it didn't really matter what condition the attic was in; he had a space to call his own, even if he owed it to his brother and his charms.

He and Claude left the shop and headed for home. "Thanks," he said after a minute. "I don't think she would have let me have it if you hadn't arrived and convinced her."

"My pleasure, little brother," Claude said, tugging at his jacket. He sauntered down the road and winked. "Let's just say you owe me a favor."

A favor. The idea bothered Phillip. He had already carried a burden for Claude all the way from New York. If anything, they were even now. They walked for several blocks in silence before Phillip couldn't keep quiet any longer. They had reached some sheds on the temple block, and Phillip motioned to Claude to sit in the shade behind one. "Come here."

Instead of joining him, Claude stared at his brother. Phillip sat in the shade and took off his hat. "Come here and sit down. We need to talk."

"About what?" Claude asked, squinting at the afternoon sun.

"I think you know what."

A palpable silence hung between them for a moment. Claude licked his lips, then hung his head and nodded. "All right. I suppose there has to be a time." He walked into the shade and sat against the shed. The air was silent behind them. Phillip wondered if the workers had taken a midday break or if this shed had been abandoned like several of the Public Works buildings throughout the block. The only thing that mattered was that the two of them were alone, with no prying eyes or ears.

Claude rested his forearms on his knees and held his hat by the brim, slowly rotating it around and around. When he didn't say anything, Phillip ventured, "I heard you and Cybil saying good-bye."

"I know." Claude continued to circle his hat as he stared at it.

"She begged you to return after what you 'did together.'"

Claude's jaw worked a bit, and he nodded. His eyes seemed to get teary. "I know," he said again, his voice low. His eyes finally left the hat, darting for just a second to the dusty ground and leaving a wet spot—a single tear.

"Yet as soon as the door closed, it was clear you had no intentions of returning to New York."

"That's right."

Silence. This time Phillip refused to fill it. Claude needed to explain himself. His face screwed up with emotion and, after a moment, one of his hands covered his eyes. "I don't know what came over me, Phillip. I'm not that kind of man. I'm really not. I didn't mean to promise things like that when I knew I didn't mean them. I shouldn't have acted like that as a missionary. I should never have kissed her. What was I thinking?" He brought up his other hand to hide his tears.

Phillip was taken aback as he stared at his brother. Claude seemed genuinely distressed.

"Kisses and false promises?" As much as he hoped that was the whole story, Phillip remembered what he had suspected in the hallway and what the look on Cybil's face had implied. So he had to press further. "That's . . . that's *it?*"

Claude's hands fell, and his mouth hung open at Phillip's question. "What are you saying? You think that I . . . that we . . ." He stood, grabbed his hat, and shook his head in disgust. "I can't believe you. Of all the low-down, dirty things to say to a brother. I'm baring my innermost soul to you, and you have the gall to . . ." His voice trailed off as if he couldn't even come up with the words. "Here I am, moments after helping my brother get a lease for his dream business, and you push me down. Well, thank you very much."

"Claude, I know what I heard, and it sounded a lot like—" Phillip tried, but Claude shook his head.

"Stop, Phillip. Just stop." Claude put his hat on deliberately. "Yes, I did something wrong, and yes, I need to make things right with Cybil. I'll send her a letter apologizing for leading her on, and from here on out, I'll never, ever let myself get caught up in the moment with a woman. I'm doing what I must to put this behind me. But no, I didn't do anything like . . . like *that.*" His face tightened, and he shook his head in horror, wiping a hand across his face. "I can't believe you'd say such a thing."

"Claude, I—"

But he wouldn't let Phillip get a word in edgewise. "And I would hope that *you* of all people wouldn't rush to judgment regarding a man's character, especially one of your own flesh and blood."

Stunned, Phillip stood in silence in the shadow of the shed as Claude turned and stalked away. Phillip rubbed his hand down his face, suddenly glad he hadn't told Ben any of this. If the matter with Cybil was all a gross misjudgment on his part, and if Claude had already begun turning around from whatever *had* happened, then there was no use in dwelling on what Phillip had seen and heard in the inn.

Even so, poor, poor Cybil.

* * *

A couple of days after the miserable onion incident, Hannah and Bethany hung fresh linens on the clothesline in preparation for their cousin Marie's arrival. She'd visited from Spanish Fork every summer for as many weeks as the girls could convince her parents to spare her. Marie's visits were the only time Bethany moved in with Hannah. Then all three slept in the same room and giggled late into the night like schoolgirls.

"We should take Marie to the theater," Bethany said, snapping a sheet open. "I don't think Spanish Fork has one, and certainly not one as big and grand as ours."

"Good idea," Hannah said through two clothespins between her teeth. She plucked them from her mouth, pushed them onto the line to hold a sheet in place, then turned to her sister. "Bethany . . ."

"Yes?" Bethany glanced up. She drew a pillowcase from the basket, shook it out, and reached up to pin it to the rope. When Hannah didn't speak, Bethany looked over. Her sister stood there, biting her lower lip and studying the grass at her feet. "Is something wrong?"

"I was wondering . . ." Hannah said quietly.

"About the theater? I hear they're doing a Shakespeare play right now, a comedy. I can't remember the name, but I think it had the word *comedy* in the title."

Hannah took a few steps closer to her sister. She leaned down, pulled out one of their father's shirts, and smoothed some creases across the front. "What do you think of Claude Adams?"

Bethany couldn't help noticing the pink flush in her sister's cheeks—and her obvious attempt at looking casual about the question, which included avoiding Bethany's gaze.

"Claude?" Bethany shrugged casually as if she hadn't noticed her sister's embarrassment. "He's the same tall, fair-skinned boy he's always been. I don't care for the way he's styling his hair now with all that fancy pomade—probably some New York fashion he picked up." She raised an eyebrow and looked quizzically at her sister, already having a good idea why she wanted an opinion. Even so, Bethany couldn't help asking why.

With a shrug, Hannah raised the shirt to the line and only then realized she didn't have any clothespins in hand. Bending down to fetch some from the smaller basket on the ground, she asked innocently, "And what of the other Adams brothers?"

Bethany tried not to show how the question ruffled her. She answered, starting with the safest brother to discuss. "Phillip's a fine man. Better looking now than he was when they left, I daresay. He's always been nice, never mean or defensive—even when certain people whispered behind his back about . . . well, you know. I've always respected that."

"No, I don't know," Hannah said, puzzled.

If Hannah hadn't been privy to town gossip, Bethany wasn't about to spread any about Phillip, so she didn't clarify.

But she didn't need to, because Hannah just shook her head and pressed on. "What about . . . Ben?" She seemed to push the name out.

"You know very well what I think of Ben Adams." Bethany put her hands on her hips. "And if you insist on discussing *him,* you'll be doing it by yourself, because I'll be inside." She made a move to leave, but Hannah grabbed her arm. Bethany sighed with frustration, then slowly turned around. "Yes?"

"Would you agree that you and I are as close as any sisters?"

"I would," Bethany said, softening her voice.

"That we confide in one another about almost everything?"

"Yes . . ." Suddenly Bethany didn't like where this was going—back to Ben, she was sure of it.

"And yet . . . after all the time that has passed, you've never told me what happened between you two."

Hannah's words landed on target, making Bethany's chest suddenly feel tight. "I'd rather not talk about it." *Even after more than two years.*

"But it's important to me," Hannah insisted. "I—I really like Claude." She said it as a confession, as if Bethany would condemn her for it. "But if my feelings get in the way of my relationship with you, I'll force them to look elsewhere. I couldn't bear it if a man came between us."

Smiling, Bethany moved to her sister and put a hand on her arm. "You needn't worry about me. I can manage the likes of Ben all by myself. If you have eyes for Claude and he returns the sentiment, you can proceed knowing that I'm happy for you."

Hannah tilted her head as if surprised. "You wouldn't mind? Honest?"

"I wouldn't mind," Bethany repeated, then smiled to confirm her words.

"I've never been courted before," Hannah said. "And I don't even know if Claude has so much as noticed me, so I know it's ridiculous to be thinking of such things, but I do wonder—if he ever wanted to become my beau . . ." She shook her head, looking distressed. "What if something similar to what happened between you and Ben happens to Claude and me? How will I know what to do?"

"You worry too much," Bethany said, trying to laugh. It came out sounding forced. She hadn't ever talked about Ben with Hannah and hadn't mentioned his name to anyone in years. Discussing it even in vague terms was like ripping a scab off a wound and making it bleed all over again. "Hannah, don't fret. The chances of something like that are ridiculously small. Claude isn't his brother's twin. If he has a particle of sense more than Ben does—which I don't doubt—you'll be fine."

Hannah nodded uncomfortably as she twisted her father's shirt between her fingers, making more wrinkles than it had to begin with. "Yes, but—but if I knew what happened with you and Ben, I might be able to prevent—"

"I will—not—discuss it." Bethany's voice was no longer sweet and sympathetic. Pushed to this point, she couldn't afford to be misunderstood, and she would *not* talk about Ben. Not even with Hannah, whose eyes grew wide at Bethany's tone. She looked as if she'd been slapped.

Guilt settled in Bethany's middle. "Hannah, I'm—sorry," she managed, but then put up a hand. "I really am sorry. But I *cannot* talk about it." She turned to go. When she reached the door, she opened it and paused. "I'll find a tick to fill with straw for Marie to sleep on," she said, offering to compensate for leaving the laundry unfinished.

Inside, she pressed her hands against her temples and sighed, then headed upstairs toward the linen closet to fetch the guest tick. Getting everything finished in preparation for Marie's arrival would help her shove away thoughts of Ben and their disastrous relationship—or what had masqueraded as a relationship.

But she didn't get any farther than opening the closet door before the unwanted memories of that time washed over her and sent tears spilling down her cheeks. The things Ben had written to her and said in her ear. Dancing with him as his girl. The night he'd kissed her . . .

She punched a stack of linens and cried out. "Ben Adams, you fool. If only you weren't . . . you."

Her arms rested against a shelf, and she leaned her head against them. She cried, hoping that Hannah would stay outside and wouldn't find her this way. No one could know—even after two years—that her heart hadn't come close to healing.

* * *

"So what *is* all this stuff?" Ben asked, looking through the crates in the attic above Mrs. Brecken's store. The three brothers were unpacking Phillip's photography supplies in the attic that would soon serve as Phillip's studio. That is, once he managed to get everything unpacked and set up. And after he had sample photos to display in the front window of the store. And after he'd put an advertisement in the paper for his services. The sooner the better, because he needed to start making some money to pay it all off.

Once he was comfortably settled in a successful business, he would be able to take a step forward in courting a wife. If he didn't hurry, there was a good chance Claude might act first with Hannah. So far his brother hadn't shown any interest in finding a professional trade or obtaining a form of income, so Phillip wasn't overly concerned. Surely if Claude had his sights set on Hannah, he would first need to make himself appear to be a viable suitor. Eventually, Claude's portion from the farm sale would run out and then what? Phillip's feelings for Hannah went back years and years, well before their mission, while Claude's seemed sparked only upon seeing her at their return.

Picking up a bottle of clear liquid, Claude held it to the dim light coming through the window and tilted it back and forth. Ever since their talk by the shed the other day, an unspoken tension hung between the two of them, but neither acknowledged it openly, and both hid it well in front of Ben.

"Hey, be careful with that." Phillip reached for the bottle and placed it in a straw-filled crate. "That's flammable—expensive, too."

They looked around the dusty room that, until today, had been nothing more than empty space above the general store. "Isn't the room perfect?" Phillip said. "Three windows on both ends. More in the gables. Easy access to the well through the store's back door. And low rent to boot."

"Not much light gets in the windows," Claude said, walking up to one and squinting.

"Not *now,*" Phillip said, "but there'll be plenty of light when they're clean."

"Looks promising," Ben said, nodding approvingly as he finished unpacking a box and stacked panes of glass on a shelf. He stood and wiped his hand on his pants, then pulled out his watch from his vest pocket. "But if you'll excuse me, the foreman asked me to drop by right about now so he could explain some of the more intricate stonework I'll be doing on the temple stones. By the sounds of it, the work is going to be downright miserable."

The two younger brothers laughed and waved him off as Ben headed down the stairs.

"So," Claude said after Ben was gone, hands on his hips as he surveyed the boxes and crates, "if I'm not allowed to touch anything, what exactly am I helping you with?"

"Start with washing the windows." Phillip pointed to a pile of rags lying on the floor. He hoped that even with Ben gone, the two of them could keep the conversation away from uncomfortable topics—like Cybil and anything remotely connected to what they had discussed by the shed. "Take a rag and a bucket of water. Mrs. Brecken brought up soap she said I could use—it's over by the banister. Like you said, I can't take photographs unless I have light."

Claude picked up the bucket. "You might have told me I would be your maid," he called over his shoulder as he headed down the stairs.

Phillip went back to work unpacking his precious cargo. So far he had found nothing broken from the long trip, and with each crate he unpacked, he got more excited to put his new skills to work. It wouldn't be too long before he'd be making enough money to pay off the equipment and make a good living. He wondered how soon he could buy some land and build a house. He rethought what his advertisement would say—*The newest photography techniques, images more realistic than any you've seen . . .* The venture would take some work, of course. He knew the basics, but he needed to practice and hone his skills.

A moment later, Claude returned with the pail of soapy water. He settled in to washing one of the big windows while Phillip unpacked cases of glass squares and inspected them for damage.

"So what do I get for helping you?" Claude asked as he reached high to scrub the grime from a top corner. "Are you going to teach me how to take photographs?"

After a grunt, Phillip responded, "Hardly. I didn't pay five dollars learning this stuff just to give away the secrets."

"Well, I'd better get *something.*" Claude rubbed a particularly stubborn pane. "How about I sit for you while you make a special portrait of me for Hannah?"

Phillip paused in his work and looked over his shoulder at his brother. "That's an idea," he said vaguely, hoping his cheeks didn't look as pink at they felt. Perhaps he could put off the favor for Claude or agree to something else in trade. Although he imagined giving Hannah a photograph, the face in it ought to be *his.*

Even so, Phillip had a sinking feeling in his stomach. Not only because Claude had eyes for Hannah but because of what had happened with Cybil. What if Claude tried something with Hannah as he had with Cybil? What if Cybil *wasn't* just a kiss? As soon as the thought crossed his mind, Phillip chastised himself. Now, he was calling his brother a liar. Who was he to judge Claude? He didn't know whether his brother was repentant or what his brother had done.

Yet there was more to the sinking sensation in his middle. As long as Phillip could remember, Claude had treated him with mild disdain, putting him down and not believing in him. And Phillip, as a loyal little brother, looked up to Claude as someone to emulate, someone he desperately wanted to please. As an adult, Phillip now knew that courting his brother's favor was a lost cause and that Claude's contempt for him stemmed from something ludicrous, something beyond Phillip's control—his paternity. Having his brother's approval now wouldn't mean much. Even so, agreeing to help Claude was almost a reflex for Phillip, as if that little boy looking for praise still existed somewhere deep inside him.

He took a deep breath, determined to lighten the mood. "You know," Phillip said with a grin, "I'm pretty good with a camera. I might even be able to make *you* look less ugly."

Claude hurled the wet rag across the room, where it landed with a squishing sound on Phillip's chest. They laughed as he took the cloth from the floor and brushed at his wet shirt. When Claude held out his hand, Phillip didn't toss the cloth back right away. Thoughts of Hannah returned, which led to his wondering about Bethany and what she might have told Hannah about the three brothers.

What prejudices would Hannah already have toward him? He was related to Ben *and* he had a muddy heritage since he was technically their half brother.

"Claude, do you—do you know what happened between Ben and Bethany?"

With a shrug, Claude grabbed another washrag from a pile and dunked it into the bucket. "Haven't got the foggiest idea—Ben's as tight-lipped as ever. I assumed you knew something." He turned to the window and kept scrubbing. The dirt was slowly coming off, and it was satisfying to see light seeping into the room.

"I don't have an inkling about it," Phillip said with a shake of his head. He threw the rag into the bucket at Claude's feet, splashing water onto the planks of the wooden floor. "All I know is what I saw that night—Bethany running out of the house in tears, Ben breaking things inside. Your guess is as good as mine."

Claude pulled up a crate and sat down. "You want to know what I think?"

"Can't wait to hear it." Phillip went back to work, moving from inspecting glass to fighting with a tripod that refused to stand.

"I think that the two of them are still in love." Claude folded his arms with an air of satisfaction.

A burst of laughter escaped Phillip, and he nearly dropped the tripod. "They absolutely hate each other. Weren't you there the afternoon we returned? I don't think I've ever seen *cats* fight like that." Phillip kept wrestling with the tripod until its leg finally slipped into place. "You do realize that you're making no sense whatsoever."

"I'm serious. I think it's all an act."

Phillip moved to the next leg. "In that case, it's an effective one."

"Hear me out," Claude said, coming over to Phillip. "I agree they're both still angry about whatever happened before. But if they didn't still care, why would they bother sniping at one another? They'd just ignore each other."

Phillip had never thought of it in those terms. No emotion toward one another *would* mean no barbs thrown. He had once heard someone say that hate was simply the flip side of love, that one couldn't truly hate someone he didn't once deeply care for. Phillip couldn't vouch for that, but Claude did have a point about Ben and Bethany.

Phillip straightened and toed a piece of packing straw out of the way. "You're almost making sense, Claude. *Almost.* But if I were you, I wouldn't say anything about *feelings* or *Bethany* around Ben. Not if you value your life."

# CHAPTER 3

Bethany stood before the vanity mirror. She stepped back and eyed herself in the slightly distorted glass on the wall, wishing she could see her whole body. Hands on hips, she twisted side to side and looked down, surveying her figure and making the hem of her skirt swish against the floor. Her waist was still narrower than most girls'—a source of pride, since she wasn't born with particular beauty. She had always suspected—hoped—she *might* be a little pretty. But one never knew for sure. Hannah's nearly black hair and fair complexion always drew attention, whereas her own reddish-blond hair and smattering of freckles went unnoticed.

She wore her white organdy with ribbon around the neckline. It wasn't her newest gown, but it was her most becoming. Besides, Ben hadn't ever seen it, so it would be new to him. She wanted him to notice her tonight, to see what he had thrown away, to make him regret everything he had done.

What would *he* be wearing at the dance? She remembered all too well how handsome he could look with his hair slicked back, wearing a crisp collar and cravat, and a coat. Her eyes stung at the memory, making her blink rapidly to chase the thoughts away.

She focused her attention on her reflection again, noting how her hair contrasted with the white dress. She had tucked a few sprigs of baby's breath behind her ear to enhance the effect. With her hair swept off her neck in an elegant twist, Bethany had sculpted tight ringlets on either side of her face—and she had a burned finger from her efforts with the heated rod. It was worth it.

She pinched her cheeks to make them pink, bit her lips for a similar effect, then let out a breath. *I suppose I'm ready,* she thought, smoothing the front of her dress, painfully aware of her trembling knees. A knock sounded on her bedroom door.

"Come in." Her voice wavered slightly, and she touched her throat. Nerves simply wouldn't do tonight.

"You're the picture of beauty," her father said as he peered into the room. He gave a slight shake of his head, as if he couldn't quite believe his daughter had become a grown woman when he wasn't looking. "You look so much like your mother did at your age, God rest her soul."

Bethany looked at her reflection again. Her mother had been considered the town beauty in her youth. Bethany hardly held *that* distinction. But of late, she had noticed something around her eyes that reminded her of her mother. Maybe there *was* a resemblance. "You think so?"

"I know so," he said.

"Thank you, Father," Bethany said, pleasure in her voice.

He stepped into the room and held out a necklace—a gold chain with a single pearl hanging from it. Bethany gasped, recognizing her mother's most expensive piece of jewelry. The gold and pearl were real. "Father, what—"

"I want you to wear this tonight." He stepped behind her, opening the necklace and securing the clasp around her neck. Bethany couldn't find the voice—or the will—to protest. She stood stunned, partly terrified at the prospect of even touching the treasure, partly entranced by its beauty—the same way she had felt looking at it as a girl.

Bethany fingered the pearl as she remembered climbing onto her mother's vanity chair. She couldn't have been more than five or six—but old enough to know not to touch Mother's "pretties." Each night she'd look over the things her mother used to make herself more beautiful—the powder puff, the tortoiseshell comb she wore in her hair, the crock of lotion, the brush, used faithfully every night on her dark red, waist-length hair.

Night after night, young Bethany would lie on her parents' bed, chin propped on her clasped hands as she watched her mother prepare for bed. Sitting in the soft glow of candlelight, Mother made one hundred long, even strokes with the hairbrush. There was something magical about the hundred strokes, so Bethany counted each and every one, piping up if her mother miscounted and stopped brushing at ninety-eight or kept going after one hundred.

Brushing her mother's hair smooth was one of the last things Bethany was able to do for her mother before she'd died and was also the final act of service she did for her mother, as she lay in her casket before the funeral.

Now, as Bethany stood before the mirror with the necklace resting against her skin, she felt a pang of loss. Perhaps her mother watched moments like these from somewhere in heaven. Bethany smoothed her bodice and nodded. "Just for tonight," she whispered. "Then it'll go back into her jewelry box."

"If you wish," Father said. "But it belongs to you. That was one of her requests."

"I know." Bethany's eyes smarted. More than a year had passed since her mother's death, but the pain hadn't gone away. It had eased slightly, in the sense that it no longer tore at her soul every waking hour. Now it was a familiar ache—except for moments like these that brought back the searing pain. After the funeral, she had wished for a dear friend to share it with. Not Hannah and not Father. They had their own grief to bear, so she held in her feelings to avoid burdening them further. More than once during those times, a thought had flitted across her mind: *If only Ben were here.* But just as quickly, she had dismissed it. If Ben had been around, he certainly wouldn't have been the friend to share her pain with, not when they had parted on such bad terms.

Father leaned over her shoulder and kissed her cheek. "The buggy is ready whenever you are," he said. "Hannah's already in the sitting room."

"I'll be right down," Bethany said, smiling as a single, shiny tear ran down her cheek. She wiped it away as Father stepped out and closed the door.

She looked up and used her hands to fan her eyes dry. Her mother may not be there to counsel or comfort her, but Bethany would sooner go to the dance in her work apron and smelling of onions than let Ben see her with red, weepy eyes.

* * *

The Hansen girls and their father entered the dance hall in the middle of a reel. The music and energy rushed over Bethany in a wave, and her stomach fluttered with anticipation. She couldn't help but look around to see who else was there—half hoping and half dreading to see Ben. Would he notice her appearance? *He'd better, after all the work I put into it,* she thought. And suddenly there he was, wearing a dark gray suit with tails as he guided Maggie Walton through a promenade.

She lightly stroked her mother's necklace and smiled, knowing that it was her crowning touch. In her white organdy she looked more than a step up from her plain old muslin—and she hoped Ben would think so, too. It would serve him right.

"Bishop Hansen, it's so good to see you," came a voice.

The family turned to see Phillip Adams crossing to them, smiling broadly.

"Good evening, Bethany, Hannah," he said with a nod to each, his eyes holding Hannah's for a second longer than necessary. It was quick enough that Bethany thought she might have imagined it, but then Phillip's ears turned pink as he glanced at Hannah a second time. No, she was right. Phillip *was* looking at Hannah with interest. Her eyebrows went up, and she almost said something, but quickly clamped her lips back together to avoid embarrassing either of them.

She wondered if Hannah had noticed his attention; by the looks of it, she hadn't. Instead, Hannah appeared to be searching the room for Claude.

"It was so good of you to stop by the other day," their father said to Phillip. "It sounds like you and your brothers had a lot of success on your mission."

"We did." Phillip gave a satisfied nod. "It wasn't easy, of course, but we had several wonderful experiences and baptized many people. Ben alone—"

"Don't tell me you let *him* baptize anyone," Bethany interjected. She raised one eyebrow and looked around the hall. "He's liable to hold a person under and consider it a good joke." As soon as the words escaped her mouth, she wished she could take them back. Such an insult would be good to throw at Ben—it would put him in his place—but she shouldn't joke about baptism like that around her father and Ben's brother. Even so, she couldn't keep the anger toward Ben from bubbling back up, and she primed her wit to be able to win against him tonight.

"I—uh—" Phillip hesitated, looking between father and daughter, clearly unsure whether Leo Hansen knew of the friction between Bethany and Ben. He tried again. "Ben was a terrific missionary, full of—"

"Yes, he's certainly full of *something,*" Bethany said. She scanned the room covertly, wondering where Ben was but hoping no one would know what she was doing.

The corner of Phillip's mouth twitched with amusement. "Clearly Ben's name is not recorded in the book of people you admire."

"Heavens no, and you know that," Bethany said with a laugh. "If he were, I'd have to burn the family library."

The reel ended, and the band's conductor informed the crowd that a quadrille would begin shortly. Leo put a hand on Bethany's shoulder as if to quiet her. "You must excuse my daughter. As I'm sure you know, she and Ben have what is called a 'merry war' between them. If I thought they meant a word of it, I'd have to lock her in her room until she promised to behave. But you know how lovers' quarrels go."

*Lovers' quarrels?* Bethany fumed. Ben was her *enemy.*

Phillip's eyebrows rose in question, and he turned to Bethany. "It's all in good fun, then?"

She opened her mouth, but nothing came out. Saying that it was all jovial banter would imply that she and Ben were friendly enough to tease one another. On the other hand, denying it would indicate that she still harbored resentment toward him. Which, of course, she did. More than two years after their row, it still had an effect on her—but an admission of the fact would be humiliating. She floundered desperately for an answer.

To her relief, instead of waiting for a response, Phillip held out a hand and inclined his head toward the floor. "You wouldn't mind dancing together, I suppose?" Couples were leaving the floor, and new couples started to replace them.

She smiled and put her hand in his. "I'd be happy to."

Phillip gave a gentlemanly bow and led her to the center of the floor—where he intercepted Ben. Bethany's heart gave an unceremonious leap.

"Here is your dance partner," Phillip said, taking Maggie's hand and putting Bethany's in his brother's. Phillip escorted Maggie away, grinning over his shoulder.

Bethany's face flushed with anger. Her first impulse was to pull free from Ben's grasp and stomp off the floor—and then pummel Phillip for his trick. But she and Ben already stood in the center of the room, and three other couples had formed the remaining sides of a square in preparation for the quadrille. Leaving a hole in the formation would draw undue attention. Besides, several people who knew Ben and Bethany already whispered among themselves and pointed at the pair. She couldn't very well make a scene without also creating a good share of gossip for the neighborhood. So instead of following Phillip, she held her ground, daring Ben to be the one to leave. *She* wouldn't be cowed. She stole a quick glance at Ben, hoping to see him sweating uncomfortably.

To her dismay, he appeared calm and unruffled as he said—without looking at her—"Good evening, Miss Hansen."

She gave a slight dip of the head in response. If he could maintain an expression of absolute detachment, so could she.

Travis Schuman walked by with Hannah on his arm. "Even if I didn't know you were your father's daughter, I could tell it by your eyes," he was saying to Hannah.

"Careful what you say, my boy," Ben called after him with a chuckle. "Women don't take kindly to being compared to elderly men."

Hannah and Travis continued toward a second square at the far side of the room, giving Ben no acknowledgment. Bethany smiled. The fact that they probably hadn't even heard Ben was beside the point. The best part was that he kept talking, raising his voice.

"If you're going to compare her to her father," he called to their retreating forms, "at least point out a feminine feature as well. That'll prevent you from getting a fat lip."

Bethany moved to Ben's side and held out her hand, ready for the dance. "I wonder why you're still talking, Mr. Adams," she said airily. "No one's paying you any mind." She smiled to the couple across from them, who also waited for the music to begin. She would appear pleasant if it killed her.

Ben slowly turned to stand beside her. Without looking her way, and with a tone as aloof as hers, he said, "I see *disdain* is alive and well. It's your middle name, is it not?" He wore a gallant smile for the other dancers and the onlookers, but when he closed his fingers around hers, he squeezed hard. Her knuckles rubbed together, sending a pinching pain through her hand, but she refused to give him the satisfaction of seeing her wince. Instead she lifted her foot and casually pressed her boot's pointed heel onto his toes. His nostrils flared suddenly, but he made no noise. They truly were terrible to one another. She wouldn't have thought herself capable of acting like this with anyone—but Ben wasn't anyone.

"How could *disdain* do anything but thrive in your presence?" she said innocently. "I don't think the most proper manners of any woman could survive two minutes in the same room with you." When the band started playing, the dancers bowed and stepped forward.

"If you're right, then all the etiquette I learned as a boy has betrayed me. But I think you're wrong," Ben said, leading her around him.

As she moved, Bethany wished she knew what insult he was about to land next. When she faced him again, she knew she was falling into his trap by saying, "Wrong about what?"

"The truth is, nearly all women love me."

Bethany snorted as the ladies moved into a chain. She put on an elegant smile as she danced around the circle with the other women. When the partners came back together, she and Ben waited for their turn at the next figure. "You're the one exception, of course," Ben said, continuing the conversation as if they hadn't been interrupted. "It's sad, for all those ladies' sakes, that I simply don't have the stomach for women."

"A great happiness to all us women," Bethany replied, stepping forward on their turn. A moment later she added, "You and I are alike in one way, I suppose—you have disdain for all women, and I'd rather hear my dog howl at the moon than hear a man declare his love for me."

"What a relief!" Ben said emphatically. "That'll prevent some poor gent from getting his face scratched off."

Bethany gritted her teeth and cleared her throat so she could speak in her most syrupy voice. "Oh, that's not something *you* need to worry about." She curtsied elegantly. "Scratching couldn't possibly make your face any worse than it already is."

The violin ended the song with a twang. Bethany tilted her head and batted her eyes, then released her hand from Ben's as she stepped away from him. She held his gaze as long as she could, knowing that even though he tried to look calm and collected, his eyes burned with anger. He was the one who finally broke the stare, and when he did, she turned away and grinned, triumphant.

* * *

Phillip walked with Claude to the temple block. He pulled a cart behind filled with photography equipment. They ran into Ben, who was leaving the block and wearing a scowl on his face. "Upset because you had to work on a Saturday or because of the dance last night?" Phillip asked.

Ben glowered at his brother. "Been a long day, and I didn't sleep well last night." He hefted his sack.

Phillip gave Claude a look that said, *Sure. And I know why he didn't sleep well.* Claude grinned back.

Ben noticed the exchange and insisted, "Listen, I've just put in a full day's work after not having cut stone in more than two years. Yet the foreman put me on an Earth stone first, so stop your carping."

"An Earth stone?" Phillip asked. "What's that?"

"Only the most difficult piece to cut on the entire building," Ben said. "I told you it was going to be miserable work." His brothers laughed, and Ben raised a hand, cutting them off before they could point out that the building was only a few feet high. "They're the most difficult stones that there will *ever* be on the entire building. They take weeks to shape just right. Tedious, backbreaking work. One stone is going to take me a good month. And if I do the cuts wrong, I'll ruin the entire block and waste hundreds of dollars of man-hours between the quarry, the hauling, the cutting—"

"Whoa," Phillip interrupted good-naturedly, he and Claude finally impressed by Ben's work. Phillip surveyed the lot, suddenly seeing it with new, more appreciative eyes. Huge gray stones of granite lay in lines, and workers milled about. Dozens of stonecutters chipped away at large blocks mounted high enough to allow the cutters to work without leaning over. They used an array of tools, from wide, clumsy-looking chisels and mallets used for cutting rough edges, to more fine-edged ones for finishing work. Ben had his own collection of these tools and had spent the last few days sharpening them.

"Now, if you don't mind," Ben said, his eyes and shoulders drooping, "I'm going home to bed before my arms fall off."

The other two waved and headed toward the north end, where the city creek cut through the block. Phillip stopped the cart and set up his tripod. He glanced at Claude, trying to figure out why his brother kept tagging along, willing to help with the studio and now with photography outings, especially after Phillip had come out and accused him. Was it Claude's way of trying to show that he had no hard feelings?

Claude adjusted a sack of supplies in his arms as he waited for Phillip to take them. "So why were you so eager to do this today?"

Phillip bent down to the level of the lens and squinted, judging the potential for a photograph. The sun was about to sink into the west, but it still provided plenty of light at an indirect angle—perfect for a clear image without any glare. He flipped the black cloth over his head and took a better look at the construction.

Claude pressed him while he examined the scene. "The foundation has been replaced and the temple walls are finally above ground, but their height isn't going to change much over the next few days. Why today?"

Phillip emerged from under the covering. "The building's part of it." Phillip took the sack, opened it, and began searching through it.

He took out bottles of chemicals and clean cloths, then set aside a box of glass squares, talking as he worked. "Of course the walls aren't going to shoot up. Unless they find a better way than oxen to transport the granite, we'll be gray by the time they finish the thing."

"So why now?"

"Look at the sky. It's rare to find such perfect conditions for taking pictures. Besides, the workers are all over the place today. Look over there—dozens of children playing on stone blocks. That's history in the making, my good brother. Someday, those boys will be able to say that they played hide and seek around those walls, and I'll have the photographs to prove it."

When Claude didn't answer, Phillip looked up at him. Facing east, Claude's eyes were trained on a brown roof a few blocks away. It stood on a rise, its distinctive stone chimney distinguishing it as the Hansen home. Phillip pretended not to notice. Of all the people in the world, *he* was not the person who should listen to Claude's notions and hopes about love, especially since they involved Hannah. Granted, Claude couldn't exactly go to Ben, either—the self-proclaimed enemy of all females.

One could hardly blame Claude for falling for Hannah. An image of her at the dance came to mind—her dress the soft yellow of buttercups, her hair in ringlets that shined in the candlelight of the hall. A smile that could melt any man's insides. Unfortunately, he also remembered her searching the room, her face lighting up when she found Claude. Phillip tried not to think about Cybil. He tried to remember what Claude had said—that it was just false promises and kisses. And Claude was sorry about it all. It was in the past. Over.

Phillip stared at the temple foundation, now above ground level. He thought back to the summer his mother had died from cancer, when he was only fourteen. Ben, at nineteen, had already been a grown man, but losing their mother had been devastating and confusing for all of them, especially since their father had died several years before they ever came to Utah.

It was Bishop Hansen who had come to their aid, not only helping to arrange the funeral and the sale of the farm, but also inviting the boys into the Hansen home for dinners. That was also the time that

Phillip noticed Hannah, who was thirteen, just a year younger than he was. She was already beautiful, and even then Phillip could have spent hours staring at her. But it was something else about her that captured his heart and bound it tightly to him.

It was June, about a month after the funeral, and Ben had taken it upon himself to support his brothers financially. He was spending much of his time with one of the men in the Parry Brothers' stone shop, learning the skills to become a stone mason. Phillip and Claude were supposed to help out with the Hansen farm and orchard to help pay for the food and other help they had received from the family—at least, that was what Ben expected of them. Phillip did his share, but Claude was rarely around, often sulking back at their house or wandering the streets with other boys and getting into trouble.

It was early evening one Saturday when Phillip found himself hoeing rows and rows of the Hansens' vegetables. He had spent most of the day working with the bishop, but now he worked alone. Suddenly an overwhelming sadness descended over him. His family had never been perfect, but now it was nothing like it had been. Ben was rarely around anymore, heading for the stone shop the moment he woke and staying until dusk. Although Claude had never been a comfort, even his familiar presence was gone. Phillip missed everything that had been taken from his life, even the simple things like sitting around the table at home for meals. As grateful as he was for Sister Hansen's dinners, he still missed his own kitchen table, the chipped dishes, Mother's gravy.

*Mother. Dear, sweet Mother.* The only person in the entire world who had loved him unconditionally and made him feel treasured and as noble as a prince. She had believed he could touch the stars if he wanted to.

Phillip had dropped the hoe and covered his face with his hands, sobbing. Wanting nothing but solitude to weep, he ran blindly away from the Hansen farm. He stayed away from home, not wanting to face Claude while crying. He ran through the city streets until he found himself at the temple block, which the workers had left for the day. All over the ground lay broken pieces of sandstone that had been ripped out of the foundation, leaving long lines dug deep into the earth where they'd once been. The old, cracked foundation would be gone soon, and a new one would have to be built.

*Starting over.* That was exactly how Phillip felt. The entire foundation of his life had just been ripped out of his chest, leaving nothing but raw holes begging to be filled. The temple foundation would be replaced, eventually, but Phillip couldn't see how his soul would ever be filled again. He went to the edge and sat on the ground, letting his legs dangle into the ditch that once held foundation stones. Without giving it much thought, he dropped down into a trench and curled up next to one of the cornerstones. With his back against the cool rock, hidden from public view, he burst into tears again, sobbing until he felt his heart would break.

After several minutes, he heard the sound of scuffling, followed by a quiet voice. "Phillip?"

Startled, he sniffed hard and wiped frantically at his cheeks. How embarrassing to be caught crying like a baby.

"Phillip, are you all right?" He looked up to see Hannah coming toward him, her dress covered in dirt. She had let herself down into the ditch.

"How did you know I was here?"

She bit her lip sheepishly. "I followed you. I was worried when you ran off like that. It's not like you to not finish a job."

Phillip scrubbed the back of his hand across his face, trying to act as if he were perfectly fine instead of red-faced, despondent, and sitting in a damp ditch in the middle of town.

Without another word, Hannah tucked her skirts under her legs and sat down beside him. "I'm sorry about your mother," she said softly, looking at her hands. "I wish I knew something else to say that would help. But I'm really sorry." Tears welled in her eyes, and when she blinked, a plump one fell down her cheek.

"Thank you," he said. "I know that's all you can say. But it helps."

She leaned against the cornerstone and rested her head against his shoulder. Just her presence was comforting, and he never wanted to leave. He hesitantly leaned his head against hers and closed his eyes, knowing that it was all right to cry in front of Hannah.

That was the moment when Phillip knew he loved Hannah Hansen. Five years later, his feelings for her had only increased, although he wasn't sure how she felt about him. For all he knew, she saw him as a sort of brother, which was the role all the Adams boys had taken on when they spent so much time with the Hansens during that summer.

*Five years.* Phillip could hardly believe it had taken that long to replace the sandstone foundation with granite. He could still remember the exact spot where he and Hannah had sat inside the ditch, hiding from the world. And here he was now, recording the progress on the temple as the walls were finally a few feet above ground level.

Letting out a breath to ease the memory back into the past, Phillip clapped his hands together. "All right, then. Claude, would you fill the pail with some water? I need it to coat the plates with collodion." He pointed to the city creek that ran through the northern side of the temple block. Being close to the creek was why he had chosen to photograph the temple from the north side. The fact that the closed-up Public Works buildings were behind him and wouldn't show in the picture was also a plus. Claude didn't answer, so Phillip picked up the bucket and pressed it into his hands. "Here."

As if in a daze, Claude grasped the wooden pail, but he didn't make a move toward the creek. "Phillip?"

Heart thudding with dread, Phillip knew exactly what his brother was about to talk about, so he tried to steer the topic in a different direction. "Fill that with water, then come back and we'll see if we can get some good images before we lose any light. Do you think the workers will detract? If they move, they'll be blurry."

*"Phillip,"* Claude said again, now turning his head away from the Hansens' rooftop to face his brother. "You have lots more book learning than I have. I'm not nearly as good with words as you are."

The statement was true enough; Phillip strongly believed in educating his mind. He had taught himself Greek and Latin and rarely had less than two books he was reading at any time—history, politics, science, he loved them all. But what did that have to do with anything? "Yes . . ." he said warily.

"I want to tell Hannah how I feel about her, but I'm afraid I'll be a bumbling fool if I say anything to her face."

Phillip stood silently. He folded his arms, not liking where this was going.

"So I'd rather tell her in a letter," Claude went on, his eyes turning desperate. "But I'm terrible with writing, too. Will you—please—help me compose it?"

*So that's why he's been so nice to me,* Phillip thought. *Because I was a judgmental prat, he figures he can guilt me into this.*

"I don't think that's a very good idea." Phillip took the pail from his brother's hand and strode to the creek himself. *It's a really, really bad idea.*

Claude hurried after him, kicking up dust with his boots. "I'm serious. I wouldn't know what to say or how to say it, and I'm sure I'd spell every other word wrong. Not to mention that my handwriting looks like chicken tracks." He touched Phillip's arm, stopping him a yard from the water's edge. "Please."

*Please.* The childhood urge to do anything to enter his brother's good graces reared its ugly head. Phillip thought back to Mrs. Brecken's store, to Claude's charming smile winning her over and getting the lease. *First I judged him, then he got me the lease. I owe him on two counts.* But if he helped Claude win over Hannah, Phillip would lose her for himself. Then again, he reminded himself, Hannah wasn't his to lose. He remembered the dance—how her eyes had lit up when she saw Claude, not him.

But what if Claude did do something to Hannah like he did to Cybil in New York? What if . . .

"Look, I'm not a poet, Claude. I can't write a love letter." Phillip closed his eyes and sighed. "I read scientific books, not anything about love and fairy tales. Any letter I could write for you would sound like a proclamation from a newspaper."

Claude snatched the bucket, leaned down to the creek, and filled the pail—as if that would win over his brother. He held it out like an offering. As Phillip took it by the handle, Claude went on. "When we left for our mission, I saw her as just a girl, but now—" His fist went to his heart and he shook his head. "I'd give anything to win her affections."

Phillip's chest constricted. He knew all too well the feeling Claude described. With their mission behind them and his financial future looking promising, Phillip had a hard time not thinking about a future with Hannah.

Apparently, Claude did too.

Again Claude gazed off toward the housetop, and Phillip's eyes followed. White smoke drifted from the chimney. That probably meant Hannah and Bethany were cooking dinner. As his brother daydreamed, Phillip took the chance to gather his thoughts.

Would he help with such a letter if Claude had asked for help courting any other girl? Of course he would. He also knew that by the looks of things, Hannah seemed to return Claude's affections. Did he, Phillip, really have much chance at winning her love? Claude was much better looking than he was, but he still clung to the hope sown during the summer of 1862 when Phillip and Hannah sat together in the trenches of the temple, so aiding Claude in his quest might very well end any chance he would have. If any letter would be written, the signature at the bottom would read *Phillip.*

With a firm shake of his head, he walked back to his equipment. He ducked under the cloth again to judge the location of the camera and the angle of the sun—and to avoid his brother.

Claude's footsteps sounded. "So?" His voice carried through the thick fabric. "Will you do it?"

"I said no," Phillip snapped. "Now, let's get back to work before the light fades." He turned to his work, thinking the conversation was over.

But Claude put his hand on Phillip's arm, and when their eyes locked, Claude said the words Phillip knew were coming. "You owe me."

Phillip grimaced. *Dash it all.*

# CHAPTER 4

*If only today had come the morning after the dance,* Bethany thought as she and Hannah headed outside to wait for their cousin to arrive. Bethany had been longing to talk to someone about Ben—and Hannah wasn't an option, given her interest in Claude. Since Marie was smack dab between Bethany and Hannah in age, the three had always been close. It was almost like having another sister.

They passed the ground-level well, which stood dangerously open. Bethany leaned down and grabbed the side of the wooden door-like cover, which had hinges on one side. She pushed it up and over on its hinges and let it slam closed over the hole. Bethany gave her sister a look.

"Sorry I left it open," Hannah said with a shrug.

"You know how Father gets riled up about an open well," Bethany said, walking to the fence.

"Thanks for closing it."

Bethany leaned against a fence post and stared into the street. Every time Marie visited, there was so much to catch up on—a year's worth—so the girls sat up late, talking night after night. Those were the times Bethany looked forward to—especially nowadays, since more and more of her friends were getting married.

Even if friends didn't move away after the wedding—which they often did—relationships with married women changed into something hardly recognizable from what they had been. It always happened. No matter how hard either Bethany or the new bride tried to keep up the friendship, it simply didn't work. The two suddenly operated in different social circles, had different responsibilities, different interests.

Bethany had seen it enough times that she no longer held the illusion it would be any different with Hannah or Marie.

*At least Marie isn't married yet,* Bethany thought.

As she leaned against the post, searching the road, she yearned to tell Marie about the hideous encounter with Ben. It was the one topic she couldn't mention to anyone in Salt Lake City, her sister included. It was too painful. Marie was the only person besides her mother who Bethany had confided in—and Marie was sworn to secrecy on the matter.

*I can talk about it to Marie. She'll understand and side with me. She'll agree that Ben's a self-important, egotistical fop.*

Just thinking the words felt good. Bethany felt smugly victorious at the thought of having said them to Ben and not just in complaints to her cousin.

A wagon rumbled down the road toward them and, like an eight-year-old, Bethany ran through the gate ahead of her sister. Bethany shielded her eyes from the sun, trying to make out the passengers. There were two, of that she was certain—but their faces remained shadowed until they drew closer—and drove right past. Watching them retreat, Bethany sighed and let her hands drop. A piece of hair fell into her eyes, and she blew it away with disdain.

"I think I see them!" Hannah called from behind. Bethany whipped around to see another wagon approaching. This time one of the two people on the bench took off a hat and waved it wildly, ribbons flying in the air.

Instantly, Bethany and Hannah cheered and ran forward. Uncle Raymond slowed the wagon and let Marie off.

"Marie!" Bethany and Hannah squealed at once. As soon as their cousin cleared the wagon wheels, the three women embraced, giggling like little girls.

"It's so good to be here," Marie said. She breathed in deeply as if drinking in the air. "Every time I visit I feel like I've come home."

"You *have* come home," Bethany said. "Salt Lake City will always be your home."

Marie smiled and laughed. "You're right. Wind aside, Spanish Fork isn't so bad, but this is where I grew up, and all of my dearest childhood memories rush back when I arrive."

Arm in arm, they walked to the house as Marie's father drove the wagon down the lane, then they stood close by as their fathers unloaded Marie's trunk. They chatted about their animals, crops, and church work, and discussed the changes in one another over the last year. They admired Marie's new brown traveling suit, with its smart jacket done up in the front with covered buttons and tailored over a three-layered skirt. She had her dark hair in an elaborate coiffure, the waves swept away from her face and then caught up in short curls behind a plait of shiny hair. Bethany wondered how Marie still looked so fresh after traveling all day in the heat.

During a brief pause, Hannah bit her lip and leaned forward. "The Adams brothers are back from their mission."

"Really?" Marie's eyebrows went up, and her gaze darted to Bethany, who shook her head disdainfully.

Hannah pressed her lips together as if trying to restrain her enthusiasm. "You should see Claude. He's so tall and handsome now." She clasped her hands together. Bethany wouldn't have been surprised to see her swoon; although had she done so, Bethany would have left her lying on the ground. She looked to Marie for confirmation that Hannah behaved like a fool.

Instead, Marie and Hannah's eyes met, and they grinned at one another. "Can you two keep a secret?" The sisters nodded, but Bethany had a bad feeling about what Marie was about to share. "He still has to ask Father for my hand, but a week ago, my beau secretly asked me to marry him."

Hannah and Bethany gasped in unison. They looked over their shoulders at their fathers, who weren't paying any attention. Turning back together, Marie and Hannah's eyes locked as if making a connection reserved for women in the middle of romance.

"Oh, Marie! I'm so happy for you!" Hannah took her cousin's hands, and the two of them practically bounced with excitement.

It was as if an invisible line had been drawn between Bethany and the other two. Bethany stood on the edge as the only one not losing sleep over a man.

Actually, she hadn't slept all that well since Ben's return, but she wouldn't have admitted it for the world—*her* sleeplessness was for a very different reason than that which kept Hannah and Marie awake at night.

"What—what's his name?" Bethany managed, trying her best to smile. It felt crooked and false.

"Ted." The name itself brought a flush to Marie's cheeks, and she couldn't stop grinning.

Their father clapped Uncle Raymond on the back and called to his daughters. "Let's get inside and find something for a light meal. They've had a long day on the road."

Bethany jumped to her feet and eagerly went into the house to get food on the table. Normally she would have lingered with Marie, slowly strolling to the house and chatting as they lit the stove and prepared some food. Now, she had to stare at the sky for a moment to let her eyes dry, refusing to let any tears fall. For the first time in her recollection, she didn't look forward to the rest of Marie's visit—not if it meant Hannah and Marie swooning over men while Bethany sat on the side and watched.

* * *

Claude paced back and forth on the porch, watching Ben and Phillip walk away. Should he call them back? Probably. Yet he wanted more than anything for them to talk with Bishop Hansen and get his approval for courting Hannah. Normally that was something a man did himself, but he just couldn't face Bishop Hansen and look him in the eye. Not after what Cybil had done to him.

It's not like he'd planned it. The night before they left he'd told her to come to his room to say good-bye. When she had arrived at the door, she'd embraced him. Sure, he had held her in return. He leaned in and smelled her hair, let himself kiss the side of her face. But then *she* was the one who came inside. She was the one who closed the door and . . . seduced *him.*

If it weren't for the wiles of beautiful women, he wouldn't be in this mess.

Because of her, he lived in constant fear that a wire would arrive any day saying that there was a baby on the way. Then *everyone* would know what they had done, and his future would be over.

A dark cloud of guilt seemed to hover over his mind, and he couldn't shake it. Especially not since lying to Phillip's face about what had happened. Phillip knew. And Claude still couldn't believe he had managed to lie so boldly and then accuse his brother of being the one in the wrong.

*I should confess before I'm discovered,* he thought, sitting on the porch bench. *But I just can't. If the bishop weren't Hannah's father, it would be another story. At least I think it would.*

What was he supposed to do now? He couldn't very well talk to the bishop and still expect to court Hannah. Logically he knew he had done something very wrong, and he felt his insides twisting when he thought about it. Yet it wasn't entirely his fault.

Women were sure wily. Isn't that what Ben had always said?

Claude stood again, pacing and wiping his palms on his pants. How could he move on with his life and still have what he wanted?

Hannah was the kind of prize every man wanted. The very essence of beauty.

*And I want her for myself.*

He went inside and headed up the stairs to pace in his bedroom, so that he wouldn't keep looking up the street to see if his brothers were coming back.

He could only hope that by the time they got home the guilt wouldn't have done him in.

* * *

*What am I doing?* Phillip thought.

The thought repeated itself time and again as he walked down the road with Ben at his side—and a certain letter in his hand.

"Are you sure you want to come with me?" Phillip asked as they rounded a final bend. "I know Claude wanted both of us there, but . . ."

"I can handle it," Ben said. Then, with a glance at Phillip's doubtful expression, he added, "I *can.* I'll be the perfect gentleman. You'll see."

"Yes, I will," Phillip said with wry smile.

"And on our way home, remember that we're stopping off to wire some money to the inn to pay for damages," Ben said. "I don't want Claude's brawl on my conscience any longer than it needs to be."

"Agreed," Phillip said. He patted his breast pocket. "I managed to convince Claude to pitch in a few dollars, since he was the one who caused the ruckus in the first place."

They lapsed into silence as they walked, for which he was grateful. Memories and emotions swirled in his mind, and the silence allowed him to sort through them.

Back at home, Claude was waiting anxiously for them to return and report on the success of the venture. And here on the street, with every step he took, Phillip dreaded that very thing.

*What am I doing?* he thought again, then added, *And why am I doing it? Why couldn't I stick with "no"?*

The answer was simple, and painful. As the black sheep of the family, Phillip felt drawn to proving himself worthy of the family name. He might not have been legitimate at birth, but he would strive to be legitimate in life and deed. At the tender age of six he had first learned the truth from some neighbor boys playing in the road.

"You have no papa," they taunted as they kicked and passed a leather ball.

Not knowing or caring what they meant, Phillip just shrugged and kept shooting marbles. His mother was a widow, so of course he had no father living at home. So what? Why should he feel bad about that? He had never known his father, so how could he miss him? As his mother said, he did have a father—he just happened to be in heaven already.

A skinny boy approached with so many freckles that his face looked splotchy. He leaned down, and with a sweep of his hand, he sent Phillip's marbles scurrying in all directions.

"Hey!" Phillip jumped to his feet. "Why'd you do that?"

The boy stuck his face close to Phillip's and said, "Your pa wasn't really your pa. I heard my mama tell Jacob's mama."

A blond boy a few feet away laughed. "Yep. You're what's called a ba—"

Before he could finish the word, the front door flew open, and Phillip's mother rushed out, fury written on her face. "Hush your mouths!" she cried at the top of her voice. With a broom in one hand, she pointed down the street with the other, every muscle in her body tense. Her face turned dark red. "You sorry boys get on home right this instant, and don't let me *ever* hear you talking like that to my son again!"

As the children scattered, Mama ran down the porch, taking a few steps along the road and waving the broom after them to be sure they stayed gone. When they were out of sight, she put a hand to her forehead. Her face looked pinched, and she shook her head.

"Come here, little Phil," she said, kneeling in the dirt. "Let's clean up this mess." Her words were nothing unusual, but he remembered it seemed she could hardly get the air out. Tears streaking her cheeks, his mother scooped up marbles and dropped them into his brown sack, then pulled the drawstring tight. She drew Phillip into her arms, oblivious to the fine dust he brought with him, and sat on the bottom stair. He held his lumpy marble bag in both hands. Her body shook as she rocked the two of them back and forth.

"My baby." Her voice was high and wavering, and she stroked his hair. "Oh, my baby boy."

"M—Mama?" Phillip asked with hesitation. He hadn't thought the teasing meant anything, not until his mother's reaction. It scared him. He looked up at her. "Mama, what did they mean?"

She sniffed hard and let out a breath of disgust. "Those boys don't know what they're talking about." Another cry escaped, and she pulled him even closer so her chin rested over his head and he could smell the soap that had cleaned her dress. "They just don't know."

But he found out later that they did know, at least in part. And as Phillip grew older, he came to understand the word that the freckled boy—Jared Foley—had been about to call him. The word was true about Phillip as far as facts went, something he learned accidentally four years later. He happened upon his mother and her best friend Adelaide discussing his papa's death. He stood outside the parlor, waiting for an appropriate moment to interrupt and ask if he could take his penny to the store for a treat.

"It's tomorrow, isn't it?" Adelaide asked.

Phillip could hear Mama sipping her drink and the teacup clinking against its saucer as she set it down. "Yes. The day is always hard for me. You'd think it would get easier with each year. It does some, but not much. I can't get through the anniversary of his death without thinking of everything that led up to it—and everything that's followed."

Adelaide sighed sympathetically. "What's it been now? Twelve years?"

"Thirteen," Mama corrected. "Can you believe it?"

*Thirteen?* Phillip's brow furrowed. *But I'm only ten.*

"I can still hardly believe I left Nauvoo without him," Mama continued.

"Two boys in tow and a third on the way." Adelaide clucked her tongue. "I can only imagine how hard it was for you to come to Zion, then face having a baby without a father to show for it."

A pause filled the room before Mama said sadly, "Some people still talk about it behind my back, I know. Of course they don't know the story, and some would still find a way to shame me even if they knew what happened. Truth be told, I don't know that I could have borne it without a friend like you—and without my sweet little boy to brighten up my days."

Phillip edged away from the doorway, feeling as if his heart had dropped into his shoes. He didn't fully understand what his mama had said, but suddenly the memory of the boys taunting him made more sense. And from that moment on, Phillip felt like an imposter in the family, in the community, in the Church. He always wondered who knew, what they thought of him and his mother. For years Phillip didn't know what had happened, but he did know one thing—his mother was true and faithful in the Church, and he didn't blame her for anything.

It wasn't as if everyone had treated him like a second-class citizen his entire life. Most didn't. Since he was born the fall after his mama arrived in Salt Lake, a good portion of the town had no idea about his family's history—that the brothers' father had died well before Phillip was born. But enough did know—and talked about it—to make life a bit uncomfortable. That was probably the biggest reason the mission to New York had been so freeing—no one there knew him as anything but a Mormon elder. No one questioned his worthiness because of his birth.

It was right before his mother's death that he learned the rest. She told him the entire story, about how she had tried to help a vagrant by giving him a hot meal and a room to sleep in for a night as he passed through Nauvoo. As a young widow, she needed as much money as she could find, and he had promised to pay her a few coins for her trouble. Instead he had paid her back in the worst way imaginable. The feelings that came with the story were like a punch in the gut every time he thought of it.

"I wanted you to know," she had said, holding Phillip's hand as she lay dying. "I can't meet my Maker knowing you might think I had been disloyal to your father. And since I was sealed to him in the Endowment House, he will be your father in the eternities, loving you as much as he loves your brothers. No matter what townsfolk may say, I've kept my covenants all my life."

As he held her hand on her deathbed, a terrible thing had suddenly become a blessing. He had an eternal family and a loving father whom he'd meet—someday. But Phillip still wanted to ask why she hadn't made sure everyone knew what had happened, that she was innocent of wrongdoing. As soon as the thought came to him, he knew better. She would still be a tainted woman in many people's eyes. And to retell such a horrific moment in her life would make her feel exposed and wounded all over again. Either way, she would come out on the losing end. God was the one who knew, and only His opinion mattered. It was best to stay quiet and hope rumors simply died.

Even now, as Phillip walked with the letter—the one he'd composed for Claude—he still couldn't decide if his mother's explaining had been good or bad for him. On one hand, he now knew that his mother was not the person he sometimes heard described by town gossips. She was no hypocrite in her faith or in her teachings to her three sons. On the other hand, he also knew that he was the product of a violent, repulsive act, and that his "real" father—whoever and wherever he was—belonged in jail.

Phillip's fingers curled, and he realized he was about to crumple the letter. He forced his hands to open, and he smoothed the folded paper sealed with red wax. The letter was written in Phillip's own hand, but signed by Claude.

Everything in him screamed that he had done the wrong thing by writing the letter. Was he completely mad to destroy his own chances of happiness? Was he leading Hannah into something akin to what Cybil had experienced—whatever that was? And would he ever find someone else to love? He had written the letter, pouring out his true feelings onto the page, only to have Claude cheering as he watched from the side, "Yes! That's exactly how I feel. How do you know? And you said it would sound like a newspaper."

Phillip shrugged off the comments, saying, "I suppose I have read a few novels." He hoped the explanation appeased any curiosity and that the light of the candle in the dim room didn't betray the emotion that was surely on his face. If Claude took a good look at him, he'd know. But Claude was so wrapped up in his own feelings that he didn't notice Phillip fighting back emotion as he wrote one word of love after another.

"Hey, are you feeling all right?" Ben's voice startled Phillip back to the present.

"I'm—fine. Why do you ask?"

"You look a bit pale." Ben raised a discerning eyebrow. "Please tell me it's this courtship nonsense making you ill, because that's what it's doing to me."

"I'm sure nothing would bring you greater joy than if I were to join the ranks of permanent bachelorhood," Phillip said, putting on a broad smile to prevent Ben from suspecting anything was amiss.

They walked up the Hansens' gravel path and stopped at the side porch, which they normally used. Phillip wondered if they should have gone to the front door, considering the formality of their errand. At the door, he just stood there, unable to move. His pulse thumped in his throat as he raised his hand to knock, then stopped it midair, unmoving.

Ben glanced over, a question on his face as he waited for Phillip. "Very well, I'll do it," he said and rapped three times. "Are you sure you're not ill?"

"Not as you mean," Phillip said, lowering his arm. His thumb rubbed the letter that would be handed over in a moment. He tried not to think of the things he had written for Hannah, sentiments she'd think came from Claude. But Claude didn't really know Hannah. How could he think what he felt was *love?* Phillip and Hannah had grown close over that summer years ago, had been practically best friends by the time the boys were on their feet enough to survive without Sister Hansen's cooking and comfort.

The brothers waited for several minutes before Bishop Hansen appeared. "Why hello, gentlemen. What a pleasant surprise." He ushered them inside and closed the door, then led the way through the kitchen. "Sorry to keep you waiting," he said. "I forgot that the girls went into town with their cousin. I'm so used to them answering." He nodded toward his cane and added, "And I'm not as fast as I used to be now that I have to use this new-fangled contraption."

He slowly led them into the parlor. Phillip closed the kitchen door behind them, noting how stooped the bishop's shoulders were. They had seen the bishop since coming home, but Phillip supposed they had all been so caught up in the excitement of talking about the mission—and thinking about the girls outside—that he, at least, hadn't noticed the bishop's decline.

When they reached the parlor, Bishop Hansen gestured toward the sofa and waited for his guests to sit before he lowered himself into a wingback chair. He hung his cane on the side, interlaced his fingers, and said, "What can I do for you today?"

Phillip couldn't help chewing on the inside of his right cheek. The moment had arrived when he would give up all chance for Hannah. "We're here to ask permission to court your daughter." He cleared his throat and tried again. "That is, we're here to ask on behalf of . . ."

*Myself.* The thought jumped into his head.

". . . on behalf of Claude."

Bishop Hansen clapped his hands together. "Well now, where is Claude? I'd think he would want to ask such a thing himself."

For the briefest moment, Phillip hoped that Claude's absence would dampen the bishop's view of him. "He's quite worked up over the matter," Phillip explained. "He asked for our help in relaying the message."

The bishop sat back and nodded. "Well, it is slightly unorthodox for him to send messengers, but I've known you boys for years, and you're all stalwart young men. Claude was a bit of a rascal in his younger days, but boys will be boys, and I suppose a mission has tempered him." The bishop laughed a bit, looking at the brothers for confirmation. Ben and Phillip both laughed awkwardly, and Phillip felt like a bit of a fraud doing so as the bishop continued. "Of course he has my blessing. Hannah, I daresay, will be pleased."

An unruly urge swept over Phillip to point out—while he had the chance—that Claude didn't have a skill or trade or any ambition to get one, but he felt his loyalties should run deeper and held himself in check. Ben also shifted uncomfortably in his seat, and Phillip laid his hand on his brother's arm in hopes of preventing Ben from saying anything uncomplimentary.

The bishop must have noticed Ben's uneasiness, because he said, "Now Ben, are you here to declare your intentions for my elder daughter?"

Ben's eyes grew wide, and he opened his mouth to protest—surely vehemently—when Phillip panicked and interjected, "Having your blessing would mean much to Ben, although he doesn't want to openly court Bethany, seeing as they haven't yet mended fences."

If looks were daggers, Phillip would have been dead. He ignored Ben and gazed pleasantly at the bishop.

"Well, both of you have my blessing, of course," he said. "And you would have had my blessing to court a daughter, too, Phillip, if it ever came to that and if I had more daughters. I hope you know that. You are all like sons to me."

"Thank you, Bishop," Phillip said, his throat tightening. The Hansen house had felt much like a second home ever since his mother's death. But he couldn't dwell on that, because their duty was only half done. Phillip pulled the envelope from his jacket pocket and wished for the hundredth time that he could admit authorship.

"Would you—give this to Hannah?" He offered the letter, now somewhat wrinkled.

Bishop Hansen took it. "Naturally," he said as he tucked it into his vest pocket. "I suppose it's written by Claude, declaring his intentions?"

*Not quite.* "Something like that," Phillip said. He clenched his teeth, wishing the situation were different, dreading the inevitable scenes of love-struck Claude and starry-eyed Hannah he would soon encounter.

He just might get sick after all. Maybe Ben wasn't so wrong.

Ben sat forward and put his hands on his thighs. "Well, that's all we came for. Claude asked us both to come, because we're the only family he has to offer our blessing to the match. Personally, I don't know how—"

"Thank you for your time, Bishop," Phillip interjected, cutting off Ben before he could share either his thoughts on marriage or on his brother's readiness for it.

Bishop Hansen put his cane on the floor and pushed hard on it to slowly stand. "Thank you for coming, elders. I'll be sure to give Hannah the letter."

"Good day," Phillip said, nodding.

Ben did the same and added, "We can show ourselves out."

"Very good then," he said, sounding somewhat relieved not to have to make the trek to the door again. "Have a good evening." Bishop Hansen sat again and opened a book to the place he had marked.

As they left the room, Phillip felt drained. What he wouldn't give for a long drink of water and a hearty piece of meat. He could use the strength. Since they had entered the house through the side porch, they headed down the hall to leave the same way. Suddenly they heard female voices and realized the girls must have returned home while they were in the parlor.

The first voice sounded like Hannah. "He's so funny, Bethany. Even *you* must admit that."

*He?* Ben stopped short of the doorway. He put a finger to his mouth, telling Phillip to be quiet, then leaned in to listen.

"We shouldn't—" Phillip whispered, but Ben waved a hand to cut him off.

"You've got to be kidding," Bethany scoffed, followed by the repetitive sound of a knife slicing on a cutting board. "Ben's greatest jokes are lame puns and comments about women's intellect."

Ben's lips tightened, but he didn't move from his spot.

"From what I've heard, he's well liked," an unfamiliar female voice said.

"Liked, perhaps, by the foolish and simpleminded." The chopping sounds increased in intensity, then suddenly ended. Bethany sighed. "Look, you two can't convince me that Ben Adams is anything but a conceited sap."

A single eyebrow arched on Ben's face, and a thick vein pulsed on his forehead. Phillip had to turn his head to keep from laughing aloud. Ben turned and quietly—but resolutely—walked back down the hall toward the front door to let himself out. Phillip followed close behind, and they walked silently past the parlor, escaping the bishop's notice. Ben turned the knob slowly and eased the door open. Once free of the house, Ben stalked down the drive, muttering to himself.

"The nerve of that woman! Talking so about me—and publicly, too!"

Phillip had to jog to catch up. "It wasn't exactly public."

"It wasn't private, either," Ben snapped back. "There was someone else in there—a woman who now thinks I have the humor of a mule's hindquarters." He tromped ahead, arms swinging in wide arcs, eyes burning with fury.

"You've said worse to her," Phillip reminded him.

"To her face, yes." Ben let out a grumble of frustration. "The worst part of this is that I couldn't defend myself. It was like standing before a militia and letting them use me for target practice. I doubt President Young himself could endure such mistreatment."

Unable to help himself, Phillip finally let out a guffaw of laughter and said, "I imagine he endures worse. Remember, he's got dozens of wives. They can complain amongst themselves and use him for target practice anytime they like."

Ben stopped, put his hands on his hips, and glared at Phillip. "Is that supposed to make me feel better?"

"Perhaps not," Phillip said, clapping his brother on the shoulder.

Grumbling, Ben kept looking back toward the house. "That's women for you—judgmental, rude, inconsiderate . . ."

"I can't help wondering why Bethany's insults bother you so much," Phillip said as they turned a corner.

"Because the woman speaks in daggers, and every word stabs." For a moment, Ben's face was unreadable. He shrugged off Phillip's hand and adjusted his hat. When he spoke again, his voice had softened. "Fine. Because it's Bethany."

# CHAPTER 5

When Phillip opened the door at home and went inside, his spirit felt heavy. He didn't seek out his brother to tell him the news. Instead he sank onto a worn chair and stared into the fireplace, where a log was burning with an orange glow.

"I'm glad *that* business is over," Ben said as he tossed his coat onto the hat rack. He filled two glasses of water from the pail, then collapsed onto a chair and let out a deep breath. He gave one of the glasses to Phillip, took a long drink from the other, then gestured behind him toward the stove. "It was nice of Claude to get the fire going for supper. I wonder if he's going to actually cook something for once as a thank-you—or if he'll expect us to do that, too. First we get him a girl to court, then we pay off his debt to the inn. The least he could do is make us a meal."

Phillip grunted in response as he sat down. He stared at the glass in his hand without seeing it. His future lay in ruins, and he didn't know how to pick up the pieces. He had to keep reminding himself that Hannah was not a prize to be won, that she had her own mind and could choose whomever she wished. Perhaps Claude might not be her choice. But such thoughts were little comfort; Phillip had seen her gaze dreamily into Claude's eyes.

But enough was enough. Claude needed to know what Phillip had done for him and what it had cost Phillip.

Footsteps sounded on the stairs. *Claude.* Phillip's fingers gripped the cup tighter, and his jaw clenched. Claude approached, stopping a few feet behind Phillip's chair.

"Did Bishop Hansen say yes?" Claude's timid voice came from behind.

Ben made a move to stand. "He—"

With a warning look, Phillip stopped him. "Don't. Let me."

Ben's brow drew together. "Very well . . ." His voice trailed off as he sat down again and waved Claude over to join them.

Claude went to the fireplace and retrieved a short stool. He dragged it across the floor and sat on it, eye level with Phillip. "So? What happened?" His hands were clasped, and he leaned forward anxiously. Phillip knew the look on his own face didn't speak of good news, and he felt bad that he couldn't muster any feelings of joy for Claude's good fortune. Perhaps in time. For now, Claude needed to know what Phillip had done for him. He knew that if their roles were reversed, Claude certainly wouldn't have done the same for him.

Claude looked worriedly from one brother to the other. "Is it bad news, then?"

Phillip gave Ben a hard look. "You might want to leave for this. I have something to say that I'd rather you not ridicule me about."

"Who, me?" Ben feigned shock, then assumed a more sober expression. "Come, you can trust me." When Phillip gave Ben an empty stare, he raised a hand as if making an oath. "I promise. I will not mock anything you say."

With a short nod, Phillip turned to Claude, hoping Ben would keep his promise. Even if he didn't, Phillip figured reluctantly, Ben needed to know.

"This is hard for me to say," Phillip began.

"Her father said no?" Claude's voice was scarcely more than a whisper. "He said *no?*"

"Just hear me out." Phillip held up his hand. He took a deep breath, then exhaled. *Here goes nothing.* "I wanted to tell Bishop Hansen who really wrote the letter."

"What? Why? I mean, you *didn't,* did you?" Claude's questions came out like a row of falling dominos.

"Listen to me," Phillip said again. "The truth is . . ." This was proving harder than anticipated. "I care for Hannah too. I wrote what I feel. I didn't make any of it up."

Claude's face went pale. "You—*you* love her?" He stood and faced the fireplace, a fist held to his mouth. "I—you—"

He whipped around, his eyes narrowed with fear and anger. "You asked to court her yourself, didn't you? You said the letter was really from *you.*" His voice rose with every statement as he shouted, "Why would you lie to me, pretend to help me, only to go behind my back to win her hand yourself? That's despicable—it's—"

"Oh, please, Claude," Ben interjected. He seemed to be taking great amusement over the problem, as if it were nothing more than confusion over whose turn it was to do the dishes.

"Oh, please *what?*" Claude snapped.

"You don't really think your own brother would treat you like that, do you?" He put a hand out toward Phillip, who gratefully saw the action as a lifeline.

But he already knew the answer to the question. Of course Claude thought so. He always assumed the worst of his younger brother.

"Who knows," Claude said angrily, with a snide glance at Phillip. "He's only my *half* brother. It's anyone's guess what character flaws his *father* gave him."

"Whoa!" Ben snapped, pointing at his little brother and cutting him off sharply. "Shut your mouth, and shut it now, or I'll—" His eyes looked at if he might really reach in and rip Claude's tongue out this time.

"Or you'll *what*?" Claude said, challenging Ben.

Ben about bolted out of his chair toward Claude, but Phillip shoved the chair away and stood, eyes flaming. Ben's attempt at defending him was too late anyway. The words had been said, and the old, festering wound had been ripped wide open.

Jaw clenching, Phillip said, "I did exactly what you asked, Claude. The bishop is thrilled beyond words that his daughter may have the illustrious Claude Adams as a suitor. I had hoped that as my brother you'd have some gratitude for what I did in spite of my feelings. Enjoy your victory."

He kicked the chair, then stormed out of the room to keep himself from punching Claude in the face.

* * *

The three girls stayed up late talking. Bethany and Marie now sat on a bed, pillows in their laps as they chatted. They'd left Hannah alone, sitting at her vanity table rereading Claude's letter with some measure of privacy.

"I wish you could stay longer," Bethany said, hugging an embroidered pillow. "Two weeks is hardly enough."

Marie sighed and shrugged one shoulder. "I've tried to convince Father to relocate a hundred times if I have once, but he feels our family went to Spanish Fork for a reason. Can you believe it's been nine years? Even Mother feels like it's home now, though she wishes she could see the progress on the temple. She was brokenhearted when the news reached us that the foundation had cracked."

"I can imagine," Bethany said. "It's amazing how long it's taken to replace it."

Nearly a decade before, both families—along with most Saints in the area—had fled south to escape the U.S. Army marching into the city to quell a supposed rebellion. Before fleeing, the temple foundation was buried, hidden under plowed soil to foil any army attempt at destroying it. When the foundation was unearthed sometime later, cracks had surfaced all over it. Attempts to preserve the temple had ruined it.

"But they say it's a better, stronger foundation now," Bethany said. "Granite, not sandstone. You'll have to tell your mother that the temple is finally above ground." The girls sat silently for a few minutes, musing on the past. Bethany remembered what an adventure it had been to live in wagon boxes on the ground during their brief stay in Spanish Fork. Some of Bethany's most prized memories were from the days of exploring the windy town with her sister and cousin, their hair flying in their faces as they ran through the fields. At the beginning of the summer, Uncle Raymond began building a log cabin, saying it was to keep the two families out of the cold if they had to be in that barren wasteland of a city during the coming winter.

Their fun ended mid-summer, when Brigham Young sent word that it was safe to return to the city. The Hansens put their wagon back together, gathered their belongings, and rushed home. The Johnsons moved into the almost-finished cabin.

"At least you aren't married yet," Bethany said to Marie. "If you had a husband—or children—there wouldn't be the slightest chance of your visiting each summer. Promise me that you and Ted won't be married anytime soon. I don't think I could stand it if we didn't have at least one more summer together."

Marie laughed and tossed a cushion at Bethany. "I can't promise something like that. I don't think Ted would want a year-long engagement. Neither would I, for that matter. As it so happens, I don't have the same aversion to marriage that you do. Besides, one of us marrying wouldn't be so terrible, would it?" When Bethany looked horrified at the idea, Marie rushed on. "No, really. After the wedding, you would still be a bachelor lady and could visit me."

"That wouldn't do at all," Bethany insisted, scooting closer to Marie as if to collaborate on a childhood scheme. "You must postpone the inevitable as long as possible. After the wedding, you'll end up a serious, mature housewife with no time for frivolous things." When Marie opened her mouth to protest, Bethany continued. "No, you will. It happens to all married women."

"It won't happen to me," Marie insisted.

"I hope not," Bethany said dubiously. "But really, you can't think any man, Ted included, would welcome a woman chatting with his wife all night—on his *bed?*"

They laughed at the image, Bethany noticeably more so than Marie, whose cheeks flushed ever so slightly. Bethany felt a wave of something. Anger toward Ted for stealing away her cousin, plus something else—jealousy toward Marie for the look of joy in her eyes.

"Is . . . Ted . . . the real reason you can stay only a fortnight?" Bethany asked the question in a quiet voice without looking at her cousin. At first, Marie didn't respond, but Bethany already knew the answer. Her stomach felt sick at the implication. She would be losing one of her dearest friends. One by one they were all jumping into the lake of matrimony, leaving her high and dry, with no one to share confidences with. The realization hurt more with Marie than it had with any of her other friends. She could anticipate two marriages soon, no doubt—Marie's and Hannah's. At this rate, old-maidenhood would be rather lonely. Bethany was already twenty-two, while most of her friends had been married for years and already had at least two children.

"Never mind," she said before Marie could come up with an answer. Bethany waved her hand and put on a broad smile to distract from her teary eyes. "You don't have to answer that." She sighed heavily and tried to change the topic by speaking to her sister across the room. "So what does Claude have to say besides the fact that he can't sleep or eat for thinking of you?"

With a start, Hannah folded the letter and clamped it shut as if someone might read it over her shoulder. Bright pink colored her cheeks, and she grinned widely. She opened her mouth, but nothing came out at first. Then she smiled and tried to find her voice "I—he—"

Marie swung her legs off the bed and went to Hannah's side. She pulled up a chair and sat knee-to-knee with her cousin. "He cares for you, doesn't he?"

Hannah could only nod shyly and smile.

"And your father already gave his consent," Marie went on.

Again Hannah nodded, this time her eyes watering.

"You care for him too, don't you?" Marie asked, taking her cousin's hands in hers.

Another nod, this time with tears spilling down her cheeks. "Has any woman ever been so lucky?" she said, looking at the letter, holding it as if it were made of gold leaf.

The cousins embraced, rejoicing, while Bethany still sat on the bed, watching the moment. Another pang of envy went through her. She had pushed Hannah away by not talking about Ben. Now Hannah would only talk about Claude with Marie.

Man hating was becoming a more lonely business all the time.

Lost in thought, Bethany didn't notice that her sister and cousin were staring at her until Hannah called out, "Bethany, I hope we aren't bothering you with such talk."

"What?" Smiling broadly, Bethany shook her head, both to dispel the idea and to shake off her emotion. "Oh, not at all. If you two are happy for any reason, of course I'm happy too." She tried to swallow the knot in her throat. For their benefit—and so they wouldn't sense anything was wrong—she added, "Of course, I will personally never understand the fascination with the other half of our species, but if one of them makes you happy . . ."

She hopped off the bed and opened the door, then turned her head partway to say, "I'm going to make some warm milk with cinnamon before bed. Would either of you like some?"

When both declined, Bethany went out, pulled the door shut behind her, and went to the stairs. She didn't go down right away, instead clinging to the banister to steady her knees. The knot in her throat returned, this time refusing to be swallowed away.

*Why does this bother me?* If only she could take a ladle and scoop out the part of her heart that still hoped for companionship and love. In spite of her protestations to the contrary, she didn't want to die an old maid. Of course, her dreams didn't include a man who called her names or accused her of things she had never done—but she wouldn't think of *that* tonight.

She would find an honest, upright, *kind* man.

Someday.

She hoped.

Yet she didn't dare hope for it, not fully. If the day ever came for her to trust someone with her heart again, it would be a frightening prospect, indeed—one that she did not look forward to. It was much safer to simply avoid the situation altogether.

* * *

A day after Phillip and Ben delivered the letter, Bishop Hansen arrived at their door. Behind him was the buggy he had driven over. "Good morning, Elder Adams," he said to Phillip, who had answered the door.

Phillip tried to appear pleasant, but he wasn't feeling well. After everything that had transpired regarding Hannah and Claude, he hadn't been able to sleep. Now, he wanted to do nothing but lie in bed all day and nurse the raging headache that pounded in the back of his head. "Bishop. Good to see you. What can I do for you today?"

Smiling, Bishop Hansen rubbed his hands together. "With the new development between your brother and my sweet Hannah, I thought it would be a wonderful idea to get our families together today and go for a stroll. You know, a first chance for the two love-birds to be together?"

Feeling his stomach drop to his toes, Phillip tried not to register any emotion on his face. "I'm afraid I'll be busy with my studio today. I believe Ben is working today as well, but I can't speak for Claude." If only the bishop would recognize what that meant—that Claude didn't *work.*

"Come now," the bishop said. "I need to go on a walk. The doctor says my rheumatism won't get any better unless I get out and about more. And I want all three of you to come. We'll do it during your midday break. You can all surely squeeze in thirty minutes for exercise and fresh air, can't you?"

Internally groaning, Phillip finally nodded. "I suppose I can," he said grudgingly. If it weren't the bishop asking, he would have refused. But Phillip owed the man a great deal. How could he say no?

So shortly after the midday dinner hour, the three brothers met at home and headed for the Hansen farm. As they approached, Phillip saw a dark-haired young woman standing beneath some trees. He caught his breath until they drew closer and he realized it wasn't Hannah.

"You must be the Adams brothers," the girl said, putting out a hand. Ben and Phillip greeted her and introduced themselves, but Claude stayed a few feet off, not even acknowledging her, and instead clung to a fence post as he stared at the house, waiting for Hannah to emerge. The girl raised her eyebrows at his standoffish behavior and shrugged. "I'm Marie, Bethany and Hannah's cousin. Just visiting for a spell. I'm not sure what's keeping them," she added, following Claude's gaze.

Ben started kicking up dirt and pacing back and forth. Claude kept to himself, biting the inside of his cheek nervously. Phillip decided it would be rude not to attempt rescuing the conversation and intended to ask Marie about herself, but she beat him to it.

"Bethany tells me you're a photographer," Marie said, leaning against the fence.

He tore his gaze from Claude, who kept his eyes peeled for any sign of Hannah. "Yes. Yes, I am," he said with a nod. "I brought the equipment back from New York. I plan to open a studio not too far from the temple lot."

Today would be the first meeting between Claude and Hannah since the letter. It would also be the first time Phillip had been around his brothers *and* Hannah since revealing his feelings for her. It wouldn't be the most relaxing stroll of his life—of that he was certain. His stomach churned as he watched Claude, standing a few yards off. Claude's eyes jumped nervously between the house and his brother as if he too knew how difficult the impending moment would be. Phillip wished now he hadn't come, but he knew that even so, he'd have to face reality at some point. Hiding at home would do no good—and would only raise questions.

"I was wondering . . ." Marie's voice trailed off. She picked at some splinters in the fence, then glanced at Claude and Ben as if making sure they wouldn't hear. "Would you be willing to take my picture? I'd love to have one to give to my—a special friend of mine."

Noting how she bit her bottom lip nervously, Phillip smiled and raised his eyebrows. "A gentleman friend, perhaps?"

"Could you?" Marie deliberately avoided the question, but her smile and eyes gave her away. She looked hopeful as she rushed on. "I'd pay you, of course."

"I'd be happy to," Phillip said. The more customers he could get, the better. Mrs. Brecken had agreed to let him use half of her store window for advertising his business, and he'd need photographs to display there. Marie would do quite nicely. He looked at her closely for the first time, noting the angles of her face, the color of her hair. She could almost pass as Hannah's twin, he thought. He wondered how much Hannah's father and Marie's mother looked alike as siblings.

"Thank you so much," Marie cried, clapping her hands.

The side door of the house slammed shut, causing both Claude and Phillip to stand up straight, as if at attention in the militia. Bishop Hansen and his daughters walked toward the fence. A wave of unease passed through Phillip. He prayed his face wouldn't give him away.

*Hannah doesn't know,* Phillip reminded himself. *And my brothers won't tell.*

He caught a quick glance from Claude that seemed guilty. For all of Claude's faults, at least he had enough of a conscience to feel a *little* bad about pursuing Hannah at his brother's expense. His heart speeding up, Phillip gripped a crosspiece of the fence until a loose nail dug into his palm.

*I won't show my feelings. I won't.*

Hannah, Bethany, and their father stopped beside the group. All of them smiled broadly, and everyone waited expectantly for Claude and Hannah to greet one another.

Claude moved away from the fence and held out a hand to her. Hannah hurried to him, her eyes bright and her face glowing. He took her hand, tucking it in the crook of his arm. They stood there for several seconds, staring at one another.

Finally, Bethany stepped forward, tapped Claude on the shoulder, and whispered rather loudly, "That's your cue, Claude. Speak to her."

Laughing nervously, Claude lowered his head in embarrassment, then ventured a peek at Hannah. "You look beautiful today."

She looked up at him through her dark lashes and smiled. "Thank you." With a sudden awareness of their lack of privacy, she eyed the group, then rose on her toes and leaned to whisper something in his ear.

"My sister," Bethany announced as if she were their interpreter, "is telling him they should walk on ahead and leave us sorry common folk behind."

Claude put a hand over Hannah's and nodded. "Very good. That's almost exactly what she said, except for the 'sorry common folk' part."

Everyone laughed as the couple turned and walked onto the road, leading the way. The rest of the group followed behind, slowly at first, to give Claude and Hannah some space. From Phillip's vantage point some twenty feet or so behind, all of Claude's initial reservation had melted. It would have been nice, Phillip thought, if his brother had held onto his guilt just a *little* longer. The fact that the two of them walked ahead so comfortably—and close—spoke volumes.

And it meant one thing: Hannah was utterly lost to him. It was something he must learn to accept.

A moment later, an eagle soared overhead. Hannah paused in her step and pointed upward. Phillip stopped to watch the bird soar majestically through the sky. He couldn't hear Hannah's words to Claude, but by the look in her face, the bird was a thing of wonder and beauty to her. Claude gently urged her forward, apparently having no interest in anything but Hannah.

"Would this Friday work?" Marie asked abruptly.

It took Phillip a moment to understand what she meant. "The photograph?"

"Since I'm not going to be here very long, I'd prefer a time when I'm not needed by my cousins. Friday afternoon Bethany is helping tend some neighbor children, and I have a feeling that Hannah won't be around much either." She inclined her head toward the lovebirds. "It would be a good day for me."

"You're probably right," Phillip said, thinking through the week. Today was Tuesday. He had hoped to get some pictures in the canyon this week as well—perhaps of the Hansens and their cousin. "I could do it Friday, but not in my shop. It's nowhere near ready yet. Is there someplace outside that you'd like? Preferably near a well or a creek, because I need to be near water."

They walked for a moment while Marie considered. A few steps ahead, Bethany stayed beside her father. Ben was on the opposite side of Bishop Hansen. Phillip almost laughed to himself at what might have happened had the elderly gentleman not been there: Bethany and Ben might have—heaven forbid—had to walk *beside* one another. If he were the wagering type, Phillip would bet that Bethany had begged her father to walk between them to avoid such a scenario.

"How about we take it here at the house?" Marie asked, signaling behind them with her thumb. "There are plenty of pretty trees and flowers, and the well is right there."

*The Hansen home would provide many beautiful spots*, Phillip mused. But he'd need to borrow Mrs. Brecken's cart again. He had hoped Marie would suggest the temple block, where he frequently saw two of the local photographers working. People seemed to like having a piece of history in their portraits. He was about to suggest as much when Marie continued.

"If you come to the house, then I might be able to have you take a couple of pictures of me in different dresses. I could wear a more serious one for the photograph for my parents, and something a bit prettier for one for . . ."

"For your beau?"

She nodded shyly. "What do you think?"

She looked so excited at the prospect that Phillip didn't have the gumption to turn her down—or point out that he hadn't agreed to more than one picture. "Sure," he said. "That sounds great. Is two o'clock all right?"

"That's perfect."

# CHAPTER 6

Ben arranged to take off work to help his brother Wednesday morning, so together they set off beside one another on the wagon bench. He glanced over his shoulder at the Hansen girls and their cousin sitting several feet away in the wagon box. "I'm still not sure how you roped me into this." The noise from the wagon wheels bumping on the ruts in the road muffled his voice. Phillip's camera, tripod, bottles of solutions, and various boxes and crates holding other supplies were piled on one side, with the girls on the far end. They had put together a picnic meal for the outing. Ben made a face. "An entire afternoon being outnumbered by women, three to two. Dismal odds, if you ask me."

"Dismal odds for what?" Laughing, Phillip snapped the reins, and their dappled pony broke into a trot. "It's not as if this is a battlefront and your life is at stake. If you recall, you came for my sake. I couldn't very well spend an afternoon with three girls up the canyon, now, could I? It wouldn't look proper, as they say, even if all I did was take their picture."

"Propriety can go hang," Ben said, rolling his eyes. "It should be Claude going in my place. He's the one who would have a chance of actually enjoying the afternoon instead of merely enduring it."

"If he had been around, I would have asked him." Phillip was secretly grateful that Bishop Hansen had asked Claude to drive with him to the north end of the valley on some church visits today. Somehow his absence made Hannah feel less lost to him. But Claude would be upset when he came home and found out he had missed spending the day with Hannah.

Ben elbowed him in the ribs. "You owe me, brother."

"Duly noted," Phillip said. "But only if you behave yourself."

"Oh, I can't possibly promise that," Ben said, leaning against the bench back and folding his arms. "Some things are up to fate—or a certain female who shall remain nameless. If she acts up, I *must* defend myself. And you'll still owe me."

Phillip looked at Ben out of the corner of his eye and shook his head with amusement. He peered at the girls, grateful that they were engrossed in their own conversation and seemed unaware of the brothers' discussion. He leaned closer to Ben and lowered his voice anyway. "Just wait and see, brother. One of these days, I'll see you look pale with love."

Ben turned and raised an eyebrow as if challenged. "Oh, no you won't. You may see me pale with anger. You may see me pale with sickness. Perhaps with hunger. But never with *love.*" He said the last word as if it were something truly abhorrent. "I can guarantee that. I despise the fairer sex. I have no desire to be controlled and nagged for the remainder of my life. I'll remain free, thank you very much. You can't change the nature of a creature."

Phillip paused only a moment before saying, "Even wild horses can be broken." He couldn't help it—seeing Ben squirm brought too much enjoyment. Deep down, Phillip suspected that Ben blustered about women because Claude was right—their older brother still cared for Bethany.

Ben rubbed his hands together and shook his head. "If I am ever broken like a common horse, you'll just have to put an advertisement in the paper announcing the demise of 'Ben the Bachelor' and plaster my face all over the paper for shame."

"That *would* be news." Phillip inclined his head, then added wryly, "*Will* be news, and I'll take the photo. But seriously, what about the next life? You know, that whole thing about men and women being saved together—through marriage."

Ben grinned. "I think I'd be pretty happy to serve as the captain of the ministering angels for eternity."

The brothers maintained an unspoken truce on the subject as they rode up Parley's Canyon. The closer they drew to the stream Phillip had found the previous week, the more excited he became to hone his skills. He knew they had reached the right spot when he heard gurgling water. One had to have a way to keep the collodion on the plates wet until exposure. Had he coated the plates before coming up, they'd have dried by now and would be useless.

He tied up the horse near a tree with long grass and shade about it, then stepped into the trees. Although he stood only a few yards away from Ben and the girls, being surrounded made him feel enclosed in a solitary, peaceful world—a sanctuary. A ray of sunlight cut through some branches and broke into several beams with dust motes floating aimlessly like leaves in a pond. He took a deep breath, smelling the pungent dirt, broken grass, crisp air. If only a photograph could capture more than just one of the five senses.

"Should we unload?" Ben asked from behind, returning Phillip to the present. He turned to see Ben and the women standing beside the wagon, watching him. He coughed, slightly embarrassed, and wondered if he had looked foolish a moment ago as he enjoyed the scenery. He clapped his hands together and strode back to the wagon.

"Let's set all this stuff up, then," he said, gently lifting his tripod. When Ben hefted two bottles, Phillip quickly added, "Be careful with those. That liquid costs a pretty penny, and it's flammable, too."

"Don't worry, little brother," Ben said, swinging a bottle around to annoy and worry Phillip. "I won't break one and cause a fire—I don't think."

Phillip raised his eyebrows in a way that told Ben his actions didn't come close to bordering on humorous. Hannah lifted out a box of glass panes, and Phillip stopped himself from telling her to be careful. Of course she would be. Bethany carried a crate of supplies, and Marie brought over the water bucket filled with rags, brushes, and other odds and ends. No one had touched his camera, for which he was grateful. He decided to carry both the tripod and the camera himself before Ben could help with them.

"Let's go that way," Phillip said, nodding toward the trees. "There's a stream through there."

The group trudged through the underbrush and trees, which opened up a few minutes later to reveal a small pond surrounded by flowers and pine trees. Cliffs of rugged rock stood in the distance.

"It's beautiful," Hannah said in awe.

*My thoughts exactly,* Phillip mused, glad someone else could appreciate the view—especially since that someone was Hannah. He walked ahead to a large rock and deposited his load beside it. Everyone else followed and put their things down as Phillip set up the tripod and attached the camera, all the while looking around for shots he wanted to take. A tree several feet away had a rugged personality; it leaned hard to the left like a drunken old man trying to right himself. At its base was a clump of wildflowers that softened the view. The spot would be great for taking shots of the girls.

Phillip sent Ben to fetch some water, and when he returned, Phillip positioned the girls by the crooked tree. He played with the arrangement until he felt satisfied with the balance. "Perfect," he said, noting Hannah's gentle smile at him.

*She's smiling at me.* Phillip's knees felt a bit weak. He looked away quickly and cleared his throat. *Gratitude. That's all her smile means,* he told himself. That's all. She was grateful to him for using one of his photography days for making sure the sisters and Marie had a memento of their summer. He knew that, yet her smile made his spirit soar. What if it could mean more than just appreciation? But it didn't. He had to remind himself of that every time he looked at her. She had eyes only for Claude, and Claude for her. Best to accept that and try to move on. *Try.*

He took several pictures while Ben stood behind him and made snide remarks to Bethany, like, "Smile much bigger and your head might break in two."

Bethany withstood his jabs surprisingly well, keeping her face straight as Phillip took the photos. More than once, Phillip wanted to shove Ben, but he contented himself with sending some jabs of his own, like, "Ben, shut your bazoo. I'm working," which stopped the teasing for a few minutes at a time.

When Phillip felt certain that he had captured a few acceptable images, he sighed with satisfaction. "Why don't you all get the food from the wagon and set up the picnic? I'll take a few pictures of the pond and join you in a minute."

Bethany left her post by the tree, brushed some grass off her skirt, and marched directly to Ben. "I deserve a medal for managing to keep a pleasant look on my face while seeing your hideous mug and listening to the rubbish spewing from your mouth. I am not about to try eating a meal if I have to look on you a moment longer. I have no stomach for such torture." She turned and, with the pointed heel of her boot, stomped on Ben's toe as she walked away.

"Hey!" Ben sucked air between his teeth and began to limp in a circle.

"Serves you right," Phillip said, picking up his tripod. "I wouldn't press my luck if I were you. Better stay here until Bethany's done eating, or you'll end up with sliced ham on your head."

Ben nodded in agreement, but he seemed distracted as he gazed into the trees where the girls had disappeared. He swallowed and sighed, then said, "I'm hungry. Join us when you're done."

"Suit yourself," Phillip called after him. "But don't blame me for what she does to you." Alone again, he looked around at his surroundings. It took only moments for the peaceful feeling to return. A group of clouds drifted past the sun, softening the light. The breeze that had kept the air cool all morning suddenly faded, leaving the trees and pond still. In that moment, the world had paused, posed perfectly for a photo.

*It doesn't get much better than this,* Phillip thought as he hurriedly set up his tripod and coated another plate. Not even a fluttering leaf would blur the photo if he caught it fast enough.

* * *

"Tell me honestly," Hannah said to Marie. "What do you think of Claude?"

*What a bunch of bosh!* Bethany thought. She stabbed her needle into the pillowcase she was embroidering and pretended not to hear the conversation. The three of them sat in the parlor. Bethany had looked forward to a pleasant evening of conversation, but Hannah's obsession with discussing Claude had reared its hideous head yet again. Unfortunately, since their father was out making calls on church business, it was safe to bring up Claude, Ted, or anything else tonight.

Marie laughed and closed the book she was reading. "Oh, Hannah. I met Claude just that once when we took that walk, and he had eyes only for you. I didn't even get to speak with him."

"I know, but even so, what do you think of him?" Hannah pressed. She had her feet tucked under her on the couch, her arms wrapped around her knees. She faced Marie as if her judgment would determine Hannah's fate.

"I think that anyone who loves my cousin and makes her happy is someone I'd like."

Marie cracked open the book again but stopped when Hannah protested, "Come. That's not an answer."

"Very well. I think Claude is handsome—not *quite* as handsome as my Ted, but you'll forgive me on that point, I presume."

With a chuckle, Hannah nodded. "Of course. I wouldn't want you to think my Claude is more handsome than your own beau. But Claude *is* handsome, isn't he?" She leaned her head against the back of the couch and stared dreamily at the ceiling. "His eyes are so blue." Marie smiled and opened her book again, but Bethany rolled her eyes—then wished she had an ally to roll eyes with. She hunkered down in her chair and kept to her needlework. The group of roses she was embroidering didn't fit her emotions. She felt in the mood to create something more like flames or a growling black bear. At least she could add thorns to the roses—that was some consolation.

"For years I've never understood my girlfriends and their infatuation with boys," Hannah said, coming out of the clouds long enough to again interrupt Marie's reading. "Seriously, what did Esther Mitchell ever see in Fred Jones? The boy is nothing more than a short, stocky bully who throws tantrums to get what he wants. He used to pull all the girls' braids in school. He broke Esther's slate when she was seven, yet they married last spring. I don't understand it. He's dreadful."

"He may have grown up," Marie suggested, putting the book on her lap as if realizing that she wouldn't be getting any reading done soon. "But love also changes the way you see people. Frankly, I'm glad that everyone finds different people attractive. It would be horrible if everyone thought the same individuals were good looking, and no one gave others a passing glance. What if a dozen other women had eyes for Ted? Besides, what a boring world it would be. Just look at the men we know—they're all so different, and that's wonderful. From what I've seen, Phillip is very much into thinking, reading, and learning, like with his photography. Claude is more outspoken and seems more eager to enjoy himself."

"True," Hannah said. "Claude's always been that way. People are drawn to him somehow. In school there was a group of boys who followed him anywhere."

"And then there's Ben," Marie said, looking pensive. "I'm not sure about him. He's outspoken for sure. He's certainly very different from his brothers."

In the corner, Bethany snorted. Her head snapped up. "I can tell you anything you need to know about Ben Adams. He's egotistical, self-important, and cruel. I pity any girl who falls in love with him—" She snapped her mouth shut, suddenly feeling anger course through her—and hating the fact that, by her own definition, she had to pity herself. After all, once upon a time *she* had fallen in love with Ben Adams. Lowering her head, Bethany kept stitching, ignoring the fact that the needle was nearly out of thread. She didn't want to raise her eyes until they started talking about something—anything—else. *I've let my emotions get the better of me! Why did I permit myself such an outburst?*

She hoped for the sake of all women that Ben kept his pledge to remain a bachelor. Bethany couldn't bear to think of seeing him with a wife—or any woman on his arm, for that matter—and she wondered yet again what her life might have been like if events had played out differently. Would she and Ben have gotten married? If so, would they have been happy together? Bethany would have given a great deal to know the answer to both questions.

After an awkward pause, where Hannah and Marie looked over questioningly, Hannah tentatively continued the conversation. "So what about Ted? What's he like?"

How much more of this could a girl endure? Why couldn't Hannah let the topic of men go? Bethany's mind thundered with aggravation.

Marie broke into a big smile, her eyes twinkling. "Ted is wonderful. He's so . . . *Teddish,* if that makes sense."

"Oh, it does! It makes perfect sense," Hannah chimed in. "Just like Claude is *Claudish!*"

*And Ben is so like Ben.* Bethany wished she knew the answer to one more question—what was Ben really like? Who was he really? Long ago she had thought she knew him. And then their world had turned upside down and made her question everything. Was the Ben of today the man she fell in love with?

*No. He's the man who humiliated me.*

* * *

The Adams brothers had just finished their dinner of burned biscuits, canned fruit, and a tough, chewy roast.

Ben leaned back and picked at a tooth. "I think it's Claude's turn to clean up."

"You're too smart to think that, dear brother," Claude said, standing up and shoving his chair under the table. "I'm going to see Hannah. I deserve that much for missing out on the canyon trip. Besides, after that hideous meal, you deserve the honors of washing up as penance for wreaking havoc on our stomachs."

Phillip laughed. "I second that."

"Serves you both right for insisting we all take turns," Ben countered. "You know I'm no chef. And I'm *not* washing up."

A knock sounded at the door. They all took a sheepish look around—muddy boots at the door, dried mud tracked into the house, two or three days' worth of dishes on the counter, piles of newspapers and other odds and ends . . . They were in no state for receiving visitors.

"Who is that?" Phillip asked grumpily, quickly grabbing the roast pan. His brothers also leapt into action, clearing the table. *They* might not care that they lived like slobs, but they didn't need others knowing it.

The brothers did a poor job of hiding the mess, but when their visitor knocked again, they had to answer. On his way to the door, Ben kicked some dirt with his foot, hoping to spread around so it wasn't so obvious. Phillip swiped the table with his arm, spilling crumbs onto the floor—and smearing butter on his sleeve.

"Bishop Hansen, what a pleasant surprise," Ben said loudly.

Phillip and Claude groaned and gave each other sympathetic looks. If it had been almost anyone else, they could have gone outside on the porch for an evening chat. But they knew from experience that the bishop wouldn't be content with that; he'd traipse through the kitchen to sit down in their makeshift parlor—and see the virtual disaster in the kitchen on the way.

"Come in, come in," Ben said, feigning joviality.

Bishop Hansen followed Ben through the kitchen to the back room, his cane sticking to the floor twice. Their guest's eyebrows rose slightly at the disorder, even though Claude and Phillip stood in front of the worst of it, trying to block the view. They smiled innocently.

"Good evening, Bishop," they said simultaneously, then followed him into the sitting room. Everyone pulled up chairs, giving their visitor the most comfortable one.

"I won't beat around the bush with you boys," Bishop Hansen said. He slipped a pocket watch out of his vest and checked the time. "I've got other visits to make tonight." He rested his hands on top of his cane. "Simply stated, I've got a job for you."

Claude's eyes grew wide, and the bishop chuckled. "Not to worry. It's not another mission, at least not yet. But it is a church assignment."

"Whatever is it, we'll be happy to help out," Ben said.

"Absolutely," Phillip agreed with a nod. It didn't escape him that Claude didn't answer. He looked almost pale, as if the assignment would tear him away from Hannah and he couldn't bear the thought.

"Glad to hear it." Bishop Hansen sat back and interlaced his fingers. "The wards in and around Salt Lake have been asked to bring in fifteen hundred loads for the temple this fall. Our ward's portion is thirty-five loads from the quarry. We have a couple of months to do it, but frankly, I'd rather have it done sooner than later. I've already assigned the other loads but we still have two more to bring in. I'm hoping you boys will do it."

Phillip's brow creased slightly. "We'd be happy to, but we don't have ox teams or a wagon . . ."

"You can borrow mine. I've got three pair that are strong enough to make the trip. A load takes about four days there and back, so two loads should take you nine days or so, counting a day to rest for the Sabbath. What do you say?"

"We accept, of course," Phillip said, looking at his brothers. "Don't you agree? Anything to help with the temple." The two trips to the quarry would postpone his opening day, but he'd manage. Ben wouldn't have trouble getting time off work since it would be considered tithing labor—and he worked for the temple anyway.

"When do we go?" Ben asked.

"In a week, if that's all right with you. You'll need a little time to get ready. I'll make sure you have enough feed for the animals, but you'll need to bring provisions for yourselves."

Phillip's first reaction—after excitement over helping raise the walls of the temple, even if only by two stones—was relief. It would be welcome respite from watching Hannah and Claude gaze into one another's eyes.

As promised, the bishop didn't stay long. Ben and Phillip walked him to the door, but when they came back, they found Claude staring glumly into the fire.

"What's the matter?" Ben asked, nudging Claude in the shoulder. "Did you just realize that Hannah will be gray and wrinkled someday?"

"Very funny." Claude stood up and walked past his brothers. "You two wouldn't understand."

"Try me," Phillip said, stopping Claude before he stalked out of the room.

Claude paused, turned around, and let out a deep breath. "Fine. Laugh all you want, but I'm going to miss Hannah. I know nine days isn't long. But it sure feels like it now that we're courting and . . . never mind." He turned and left, going upstairs.

Phillip watched him go, feeling a bit of sympathy for the poor man. What would be a relief and an escape for one of them would be a trial for another.

* * *

The following day, Claude went to three stores in downtown Salt Lake City before he found what he was looking for—the perfect gift for Hannah. He didn't want to tell his brothers about it; they'd just laugh at the idea of giving her a going-away present before their temple assignment, say he was being nothing but a heart-sick fool. Sure, he'd be gone only a week and a half, but he'd miss her, and he was quite sure she'd miss him equally. Since they'd be packing over the weekend in preparation to leave Monday morning, he wouldn't be able to see her much before they left. This way she'd have something tangible to remind her of him, to keep her connected to him in his absence. Besides, it was a way to show that Hannah was really his.

"I'll take that one," he said, pointing into the glass case at the beautifully carved tortoiseshell comb with a cluster of pearls in the center.

"Good choice," the woman behind the counter said as she placed the comb into a small box. "A gift for someone special, I assume?"

Claude dug into his pocket for money. "Yes," he said, smiling awkwardly. "I hope she likes it."

"I'm sure she'll wear it with pride," the woman said, taking the coins from Claude and handing over the box. "Good luck."

"Thanks." Claude left the store, turned onto State Street and bit his lip. Should he take the comb to Hannah right now? He had no idea if she was even home, but he couldn't wait to see her face when she saw his gift. He'd take it out of the box and slide it into her hair—the perfect accent to her dark waves.

He headed left toward the Hansen place, hurrying along so he could get there quicker. A part of him knew that even if Hannah were home, he shouldn't stay long anyway; his brothers would be looking for him, especially since it was his turn to attempt making supper.

Bishop Hansen answered the door and let Claude in with a hearty, "Come in, come in." Leading Claude to the sitting room, he left to find his daughter.

Claude sat on the hard sofa and waited. To his relief, Bishop Hansen didn't return along with Hannah. Instead she appeared at the door alone. "Hello," she said.

He stood as she entered. Her hair was loose, instead of in its usual twist. It fell in waves, and a few tendrils curled around her face. She was beautiful. Perfect. A greeting caught in his throat, and he had a sudden desire to take her in his arms, to kiss her hard, to call her his own. He remembered what kissing Cybil had felt like, felt his heart hammering . . . and quickly shoved such thoughts out of his mind.

"It's nice to see you again," Hannah said, stepping into the room.

"Likewise," Claude managed. She took a seat across from him, and he returned to his spot on the couch. They sat awkwardly for a moment, Claude turning the box in his hands and Hannah looking around the room at everything but him.

Why were they suddenly so bashful with one another? On their walk the other day, they were comfortable talking and laughing. Maybe it was the formality of the room—and being truly alone for the first time. He eyed the candlesticks on the mantel, the rug covered with elaborate roses, the bust of some long-dead composer sitting on the piano. He didn't feel comfortable in the fancy room, so he found himself acting as stiff as the starched, crocheted antimacassars on the armrests. It was clear from Hannah's prim posture and clasped hands that she too felt awkward.

He finally ventured to speak. Holding out the box, he said, "I brought something for you." He almost added, *Miss Hansen.*

Her eyes lit up. "You did?"

There was the face that turned his heart. More relaxed now, he nodded. "It's not much. Just a little something before I leave for my temple assignment."

Hannah crossed over to the sofa and sat beside Claude. "What is it?" She took the box and lifted the lid. With a gasp, she exclaimed, "Why Claude, it's beautiful!"

Satisfaction warmed him head to toe. "You like it?"

"I've always admired tortoiseshell combs. My mother had one, and I was hoping Father would buy me one for my next birthday." She gently removed the comb and held it in her palm. "Thank you. I'll treasure it."

"May I put it in your hair?" As soon as the question left his mouth, he clamped his teeth together. She might see him as awfully forward to make such a suggestion, and that wouldn't do. He had hoped to slide the comb into her dark hair, but shouldn't have actually *suggested* it.

But Hannah just took his hand, placed the comb into the palm, and turned her head to the side. She hesitated only slightly before saying, "Please do."

Claude's hands trembled with anticipation. Gently, he smoothed back a section of her hair. At his touch Hannah closed her eyes, a smile still on her lips. He slid the comb in but let his hand linger, resisting the urge to lean in, smell her hair, kiss her neck. *Not now,* he told himself. *Later . . .*

Hannah reached up to touch the comb, then stood and crossed to the fireplace, over which hung a large mirror. She tilted her head to see the effect, then lifted her fingers to touch the pearls. "It's beautiful, Claude, thank you."

"A beautiful gift for a beautiful woman." He came up behind her, placed his hands on her shoulders, and admired her. Hannah seemed to take a sudden breath at his forwardness, but she didn't protest or pull away.

As they gazed at one another in the mirror, the moment felt so perfect that Claude didn't want to risk ruining it by letting it go too long. He leaned down and kissed her cheek. "I'll see you as much as I can before I leave."

With that, he strode to the sofa, picked up his hat, and left the house—hoping he had left Hannah in a state of romantic bliss.

*This is why Ben never managed to convert me to his way of thinking,* Claude mused as he walked home. *I'm made for wooing women.*

# CHAPTER 7

"What do you think?" Marie asked as she emerged from the house Friday afternoon. She wore Hannah's pale-yellow silk dress, which fit perfectly.

Phillip stood from his work of preparing glass plates and nodded with approval. "Looks like it was made for you." That dress was his favorite of Hannah's.

"Thank you. I'm glad you suggested it." Marie turned to a window and looked at her reflection. She smoothed the neckline and turned so she could see the back of the dress. "It's so much nicer than anything I brought with me from home—perfect for Ted's photograph."

"And Hannah won't mind?" Phillip asked.

"Oh, no." Marie laughed, a tinkling, musical sound. "We used to share clothes as girls. Haven't in years, of course, but I asked her this morning, and she was happy to let me borrow her things." She smoothed back her hair and came to Phillip. "Where shall I stand?"

"Let's see . . ." He bit his lip as he surveyed the yard. They had already taken several photos of Marie in her dark brown dress, using the old pine tree for a background. Something more interesting—more romantic—should serve for the photo intended for her beau. He needed to hurry, because back at home his brothers were already trying to pack. If he didn't help them out, he'd hear about nothing else the entire trip. They didn't know he was taking pictures of Marie, just that he was working on getting the studio ready to open. She had seemed reluctant to talk about her beau openly, so he'd respected her privacy and kept the information to himself.

Several aspens and a birch grew beside the fence that ran along the front of the Hansen property. The shade would soften any harsh sunlight and make a beautiful frame. "Over there," he said, pointing. He lifted his tripod. Instead of taking her spot right away, Marie picked up a box of supplies and followed Phillip.

"Thank you," he said, then took the box and set it on the ground. "Now, stand there with your hands resting on the fence post."

He worked quickly before the plates dried, and as he directed, Marie stood as still as possible so the image wouldn't be blurred. He drew the camera into the shade of a tree, then slid the plate into place, thinking wistfully that if he couldn't have love in his life, he might as well help others have their own. He peered through the viewer at Marie, to adjust the camera's angle and her pose.

As Phillip ducked under the cloth, a sudden cry of surprise burst from Marie. Clearly visible through the viewfinder was a dark-haired man standing on the lowest fence rail. He leaned over the edge and held his hands over Marie's eyes. The camera was largely hidden by a pine tree, so perhaps the man didn't notice it, Phillip thought. Before he could be overly concerned, however, the man's harmless tone reached Phillip's ears.

"Guess who?" he said.

Even with her eyes covered, the smile on Marie's face registered shocked joy.

*"Ted?"* Marie's hands went to the man's fingers. She pulled them away and turned to face him. Her cheeks flushed. "My goodness. What are you doing here?"

"Came up to deliver some papers to Church headquarters from Bishop Green. I'm only here for the day, but I couldn't leave without seeing you." Ted glanced both ways down the street—either not noticing the camera and Phillip, or not caring about them—and drew Marie close. The two shared a sweet kiss. Phillip caught the moment on a plate. He pulled his head out from under the dark cloth, grinning—grateful that the newest photography techniques didn't require the shutter to be open very long to produce a usable image. Taking such pictures would have been inconceivable ten or fifteen years before.

"Hello there," Phillip said, holding out a hand and walking toward the couple.

With a start, the two broke apart. Marie flushed bright red and covered her mouth shyly, as if she had forgotten in that fleeting moment that she wasn't alone. Phillip wished he knew what such a thing was like—losing himself in a tender kiss.

"Phillip Adams," he said. "Friend of the Hansen family. I was just taking some photographs of Marie. I assume you're Ted."

The couple eyed one another with a combination of embarrassment and happiness. Finally Ted nodded and shook Phillip's hand. "Good to meet you."

Marie sidled awkwardly toward Phillip, gripping and ungripping her fingers nervously. "Would you not mention this to anyone?" She waved her hand between herself and Ted. "Only Bethany and Hannah know about us. I'd rather my parents found out from me instead of someone else. They know we're courting, but they don't know that he proposed the day before I came up here. We wanted to tell them together."

Phillip made as if to button his lips together. "You have my word," he said, glad he had already kept the secret so far. How easy it would have been to mention it to Ben or Claude.

"Thank you," Marie said, relief washing through her voice. She leaned forward and said, "I know I can trust you." Ted came around, and she put her hand through his arm. For a second Marie hesitated, looking at Ted longingly, but then eyeing Phillip's camera a little guiltily.

"Don't worry," Phillip said with a smile. "We can finish later."

Of course, he now had four plates that would be ruined, but he couldn't quite bring himself to anger over it, not when Marie and Ted looked so happy together. Besides, he needed to get home to pack.

"I'll be right back," Marie promised Ted as she held out her skirts. "I need to change."

She lifted her hem and hurried inside the house. While she was gone the men chatted amicably, mostly about Phillip's equipment. It was a safe topic, one unlikely to embarrass Ted further, and one Phillip found easy to discuss.

When Marie returned a few minutes later, she and Ted left for a walk. Once they were out of sight, Phillip loaded his supplies onto the cart he'd borrowed from Mrs. Brecken. At the last moment he remembered that he hadn't closed the well. He pulled the wooden cover over the opening and returned to his cart just as Claude and Hannah appeared at the end of the lane. Phillip's stomach flipped over.

*If only I'd managed to leave a few minutes earlier,* he sighed.

"Phillip!" Claude hailed him. "What are you doing here?"

Pushing his lips into a smile, Phillip waved back. "I could ask the same of you. I thought you and Ben were home getting ready for the trip." He warily glanced at the cart piled with his things. He would have to tread lightly to avoid telling Marie's secret. "I'm just taking some pictures. Why aren't you home?"

"Ben had to run some errands, so I decided to see Hannah again before we go." He kept his gaze on Hannah as he spoke.

Hannah eventually tore her eyes from Claude's. "You're taking pictures all the way out here?" She stood close enough that Phillip could almost smell the white carnation tucked behind her ear—something Claude had surely put there himself.

"Well, I . . . Marie just wanted a photo for her parents." The sight of Hannah still made him lightheaded, making it hard to think clearly. Even so, that much information surely couldn't hurt. It was the truth—part of it.

"That's right," Hannah said, then looked around. "Where is she? Did she go back inside?"

"She went on a walk after we finished," Phillip said. Again, the truth, yet safe enough. Hannah knew the secret, but it wasn't his place to tell Claude about it.

"I wanted to show her the new calico I bought, but no matter," Hannah said, pointing at the package she carried in one arm. "It can wait. Don't go, Phillip. Come inside for a bite. I think we still have some of Bethany's cherry pie."

Being around Hannah produced a paradoxical effect in Phillip—he had equal desires to run away and to linger forever, even with Claude standing close by. Plus, there would be work to do at home if he left. But if Claude was skipping out on chores, why did Phillip have to be the responsible one? His appetite tipped the scales, and he found himself following the two of them inside. The men sat at the round kitchen table while Hannah rummaged in the pantry and appeared triumphantly a moment later with the pie tin raised in both hands.

"Here it is!" Hannah placed the tin on the table between them and cut two thick slices, then a thinner one for herself. She returned the tin to the pantry and sat down. The three of them had scarcely touched their dessert when Bethany returned from tending the Anderson children, whose mother had been ill with pneumonia for some time.

"What a day," Bethany said, collapsing in the last chair at the table. Her face was drawn, her eyes droopy. Wisps of hair had escaped her bun, and they hung around her head like a disheveled halo. "I've always liked children—until now."

Phillip and Claude gave each other amused smiles. But when Hannah spoke, she was clearly concerned. She touched her sister's arm and asked, "What happened?"

"The Andersons are not children. They are utter terrors. Devils. No wonder their mother is ill so much of the time. Anyone living under that roof would have to be ill or mad." She leaned her head onto her hands and groaned. "It's a wonder their house hasn't burned down or that my hair isn't entirely gray." She sighed, rubbed her forehead, and sat against the chair back, adding, "Or that I didn't kill one of them. I don't know that I can handle one more upsetting thing today. It's just not in me."

Hannah's lips bit shut into a tight, white line, and she suddenly sat up straighter, staring at the side door. Phillip shifted in his seat and had to hold back a laugh at what he saw. Bethany wasn't done with her upsetting day, not yet.

Bishop Hansen was walking up the drive. And beside him was Ben.

* * *

"Any pie left?" Bethany asked, heading for the pantry before anyone answered. She stepped inside and scanned the shelves just as the outside screen door opened and slammed shut. She figured her father must be home.

The pie sat on the top shelf. Bethany reached for the tin and looked into it. *Good. One piece left.* She stepped into the kitchen in time to hear an all-too-familiar voice say, "Oh, no."

Her fingers tightened on the tin, and her step came up short. Before her stood not only her father, but Ben at his side. She felt exposed, as if someone had walked in on her while she was dressing. Mind reeling for a snappy retort, she floundered for something to say.

"I'll let you young people sit around and chat awhile," her father said. "I have some work to do in my study." Apparently he hadn't noticed what Ben said—or what he'd meant. Her father walked right past her, oblivious to her seething.

"I don't know that I'll stay," Ben said, eyeing Bethany directly, even though he seemed to be speaking to everyone else. "Claude, do you think if I called the bishop back in here, that he'd send me on another mission right this instant? I'd rather swim the ocean and climb Mount McKinley if it meant not wasting three minutes' conversation on this *harpy.*"

Bethany's hand began trembling with pain as Ben's last word repeated itself in her head like a hammer striking an anvil again and again. Her teeth clenched, and she couldn't speak.

Her mind searched for a retort but remained blank. *He's won this time,* she thought, angry that she had been taken by surprise. *I have no barbs left to fling.*

Their eyes locked, and she searched his gaze for any shred of evidence that he realized how mean he was, for any regret for inflicting such a deep verbal wound. Surely he remembered the last time he had used that word. But with his folded arms and raised eyebrows, he looked nothing but smug and self-righteous.

In spite of her throat constricting, she managed a few words. "You won't have to leave," she said, smacking the pie onto the table. If she had had the nerve, she would have flung the dessert into his face, but it wouldn't have given her any satisfaction. Right now she just wanted to run. "*I'll* leave."

She turned and fled down the hall, shoes tapping a staccato rhythm on the wooden floor. She didn't stop until she reached her bedroom and collapsed at the head of the bed. As if she were a little girl, Bethany pulled her knees up to her chest and cried. The white pillowcase soon had a damp spot. She clutched a smaller pillow between her arms and stared at the wall. The pink roses on the wallpaper blurred through her tears.

Wasn't it enough that Ben had publicly humiliated her so long ago? Did he have to keep opening the wound every time they met? If he was that coldhearted in her presence, heaven only knew what he said to others when she wasn't around. Maybe her father *could* call him on another mission. He could make it for five years at least—and to somewhere across the ocean this time. Everything had been simpler when he was gone.

*He's always been pigheaded,* she reminded herself. *It shouldn't be a surprise that a mission didn't change that.* And he probably hadn't changed in any other significant way, either. Part of her wanted to confront him, to at least make him listen and understand that she had done nothing wrong—well, nothing except engage in this miserable war of words. But if he wouldn't listen to her side of the story before he left, why would he listen to it now? Things couldn't get any worse—unless she attempted to reason with him and he chose to call her names.

Bethany sat up and wiped her eyes, accomplishing little, since new tears wet her face the moment she pulled her hand away. She slid off the bed and lifted the edge of her mattress. Underneath lay a hardbound volume and a small stack of folded papers. Clutching them to her chest, she crossed to the door and secured the hook that locked it.

Once again she sat on her bed. She lay the journal aside and unfolded the papers. They were letters from Ben, dated years ago before everything had fallen apart. His uneven scrawl made her smile sadly, but his words brought back a pain that she was now certain would never heal. The way he described her on the page—sweet, gentle, beautiful—couldn't be more different than the way he saw her now.

*Harpy.*

*What have I done to deserve being called that?*

If that was how men were, she'd rather do without one, thank you very much. But she couldn't help remembering the good times, when she and Ben had been far kinder to one another, where just a glance from him was enough to make her happy for an entire day. Could such a feeling ever last? With a sigh, she carefully folded the letters and set them aside, then looked at her journal, unsure if she wanted to reread the entries. Her finger traced the embossed design on the cover as she recalled some of the events that were recorded on the pages.

Even now she wondered if she could have handled the situation differently, but she still hadn't figured out how she should have mended it. It all happened so quickly, over the course of less than twenty-four hours—a one-two punch of elation and then despair.

The memories stood out in stark contrast against one another and always would. First was the night of the dance at the Perkins home, a favorite place of young people. It had a large parlor area with a smooth wood floor, and with the furniture pushed and stacked against the walls, and some pieces removed altogether, there was room for dancing. A small band traditionally played in the corner by the fireplace.

For several months both Ben and another boy, Matthew, had been showing Bethany extra attention, openly competing against one another for her favor. The memory stilled her tears, and Bethany picked up her journal and held it to her chest, smiling at the memory of the two of them racing across the room to ask for her hand—and of Ben's foot catching on a lady's train, sending him sliding face-first into a wall. Matthew won that time due to sheer luck, but Ben was champion on plenty of other occasions.

Even before those days she secretly harbored feelings for Ben, but at first it seemed he was more interested in competition than in the girls he competed for. About a year before his mission, she had begun to truly care for him. But she had watched him compete against Clark MacKenzie for Daisy, and against Garth Wilkin for different girls, so she'd assumed he wasn't serious in any of his attentions.

And then he began writing those letters. She shyly answered them, confessing her own feelings, then noticed that he had stopped chasing after other girls. He wasn't openly courting her, but something was definitely different between them. Their eyes would catch across a street, or at church, they'd smile, and her heart would hammer against her rib cage.

Ben's letters spoke of admiration, of sleepless nights, of his dreams for their future together. He wrote sonnets. The passion in his letters was such that it left Bethany breathless—and at times she wondered if he could mean it all. Could Ben Adams feel so deeply for her, Bethany Hansen, a little old farm girl? She certainly hoped so and said as much in her letters back to him, pouring out her very soul with her pen. Ben knew things about her that no one else in the world ever heard. She trusted him, and, she believed, he trusted her with his innermost thoughts and feelings. It was only a matter of time until they could speak to one another openly about it.

At dances, Ben would always try to beat Matthew in asking her to the floor first, then as the music ended, he'd squeeze her hand gently, winking as he led her back to her seat. At night she often fell asleep with the words of his letters flitting through her mind. But every so often she'd remember his past flirtations with other girls and wonder if he were merely playing a game with her, though it did seem he had stopped such shenanigans long before.

Their feelings for one another had been shared only on paper, until that final eventful night when Matthew had been pirated away by Polly Law to the dance floor. Ben seized the opportunity to catch Bethany alone. "Come outside and walk with me," he'd whispered in her ear.

She'd jumped, not realizing he was there, and turned to face him. He stood close, and when their eyes met, his looked deeply into hers, making Bethany's entire body tremor with delight. "Come with me?" he asked again, then nodded toward the dance floor, where Matthew clapped in rhythm to the fiddle with Polly. "Before *he* sees us."

Butterflies came to life inside her stomach. *Could Ben Adams really care for me as more than a prize? Do his letters really say what he feels?*

Even as she wondered, she had the good fortune of overhearing a spot of gossip about them from her friend Marilyn. "Just look at that Ben Adams. He thinks he's so much better than everyone. Do you realize he hasn't danced with anyone but Bethany Hansen since Christmas? The nerve."

Ben flushed red, and Bethany bit her lips with pleasure. She had noticed that Ben wasn't chasing other girls, but she hadn't realized she was his sole invitee to the dance floor. "Let's go," she said quietly, secretly grateful for once that Marilyn was such a gossip.

Ben took her hand and wove the two of them through the edge of the crowd and out the Perkins' front door.

Once outside, he tugged on her arm and whispered, "Come on!" Together they ran behind the house, not stopping until they reached a thick stand of trees hidden by the stable. The dark night shadowed them. A waxing moon and bright stars provided just enough light to illuminate Ben's face.

Breathless from running—and from the spontaneity and daring of Ben's proposition—Bethany didn't say anything. Then Ben took both of her hands in his and gazed into her eyes. She swallowed hard, painfully aware of her ragged breath. Her world seemed to be spinning, and the sensation was intensified by his touch.

*I like you, Ben,* she wanted to say. *I really like you. Very well, I love you.* But she couldn't let loose a sound.

"Forget Matthew," Ben said suddenly. "This is all just a game to him, but for me . . ."

"For you?" Bethany repeated, her heart hanging on his reply.

He drew her closer and leaned down to whisper in her ear, even though no one was around to hear them. "I'm fixin' to marry you someday, Bethany Hansen. Will you be my girl?" He pulled back just enough to look at her as he waited for her answer, but he stayed close enough for her to feel his breath and smell his musky scent.

Her knees felt as weak as tapioca. "Are you . . . are you toying with me?" If he didn't really care for her, she wasn't about to be played for a fool. "Because if you're just trying to beat Matthew again—"

He drew back a few inches as if something had physically struck him, and she instantly regretted saying it. "You don't believe me?" he said. Releasing her hands, he dropped his eyes and shifted uncomfortably on the grass. "Or maybe you don't feel the same way. I thought you knew . . ." He shook his head. "Never mind. Forget I said anything."

The devastated look on his face shot joy through Bethany's entire frame. Even Ben was incapable of acting a part that well. He *did* care. "Ben!" she called out as he took a step to leave. He paused with his back to her and cocked his head slightly, but he didn't turn around. She tried again. "Don't go. I've wanted to be your girl for ever so long—since your very first letter."

There. She'd said it. She covered her flip-flopping stomach with both hands, waiting for him to look at her. Each second that ticked by felt like a full minute, and the wait was agonizing. Ben finally turned around, the crooked grin she loved slowly breaking across his face, his silly cowlick curling over his forehead.

"Really?"

She nodded, feeling her face ready to split from her own grin. She reached for him, and Ben returned to her in two long strides. Instead of taking her hands, he wrapped his arms around her and pulled her close. Stunned, Bethany caught her breath and looked up at Ben, whose face was only a few inches away. His smile had softened, and now he leaned closer. Rising on her toes, she leaned toward him, allowing him to kiss her.

As their lips met, the butterflies in her stomach went into a frenzy, making Bethany's fingers curl around his shirt. She could feel his heart beating hard inside his chest, which only made her own heart rate speed up. He pulled away, let out a breath, then said, "My girl?"

Emotions coursed through Bethany that she had never experienced. Their power was so overwhelming she could only nod and whisper, "Yes."

Ben hugged her, and she embraced him back, wishing the moment would never end. After breaking apart, they looked at one another with new eyes and suddenly felt a bit shy. Both laughed nervously. Ben put out his arm, Bethany took it, and together they went on that walk he had first suggested. Neither said much the rest of the evening, but Bethany didn't care. She reveled in the glow of her love for Ben as she strolled beside him, knowing that he cared for her as she did for him.

He walked her home by the light of the moon and stopped at the end of the drive. Ben brought her hand to his lips and kissed it. She walked toward the house, unaware of her feet touching plain old earth. Instead her mind was filled with the knowledge that Ben—*her* Ben—watched from the gate. She still felt his kiss on her lips, his touch on her hand. She reached for the door and opened it, then paused and looked back. At that distance, she could make out only Ben's dark outline. Hoping he could see her better, she kissed her fingers and blew.

She had no idea that the very next day would destroy the happiness she'd found—destroy it completely.

*Why did I think I'd want to read my journal?* Bethany slipped off the bed and shoved the book and the letters back under her mattress. She wiped her hands as if she needed to remove the stain of memories from them.

A door banged shut outside, and Bethany looked through the window. Ben was leaving. Supposedly all three of the Adams brothers would be hauling rock from the temple quarry next week. It wasn't a mission across the ocean, but she would welcome a few days without having to worry about crossing his path. She watched Ben walk away, his posture somewhat stooped and his pace slow. At the end of the drive, Ben paused and turned toward the house. Bethany gasped and drew deeper into her room, even though the slightly sheer curtains would certainly prevent him from seeing her at a distance.

He stood far enough away that she couldn't make out his face, but he didn't seem to wear his usual look of self-congratulation. Bethany stared at him, unable to move until he did. Perhaps he did see her after all, because his gaze seemed to penetrate her soul. He raised his hand, but then must have thought better of it and shoved his hand into his pocket. He turned away and headed down the street.

Bethany released an uneasy breath. She left the window and lay on her bed, then drew her knees back to her chin and relived Ben's kiss. Once, twice, three times. That was the happiest night of her life. For now she let herself remember it, not allowing her mind to step to the inevitable—the day that ruined everything.

# CHAPTER 8

With sudden awareness, Ben rubbed his fingertips and thumb together and lowered his hand. He took a backward step and another, then turned and walked away, hands deep in his pockets. He was taken off guard by strong memories of the night he had walked Bethany home. He hoped she hadn't seen him almost blow a kiss toward her window. At least, it had been her window two years ago, and he assumed she still slept there. The same lacy curtains hung, swaying in the breeze. The window must be open for them to be moving like that. Was she watching him? He dismissed the idea as soon as it came. Why would she bother looking at someone she despised?

As he turned down the road and headed for home, the past few minutes repeated themselves in his mind. After seeing Bethany flee from the kitchen, he hadn't enjoyed himself. Normally he would have reveled in yet another point in their never-ending game of verbal swordplay. But tonight, he knew his jab had wounded her deeply.

Why did it come as such a surprise that he could hurt her? Did he really think all this time that she was unfeeling? To escape his guilt and discomfort he had made some lame excuse about having a matter to attend to, then left the house before anyone could ask what he meant.

At the end of the lane, Ben paused. He smoothed the wrinkles out of the hat and put it on, then turned back and looked at Bethany's window.

With a sudden pang, he lingered on thoughts of the night he'd walked Bethany home, when she had blown him a kiss from the side door, and he had waited by the fence until he saw candlelight in her room. She had stood at the window and watched him walk away. With only a flicker behind her for light, he couldn't make out anything but her outline, but he'd always imagined that she was smiling as he left.

He didn't want to think about what had happened the first time he saw Bethany after that fateful night. But he couldn't keep the memory from surfacing. It was like trying to hold a wooden raft under water; eventually one's arms grew tired and it popped above the surface again.

*I shouldn't have assumed she'd take me seriously that night,* he thought. *Of course she didn't think I meant it, even given my letters—in her shoes, I might not have believed me, either.* He had to admit that his record with ladies prior to Bethany wasn't one he was proud of—not anymore. There had been a time when he enjoyed the long line of girls eager for his attention, all of them vying to be his pick. He couldn't blame Bethany for assuming she was just one more on the chain. But she wasn't. Even though he'd flirted with other girls in years past, Bethany had been his sole interest for months; then when Hannah dropped a comment that made him think perhaps Bethany cared for him, he abandoned any interest in other town girls and focused only on her. Unfortunately, Matthew did, too. Ben always hoped that his letters to Bethany would sway her in his direction, convince her of his feelings.

One day, several months into Ben's attempted courtship, Hannah found him after church and slipped him a letter written on pale pink paper. He knew immediately whom it was from.

He had secluded himself behind the blacksmith shed on the temple block and read it alone. *Thank you for your letters,* it began. *I admit to having similar inclinations . . .*

After that Bethany answered every letter. Her tone was formal and sometimes awkward, but then, his was too, at first. It was hard to be one's self on paper, writing to an audience you were unsure of. Months passed, and gradually they became more comfortable writing to one another and sharing their deepest, truest feelings. Eventually, Ben mustered the courage to sneak Bethany away from the dance and bare his soul in person—much more naturally than he ever could through pen and paper. It was a night he thought he'd always remember.

And he did. But with pain.

Who knew that Bethany had it in her to trail along more than one boy?

*I suppose I deserved that,* he thought. *I'd done the same to plenty of others. But never to her. And I never wrote letters like that to anyone else.*

She had asked if he were just playing with her. Ironically, it turned out to be the other way around. Shortly after the debacle, Ben considered asking Matthew what had gone on in the orchard—had he just found Bethany there picking fruit, or had they gone together specifically because it was a romantic spot for his proposal? Such questions were easy to put off, after that, when Ben went straight to the bishop and volunteered for a mission. He never did see Bethany and Matthew together after that day. At the time, Ben felt rather smug that things hadn't worked out between them, but never found out why. And now Matthew was married to someone else and living in Tooele.

Ben thought with frustration of the afternoon after their magical night at the dance. Ben had walked to the Hansen place, hoping to see Bethany and be invited inside. When he knocked on the door, Bishop Hansen answered. "You're looking for Bethany?" He seemed puzzled at why Ben would be asking for his eldest daughter. "I think she's out back in the orchard."

"Thank you, Bishop," Ben said with a nod. He wove his way through fruit trees in bloom, the setting sun painting hues of pink and orange on the blossoms that burst all over the orchard. Ben felt as if he were walking through heaven. He caught a glimpse of Bethany's hair through the trees. He picked up his pace, eager to see her again.

Someone spoke, and Ben paused. It wasn't Bethany. Or Hannah. It was a man. He peered through the branches and jumped when he recognized Matthew Pierce standing before Bethany. Drawing closer, Ben squinted between some tree limbs, crouching down to watch. Kneeling, Matthew took Bethany's hand in his. Her face was flushed, and she held her fingers to her lips as if overcome with emotion. Matthew held out a ring, ready to put it on her finger. Ben's fingers curled around a branch, a piece of bark biting into his skin. He leaned forward, his other hand leaning against a low branch. Matthew leaned in and kissed Bethany's cheek.

A crushing sensation of absolute betrayal descended on Ben. He leaned forward, his foot snapping a twig on the ground. The two looked over with a start. Bethany pulled her hand away from Matthew's.

"Ben!"

He shook his head in disbelief, his body trembling with rage. He pushed backward off the branch and slammed his boot into the trunk before stalking away.

"Ben! No, come back!" Bethany called after him. He didn't answer. When her footsteps sounded behind him, he raced off without acknowledging her. He ran all the way home without looking back, then locked the door. He collapsed on a chair and dropped his face in his hands.

Anger and betrayal quashed all the love he felt for Bethany. He sat before the cold fireplace, staring at the blackened bricks, feeling alternately hollow, then filled with burning rage. At least Phillip and Claude weren't home. He couldn't have borne trying to pretend all was well—or worse, seeing looks of pity if they found out.

He hadn't been home more than five minutes when a knock sounded on the door. "Ben!"

It was Bethany. His gripped the sides of the chair but made no move to answer.

"I know you're in there. Please, let me in. I need to explain."

He didn't speak or move. He watched his hands shake and realized it must be from emotion—emotion he was trying with everything in him to stifle. He gripped his hands together and squeezed them hard.

"Ben! Ben, please!" Bethany kept pounding on the door. Five minutes passed, then ten. Still she didn't leave. She called through the window and banged on the door again. Then kicked it and knocked again. "What happened isn't what you think."

*Her hands must be sore from all that knocking,* Ben thought absently. *And her voice sounds strained.*

"Let me in!" Her tone was no longer pleading. Now she yelled with clear anger. She kicked the door hard.

*How dare* she *be angry with* me?

"You stubborn, pigheaded fool! You open this door right now!"

*Fine.* Ben stood up so quickly the chair skittered several inches and turned over. He stormed to the door with long steps, then yanked it open, making it slam against the wall. He stared her down. "What?"

At his sudden outburst, Bethany drew back, startled. *Good,* he thought. *She's feeling guilty and intimidated.*

"It wasn't what it appeared to be," she said, voice slow and deliberate as if she were trying hard to keep it even.

"Let's review what it was and what it looked like. Were you alone in the orchard with Matthew Pierce? Yes, I believe you were." Ben ticked the item off on a finger. When Bethany opened her mouth to protest, he held up a hand to stop her and went on. "Did he kiss you? By golly, he did." Bethany flinched, which only egged him on. "And—oh yes—did he then get down on one knee, hold out a ring, and ask you to marry him? Guilty again. Who knows what else happened before I got there—or what has gone on for weeks or months to encourage him that way. And after what happened last night . . ."

Bethany's eyes narrowed, which unsettled Ben. She didn't look penitent or intimidated. Both arms raised, she pushed hard against his chest, sending him stumbling backward. She stormed into the room after him as he lost his balance and fell. Leaning over his form sprawled on the floor, she wagged a finger at him. "If you'd just listen to me for half a minute, you'd—"

Ben scrambled to his feet and regained his composure. He stepped forcefully in her direction. "Get out." He spoke with finality, with a tone that cut Bethany off.

She took a strong step forward. "Can you even remember how many times you've been alone with other girls? Or how many girls you've taken out of dances and whispered to? Flirted with? And then you have the audacity to suspect the worst of me without learning the facts. You accuse *me* of wrongdoing? How *dare* you!"

"None of those girls meant anything to me."

"I suppose I should be honored to join their ranks." Bethany's tone was icy.

"You know that's not how it is with you," Ben started.

Bethany's face flamed. "*Do* I? How can I know that? Especially since you assume the worst of me. How can I think you really care for me one jot when you fly off the handle at the very thing you've done a hundred times?"

"This is different, and you know it."

"It *is* different, but you're too caught up in your own pride to find out how." She pressed her trembling lips together. "You're different, Ben. You aren't the man I stood behind the barn with last night. *That* I know." Her mouth drew into a tight line. She lowered her eyes and sniffed.

Ben took the moment of weakness to speak out. "I'm not the one who changed—you are." He pointed to the door. "Now leave."

Bethany raised her face, tears brimming in her eyes. "Don't do this, Ben . . . If you'd only let me explain . . ."

"I said, get out." Anger pounding in his temples, he couldn't see straight or think clearly. The only thing he knew for sure was that Matthew had kissed Bethany—and she certainly hadn't stopped him. Granted, over the last while she had encouraged Ben, but apparently she had strung along Matthew as well. What else about her did he not know?

She took a step toward him, holding her hand out. "Ben, will you listen? Matthew means nothing to me."

He instinctively stepped back as if doing so would protect him from further harm. "Just go!" He grabbed a vase from an end table and smashed it against the wall. Bethany covered her ears, then hurried to the door. She paused at the threshold and gripped the edges of the doorframe.

She turned, and when she spoke, her voice was painfully quiet and even, but her eyes were filled with tears. "You'll regret this someday." She opened her mouth as if to say something more, but then closed it and walked out.

Ben watched her leave, step down the porch, and walk toward home with her head bowed. The sight didn't stop his insides from boiling with rage and humiliation. Soon he would be the laughingstock of the entire stake.

Unless . . .

He ran out after her and, in front of at least a dozen people on the street, called as loudly as he could, "Bethany Hansen, you had no right to mislead and deceive me. From here on, everyone will know what you are—a *harpy!*"

Bethany stiffened and stopped, but she didn't turn. She looked around at the crowd of people staring at her. Then, after a pause, she lifted her chin ever so slightly and walked away with the shred of dignity she had left.

And so the war began. From that day on, they couldn't see one another without exchanging barbs. Ben had always known she was clever, but her ability to insult was unparalleled. He couldn't stand the onslaught for long, and volunteered for a mission at his first opportunity. At the time, he thought the years away would make him stop thinking about Bethany, stop caring for her—or any woman, for that matter. Female folk weren't to be trusted. At least, he thought so then. But he wasn't proud of how he'd behaved that day, knowing how it had hurt her.

Today in the Hansen kitchen, after seeing the expression on Bethany's face before she fled, he knew the mission absolutely, positively, hadn't worked. He flinched at remembering what he'd called her.

*Harpy.*

When he'd said it, he hadn't been thinking of the first time he'd called her that. But by the look on her face, she hadn't forgotten the sting of that day any more than he had. She clearly despised him.

He didn't know if he could get over her deceit enough to make amends. After all, when she came to defend herself, she had never denied what had happened in the orchard. How could she? Matthew *had* kissed her and proposed to her. She had never worn his ring, but that was immaterial.

She had betrayed him. Ben had seen it himself.

# CHAPTER 9

After Ben left on his unexplained errand, Phillip sat in thought as he slid a fork from his lips. Claude and Hannah were talking, but Phillip had started thinking about Ben and Bethany—what had happened and what it meant. An idea began growing in his mind. He didn't realize he was grinning until someone spoke.

"What is it?" Claude asked, nudging his brother with the toe of his boot. "How about you share the joke with the rest of us?"

Phillip put down his fork. "What would the two of you say to undertaking one of Cupid's tasks with me?"

Hannah's brow rose in question, but Claude smiled back knowingly. "Sounds like a great idea."

"Wait a minute." Hannah planted both hands on the table and leaned forward. "What are you suggesting? I don't want my sister getting hurt."

"She won't be hurt," Phillip said, then added a little less than reassuringly, "I don't think." He leaned toward her and said, "Ben and Bethany"—he paused for effect—"love each other."

"Oh, please!" Hannah snorted with laughter, but quickly stopped when no one else seemed to be joining her mirth. "You—you can't be serious," she said as she looked from Claude to Phillip and saw that neither of them was laughing.

Claude nodded. "I've had similar suspicions for some time now, but I never dared broach the subject. You know how Ben is. Ever since we returned, Phillip and I have noticed the two of them interacting. And today—" He nodded toward the door where Ben had just left and then to the hall where Bethany had fled moments before. "Now I think it's true."

"What's your idea?" Hannah asked. She scooted her chair closer to the table, pushed her pie plate away, and leaned in.

Phillip glanced over his shoulder, making sure that Ben hadn't returned and that Bethany was still upstairs—then began. "The two of them had some misunderstanding—we know that much. They both accuse the another of humiliating them, but that's all either Claude or I know. Do you know what happened?"

Hannah shook her head and added, "That's as much as I've ever been able to figure out."

"I get the sense," Phillip went on, "that it's just their own pride standing in the way. That if they knew the other still cared, they'd both find a way to let go of being so obstinate. They'd mend fences and live happily ever after."

"Maybe," Hannah said dubiously. "But why do you think *we* can make it happen?"

"That's the best part," Phillip said, his face breaking into a grin. "The three of us are leaving Monday to haul rock for the temple. We'll be gone over a week. When's Marie going home?"

"A week from tomorrow," Hannah said. "Why?"

"Good. Plenty of time for my plan." Phillip settled into his seat, relishing the moment. "You see, the trick is to talk amongst ourselves about the situation, with Ben or Bethany listening but not *knowing* that we're perfectly aware that they're hearing every word."

"Interesting," Claude said, folding his arms. He leaned back in his chair. "Assuming we can make that happen, what do we talk about?"

Phillip gestured between himself and his brother. "Claude here will tell me all about Bethany's late-night confessions to Hannah."

"But Bethany has never confided in me about *Ben,*" Hannah protested.

"Ah, but does *Ben* know that?" Phillip asked. "Claude will say how Bethany can't sleep for thinking of Ben, how she *pines* for him and wishes he would love her in return. You know, anything that sisters might confide—pretending, of course, that she would say such things. Ben won't know the difference."

Claude fiddled with his fork, rotating it between his fingers. "But why would I know these things? How likely is it that Hannah would just decide to tell me Bethany's secrets?"

"That's easily explained." Phillip began talking faster as his excitement mounted. "Hannah's worried for her sister and must find someone to counsel with. Claude's the obvious choice. When he tells me all about it—with Ben listening, of course—I'll insist we tell Ben, but you'll swear me to secrecy so he can't mock her, and so a battle over sibling loyalties won't divide Hannah and Claude."

"Let me guess my part," Hannah interjected. "I tell Marie confidences supposedly given me through Claude—confidences about Ben's deep affection for Bethany." Her mouth curved, and she nodded, warming to the idea. "And I insist we never tell Bethany about it, because she'd scorn Ben if she ever found out his true feelings."

"That's the idea." Phillip sat back, pleased. "The way I figure, what we'll be saying is the truth. I'm sure they both really *are* losing sleep over each other—inside they're aching to be together. They haven't said as much, but that doesn't mean we can't pretend in order to force them to admit their feelings."

"I don't know . . ." Hannah shook her head, wavering. "If it doesn't work . . ."

"But imagine if it *does,*" Phillip insisted. "They'll both be happy. All of us will be able to be around one another without having to worry about what's going to happen next between them. No more outbursts, no more awkward moments. No more preplanning to make sure your father is present as a buffer between the two of them. It's perfect."

Hannah hesitated before finally nodding, a smile breaking across her face. "We'll do it. Marie won't be here long enough to see the effects, but it'll be grand fun making it happen."

* * *

Phillip spent Saturday evening in his photography shop doing as much work as he could before bed. Tomorrow was the Sabbath, and the morning after that he and his brothers would be off hauling granite for over a week. They'd spend even the Sabbath on the road.

This was his last chance to work and get the shop closer to opening for business. Their provisions were ready to load into Bishop Hansen's wagon, so he didn't feel guilty spending an hour or two here tonight. His creditors would be expecting their first payment soon, and Mrs. Brecken had been more than clear that she didn't like waiting on his rent. The sooner he could open up and start making money, the better. The fee he'd charged Marie wasn't nearly what it should have been, and it didn't come close to paying for next month's rent.

Most of his supplies were stored in a row of shelves along the right wall. His tripod and backdrop were at one end of the room, his makeshift darkroom at the other, complete with thick black curtains he'd ordered through Mrs. Brecken. The setup wasn't ideal, and it wasn't nearly as fancy as some of the portable darkroom caravans he had seen back East, but it would do for now.

He sorted through his latest photos, deciding which to display in the window. Marie's portrait had turned out quite well, and he made two extra copies for advertising. He came across the picture of Ted with Marie. He paused. It was a beautiful shot—slightly blurred from movement, but not as badly as he'd feared. The composition couldn't have been planned better.

But he certainly couldn't use the picture for promoting his business. Aside from the blurring, it was a private moment captured, a secret that wasn't his to share. He wondered if he should deliver those pictures to Marie before leaving for the trip, but decided against it; arriving at the Hansens' with a mysterious envelope would only provoke questions. He'd simply mail all of her pictures to Marie when he returned. That way she could slip the one of her and Ted out of the package before presenting her parents with the formal portrait.

"Phillip, are you still up there? It's late," Claude called from the back door. Phillip glanced at the clock. He had arrived when Mrs. Brecken was closing for the day—nearly three hours ago. He hadn't realized how late it was, how dim the room had grown with twilight coming on.

"On my way," Phillip said. "Just setting everything straight before the trip."

"Hurry up," Claude called. "Ben's threatening to cook biscuits if you don't get home, and I'm not about to eat his charred lumps."

Phillip laughed and set the stack of pictures back on the shelf. "My cooking's not much better." He brushed some dust off the wooden edge, then headed for the stairs. From the top he could see Claude standing by the back door, holding it open. Phillip paused and looked back. The room was starting to take shape. It wasn't fancy, and it wasn't large, but it was all his.

He grabbed his coat from a hook on the wall and headed down. "Let's go. I'd hate for my brothers to starve on my account."

Phillip paused at the top of the stair and looked back again. Would his business be successful? If not, where would he turn next for work? And if he did manage to make a living, would that help him have a chance for a happy life? He couldn't imagine happiness without Hannah, yet he couldn't see how a life with her was possible. He descended the steps, knowing that everything he left upstairs would be a big part of determining his future.

His brother had already headed for the door. "Claude?"

He turned back. "What?" The setting sun came through one of the store windows, putting his face in shadows.

"Listen, I'm—I'm sorry for what I said before. You know, back at the shed. I shouldn't have judged you like that. I was wrong."

Claude lowered his face and didn't answer right away. With the shadows, Phillip couldn't read the expression in his eyes. "Thanks," Claude finally said. "I shouldn't have yelled at you like I did. You were just trying to be a good brother. You always have been, you know." Claude looked up and smiled, then patted Phillip's shoulder before heading out the door.

Suddenly, Phillip's eyes smarted with tears. Claude's words were the closest thing to a compliment he had ever uttered, and until that moment, Phillip hadn't realized just how desperately he had wanted to hear praise from his older brother.

Phillip wiped his nose, cleared his throat, and followed Claude out the back door.

* * *

Monday morning, Phillip sat on the front porch and rested his arms on his knees. "Sending Claude to fetch the bishop's wagon was a mistake," he said to Ben. "You should have gone instead." The brothers were supposed to be on the road to the quarry. Claude had insisted on going to get the team and wagon. He had already said good-bye to Hannah, but he couldn't pass up the chance to see her just once more before their heart-rending separation of nine days. Ben and Phillip had reluctantly agreed to let him have one last good-bye—two hours ago.

"So it wasn't the best idea," Ben agreed. "But why do you think I should have gone? I know—maybe my getting into another fight with Bethany would change the bishop's mind so we couldn't borrow his team, and we wouldn't have to go after all?"

"Hardly." Phillip laughed, then straightened. "I don't mind helping out with the temple at all. Even if it takes time away from the studio, I figure I'm serving the Lord, and He's bound to give me blessings for it, right? I could use some blessings about now." He eyed the sky, where the sun slowly climbed. It was still morning—barely—but much later than they had wanted to start out. He knew that Ben's comment was in jest; neither of them would seriously consider not doing their tithing work. But Phillip had a bigger reason for wanting to be gone. Every day Claude and Hannah grew closer, and Phillip had no choice but to witness much of it. A week or more away would simplify matters considerably. "It's just that at this rate, we might not make it to the quarry by sundown."

Ben sat beside him and shrugged. "I'm not worried. We're ready to load up the wagon the minute he arrives. And it's what, only twenty miles or so to Little Cottonwood? We can make it if we hurry." He nodded toward their pile of provisions. "But why'd you insist on bringing along so much food? There's no way the three of us will eat it all."

"It's good to be prepared," Phillip answered vaguely. The truth was, he hoped to stay behind for a third load with another group. That would mean additional time away from Claude and Hannah. Granted, it would also mean more time away from his business, but he didn't want to think about that.

The steady clopping of hooves finally reached them. Down the street, barely visible but growing steadily larger, was Claude and the three pair of oxen pulling Bishop Hansen's wagon.

"So, our brother finally managed to pull himself away from his beloved?" Ben called as he stood. "I don't suppose the two of you carried on like Romeo and Juliet or anything? 'Parting is such sweet sorrow' and all that nonsense."

The oxen came to a stop. "Very funny," Claude retorted from his perch on the bench, but it was clear from the flush in his face that he was still overcome by his farewell to Hannah.

Ben rolled his eyes. "It's a week and a half they'll be apart. Land sakes, it's not as if he's leaving for another mission," he muttered. Then louder he called, "Let's load her up."

Phillip began loading the supplies. Starting with cans of dried fruit and jerky, he moved quickly, without much talk. Claude stayed put, waiting for Ben to take the reins. Within ten minutes the brothers were packed up. Phillip and Ben hopped into the back of the wagon and made themselves comfortable on top of the bedrolls.

"Let's move out," Ben said, slapping his little brother on the shoulder.

Claude eyed the team warily. "I'm not used to driving oxen. Coming back from the bishop's was plenty on my nerves. Someone else take over."

"Here. I'll do it," Ben said, hopping over the wagon box and sitting beside Claude. "I forgot that you only ever drove the horses and the old mule. Oxen are a bit different handling. Move over."

Ben took the reins. Claude stepped into the wagon box and eyed the sun above them. "It's not going to be pleasant driving in the heat like this," he said, squinting in the bright light as he settled in the open wagon across from Phillip.

"It's not that hot, so stop your bellyaching," Ben said. "It's not like we're traveling from Winter Quarters in the summer without a wagon cover. We'll be there by evening." With a flick of the reins, the oxen moved forward in their slow, plodding way.

A block or so down the road, Claude gave a sideways glance at Ben, then leaned close to Phillip and whispered, "Should we start talking about *you know what?*"

Phillip kicked his brother in the shin and shot him a look intended to mean, *Not if you value your life.*

Sucking air between his teeth, Claude rubbed his leg. "Sheesh! What did—"

But Phillip leaned closer and formed a fist. The action got the message across. Claude raised his hands in surrender, then sat back, arms folded, and watched the road creep past.

Shaking his head, Phillip swatted at a horsefly, grateful Ben hadn't seemed to notice the exchange. What was Claude thinking? That the two of them could discuss Bethany and her "midnight confessions" while Ben sat only a yard away? No man was stupid enough to think that such a conversation was supposed to appear secret.

For the plan to work, they'd have to be patient—willing to wait days if need be for the right moment, or to seize an unexpected opportunity. They had over a week to get the job done, so there wasn't any rush. With Claude chomping at the bit, Phillip knew that deciding when and how to begin the scheme would be up to him. He'd have to keep a close eye on Claude.

Phillip mused about the plan. Their best shot would be during their evenings camping on the road. Maybe they could send Ben fishing and talk of Bethany when they knew he was on his way back. They'd need to find a way to secretly observe his approach, though. A signal of sorts, since Ben was a smart one—a bit brighter than their middle brother, apparently.

Phillip looked up at the sky, pale blue and clear save for a handful of white puffs. He willed his thoughts heavenward. *If it is Thy will for Ben and Bethany to forgive and unite, help us accomplish this desire.*

He imagined what it would be like to see the two of them together as a couple and smiled. But immediately following in his mind was the picture of Claude and Hannah together. A knot formed in Phillip's throat.

What would life be like if both of his brothers ended up marrying Hansen girls? Would he spend his days feeling awkward and uncomfortable around Hannah, with thoughts unbecoming a brother-in-law?

*Help me know what to do about Hannah. I can't go on like this much longer.*

# CHAPTER 10

Several hundred yards from camp, Ben waited for a bite on his fishing pole. *No wonder it's so hard to get enough men to haul the temple rock—doing nothing but hauling a heavy wagon for days on end is duller than I imagined.*

Glad the day's work was done, he had just moved to another spot, hoping for better luck. In an hour he had caught two small fish, but that wouldn't amount to much among three men. If he didn't catch more, they'd end up eating beans, dried apples, and rock-hard biscuits to satisfy their hunger again. He made a face as he drew in the line, then cast again. *Come on and bite, fish. Just one more.*

But truth be told, he was in no hurry to return to camp. He and his brothers had spent one day heading to the quarry and two days going back, with one more to go. For the entire trip, he had felt pulled between his brothers. Any chance Claude found, he'd corner Ben and drone on about how much he missed Hannah, how beautiful she was, how much he loved her with his very soul. It was enough to make a man lose his beans and dried apples. But apart from that, it was hard to hear such things and be sympathetic when Phillip, who also cared for Hannah, was there listening to it all.

In the last day, Ben had managed to force it into Claude's head that such talk in front of Phillip wasn't very courteous. But that had only made it worse for Ben, since he was now the only target for all this women talk. Why Claude thought it was a good idea to tell these things to *him* of all people—the one person Claude knew who held love and romance in disdain—Ben would never know.

The river moved quietly, the water making little noise save the splashing of small waterfalls as it fell over stones near the bank. The sound drained away his fatigue, and as he drew in the line again, he found himself thinking about Claude.

While they were in New York, Claude appeared to scorn the concept of being in love as much as anyone. *Look at him now!* Ben shook his head regretfully. He had been so proud of Claude back then. *I thought I had trained him well and that the effects would last. Yet what does he do the first chance he has when we return? Fall over his own shoes because of a girl.*

The tip of the fishing pole jerked and bent downward. Ben carefully reeled in the rainbow trout on the line. It was a big one, well over a foot long. After removing the hook and hitting the fish's head against a rock, Ben strung it onto a chain and headed off to camp, three fish in tow, still grumbling inwardly about his brother. If one of Ben's own pupils could be transformed into a lovesick fool, then that meant just about anyone could. Ben stopped in his tracks and cocked his head. "Anyone *but* me," he said aloud.

He considered for a minute, shook his head, and kept walking. "Nah. Not me."

He'd seen plenty of beautiful women in his time—sweet ones, virtuous ones. But until he found the perfect woman with every perfect trait, he'd be safe from love. *Which of course will never happen, so I'll die a bachelor.*

Ben's lips curved into a thoughtful grin. He pushed aside branches of quaking aspens and kept walking. He began thinking about what kind of woman would constitute a perfect one—pretending for a moment that he could be lured into following Claude's footsteps.

He decided that any woman for him would have to be strikingly beautiful. Riches would be a nice bonus, although unlikely in Utah. Kind, sweet, and virtuous, naturally.

*I'd insist on someone with a mild temperament—unlike a certain woman. I'd want someone who is an elocutionist, an excellent cook, a seamstress. Oh, and she must play an instrument and sing like an angel. And her hair—well, I suppose I can't be too picky. It can be any color, so long as it's got some curl to it.*

Through the trees, Ben could now see Claude at the fire pit, one of many used by the teams hauling temple granite. With his back to Ben, Claude arranged sticks and kindling for a fire. For a moment, Ben fancied bopping Claude across the head to knock the romantic notions out of him.

"The area's pretty picked over for firewood," Phillip said, coming through the trees. "What were you saying before about Hannah and Bethany?"

Ben stiffened, hoping to go unnoticed and escape having to hear Claude's romantic talk again. Best to wait a few minutes, then return to camp as if he had just come from fishing.

"I was just wondering what you thought of—you know—what I told you about what Bethany said to her."

"Where's Ben?" Phillip asked, looking around. "This isn't something he should hear."

Ben sneaked behind a leafy branch and watched, listening carefully now that his interest was piqued.

Claude shrugged. "Still fishing, I guess. I haven't seen him since he left."

"Good." Phillip sat across from Claude, right in Ben's line of sight. If his brother looked up at the right angle, Phillip would see him easily. "First of all, are you sure it's true what Hannah said?"

Claude glanced about as if making sure they were alone. "You mean about Bethany being in love with Ben? Absolutely. I wouldn't joke about something like that."

Ben nearly lost his balance. His eyes grew wide, and his jaw fell slack. He set the fishing pole down and gripped a branch to steady himself. Eavesdropping might be improper, but in matters that concerned himself, a person had to break with convention.

Phillip shook his head and leaned back. "It's such an impossible idea. Who would ever have thought Bethany would still love Ben after the way he's treated her? I don't know what happened before, but he's been atrocious to her since we got home. She probably can't be trusted to treat any man with kindness—look at how sharp-tongued she's become."

Claude laughed. "I count myself lucky that I'm in her good graces for now. I hope to stay there."

"Me too," Phillip agreed, leaning forward with his arms on his thighs. "But if you had asked me to guess who she'd end up caring for, Ben would be the last person on my list."

*Am I so repulsive, then?* Ben thought, indignant. *Remind me to bop your head too.*

"She certainly seems to abhor him, doesn't she?" Claude finished with the sticks and kindling and now sat on a stump. He shrugged. "Just goes to show that you can't ever know for sure what someone's thinking."

"Hah!" Phillip laughed. "You can always tell with Ben. It's clear as day what he thinks of Bethany."

*I'm not the open book you think I am.* Ben's fingers closed angrily around the chain holding the fish.

Claude went on. "Hannah says that Bethany rarely feels anything halfway, that her feelings for Ben are so intense they're almost beyond comprehension."

Ben's mind raced. It was true that Bethany showed every emotion full-blown—and what he usually saw was hatred for him. It hadn't always been that way. Over the course of the months they had written to one another, she had looked on him with love and happiness—*pure* love and happiness. So what if now all the hateful comments and looks were just an act for his benefit, a way to protect herself? Ben's mind reeled, and he had a sudden urge to hold Bethany and tell her he was sorry for hurting her as he had. No one deserved what he'd done to her. Even if she had been the one to wrong him first, he had gone too far in evening the score.

Ben gripped the branch tighter and, for the first time, admitted to himself the main reason he enjoyed making Bethany angry—the flush in her cheeks and the fire in her eyes did something to him. He was addicted to seeing her face light up like that.

Pressing his lips together, Phillip spoke, his voice unsure. "Maybe Bethany's making it up just to get a reaction from Hannah."

"Doubtful," Claude said. "Unless Bethany's one amazing actress."

"An actress?" Phillip asked, picking up a piece of wood. He began whittling with his knife. "How so?"

Clutching a branch, Ben craned his neck to hear the next words. He wondered how his brother could appear so calm discussing something of such magnitude.

Claude lowered his voice, and Ben closed his eyes to concentrate on hearing every word. "According to Hannah—she was really upset by it all, that's why she told me—Bethany hasn't been able to sleep since we got home. She lies awake for hours and hours. And when she finally dozes off, sometimes crying herself to sleep, she wakens Hannah in the middle of the night by talking in her dreams—about Ben. Then, the other night, Hannah walked in on Bethany crying at her bedside saying, 'Ben will never be mine!'"

Thoughts and emotions swirled so hard that Ben could hardly think. His mouth had gone dry.

Phillip's knife stopped midstroke. "Sure sounds genuine. I can see why Hannah was so upset. I don't suppose Bethany has told Ben how she feels?"

Claude let out a loud laugh. "Hardly! Bethany swears she'll never tell, and that's what makes her suffering so much worse."

"Even so, it's probably for the best that she keeps it to herself," Phillip said with a sigh. "You know Ben. He'd make a joke out of it and torment her if he found out. Poor girl is doomed to love a man who has no heart."

Taken aback, Ben scowled. Was he so hateful that even his brothers thought of him that way? Would he really treat anyone in such a manner—especially a woman like Bethany?

*I already have,* he reminded himself. He ran his fingers through his hair in frustration. Of course his brothers had no reason to believe otherwise. But all of that was because he thought Bethany had betrayed him, because he thought she hated him, and because he refused to be made a fool again.

But at what cost? He might win a battle here and there. In the end, he might be the winner, but a pretty miserable one. Better to be humbled but happy. He stepped back from the tree, his hands none too steady as he thought of Bethany up at night, crying over him. He thought about their brief moment of happiness behind the barn, of how much he loved her then—and probably even now, if he were entirely truthful with himself. If he cared nothing for her, he wouldn't bother trying to see her eyes light up, and he certainly wouldn't care whether she noticed him. The reality was, he did care. It would be unacceptable to be in the same room and have Bethany *not* notice him, even if that was through his insults.

Phillip's voice broke through his thoughts. "Neither of us can say a word to Ben about this, for Bethany's sake. Agreed?"

"Agreed," Claude said. They shook hands over the fire pit to seal the deal.

Phillip sighed again and continued whittling. "If only Ben could see how undeserving he is of such an amazing woman as Bethany Hansen."

In a daze of emotions and thoughts, Ben walked away after dropping the fish to the ground. The pole leaned against the tree, abandoned. "I'm a cad," he whispered to himself. "I'm a mean-spirited, hateful cad. I've hurt a sweet girl whose only weakness is loving me." He sat on a fallen log and put his head in his hands, trying to sort out everything he had just heard.

*In spite of everything that's happened, she loves me.*

"Bethany loves me. *Bethany* loves *me.*" He had to repeat the words to come anywhere close to believing them, and even then he had a hard time grasping their meaning. He looked up and asked the tops of the trees a single question. "Why?"

The only answer was silence. He thought of Bethany—beautiful, kind, sweet Bethany. Even a confirmed bachelor couldn't deny she had those qualities, even if she had a tongue and a temper. He remembered the list he had just made about a prospective wife. Kind, sweet, virtuous—she was all of those things. *Mild? Not so much,* Ben thought with a smile. But he wouldn't trade her spunk for a woman with no backbone. Such grit would make life interesting if they were to . . .

His thoughts trailed off, resisting the word that managed to squeeze into his mind anyway—*Marry.*

*Marry.* He ran a hand down his face and laughed. *Marry? I must be mad.*

He forced such an absurd notion from his mind immediately, but he was still faced with a very real dilemma—what to do the next time he saw Bethany. Doubts about the past still lingered in his mind. There was everything that happened in the orchard to consider. But in the end, Matthew was gone, and did she deserve to be tormented if she really did care about him?

*I'll treat her as a woman ought to be treated,* he finally decided. *Even if that means getting teased by certain brothers who are bound to think it hilarious.*

* * *

The following morning Ben remained quiet. When Claude came close, Ben turned the other way to break camp. He couldn't afford to listen to more pining over Hannah, afraid he was liable to join in the conversation and talk about Bethany. The more he thought about her, the more he realized how amazing she was. Instead, he stayed silent and thought out how he could talk around Bethany and not look like a fool.

Keeping quiet was easiest when they pulled out with Ben driving. With a 2,500-pound stone already in the wagon, Phillip and Claude couldn't add additional weight by riding. As it was, the load might break a wheel. The granite block was already shaped for the precise spot it would go—one of the eastern towers. It was wider at one end and tapered slightly at the other. A black *J* was scrawled on one side with paint, indicating the stone's location on the wall.

The oxen plodded so slowly that keeping up was easy, and Ben's brothers weren't remotely winded as they walked beside the wagon, talking at times and not expecting Ben to join in. That would have been different had they been able to ride along, and Ben was grateful for the distance, which allowed him to be alone with his thoughts about Bethany. He was a bit disturbed at how quickly he had gone from *I'll treat her well* to *I can't stop thinking of her.*

The last day of the return trip through the rough canyon was smoother than the others—far fewer dips and ruts for the wagon to get stuck in, and eventually city roads ahead. But shortly after they left camp, a harness strap broke from one of the oxen, making it trickier to control the wagon. It slowed them down enough that getting to the temple block took several extra hours.

*Good thing it didn't happen until today,* Ben thought. A broken harness a few miles back would have made getting through some parts of the canyon an unthinkable challenge. Now that they were returning to the city, they could get it fixed or replaced and still be on schedule to leave the next morning for their second trip to the quarry. Surely Bishop Hansen either had a replacement strap or could repair the broken one.

*Bishop Hansen. Bethany's father.* Ben managed a quick intake of breath at the thought of going to Bethany's home to get the repair—and seeing her. He licked his lips and shifted in his seat, wishing he were there already. Knowing what he now did, nothing Bethany could say would ever bother him again. He would show her that she no longer had to be defensive. How he would manage that, he hadn't figured, but somehow . . .

It wasn't quite dusk when they entered Salt Lake City proper, with Phillip taking his turn at maneuvering the wagon through the wide city streets. Ben purposely walked on the opposite side of the wagon from Claude, and he eyed the sky where the sun had just dipped past the horizon. The Hansen sisters were probably getting their evening meal ready. He and his brothers would be able to eat at home tonight, but Ben had a hankering to dine across the table from Bethany, to eat her delicious food and see her bright eyes watching him.

When they reached the temple site, a man carrying a thick notebook consulted an architectural drawing of the current course of stone, noted the J written on the granite block, then waved Phillip ahead. He pointed to the southeast corner tower. "This way. It goes right over there."

Ben eagerly glanced in the general direction of the Hansen house, northeast of the temple block. Over building tops and trees, several threads of smoke rose from chimneys. He wished he could tell from here which chimney was Bethany's.

"So . . ." He glanced over his shoulder again. "We need to get that harness fixed . . ." His voice trailed off, and he shifted his feet, trying hard to sound disinterested. "While you two take care of the load, why don't I walk on over to the bishop's and see what we can do about the strap?" He reached onto the bench for the broken pieces of leather—at the same moment Claude did.

"You don't have to do that. I'm happy to go," Claude said. "I could see Hannah."

Ben froze. What excuse could he possibly give for wanting to go? *You aren't the only one who wants to see a girl?* Instead Ben scoffed. "Oh, please. That's the last thing we need." He yanked the straps from his brother's hands. "If you go, I know exactly what will happen—you'll hang around for hours like a lost puppy staring into her eyes all night, and when you finally decide to come home, your head will be so high in the clouds you'll be useless to us tomorrow. No thanks. Right, Phillip?"

Ben could feel his face burning to the tips of his ears. Did they believe him? His brothers exchanged glances, and Phillip looked amused, but otherwise Ben couldn't read their expressions.

"Go ahead," Phillip said offhandedly. "We'll be fine here." Ben nodded and started walking away, when Phillip added, "Of course, if *I* go, we'll still keep Claude away, and you won't have to deal with that *harpy.*"

Ben paused in his step. *I deserved that.* "I can handle *Bethany,* but thanks anyway." He tossed the words over his shoulder a little pointedly, then turned and fisted his hands. *Be careful,* he said to himself as he left. *That almost sounded like you were defending her.*

He hurried on through the city streets without looking back. Quickly—but not quickly enough—he reached the edge of the Hansen fence. He stopped behind a stand of trees and caught his breath. Just a few more steps and her home would be in view. Was she outside? What would she do when she saw him? What would *he* do?

Ben scrubbed his sleeve across his face, smoothed his hair, then tucked in his shirt. Campfire smoke surely hung around him like a cloud, but there wasn't anything he could do about that. *Here goes.* He took a brave step forward and another and another until he reached the end of the lane. He looked around, searching for Bethany, but didn't see her. While he hadn't expected her to be waiting for him in the yard, a twinge of disappointment came over him anyway.

Then he saw her inside. There was her shape, outlined in the kitchen window as she lit a candle and resumed her work. Ben gripped the leather straps. The light created a halo around her hair, which was loose tonight, falling in waves around her shoulders. In shadow, her profile looked smooth and delicate. He wanted to hold that face in his hands and kiss it.

The side door opened and banged shut, and Ben started with a jolt. "Bishop. Hello," he said, hoping his voice didn't reflect his nervous state.

"Why Ben, what are you doing here?" The bishop hobbled the distance and put out his hand. "You aren't done with your quarry assignment, are you?"

"N—no. We're not," Ben stammered. "Halfway. We just completed our first trip this evening. Stone's being unloaded right now." He held up the broken harness. "I'm here because this broke this morning. I'm sorry about it. I'm not sure why it snapped. But I was wondering if you could fix it since we're due back at the quarry tomorrow." The words tumbled out of his mouth, and when he finished, the silence was deafening, save for the pounding of his pulse in his ears. All of his senses were heightened. He felt sure that his thoughts and emotions were plain to see on his face and that at any moment Bethany would appear. He half hoped, half feared she would.

The bishop took the strap and inspected the ends. "I can fix that easily enough. I doubt this harness has ever dealt with as heavy a load as yours, and it's on the old side to boot. No wonder it broke on you." He handed the strap back. "Here, you take this out to the shed. I'll go tell the girls to put on an extra plate for dinner, and I'll join you in a minute."

"Thanks," Ben said, but his voice was suddenly dry, and the word had barely made it out. Once inside, he waited for twenty minutes or so and began wondering where the bishop had gone and what was keeping him. Then finally he heard a step at the open door.

"Bishop," Ben said, looking at the torn ends. "I have to admit that I don't know as much about leatherwork as I ought. I'll be a willing pupil." When he received no answer, he looked up to find Bethany standing before him. She held something in one hand. He stood straight and gulped a breath of air. "Bethany!"

"My father sent me to tell you that he's been called away on church business," she said. "He asked that I give this to you. It's a spare strap he found in the barn. It's a little on the short side, and it's old—he said it might break on the return trip—but it's the best we've got right now."

Her voice was even and formal. She took three steps into the barn, the harness in her outstretched hand. Ben reached forward, his entire body tingling with the rush of being in her presence. As he took the harness, his fingers brushed her hand.

"Thank you, Bethany," he said in the most sincere voice he possessed. He tried smiling. "I appreciate it so much that you took the trouble to help me."

Bethany tilted her head in bewilderment, and her mouth hung slightly open as if she couldn't figure out whom he was speaking to. "Trouble? It wasn't . . . any . . . trouble . . ." Her voice trailed off, and her eyes held a mixture of confusion and suspicion. She would see soon enough that he wouldn't attack her anymore. He wanted to race forward and take her in his arms, but she would likely punch him if he tried that—until he could convince her that he felt the same way she did.

"No trouble?" he said, taking a step closer and testing a smile. "Coming to see me was a *pleasant* task then?"

"Pleasant?" She folded her arms and laughed derisively. "Oh, I find *much* pleasure in coming to see you—about as much as our poor oxen have felt dragging that wagon for days." She rolled her eyes and turned for the door.

*Don't go,* Ben wanted to say, but instead he scrambled for something else to talk about, a reason for her to stay. "Your father said something about me staying for dinner?"

Bethany paused at the door and looked back, her brow raised. "Oh, now *that* would be pleasant." With a sharp laugh, she walked away. Ben hurried to the shed door and watched her go.

He leaned against the barn wall. "'It wasn't any trouble,'" he murmured. "No trouble at all. And my staying for dinner would be *pleasant.*" He knew he wasn't actually invited inside—and wouldn't have tempted fate by trying to make good on her father's invitation anyway. He watched Bethany walk toward the house.

He tossed the strap from one hand to the other and grinned.

*"Now that would be pleasant." There's another meaning in that.*

# CHAPTER 11

When Bethany left the shed, a crease furrowed her brow. Halfway to the house, she turned and looked back, reliving what had just happened. Had Ben Adams just *smiled* at her? Had he said *thank you* and that he *appreciated* her? *Was* that Ben Adams? She wouldn't have thought it possible, yet she had seen it with her own eyes, heard the words with her own ears.

She shook her head to clear her thoughts and headed back for the house through the darkening twilight. The biggest puzzle was that Ben had kept a straight face through it all. She had expected him to laugh, to catch her in a snare and then mock her for taking him seriously. She knew better than to fall for such a thing, but why would he act that way? Probably to confuse her, to get her off balance for the next time they faced one another.

The screen was closed, but the house door stood open behind it, leading into the kitchen. The warm orange glow inside was inviting, and Bethany looked forward to spending some time talking around the kitchen table with her sister and cousin. Her hand rose to reach for the screen door when Marie spoke.

"Don't ever tell Bethany. She can't know."

Bethany pulled her hand back as if the handle were a hot coal. She had never known Hannah or Marie to hide anything from her; the three of them shared everything. They were the only ones who knew about Ted, for starters. What on earth could they be talking about? *It probably has something to do with Claude,* she thought sadly. Something Hannah wouldn't confide in her.

"But this is *Ben* we're talking about," Hannah insisted. "Don't you think she has a right to know something this important?"

Eyes wide as saucers, Bethany leaned in and listened.

"Normally, I'd say yes," Marie answered. "But Bethany and Ben don't have what I'd call a normal relationship. His secrets should stay his."

"True," Hannah conceded.

Bethany scoffed and shook her head. So this was about Ben. As if she could possibly care any less than she already did about a secret he might hold. Again she reached for the handle, but this time she was stopped by Hannah's voice.

"So you also think that Ben really is in love with Bethany? It seems impossible. I wouldn't believe it myself if Claude hadn't been the one to tell me."

Bethany's heart seemed to stop in her chest, and her hand dropped to her side. What had they just said? She must have heard wrong. Just the same, her hands started trembling, and she clasped them together to stop them from shaking.

"Ben may have his faults," Hannah went on, "but he's one of the best men alive. So hardworking, willing to do anything he's asked by the Church or Father. He's always been kind. Remember that cat he saved when we were young?"

"The one that fell into the well?" Marie asked. "I had forgotten about that."

Hannah sighed. "But in spite of the fact that he's one of the best catches in the city, Bethany's been awful to him ever since they got back. Imagine how bad it could get if she found out. Ben would end up retreating with his tail between his legs every time he saw her."

A wry smile crept across Bethany's face. So at least they acknowledged her superior wit.

"Exactly," Marie said. "She's too proud to admit she's done anything amiss toward Ben, and she's bound and determined to squash him flat any chance she gets. Can you imagine what she'd do if they ever married? He'd die within the week from being pummeled by her words."

Bethany took a step back, sadness filling her at how Hannah and Marie viewed her. *Did I* deserve *to be called a harpy?*

The shed door banged shut in the distance, and Bethany's head whipped around. Ben walked toward the road with swift strides. When he noticed her, his step came up short. For what felt like a moment suspended in time, they stared at one another. The purple of dusk had set in, making it hard to read his expression so far off. Her throat tightened, and she swallowed hard to clear it. If Ben were to speak, she wouldn't manage a coherent response. He'd certainly win this round.

Unless he had no intention of insulting her tonight.

She glanced at the kitchen door, then back at Ben. Could it be true that he loved her? It would certainly explain his behavior in the shed a few moments ago. But . . .

When she said nothing, Ben nodded, touching his hat, and headed toward the road again, this time wearing a grin. Confusion washing through her, she watched him leave. *Wait—no patronizing remarks?*

As he retreated, she felt a sudden urge to run after him and say, "I love you, Ben. I always have. Is it true you love me too?" But fear, hurt, and confusion kept her feet rooted to the ground, so instead she watched him leave until she could no longer see his shape. Then she dropped to the porch step, stunned. She stared into the darkness, her mind reeling. Claude had told Hannah himself. And he of all people wouldn't dream up something like that.

*It must be true.*

She had a few more days before Ben returned from his quarry assignment. It would have to be enough to decide what to do.

*Good-bye, girlish pride,* Bethany thought. *It's time for me to grow up and let you go.*

Would a few days be enough to change such a big part of herself? For so long she had worked at being witty and thinking in terms of beating Ben at his game. It would be hard to unlearn that. And assuming she managed to, what could she possibly say to Ben when he returned to let him know she cared for him as well?

She thought back to the scene he had made in the orchard, and her stomach turned. Had he finally realized that he hadn't ever given her a chance to explain? That he had overreacted and wounded her deeper than anyone else could?

Unwittingly, her mind trailed back to the night before the orchard—when Ben had kissed her. One kiss was all they had ever shared, but the memory of that moment was as clear as a freshly washed windowpane. She could still remember his smell, the feel of his lips on hers, the touch of his hands. And the joy that surged through her at that moment—a moment she had never wanted to end.

Could she be that happy again?

* * *

Ben moved in a daze on his way back to the temple block, unaware of the ground beneath him or even of the harness in his hand. He could have dropped it in the middle of the road and not noticed. All he could think of was Bethany looking at him from the side of the house. She hadn't gone in when she returned from the shed—why? Maybe she had wanted to come back and talk to him.

When their eyes met, he had felt a connection, a pull toward her. Surely she'd felt it too. If she hadn't, she would have spoken, perhaps ruining the moment with her usual fare of words. Instead, neither ventured to speak, just gazed at one another as if they could communicate without words. If only he could know for sure what it was she had been communicating.

Just as he rounded the final corner, a thought wormed into his mind: What about that scene in the orchard?

*If you'd just listen.* Bethany's voice from that horrible day echoed in his mind for what had to be the millionth time since it had happened. *It* is *different, but you're too caught up in your own pride to find out how.*

Ben paused in the street, his heart nearly stopping. What if the whole thing had been some ridiculous misunderstanding? After all, Matthew and Bethany hadn't ended up as a pair. Could the last two-plus years of hatred and anger have been completely avoided if he had just stopped raging and listened to her?

In a perverse way, he hoped so, because it meant that he and Bethany might have a chance for happiness together after all. Perhaps he could change the outcome of that fateful afternoon. *Either that or I'm about to* really *be made a fool of this time.*

He tugged his hat down lower, only now noticing the lamps and candles lighting in the windows bordering the street. A smile curved his mouth. *Somehow I don't care if I look the fool, if it means I can earn her love.*

A few minutes later, his step light, Ben entered the temple block and looked around for his brothers. He found the wagon and the team, but instead of Phillip and Claude, another man tended the animals. The huge boulder they had hauled from the quarry was gone, and the oxen were at a watering trough.

At Ben's quizzical expression, the man spoke. "You the other Adams brother? Good to meet you—I'm Joseph Adler. Just watching out for you. Promised your brothers I'd take care of the harness when you got here while they took a look at the Tabernacle. It's nearly finished, you know. They said the three of you hadn't been by to see the progress. You ought to go."

"Oh—thanks," Ben said. "Here's the harness. Can I help you with it?"

"Nah." Joseph waved Ben away. "You go take a gander at the Tabernacle. The doors are open tonight. Magnificent how there's not one column holding up the roof."

"Thanks, maybe I'll go," Ben said, but he moved without giving it much thought. He'd look for his brothers, but at this point he had a difficult time thinking about much more than Bethany looking at him—loving him.

He stopped before the windows of the Tabernacle, which were nearly shoulder high. He peered in but didn't see his brothers—only row upon row of brown pews and on the far end, the largest and most beautiful organ he had ever seen. Even in the light of dusk, it looked stately, as if it were reigning over a kingdom.

As he took a step back to look elsewhere for his brothers, he noticed his reflection in the glass. After a quick glance around him, Ben stepped closer and took a good look at his face. His mother used to say he was handsome, but he knew mothers were biased. His fingers rubbed against his stubble, and he wished he had shaved that morning even though he had been on the road.

He studied his hair. As a boy his had been blond, but the older he got, the darker it grew. Right now it looked atrocious, thanks to several days on the road with a hat firmly planted on his head. Running his fingers through his flattened hair, he wondered if women cared about such things. Did Bethany think him handsome? He had never given his looks much thought, but now he desperately wished for a comb and a basin of water with some soap.

Belly laughter erupted behind him, and Ben started. His hand flew down to his side, and he whipped around to see his brothers laughing so hard they were crying and leaning on one another for support.

So he had been caught preening. So what? But they needed an explanation, and now was as good a time as any. They would find out about his change of heart soon enough. He took a deep breath and spoke. "As my brothers, I suppose you should be the first to know that . . . well, I am not the man I once was."

The brothers burst out with new joviality, and Phillip's face wrinkled as he said, "Nope. Now you're even sadder!" He broke into another gale of laughter, slapping his thighs and trying to catch his breath.

Heat climbed up Ben's neck and filled his face, ears, and then his entire body. His hands clenched and unclenched. Telling them now would only invite mockery. "I don't need to be abused this way." He gave them a stiff nod and tried to walk away with some shred of dignity, when Claude spoke, his voice high and lilting.

"Maybe he's in *love*."

Ben's boot caught on a shovel handle, and he stumbled for a few steps, nearly plunging headfirst into the dirt. He stood straight and wiped dust from his trousers, ignoring a new wave of chuckles behind him. He whipped around. "I have a toothache, that's all. I think my cheek's swollen."

Phillip took a few steps forward and leaned in as if inspecting Ben's face. "I see no swelling. Nope, I think Claude's right. You're in love."

"What did I do to deserve that kind of insult?" Ben knew it wouldn't be long before he would have to admit that they were right. But it wouldn't be after they caught him preening. "After all my years of ridiculing lovesick fools, how can you accuse me of something like that?"

He turned on his heels and stalked away. *Let them bring the wagon home,* he thought. He wasn't about to offer himself as a verbal punching bag. At the edge of the block, he had an insane urge to turn left and go back to the Hansen place. But that would accomplish nothing. Besides, his brothers might still be watching. So after only the slightest hesitation, he turned right, toward home. He sighed. With the Sabbath ahead, a five-day round trip loomed in his future before he could see Bethany again and tell her what was in his heart.

Five days of being apart from her.

Worse, five more days of putting up with a pair of jokers.

And *where* had they gotten the idea that he cared for Bethany?

* * *

"Aren't you going to sleep in here?" Hannah asked as Bethany gathered her things. "Marie has only two more nights before she goes home."

"I know, and I won't miss her last night, I promise." Bethany adjusted the quilt in her arms. "But I—I'm not feeling well. I wouldn't be good company. You two will have a more pleasant time without me and my upset stomach, and I'll sleep better in my own bed instead of on the floor." She gave a pained smile and headed for the door as gracefully as she could with an armful of blankets and clothing.

"Let us help you carry those things," Marie said, hopping off Hannah's bed.

"I'm fine, really," Bethany said as she went through the doorway. "And I'm sure I'll be better tomorrow."

Before her sister or cousin could venture another concern, Bethany hurried to her room. She plopped her burden onto her bed, then went to the door and slipped the hook into its place. She leaned hard against the wood. Her gaze drifted to her bed, and she bit her lip as she thought about what lay beneath her mattress.

She pressed a hand against her eyes to prevent the stinging from turning into anything else. She glanced over her shoulder in the direction of her sister's room. It wasn't untrue that her stomach was upset; how could she possibly have a settled stomach after hearing about Ben's confessions to Claude?

Hesitantly, she stepped toward her bed, knelt, and lifted the edge of the mattress. Fingers trembling, Bethany slid the letters and journal out and held them in her lap as she sat on the rug. She rested against her bed and traced the edge of the stack of letters with her finger. She could recite several of them verbatim, and as she remembered the words, she held the stack close to her chest, leaned her head back against her tick, and let two years' worth of tears slip down her cheeks.

*He still loves me. Or is it that he's started to love me all over again? Can I forgive him? Can I ever let him know that I still care, too?*

She felt almost dizzy as the thoughts spun in her mind. Unable to think clearly, she decided to do what always helped clear her mind and put problems into focus. She crossed to her writing desk and lit a candle to work by. From the drawer she pulled out a sheet of paper, and with a freshly sharpened pencil, began to write.

*Dear Ben,*

Her pencil hovered over the words, and for a moment she wondered if she were crazy to write him a letter. *He never has to read it,* she reminded herself. *And it doesn't have to be a letter.* She scratched out the words and began again.

*I hardly know what to think or feel. It's all so sudden*
*and yet it seems like an eternity since it began.*

Her pencil kept moving across the paper, hardly able to keep up with the thoughts and feelings pouring out of her. Four sheets were filled before she laid the pencil down and sat back. She closed her eyes and sighed, feeling spent—and no closer to knowing what to do the next time she saw Ben. Her eyes were drawn back to the last line.

> *If there were a chance I could have the old Ben in my life again, I'd take it in a heartbeat.*

But was that possible? Did the old Ben still exist somewhere? Could they ever forget their angry words to each other?

# CHAPTER 12

At the Little Cottonwood Quarry, the Adams brothers stood beside several large blocks that were shaped and ready for transport. One wagon at a time rolled down into a pair of ruts that had been dug so deep that a wagon bed was nearly level with the ground when it reached the bottom. That made it possible for the workers to load a stone without lifting it much. Marked with its correct letter, each stone was hoisted onto a wagon, where it was secured with chains before the teamsters brought it back down the canyon. Phillip had seen them perform the feat several times, and it was a sight he could watch for hours. The sheer weight of each block made it staggering to contemplate how large an undertaking this temple really was. At the rate the work was going, he wondered if he'd live to see it completed.

"Are you sure about staying?" Ben asked, breaking Phillip out of his thoughts. "I mean, it's nice of you to volunteer to help another ward, but do you really want to be gone another week?"

Phillip shrugged. "I know it's not the most exciting thing I could be doing, but I think it's important." He still hoped that heaven would smile on him for sacrificing more time at his studio. But he had a sliver of doubt about it, because his motives weren't entirely pure on that front. He wanted to stay away from home just as much as he wanted blessings.

"You coming, Phillip?" One of the men from the Tooele ward called to him from their wagon, where they had just finished securing their block with chains. They were ready to move out on the three-day trip back to Salt Lake. Following that, Phillip would take a four-day trip with them for another stone before heading home.

"I'll be there in just a minute," he called back, then spoke to his brothers. "They started short one man, and another just broke his leg, so I'll be taking his spot—unless that's a problem. I figured you two could manage the last load without me."

His two older brothers looked at one another. "I think we'll be fine," Claude said. "Don't know that *I* would be willing to stay longer. I'm itching to be home something fierce. Life on the road doesn't suit me." He and Phillip exchanged meaningful glances.

He found his feet shifting awkwardly in the dirt and forced them to be still. "See you later then. I'll be home in about a week." He turned to head for the Tooele wagon, where the men from that ward eased the oxen back up the embankment. With his back to his brothers, Phillip closed his eyes and breathed out in relief. He didn't think they'd noticed anything.

Phillip hoped one week was long enough to compose himself and accept things. Hannah would be his brother's wife, and he would be happy for them.

* * *

Saturday morning, Bethany and Marie walked through the orchard, picking the first of the late-summer peaches and filling baskets with them. Bishop Hansen always sent whatever food they could spare with Marie and Uncle Raymond on their way back home. Marie was leaving this morning, as soon as her father had the horses harnessed and the wagon loaded.

A peach tree branch bowed low under the weight of its fruit. The two women hadn't said much over the last several minutes, although Bethany kept trying to decide what she could say. Marie was leaving for the summer—and this had quite possibly been her last carefree visit, since next summer she would probably be married. And yet here they were, with but a few more minutes together, and they said nothing.

After putting her bushel onto the ground, Bethany held the heavy-laden branch and picked the golden fruit. "I was about to say that I wish you could stay longer, but considering you're leaving early to see Ted, I don't suppose I can really object . . ." Her voice trailed off, fearing that if she said more, it would sound as if she resented Ted, the faceless man who had managed to win Marie's love, removing her from Bethany's future.

"I'm sorry," Marie said, sounding regretful. A finger to her eye came away wet. She put down her apron's load of peaches and crossed the distance to Bethany, opening her arms. Bethany welcomed the embrace, and the two women held one another.

"I can't bear the thought that this is your last visit," Bethany said.

"I know," Marie said quietly.

Marie pulled back and wiped her cheeks. "This is one of the most confusing times of my life. On one hand I'm terribly sad to leave. It's dreadful to think that we will likely never have another summer like this again." She lowered her gaze and nodded unhappily. "Because you're right, Bethany. Things *will* change. But I want to be with Ted. I want to marry him and spend my life with him. He makes me so happy—he's worth giving up almost anything for."

*Even me,* Bethany thought, then sighed. *That's the way it should be, of course.*

"I'm sorry I haven't been much fun during your visit," Bethany said with a shrug.

"And I'm sorry for being so caught up with Ted that Hannah and I have talked of little more than weddings and marriage since I got here," Marie returned.

In the distance, Uncle Raymond called to them. "Marie, it's high time we go if we want to get home before dark."

With an unspoken agreement, Bethany and Marie picked up their bushels. They set their burdens next to the wagon, and as they watched Uncle Raymond load them inside, Bethany leaned over and—making sure Uncle Raymond couldn't hear—whispered, "Can I at least be your maid of honor?"

A smile brightened Marie's face. "I'd like that very much." She cocked her head to the side. "Unless you get married first." Before Bethany could come out with a retort, Marie continued, "In which case, I reserve the right to be *your* maid of honor."

She poked Bethany in the shoulder as Bethany guffawed loudly. "Oh heavens," she said, covering her mouth. "That's preposterous. *Me?* Get married?"

"Preposterous or not," Marie said, extending her hand to seal the agreement. "Will you agree to it?"

"Very well. You have a deal," Bethany said, shaking hands. The words almost caught in her throat as she thought about what it would mean for her to marry before her cousin—there was only one man she cared enough about that could possibly become her groom in so short a time.

Her stomach turned, and she put her hand on the wagon side to steady herself. If only she could know once and for all whether Ben really cared for her. If only she knew how to ask Ben—and then tell him she felt the same way.

Now that Marie was leaving, Bethany wanted to discuss the nuances of romance she'd been ignoring for two weeks. Besides being too late, she had to hold her tongue as she couldn't reveal that she'd been eavesdropping.

"One cannot predict the future," Marie said. "But it wouldn't surprise me at all to find out in another few months that I'll be back as your maid of honor."

Hannah came out then, looking from side to side frantically. She breathed a sigh of relief when she saw the wagon still standing in the yard. "Oh good. I thought you might have left without me saying good-bye."

"Never," Marie said, crossing to Hannah.

As they hugged, Hannah said, "I'm going to miss you so much. Be sure to write and tell us everything about—" Her voice cut off, and she glanced hesitantly at her father and uncle. "About everything you're up to," she finished, flushing. As they broke apart, Uncle Raymond came up and held out a hand to his daughter.

"Ready to go?"

After one more look at Bethany, who smiled back, Marie nodded. "Ready."

He helped her into her seat, then climbed up saying, "It's good to see you again, girls. Marie looks forward to these visits all year. Maybe we can bring her up earlier next time, because as soon as the trees start budding, she gets antsy to head north."

From her spot on the wagon bench, Marie suddenly looked at Bethany with guilty eyes—they both knew that next spring's buds wouldn't mean the same thing. Bethany just smiled back and said, "That would be great, Uncle Raymond. She's always welcome, but we don't want to take her away from home too long."

Marie gave her a look full of gratitude for understanding.

"Have a good trip home," Bethany said, moving beside Hannah. The sisters and Bishop Hansen waved as the wagon lurched and moved out.

"See you soon," Marie called over her shoulder. "And Bethany, remember your promise!"

When they had rounded the corner and were out of sight, Hannah and their father turned to Bethany. Their father adjusted his hat as he said, "So, what's that promise Marie mentioned?"

"Yes, what was it?" Hannah insisted.

Bethany laughed but felt her neck growing warm. "She was just teasing. It's nothing." She wiped her hands on her apron and headed inside. At the door, she paused and looked back to where she and Marie had stood moments before.

Wouldn't it be grand if Marie's words were prophetic?

She smiled grimly to herself and went inside, knowing such optimism was silly. She took a deep breath, shook off her thoughts, and turned to cleaning the morning's dishes.

* * *

Claude and Ben got lucky with their second granite block; it weighed less than their first, and they made good time. Both had extra motivation to get home quickly to see the Hansen girls, so by unspoken agreement, they pushed farther each day before making camp, knowing they had the Sabbath in front of them when they wouldn't be traveling at all. They arrived early on Tuesday and, after unloading their second granite block at the temple site, Claude and Ben headed for home.

Driving the team, Claude turned the wagon toward home, wanting to shave and clean up before returning the animals and the wagon to the Hansen place. Ben didn't object, and Claude figured he wanted the same thing but was unwilling to say so aloud. They unloaded their things and washed up in no time, then headed to the Hansen place, this time with Ben driving. Claude didn't ask—and didn't need to ask—why Ben came along or why he had cleaned himself up.

As they turned onto the lane, Hannah and Bethany were working at the well. Bethany knelt at the edge, drew the bucket, and passed it to Hannah, who dumped it into a washtub, then handed it back to Bethany. At the sound of the wagon, Hannah looked up at Claude, broke into a big smile, and waved. He gripped the reins and sighed happily. It had been nine days since he'd seen that face. Nine long days since he had been able to walk with her at his side and know she belonged to him. He hopped down and crossed to Hannah, whose hands were extended toward him.

"Welcome home," she said, smiling bashfully and looking at him through her lashes. He loved the way her eyes flashed when she saw him.

Bethany hadn't said a word, but her gaze was fixed on Ben atop the wagon, who tipped his hat toward her and said, "Afternoon."

"Hello, Ben," she said quietly. Her voice seemed to stick in her throat. Both blushed and seemed unable to quite look one another in the eye.

Claude eyed them both with satisfaction. His brother didn't seem able to keep his eyes off Bethany. While he would have given a lot to witness their reunion, he knew they likely wouldn't reveal anything while he was around. Best to take Hannah on a walk and leave them some privacy, which suited him fine—he and Hannah could use some privacy too, and there was a photo of him in Phillip's studio that he wanted her to see.

"Father's not home right now," Hannah said a bit shyly. "He left yesterday on church business and won't be home until morning. He was afraid he might miss you coming back."

"Give him our regards when he returns," Ben said, still eyeing Bethany. He nodded toward the oxen. "So Claude, are you going to help me put up the animals out back?"

Claude groaned inwardly, not wanting to interrupt his reunion with Hannah. *Do it yourself,* he almost said, but what would Hannah think of him? So he smiled at her and said, "I'll be right back."

He trotted behind the wagon as Ben drove it to the stable out back. They quickly got the oxen unhitched, wiped down, and fed, and the wagon put away. In no time at all, the men had returned to the ladies, who stepped aside from their work, quite happy to leave the pail and washtub sitting on the well's wooden cover.

"So," Claude said, trying hard to be casual. He rocked on his heels. "Hannah, would you like to take a stroll?"

"I'd love to," she said, putting her arm in his. Then, turning to the other two, she asked, "Would you like to join us?"

Claude gave Ben a look that threatened bodily harm. Ben took the hint and shrugged. "Go on ahead. I could use a little rest and a drink of water instead."

Bethany didn't protest, roll her eyes, or otherwise show irritation. *So far so good,* Claude thought. *Looks like Hannah and her cousin played their part well.* "We shouldn't be long," he said, leading Hannah toward the main road and leaving the two unwitting lovebirds behind.

When they were at a distance, Hannah leaned in. "I would give my small toe to find out what they're going to say to one another right now."

"So would I," Claude said, laughing. "But of course they wouldn't say a word around us."

"Hence, your suggestion of a walk," Hannah said, waving back at her sister and Ben.

"In part, yes," Claude said. "But there's also something I want to show you. It's a surprise that can't wait."

"What is it?" Hannah asked, clearly pleased.

"Come with me." Claude took her hand.

He drew her quickly through the hot city streets. At times Hannah could hardly keep up. When they reached the general store, they both breathed heavily, and Hannah's eyes sparkled. "What is it?" she pressed again.

They went inside, and at the front counter, Claude paused and said,

"You'll see in just a minute. You wait down here, and I'll be right back."

"All right," Hannah said, curious. She meandered over to a wall of fabrics and looked them over while he found the shop owner. "Mrs. Brecken, do you mind if I go up to Phillip's studio for a moment?"

Mrs. Brecken's eyes flitted to Hannah, then back to Claude. She pointed between the two of them. "Are you two courting?" she asked, rather abruptly.

Claude blushed. "You could say that." Their relationship wasn't common knowledge, and it was awkward to have someone be so brazen about it. He glanced around the store to see if anyone had heard. A good dozen people were shopping.

"I've always liked you, Claude. You know that." Mrs. Brecken's mouth tightened into a harsh line. "Go up if you want. But I don't think you'll like what you're going to find up there." Mrs. Brecken's cryptic warning made no sense. She shook her head and began sweeping the floor. "I felt in my gut from the start that letting the attic to him would lead to trouble."

"Excuse me?" Claude said. He had no idea what Mrs. Brecken was talking about. He felt a sudden foreboding, knowing that he was the one who had convinced her to let the space to Phillip. What was wrong upstairs? Claude couldn't imagine Phillip doing anything suspicious, although it would be a bit satisfying to find a flaw in the perfect brother for once. But what was Mrs. Brecken referring to?

After another look at Hannah, Mrs. Brecken paused in her work, rested her hands on the top of the broom, and jerked her head toward the studio upstairs. "I went up the other day to do some cleaning, as I promised your brother I'd do while he was away. Didn't mean to snoop, but I—well I guess I did look around a bit more than I maybe should have, and I found a picture." She glanced at Claude's hair. "You're blond, so there's no mistake—nope, you aren't going to like it at all." She waved a hand and walked away to help a customer, muttering under her breath words that Claude couldn't make out.

As he headed for the stairs, he thought back to how he had defended Phillip when they'd first approached her about renting the attic space. He remembered her wariness and how sure Phillip had been that she would have turned him down without Claude intervening. What had convinced her that her premonition was right? He paused at the base of the staircase to look at Hannah. She must have sensed his gaze, because she turned around, and they smiled at one another, sending a thrill through him. "I'll be right back," he said, and she nodded, still smiling.

He climbed the stairs and went straight to the metal shelves that bordered one wall. Glass canisters of fluid and boxes with glass squares filled the lower shelves, while paper, film, and photographs filled the upper ones. Somewhere in the piles were copies of the photograph Phillip had taken of Claude. They still hadn't decided which size to give to Hannah. He wanted to give her the largest one, but Phillip insisted such an act would appear presumptuous and that she would prefer a smaller photo—something she could tuck away inside her scriptures, perhaps.

Claude rummaged through several stacks of photos, wondering where in the world Phillip had stashed his portrait and thinking that his little brother wouldn't have much business success if he didn't organize his things better. *How many times has he photographed the temple foundation, anyway?* There were pictures of landscapes, their home, even a few of Mrs. Brecken and some ward members.

Then, at the bottom of a pile, Claude came across a photo that made his mouth hang open. At first glance he didn't believe his eyes. He slid the picture out and walked to a window to see it better in the light, as if that would change the image. But there was no mistaking it, although he wished so badly he could disbelieve what he saw.

In the picture, Hannah wore the same dress she had worn to the dance. Of course the photo had no color, so he couldn't tell for sure if the dress was yellow, but it had the same lace petticoat showing beneath the skirt, which was hitched up in a scallop around the bottom. Because the image was slightly blurred from movement, he couldn't make out the pattern of the fabric.

But she was clearly kissing a man with dark hair. Claude's insides twisted. How could this be? Who was this man? When was the photo taken? And how dare Phillip take such a thing, then let Claude go about with Hannah on his arm, knowing she wasn't trustworthy?

The girl was clearly Hannah, no matter how much Claude wished it otherwise. Only part of the left side of her face was visible, since the man's face covered her eyes, but the cheekbones were hers. So was that dark hair swept off her neck. If there had been any doubt, the background would have confirmed it—the aspens growing behind them, the fence with its broken crosspiece—he had seen these enough times to know they belonged in the Hansen front yard.

But the most telling detail was one he couldn't tear his eyes from. Tucked into the side of her hair was the tortoiseshell comb with a cluster of pearls in the center.

His emotions boiled inside him. This made no sense. Hannah was supposed to be beautiful, virtuous, and pure. She was to be his badge of honor, his prize.

But if she had kissed another man, what else might she have done? He knew all too well how one small act could lead to another, and then another . . .

Could she have done with that man what *he* had done with Cybil? The thought exploded in his mind from a simple imaginary possibility into reality. He suddenly believed that Hannah *had* done that. The idea of her touching another man, being *touched by* another man. Even *looking* at another man . . .

He shuddered. It was too much. Hannah was *his.* She belonged to *him.*

Anger roiling inside him, Claude gritted his teeth and in one swift movement kicked the metal shelves as hard as he could. Photos tumbled to the floor. Bottles fell—one cracking and spilling its contents. He didn't care. He shoved the tripod to the side and raced down the stairs, taking two at a time even though they were so steep he could have fallen and broken a leg.

He strode to Hannah's side and tried hard to spit out some intelligible words. "Mrs. Brecken warned me about you. Would you have any idea what she meant?"

Hannah looked over Claude's shoulder at Mrs. Brecken, who was arranging items on a shelf while watching the pair out of the corner of her eye. "Mrs. Brecken? I have no idea what you're talking about."

Claude shoved the photo in her face. "What have you got to say about *this?*"

Hannah had to lean back to even see the picture. "What is it?" she asked, alarmed.

*As well she should be.*

She took the photo and looked at it. Eyes narrowing, she said, "I've never seen this."

"But it's you."

"No, it looks like my cousin Marie."

Claude looked at her in disbelief. "So now you compound it by *lying* to me?" He shook his head. "Ben was right all along. Women can't be trusted." He gripped the picture between his fingers, jealousy rearing inside his chest like an animal. Claude wished he could reach through the image and rip the couple apart, then throttle the other man thoroughly.

"It's Marie, I'm sure of it," Hannah said. "Look closer. Don't you recognize her?"

"I don't know what Marie looks like," Claude snapped, deliberately looking away from the picture now that she asked him to study it. He pushed Hannah's arm away with the photo.

"You do know Marie," Hannah insisted. "You must have seen her many times. She was just here visiting. She came up the canyon when Phillip took our picture."

"I wasn't there, remember?"

"Oh . . . right." Hannah's forehead wrinkled, and she thought some more. "What about the day after your letter? She came with us on that walk." Her voice wavered as she went on. "You must remember her."

"That day I had eyes only for you." Claude gazed into her eyes, hoping she'd see how deeply he felt for her. Didn't she understand how much he cared? "Besides, everyone else walked behind us. An elephant could have come along and I wouldn't have noticed—unless she looked this much like you."

Hannah pointed at the girl in the picture. "But it *is* her. It's not me."

"It's your dress, isn't it?" He shoved the image before her. She took it in her hands and studied it.

"Yes. I said she could borrow it."

"And that's the comb I gave you. Even you can't lie about that."

Hannah's head snapped up. "Even I?" She took a step back from him, her head shaking back and forth in disbelief. "Claude, I've *never* lied to you about anything. Yes, it looks like my comb. I told Marie she could borrow anything she wanted. Who *are* you, Claude? What right do you have to accuse me of something so ridiculous?"

He went on as if she hadn't spoken. His insides were raging. Claude felt like a bull with its sights on a target, charging forward. Sheer jealousy and lost hope fueled his anger. "And that's your front yard, complete with the quaking aspens and the broken fence piece. What else did you do with him, hmm? I'm sure it wasn't just a kiss. What else? What else have you done?"

"What on earth do you mean? I've done nothing!" No longer able to control her own anger, Hannah raised her voice and looked him in the eye. "Marie was wearing my things in this picture. But it isn't me, and I've never seen that man in my life."

"A likely story," Claude spat. He narrowed his eyes. "Who is he?"

Hannah smacked the picture into Claude's chest. He didn't take it. "He must be Marie's beau. She said he stopped by one afternoon out of the blue."

"All the way from Spanish Fork? Hardly." Claude went on, not giving her protestations any credence. They made so little sense, and the most obvious answer was the most likely, anyway. "So someone else just happens to be wearing your dress, wearing a gift I recently bought you, standing in your yard, looking like your twin?"

Hannah took a step closer, painfully aware of customers staring. "Please, Claude. You're making a scene."

"I have every right to make a scene!" Claude was nearly shouting now. "I have proof of the kind of person you really are."

She flinched as if he had struck her. Her mouth twitched, and she was visibly trembling. She looked at him helplessly, shaking her head back and forth as tears ran down her face, but he felt no compassion for her.

"I thought you were different, Hannah Hansen. But it looks like you're nothing more than a tease and a flirt. I should have listened to Ben. Women are fickle creatures without a shred of loyalty. Especially Hansen women."

Hannah let the photo drop to the floor. "How can you say such things to me? I thought I knew you."

"I thought the same." Claude's voice was toneless.

She covered her face and ran out of the store, crying with what Claude assumed was humiliation and shame. *Serves her right,* he thought, picking up the photo. He walked to the door, giving the customers a pained smile. "Sorry for the commotion," he said, then he put on his hat and left, crumpling the photograph in one hand. He narrowed his eyes and headed for the Hansen home. Not for Hannah. She was already out of sight around the corner, and he wasn't going after her.

*Ben was right all along,* he thought as he stalked down the street. *I should never have gotten involved in playing Cupid with Phillip. Now I'm going to have to save Ben from himself.*

# CHAPTER 13

Standing alone with Ben, Bethany couldn't manage to keep eye contact with him. After Claude and Hannah had left them behind, they had to make painfully awkward small talk to fill the silence. Bethany didn't know if she could tolerate it much longer.

What made things worse was how Ben looked. It might have been easier to stand there looking disinterested if he had arrived wearing travel-worn clothes and smelling of campfire smoke. Instead he looked as if he had bathed before coming over. His hair even looked damp. His face was clean shaven, although she secretly preferred him with a little growth, like he'd had in the shed the other day. It made him look rugged and more masculine.

Instead of wearing dust-covered, wrinkled clothes, he had on clean, black trousers, a white shirt, and freshly polished boots. Maybe, just maybe, his attention to his appearance was not coincidence. But she didn't quite believe that yet, not until she heard it from the horse's mouth. She hid a smile at the thought of calling Ben a horse. Insults were still second nature.

"So . . . how was your trip?" she asked, toeing a weed as she tried to find another topic of conversation. If only they hadn't been left alone. She wanted to talk with Ben—really talk—but how could she bridge the gap that had grown between them? She'd have to be careful not to be mean or rude; with all the practice she'd had, it would be a little too easy to throw a barb without thinking. On the other hand, if Ben were mean first . . .

"The trip was good," Ben said. "Long. Hot." He nodded and

pressed his lips together, then scanned the area. "Yep. Long and hot. Your house looks good. Flowers new?"

"Not really. We planted them a couple of months ago."

"Well, they're sure pretty. Tulips?"

"Pansies."

"Ah."

They continued avoiding one another's eyes. Bethany was ready to scream if the conversation continued as painfully as this. It was almost worse than hurling insults. At least when they fought, they looked at each other and could find their tongues. They actually *said* something.

"Anything interesting happen on the road?" Bethany asked.

Ben visibly started, as if she had poked him. He took a deep breath and paused. Sighing, he finally tilted his head and said, "Well . . . Now that you mention it, something did."

She hadn't expected her question to elicit a response like this; she had hoped to merely avoid more hemming and hawing. Ben's face was turning red around the edges, and by the intense look in his eyes, she wasn't sure if she dared ask what had happened. She contented herself with a vague, "Oh, really?"

He nodded uncomfortably and looked around as if someone might be watching. He took a step closer and leaned in. Whispering, he said, "Bethany, what if—what if I told you that . . ." His eyes held hers, and his voice caught.

Bethany could hardly breathe. Everything Marie and Hannah had said was true. She knew it. He was about to tell her as much. When he didn't continue, Bethany found her voice and prompted, "What if you told me . . ." She spoke breathlessly, her voice trailing off as she took a step closer. He took a matching step toward her, and now they were so close she caught the scent of soap on his skin. The hair on her arms stood on end as she raised her head, hardly daring to look into his eyes—the deep brown that once melted her insides like maple syrup. She quickly looked down again, but it didn't help much. Now she stared at his hands, his strong arms, the freshly pressed clothes he had worn just for her. She wanted so badly to pour out her innermost thoughts to him, but she didn't dare. Something held her back from letting herself be totally vulnerable again.

"What if," Ben began again, speaking softly in her ear. The tenderness in his voice was maddening, sending Bethany's heart racing. "What if I told you . . ."

Tears pricked her eyes. Was he about to say what she thought he was? She swallowed hard. And if he was bridging the gap that had been between them for so long . . .

*But what about . . . everything?*

He brushed a stray curl from her face, still not finishing his sentence. She closed her eyes, allowing herself to feel his touch on her face. But when quick footsteps came from behind, she opened her eyes. Hannah came toward them from the street, her hands covering her face. She was sobbing.

"Goodness, Hannah, what happened?" Bethany stepped away from Ben.

Hannah paused and shook her head, tears coursing down her cheeks. "It's Claude. He thinks I—" She covered her face again and shook her head.

"He thinks you what?" Bethany asked.

"He says I'm a disloyal flirt. That I've been secretly courting—and kissing—another man—and—and *worse!*" Hannah looked at Ben as if gauging whether she dared speak ill of his brother. "He accused me in public, in the middle of the general store. It was horrid!" Bethany tried to reach for her sister, but Hannah shook her head. "No. I have to be alone." Overcome with emotion, she practically ran backward toward the house in escape. One of Hannah's feet landed on the edge of the well, her heel slipping inside. The misstep sent her stumbling, arms flailing in the air.

Ben and Bethany ran forward, Ben throwing himself onto the ground toward Hannah, reaching out with all his might. She slipped just past his hands and fell backward, landing inside the well with a thud and, a second later, a splash.

"Hannah!" The word ripped from Bethany's throat as she knelt at the edge of the well and looked down, her insides leaden. "Hannah, can you hear me?" No answer came from below, and all Bethany could see was a mass of fabric.

Ben jumped to his feet and raced to the shed, returning a moment later with rope strong enough to hold a grown man. Without a word, he dropped the coil to the ground, tied several knots along the length, then securely tied one end around a tree by the porch and dropped the other into the well. He yanked on the rope to make sure it would hold him.

"Hannah, can you hear me?" Ben searched the darkness for her shape then said over his shoulder, "I can't tell what position she's in. I'm going down."

As he lowered himself, Bethany tried not to think about what he was doing or what condition Hannah was in, but it was hard not to imagine her sister's crumpled form in the wet, narrow well. Was she bleeding? Conscious? Breathing?

Bethany paced between the well and the house, hating that there was nothing for her to do while Ben went into the darkness. She buried her face in her hands as his head disappeared below ground. She felt sick inside, and her stomach clenched. She shook her head to force the thoughts away and gritted her teeth, determined to be strong for Hannah. Even so, cold fear coursed through her veins.

"I made it," Ben called.

"How is she?" Bethany gasped, the images of Hannah finding their way back to her mind.

"I can't see anything." His voice echoed as it came up the well. He didn't say anything else, and all Bethany could hear was splashing sounds and grunts. She resisted the urge to go to the edge and look down, knowing she wouldn't be able to see anything anyway, but she kept her eyes on the rope, lying slack on the lawn. Her heart leapt when the rope grew taut again, and soon afterward Ben's head appeared at the edge of the well, with Hannah's limp form braced over his shoulder. She and Ben were both dripping wet, making it hard to tell where Hannah was bleeding, but it was clear she had a head wound.

It took all of Bethany's inner strength to keep herself from crying out at the sight of Hannah's body flopped lifelessly.

"Help me," Ben said between gritted teeth. It took Bethany a second to move her shocked feet and rush to the edge. She reached for Hannah and hoisted her onto the ground. Ben braced his hands on the well's edge and pulled himself out, panting hard.

Tears threatened, but Bethany swiped them away. *Not now. Hannah needs me.* Hannah lay unconscious, with most of her face covered in blood, so much so that Bethany couldn't tell at first where she was hurt or how large her wounds were. Hannah didn't move, and if she was breathing, it was so shallow Bethany couldn't see it. She dropped to her knees and put her head to Hannah's chest. When the sound of a heartbeat thrummed softly and Hannah's chest rose and fell, Bethany nearly cried.

"She's breathing," she said, her body suddenly trembling.

"Good," Ben said, still breathing heavily. "Then I don't think she took in much water. But we need a doctor." Ben took off his shirt, wadded it up, and swabbed the blood from her face. He found the cut, which was over her left ear and still bleeding. He pressed the shirt against her head and looked up at Bethany. "Go get help."

For just a moment, she hesitated leaving Hannah, but she trusted Ben to care for her, so she scrambled to her feet and raced down the lane. When she reached the road, she spotted a dark-haired boy of about ten years walking along with his head down, dragging a stick in the dirt behind him.

Instinctively, she called to him. "Do you want to earn some money?"

He looked up in surprise, and when she saw his features, Bethany was taken aback. Although dressed in regular clothing, the boy looked like an Indian with high cheekbones and dark eyes. His sad little face broke into a smile. "Sure. What do I have to do?"

Bethany didn't recognize the boy and didn't have time to not trust him. "Do you know where Dr. Wood's office is? It's next door to the feed store on Third South."

"The one with the green awning?" the boy asked, drawing shapes in the dirt with his stick. "Sure. I know the place."

Bethany took the boy by the shoulders so he'd look directly at her. He had a bruise around one eye and a goose egg on his forehead. Typical of a boy that age, she supposed. "What's your name?"

"Abe."

She had half expected "Red Bear" or something. "All right, Abe. Listen. I'll pay you a half dollar if you run to Dr. Wood's office and bring him back—right away. It's an emergency."

"A half dollar!" The boy's eyes opened wide. "That's more money than I've ever seen in my whole life." It was a lot of money—nearly all Bethany had saved up in her coin box. But if it meant motivating this young man to get a doctor fast enough, she was willing to give it away. By the look on his face, it was plenty of motivation.

Abe looked over her shoulder at Ben, who was bent over Hannah in the distance. "Someone's hurt pretty bad, aren't they?"

Bethany's throat tightened, and her chin trembled, making it hard to speak. "Yes. It's my sister. Please hurry. You can reach him faster than I can."

"Sure can. I'm a good runner," Abe said in agreement. "I'll be back right away." With that he dropped the stick and burst into a run, his arms and legs pumping.

Bethany held her breath, praying that Dr. Wood was in his office and would come right away. A moment later, someone came around a corner and nearly ran headlong into Abe.

Claude.

Abe collided into him, stumbling and backing up. "Excuse me. Sorry, sir," he said, head lowered in an attitude of penance and fear of reprisal.

"Get out of my way," Claude said with a shove, sending the boy sprawling to the ground. Bethany winced. For the briefest flash, a look of rage crossed Abe's face, but then he looked back at Bethany and brushed off his trousers. "I'll be back with the doctor. Don't you worry." He threw Claude a look of absolute hate before running down the road again.

Bethany turned back down the lane and hurried back toward Hannah and Ben.

"Doctor?" Claude called after her. "What was that all about?"

She ignored him, holding her skirts and running back to her sister. Claude raced up to her and grabbed her arm. He turned her around. "Why are you calling a doctor?"

"Because of you," she said, then ripped her arm away.

"What are you talking about?" Claude leaned to look around Bethany. Rage boiling inside her, she shoved him backward as hard as she could. He stumbled and fell, looking bewildered and almost afraid at the sudden appearance of a madwoman.

"You nearly killed my sister! She fell down the well, all right? Now go away."

Claude's face immediately fell. He peered around Bethany at Hannah's form lying on the ground. "Is she all right?" he asked, scrambling to his feet. He tried to get past Bethany to Hannah.

She blocked the way, intent on protecting her sister from further harm. "Don't you dare go near her."

"Why shouldn't I?"

The sound of Ben's voice coming up behind her brought her sheer relief. "Because if you don't get your sorry carcass out of here, I'll knock you down so hard your teeth will fall out."

"Fine. Consider me gone." Claude raised his hands in surrender and left.

Bethany dropped to her knees and put her arms protectively across Hannah. "Thank you," she told Ben, watching with a mix of satisfaction and pain as Claude left. This was supposed to be the man who would cherish her sister. Without a word, Ben raced back to the sisters and knelt beside Bethany.

Ben continued putting pressure on Hannah's head wound. "Her head won't stop bleeding, and I can't get her to wake up. Is a doctor coming?"

"I sent for one," Bethany said without elaborating. "I'll get some blankets."

She raced inside and brought out two quilts to cover her sister, who was pale and cold. With nothing else either of them could do, they silently prayed as they waited. Bethany tried to wake Hannah more than once, but to no avail. Her shoulder, arm, and leg seemed bent at odd angles—perhaps they were broken. Other scrapes and scratches crisscrossed her body. It wouldn't be long before bruises would start to show up as well.

Several minutes later, young Abe arrived carrying the doctor's bag, looking over his shoulder repeatedly and calling, "Hurry, Doctor! Hurry!" The boy nearly slid to his knees beside Bethany. "We're back," he announced, presenting the bag. He looked at Hannah. "So what's wrong with her?"

"I don't know." Bethany stood and gently nudged the boy to the side to make room for the doctor. She put her arms around Abe, and he seemed willing to stay.

The doctor felt Hannah's pulse, looked into her eyes, and probed the cut on her head. "You've slowed the bleeding. Good." Near the porch, he spotted a piece of wood several inches wide and almost six feet long. He had Ben fetch it and then strapped Hannah to it. "Let's get her to a bed," he said to Ben. "Watch that we don't move her neck."

The two of them carefully lifted Hannah, and Bethany followed behind. At the door, she whispered to Abe, "I'll go get you the money," expecting him to wait outside. Instead, he came in with her and stood at the base of the stairs.

"Her room is on the right," Bethany called behind them as the doctor and Ben carried her up. Bethany raced to her windowsill and emptied all of the coins of her heart-shaped crock into her hand. It was more than half a dollar, but the boy's service was worth that. She returned to him a moment later and pressed the money into his palm, eager to get back to Hannah. "Here you go. Thank you for helping."

"What's her name?" Abe asked, looking up the stairs.

"Hannah."

"What's yours?" He wrapped his slender brown fingers around the coins without counting them.

"Bethany."

"Thanks for the money, Bethany. I'm going to buy a new hymn book for my mother with it before my stepfather can take it away from me." Abe smiled and raised the fist that held the coins. "Hope your sister gets all better." He paused at the door and gave her a crooked grin.

"Me too," Bethany said. "And thank you, Abe."

# CHAPTER 14

Dr. Wood came out of Hannah's room and closed the door behind him. He looked haggard, his eyes weary and the lines around his mouth more pronounced than usual. Bethany left her place against the wall and came to him. Ben stood beside her for support, now wearing an ill-fitting shirt he had borrowed from the bishop's closet.

"How is she?"

"To be honest, it's still too early to tell," Dr. Wood said. "For now we need to watch and wait. There isn't anything else I can do for her."

He made a move toward the stairs, and Bethany put a hand on his arm to stop him. "What do we wait for? What should we be looking for?"

"Any improvement. Keep trying to wake her every few hours. The longer she stays unconscious, the worse we'll know her injury is. Head wounds are tough to diagnose. I'll be back tomorrow to check on her."

"Wait—she's *still* not awake? What does that mean?" Bethany wanted to wring the doctor's neck. He seemed reluctant to tell her anything, which only made her worries escalate.

"It may mean she has a brain bleed, causing pressure. I don't know how serious it is. On one hand, it still could be just a severe concussion, or it could be . . . worse."

Ben came to Bethany's rescue. "What do you mean by *worse?*"

Dr. Wood sighed. "Do you mind if we sit to talk?"

"Not at all," Bethany said, throwing Ben a grateful look. She doubted a woman could have squeezed more information out of the doctor.

They went downstairs, and after the three of them had settled in chairs at the kitchen table, Dr. Wood continued without preamble. "Head injuries are complex. If she has a brain bleed, swelling, a blood clot, or any number of other complications . . ." His voice trailed off, but when he saw Ben's look of determination, he finished the sentence. "In the worst case, such complications would make any kind of recovery almost impossible."

"You mean she'd—" Bethany could hardly get the words out.

Dr. Wood nodded, but seemed hesitant to commit to the reality. "Theoretically, we could lose her. Then again, she might just have a severe concussion. In that case, she should wake up soon enough—quite possibly with some memory loss at first. She'll be in a great deal of pain as well. She's got a few broken bones—collarbone, upper arm, and her left foot. I've put her arm in a sling for now, but I may need to plaster it if the sling can't hold it steady enough. I'll also bring supplies in the morning to plaster the foot."

"What else?" Ben asked. "We want to know everything." At least Ben managed to keep a clear head and continue asking questions. The idea that her sister might not survive made thinking almost impossible for Bethany.

"There are some other possibilities," Dr. Wood acknowledged. "It's just too early to tell. A neck injury might mean the loss of leg movement."

Bethany gasped, putting a hand to her mouth.

"Now, let's not assume anything yet," Dr. Wood said, putting up a hand to calm Bethany. "We just don't know. Don't worry."

*Don't worry?* Bethany could hardly speak or move, but for that comment alone she wanted to shove the doctor off his chair.

"Anything else?" Ben probed. "Please tell us anything you think would be helpful." He put a hand over Bethany's in a gesture of comfort. He was keeping remarkably calm. How he could do that in the face of such daunting possibilities was beyond Bethany. She wished some of his strength would seep into her through his hand.

"I want someone with her overnight," Dr. Wood said, standing. "Check to see if her pupils are the same size. Watch for any changes in her consciousness and record them—whether she wakes up, falls back asleep, or appears disoriented. Write it all down, along with the times. Remember to try to wake her every few hours." He moved to the door, reached for the handle, then added. "Oh, and whatever you do, *don't* move her. If she has a neck injury, you'll only make it worse. I'll be back in the morning."

"Thank you, Doctor," Ben said, seeing him out.

But at the door, Dr. Wood stopped and turned around. "One more thing. I shouldn't have said as much as I did about her prognosis. Don't tell her any of that. You see, with this type of injury, it's paramount that you not upset the patient if at all possible. Her mental stability may be compromised as it is, since she's already been through a great deal of trauma. So please, do not discuss the accident with her, and do not talk about what the outcomes of her injuries might be."

Bethany shook her head with confusion. "But what if she asks? I'm sure she will. We can't lie to her."

"Just change the subject," Dr. Wood said. "Avoid the topic. And for that matter," he added, wagging a finger, "consider Hannah the center of the universe for now. What she says, goes. The fewer bumps she experiences for the next few weeks, the quicker I believe she'll recover. So if she wants a roast for dinner, she gets it. If she says the sky is red, it is."

Ben folded his arms. "Except she can't discuss the one thing she probably wants to, and she can't get out of bed."

"Well, yes," the doctor admitted. "But please accommodate her as best you can. I know this may sound silly, and I'm probably the only doctor around who thinks that a patient's mental state can affect their healing this way, but there you are. Will you abide by my orders?"

"If she says the sky is red, it'll be scarlet," Bethany said, smiling wearily.

"Thank you." Dr. Wood tipped his hat and walked out.

Bethany sighed heavily and closed her eyes. Ben came to her and gently urged her toward the stairs. "Let's go see her. I'll stay with you."

Together they went up to Hannah. Bethany wished her father wouldn't be gone overnight. They had sent word about Hannah's condition with one of his counselors, but she knew it would do little good; he wouldn't be able to get home much quicker anyway, since he was probably already on the road home. Ben and the doctor had given Hannah a priesthood blessing, but Bethany wished her father had been home to do it. The doctor hadn't let her in to see her sister yet, so Bethany didn't even know what the blessing had said.

As they went into the bedroom, she held her breath. But when she saw Hannah, she let it out slowly. At first her sister looked like she was just taking a nap, although she had a white bandage stained with blood wrapped around her head. As they drew closer, more evidence of the accident was visible. The wood plank still lay underneath her—to support her neck, Bethany presumed. Either that or Dr. Wood didn't dare move Hannah to remove it. Her eyes were closed as if she were merely dozing. The first signs of bruising were just starting—red, puffy areas on her face and arms that would eventually change to darker colors. Her left arm was in a sling.

Bethany sat at the edge of the bed, and Ben pulled up a chair from the corner. "She's going to be fine," he said, sitting down.

"I hope so," Bethany said weakly. "She might be perfectly well in a few days, or . . ." She forcefully bit her lips together to keep emotion from taking over.

"She'll be fine," Ben repeated, reaching for her hand.

"How can you keep saying that?" Bethany said, pulling her hand free from his. "My sister could have died a few moments ago, and she's lying here fighting for her life, and all you can say is that she'll be *fine?* We don't know that she'll be *fine.* I am not *fine.* And right now she's *certainly* not fine."

She stood and stormed to the other side of the room. Her hands covered her face, and all the tears that she had held back for the last hour came streaming down her face. She had managed to be so strong for Hannah, but now that exterior crumbled, and she sobbed uncontrollably. Ben's chair scraped against the floor, and a second later, he touched her shoulder. She needed comfort from someone. And maybe Ben could be that person, one day—but now? She still hardly knew him. The chasm between them hadn't been crossed. She pulled away as if his hand were a hot poker.

"Bethany," he said.

"What?" She spat the word and stalked to the other side of the room, to the window, trying to escape his touch. Somehow she knew that if she let him touch her, any remaining protective barrier she had would come tumbling down. She already felt as weak and helpless as a newborn lamb. If Ben managed to put his arms around her and make her even more vulnerable . . . She couldn't allow that. Not now, not around Ben. This new Ben, whom she didn't know. She had too much to manage right now, too many emotions, thoughts . . .

She stood by the window for several seconds without Ben following. He finally asked, "What can I say that might help? What can I do?"

She squeezed her eyes tight shut, sending plump tears down her cheeks. A part of her wanted to reach out and let Ben hold her, but another didn't dare, told her that if she opened that door, that she'd just be wounded more than she already was with her sister lying in the bed, hurt. What guarantee did she have that Ben wouldn't strike back after all?

"There's nothing anyone can do. Just . . . just go."

"Are you sure? I could—"

"Go. Please."

"Very well." Ben tilted his head toward her and left the room, closing the door behind him.

She stayed at the window for several minutes, staring into the sky until her sobs had lessened and she felt like the elder sister again. She wiped her cheeks and took a deep breath, then returned to Hannah's bedside.

"Wake up, Hannah," she said, gently patting her sister's cheek as the doctor had suggested. When she got no response, she tried not to be disappointed. Instead, she checked her sister's pupils, monitored her pulse, and made a note of all her observations—including the times—in a notebook.

Then she pulled up a chair and sat down to begin an all-night vigil.

* * *

When Bethany sent him packing, Ben had planned to go home. He really did. But as he headed for the door, the Frandsens, some well-wishing neighbors, dropped by to check on Hannah. Ben acted as the doorkeeper, sharing little and sending them on their way. He did the same an hour later when Sister Hornby arrived after hearing about Hannah's accident. And again when the Hill sisters came, asking whether the rumors they heard from Mrs. Brecken's store were true about Hannah having some strange man's baby. Ben sent them all packing—especially the last ones—and decided at that point that for Bethany's sake he couldn't go home.

The sun had set when Claude tried to force his way into the house, insisting that it was his right to see Hannah.

"She's mine. I love her, and I'm going to see her," he declared, pushing his way into the house.

Ben shoved him right back out. "You have no rights to any woman," he snarled back, "And you never will. It'll be good for you to remember that. Women aren't property."

"But how *is* she? I have to see her."

Ben felt a twinge of sympathy. He could tell Claude was worried about Hannah. The boy did have a heart in that chest of his after all. But in the end, he had also managed to cause a lot of pain. *Maybe I'm wrong to do this, but I'm going to do a bit of the same to him,* he thought.

"She's clinging to life, if you must know. Doctor says she might die." Ben figured Claude deserved the shock.

Claude went white and pulled at his chin. "That's right," Ben said, watching Claude pace in a tight circle next to the porch. "Or she might lose the use of her legs. It's too early to tell. But even if she recovers, I'm already hearing rumors that she's done all sorts of things, none of which are true, and you know it."

"Let me in, Ben," Claude said again, coming back to the porch. "Please," he begged, no longer trying to force his way in. None of it swayed Ben one bit, because he knew Bethany would have his hide if he let Claude upstairs.

"Not unless you beat me senseless first," Ben said, bracing himself in the doorway. They both knew from childhood that Ben could whup both of his brothers. Ben raised an eyebrow. "Game tonight?"

"You're cruel, you know that?" Claude said, glowering at Ben as he stormed off.

"If you only knew," Ben said under his breath as he went back inside to keep watch.

He waited another few hours until it was well past dark, debating whether he should go home and leave Bethany to tend Hannah alone, or whether he should stay in case she needed something. On one hand, it wasn't socially acceptable for two young people to be unchaperoned under the same roof all night, but this wasn't a normal situation. Granted, Bethany had basically kicked him out of the house and didn't know he had stayed. She needed support, even if she wasn't aware of it.

He glanced at the clock. Ten past midnight. Bethany hadn't left Hannah's room since she went up around six o'clock. He had no idea when she had last eaten, but she had to be ravenous. Knowing her, she wouldn't leave her sister's side even for food. He eyed the stove. He wasn't the best cook, but she needed to eat. He found a pot with potato soup and managed to warm it up without burning it. He tried making a batch of biscuits but somehow the insides were soggy while the outsides were hard and black. Three were less dark than the others, so he put them on a plate, then sliced an apple.

With the makeshift meal on a tray, he went upstairs and knocked on the door. He heard a sudden gasp from the other side. "It's just me—Ben. I brought you some food."

He waited, hoping she wouldn't send him away, and was relieved to hear her say, "Oh. Come . . . come in."

Ben pushed the bedroom door open with his shoulder. "I figured you'd be getting hungry," he said, placing the tray on the bedside table.

"Did you make all this yourself?" she asked, amazement in her voice. She leaned down and inhaled the aroma. "Didn't you go home?"

He shrugged apologetically. "No. And sorry that the apple's bruised. It's the only one I could find. The biscuits are barely edible, but you can probably choke one down with butter."

"I . . . thank you," Bethany said, smiling up at him. "It looks wonderful." As if in confirmation, her stomach growled. Her hand covered it. "Have you eaten anything?"

Ben shook his head. "Not yet. I'll have some soup and some *really* black biscuits later." He picked one up and slathered butter on it. "Just close your eyes and pretend it's golden brown."

Laughing, Bethany took a bite of the biscuit, catching crumbs as she did so. "Thank you."

"It's the least I could do." He pulled up a chair and sat beside her. With a look at Hannah, his eyebrows drew together, and he said, "Any change?"

Bethany shook her head and stirred the soup slowly. "None." They sat silently for a minute. Then Bethany sighed and looked over. "I'm sorry I snapped at you earlier."

"It's all right," Ben said, smiling. "That's what you and I do, right?"

"But I shouldn't have." Bethany looked into his eyes for a minute as if trying to read them. Ben wished he knew what was behind hers. He lowered his gaze and changed the subject.

"What happened, do you think?" he asked. "I mean between Claude and Hannah?"

"Exactly what she *said* happened," Bethany said a little tersely. "You don't think she did what he accused her of, do you?"

"No," Ben said slowly and—he knew—somewhat hesitantly. It wasn't that he doubted Hannah, but he wondered if there were more to the story than they had heard. Certainly not what the Hill sisters had suggested—not even a particle of that. *Yet every dime has two sides,* he thought. The past still colored his perception of things. He loved Bethany, and yet he had seen what he saw in the orchard. It was inescapable.

She remained impassive. "If anyone is in the wrong, it's not Hannah. I'm sorry to say something like that about your own flesh and blood, but there it is."

Ben didn't answer right away; he remained deep in thought. "Do you think Hannah is *completely* innocent? Is there a chance she did anything wrong? Even something that Claude could have misunderstood?"

Bethany shook her head adamantly. "If anyone in the world knows Hannah, it's me. She loved Claude and trusted him with her soul. She would never do anything to jeopardize that." She searched Ben's face for agreement. "You've known her most of your life, Ben. Have you ever known her to be a flirt?"

"No," Ben admitted, sitting back in the chair and looking at Hannah's figure in the bed. "Never."

Bethany tore one of the biscuits into pieces as if trying to find the best way to ask her next question. "And have you ever known Claude to overreact or be suspicious?"

With a reluctant nod, Ben said, "I have. Even recently—and about Hannah." He sighed and leaned forward, his elbows resting on his thighs. "It was the day Phillip and I came over with that letter from Claude, when we asked your father for permission for the two of them to court."

"I remember," Bethany said with a nod. "What happened to make Claude upset? I would have thought he'd have been ecstatic."

Ben thought back to that day as he stared at the wall above the bed. "When we got home, Claude suspected that we didn't do what he'd asked."

"That's strange," Bethany said, shrugging. "What else would you and Phillip have done? Unless he thought you had caused a scene about bachelors and romance."

With a pained laugh, Ben shook his head. "No, it wasn't that. But I wouldn't have put such a thing past me—at one time." He and Bethany locked eyes for a moment, smiled, and shyly looked down. Something was there between them, but nothing had been spoken openly yet. It was maddening.

"Claude exploded when Phillip confessed that—" Ben cut off abruptly.

"Confessed . . . what?" Bethany suddenly raised her head, and a sudden look of understanding dawned on her face. "He confessed his feelings for Hannah?" she ventured.

Startled, Ben looked over. "You know?"

"I guessed. Call it sisterly intuition. I noticed Phillip looking at her during that first dance after you returned home." She looked at the biscuit, which now lay crumbled on the tray. "What did Claude say?"

Ben summarized the accusations that Claude leveled at their brother and finished with, "I've seen him rage about other things in the past—call people names, even." He swallowed after saying that one. He had purposely avoided telling Bethany about the part of the fight where Claude brought up Phillip's biological father. If bloodline were tied so closely to character, one would hope that Claude would have gotten some kindness from his own father.

Bethany touched Ben's hand, and he looked up. "Claude thinks he saw evidence of her being unfaithful to him, but he's wrong. He has to be."

"But if he saw the proof with his own eyes . . ." Ben's voice trailed off.

Bethany withdrew her hand and shook her head. She stood, ignoring a biscuit piece as it tumbled to the floor. "You still can't understand how to look with your heart instead of your blasted eyes all the time, can you? You probably still think I was stringing along both you and Matthew all those years ago."

Ben stood up. He didn't want to bring that up right now—even if he was thinking about it. "Bethany, the past is the past."

"You *do* think I was playing you against Matthew, don't you?"

Her eyes closed tightly, and she shook her head. "The past isn't the past, not today. It's right now. It's happening again, and you'd better not be such a fool that you can't see it." Bethany's eyes watered.

A practiced reflex made him want to yell back and defend himself, but at the same time, she had a point—he had never heard her side of the story.

As Bethany paced the room, Ben tried to follow, but she jerked away from his touch. Turning on him, she said, "Matthew came to talk with me that day. That much is true. I agreed to walk in the orchard with him—but only so I could tell him that I didn't return his feelings. That I was *your* girl." Bethany glared at Ben, and it took a minute for him to respond. Their eyes held one another's, and Ben repeated her words in his mind. *Your girl.*

"What happened?" he asked, hardly trusting his voice. Trying to be humble and willing to listen took all his effort, but he had wanted to know this story for so long. Even now he hesitated, his heart questioning, but this time he restrained himself. He *would* listen. He'd hear her out.

She took a deep breath and hugged herself, then laughed sadly. "The first two times anyone ever kissed me came two days in a row. One I wanted, and the other was simply thrust upon me." She turned to Ben. "I was walking through the trees as Matthew talked, not hearing a word he said because I was so busy trying to come up with a way to explain my loyalties without wounding his pride. Then out of the blue, he knelt in front of me, took my hand, and proposed marriage." Ben's eyes narrowed in disbelief, but Bethany hurried on. "I know it sounds fantastic that I didn't expect it. But it's true. I didn't believe it was happening, and there I was in the middle of it. I didn't know him that well, and we certainly hadn't been courting. Why would he ask me such a thing?"

Ben took a step back with understanding. "Because he saw us leave the dance the night before and didn't want to lose his chance with you."

She nodded. "He knew, but he hoped I'd change my mind. When I said no, he pleaded. Then he stood up and said, 'Just give me a chance. I can be the man for you, you'll see.'" She closed her eyes and pressed her fingertips to her forehead as if trying to forget the moment. "He had the audacity to lean in and kiss me. It happened so fast—I was totally surprised—that I didn't have time to even pull back before you showed up."

"And left."

"And left," Bethany said with a nod, crossing to him. "When I first saw you through the trees, I about collapsed with relief. I felt sure that you'd save me from Matthew's advances. He'd finally see that I really was your girl. I called out to you, hoping you'd save me."

"And instead I ran." Ben looked up at the ceiling, his head going back and forth. "What a fool I was."

"You believe me, then?" Bethany took a hopeful step toward him.

He looked at her and reached a hand out for her to take. "Of course I do. I wish I would have listened to you when it first happened."

Bethany took his hand in both of hers and studied the rough knuckles. She raised her head and looked at Hannah's limp form, then at Ben. "Then believe my sister. You know as well as anyone that seeing isn't always proof."

He nodded. "I will."

# CHAPTER 15

It took half an hour for Ben to convince Bethany to eat more food than would satisfy a small child. He returned the plate to the kitchen, and when he came back, he found her leaning against the headboard, asleep. Hannah still showed no signs of change, for better or worse.

He unfolded a blanket, put it over Bethany's sleeping form, and walked out, closing the bedroom door behind him. After washing a few pans and putting away the food he'd used in the kitchen, he headed for home.

Walking along the dark street by starlight, he wondered about the mess his brother had created, and the pain it had caused so many people. *What if Hannah is left a cripple? What if the family can't care for her themselves? What if she . . .*

Ben breathed out heavily and tried to clear his mind. *I'll just have to knock some sense into the boy,* he thought as he climbed the porch steps. *Claude needs to fix this.* A tiny seed of doubt tried to wiggle its way into his mind again, but he squashed it. He had to have faith in Hannah, for his sake and Bethany's.

Pausing on the top stair of the porch, he looked at the sky. Bright stars glittered above him like pinpricks of light through a piece of black velvet. At times like this he wished more fervently than usual that his mother were still alive, that it wasn't just three brothers living together and driving one another mad. It would be a nice change of pace not to be the one responsible, the one who felt the greatest duty to make sure the others were provided for and coming along well in life.

"I've tried to care for them as I promised, Ma," he said to the sky. "But I don't know what to do about your pigheaded middle son."

In frustration, he pulled the screen open, turned the knob, and went inside, fully expecting to see nothing but darkness at this hour. Instead, a lamp burned low in the family room. "Claude, what are you doing in here?" Ben went through the kitchen and found his brother slumped in a chair.

"About time you came home," Claude retorted, glancing at Ben beneath his hat, which was pulled down over his eyes. His arms rested on the sides of the chair, and in one hand was a bottle of liquor. Two other bottles lay empty on the floor at his feet.

"You're drunk." The obvious spilled unbidden from Ben's mouth. He reached for the lamp to extinguish it, unwilling to risk the fire that could be sparked from his brother's alcohol. Like most Saints in the city, they had some wine in the house and drank it on occasion, but these bottles weren't from the wine cupboard. Claude had to have bought several bottles of hard liquor somewhere in town. "Drinking a little on a special holiday is one thing, Claude."

"So what if I am stinkin' drunk?" Claude deliberately put the bottle to his mouth, took a swig, smacked his lips, and smirked at Ben with a look of bravado.

"You make me sick," Ben said, turning around to leave.

"I could say the same about you," Claude said, leaning over the edge of the chair to see Ben better. "Hanging around all day in a house full of lyin', loose women." Claude let himself fall back into the chair. But before he could raise the bottle for another drink, Ben clutched his arm and ripped the bottle away. He threw it into the cold fireplace, shattering the glass, then thrust his face inches from Claude's.

"Don't you *ever* say such a thing about the Hansens again. *You* are the one who humiliated an innocent, sweet girl—a girl who might not live through an accident for which *you* were partly to blame."

Claude used both hands to push Ben away by the shoulders. Ben backed up, but not because of his brother's strength—he couldn't stand the stench of Claude's breath. Claude pulled himself out of the chair and tried standing straighter, as if that would make him look stronger, but he teetered off balance. Then he spoke with the thick tongue of a muddied mind.

"Listen, I'm *sorry* anyone got hurt. That wasn't *my* fault." He took an unsteady step to the left, caught his balance on the mantel, then pointed a finger at Ben. "You didn't see the photograph." He jammed a finger at his own chest and nodded. "I did. You should heed your own advice. Stay away from those wily women creatures, Ben. Bethany's no better. You've said so yourself a thousand times. They're all whores." Claude raised his hand as if trying for another drink, then noticed the bottle was gone and scowled.

*Is that what I taught him?* Ben had never, ever used that word about a woman, he was sure. He couldn't believe his own brother just had.

Pained and furious, Ben gripped Claude's shirt and yanked him close. Holding him with one hand, Ben laid into him with the other fist. A well-placed punch landed on his jaw and sent Claude sprawling to the floor. Ben picked him up and hit him again—this time in the nose, which started to bleed.

"Don't ever talk about a woman like that again!" Another punch, this time in the gut. Claude doubled over in pain and vomited on the floor.

Ben stood back to avoid the smelly mess. "Our mother was one of those women you just denigrated," he said, panting heavily. "You will *not* speak of women in such terms in my presence."

Claude groaned as he moved shakily to his knees. "Why'd you do that?"

"Because you're a good-for-nothing scoundrel. Hannah and Bethany are just as dear and pure as our mother was, and you will show them respect." Ben leaned over and shoved Claude's head to the side. Weak and unsteady from the alcohol, he fell to the floor with a flop and landed on his face with a thud and a groan.

"Serves you right," Ben said, then stalked out and went upstairs, his feet pounding the wooden boards as he went to his room and slammed the door. Still in his clothes, he landed on his bed and rolled to his back. Arms folded tightly, he gazed out the window at the stars. Not so long ago he thought he knew the people in his life. Suddenly a former ally had become his enemy, and he was siding—with Bethany of all people—against his own flesh and blood. His eyes stung with anger and pain.

If only Phillip were home, instead of somewhere between here and the Little Cottonwood Quarry. It would be days until he returned and the two of them could figure out a solution to the problem. Phillip had always been the most levelheaded one in the family. *He wouldn't have hit Claude like that.* Ben groaned and rolled toward the wall. Sometimes being the oldest was nothing but a pain in the rump.

* * *

Phillip reached the temple block with the Tooele ward's load late Thursday afternoon. The extra time away didn't bother him one lick. But if he wasn't careful he'd have creditors breathing down his neck soon. He couldn't stay away much longer. He itched to get the stone off the wagon so they could turn around and head back to the quarry. Being in the city made him on edge—it was too close to Hannah and Claude. A young man of about twenty approached, introducing himself as Charles Lyon and distracting Phillip from his morose thoughts. Charles consulted his notes, told them where to take their load, and nodded at the men.

"I've got news for you after you unload," he said. "It's not so good for the temple, but it is for you. They're shutting down the quarry temporarily. You're free to go home."

*Home?* That was the last place Phillip wanted to be.

Charles turned to walk to the next team, but Phillip grabbed his arm. "What do you mean, the quarry is closed? We're supposed to bring in another load."

"Good luck," Charles said with a laugh. "I just know what I was told. They're trying to find a quicker way of hauling the stone, so they're contracting out a railway. The quarry is closed until further notice."

Sam, one of the Tooele elders, shrugged. "Sounds good to me." Everyone but Phillip looked excited at the prospect of going home early. His fists worked uneasily. Four days. That's how long he was supposed to have until he had to face Hannah again—and see her gazing with longing at his brother.

Charles shrugged. "That's the way it is, brother. I thought it would be good news."

"But—" Phillip floundered, trying to find a way out, but he couldn't see one. Then another thought suddenly hit. *Ben.* "What happens to the stonecutters?"

"As soon as they're done with the stones we've already quarried, they're out of work, I'm afraid." Charles shrugged unhappily. "For that matter, so am I. But some of those stones will take a few weeks yet."

"Like the Earth stones, I imagine," Phillip said offhandedly.

"That's right," Charles said, surprised.

"My brother is one of the stonecutters," Phillip explained. "So what is he going to do when his work here is done? What are *you* going to do?"

"Good question. Maybe try the railroad—they haven't started on it yet, but I imagine they'll be looking for workers."

Pete, the leader from the Tooele group, clapped Phillip's shoulder. "Thanks for helping out. We sure appreciate it."

"Yeah, sure," Phillip said with a shrug. He lifted his sack from the back of the wagon, leaving behind a couple bottles of food that he didn't want to bother carrying, and trudged off. *I should find Ben.* The men he had spent the last few days with were already leaving. He waved to them and started looking for his brother.

He walked through a virtual maze of stones, which lay all over the lot where the teamsters had dropped them. After three rounds with no sight of his brother, Phillip stopped a stonecutter in his work on a massive block nearly as tall as he was. It had to be an Earth stone, judging by its sheer size. "Excuse me, do you know Ben Adams?" he asked, figuring they might all know one another.

The man put down his facing chisel and single jackhammer, which he'd been using to smooth one side of the rock. He wiped his brow and stretched his back. "Sure do," he said, his voice tired. "Worked next to him on my last block over there."

He pointed to the east side of the rising walls, which already had the first row of Earth stones in place, plus a long horizontal line of stone jutting out at an angle above it, right over the window holes. At a distance it looked right pretty, and then when you walked up close, you realized that the long line was well above your head, maybe ten or twelve feet high. Phillip could barely touch it if he reached up with his arm outstretched. He almost had to jump to touch it. Ben had called the line something odd—a water table, Phillip thought it was—because it helped shed water from the sides of the building, even though this one was primarily decorative. Other sides of the walls weren't nearly so tall yet, some barely above ground level. Looking across the walls, one could already tell that the water table would circle the entire building, including the corner towers.

"I think Ben is assigned to another Earth stone on the west end now," the man continued. "And will be for a while. Those things might just take until the Second Coming to shape."

Turning west, Phillip strained to see Ben, but was pretty sure he wasn't over there, since he'd already searched the area thoroughly. That side of the temple was one of the two shorter ends of the building, and it wasn't as high as the east side yet.

The stonecutter went back to work, striking his chisel with a heavy blow from the hammer and getting only a small bit of rock off for his effort. "But you might look for him at home," he said, still chipping away at the block. "I think he only worked until about noon today."

That didn't sound like Ben. Curious, Phillip thanked the man and wandered off, wondering if he should find Ben but not wanting to go home. No one expected him there yet. Instead, he decided to head for his much-neglected studio. He needed to get some work done anyway. Besides, he wanted to be alone for a bit before facing the rigors of earning his daily bread and watching Claude make eyes at Hannah. It would also give him some quiet time to reflect and find answers. There was a set of scriptures on one of the shelves. Reading the hopeful words in solitude would be nice.

As Phillip went in, Mrs. Brecken looked up from her ledger book with surprise. She glanced quickly toward the stairs. "Back already? Your brothers said not to expect you for almost a week yet."

"I didn't think I'd be back so soon, but plans changed." Phillip wasn't in the mood for small talk, so he didn't say anything else as he crossed the floor.

Mrs. Brecken pumped her arms as she scurried in front of Phillip, stopping him at the base of the staircase. "I was going to clean it up," she said, putting her hand out. "But I haven't had the time since it happened Tuesday, and I didn't think you were coming home yet."

Phillip's stomach sank. "What happened on Tuesday?" He looked up the stairs. If his studio was damaged in any way . . .

He pushed past Mrs. Brecken and climbed the steps two at a time. At the top, his mouth fell open. All but one set of shelves lay on the floor, their contents splattered everywhere. Two canisters were shattered, their fluid spilled and nearly dry in a great puddle. In the middle of it all lay his photographs, now warped from bathing in chemicals. A box of glass plates had fallen to the ground. Shards were spread across the room. His tripod lay awkwardly with a broken leg, like a wounded animal. The sight nearly choked him, and Phillip had to grip the banister so he wouldn't drop to his knees.

"What happened?"

Mrs. Brecken still stood at the bottom of the stairs. "It was your older brother," she called. "Claude, I believe? He saw that picture of Miss Hansen with a strange man and pitched a fit."

For a second Phillip just furrowed his brow. *What does she mean?* Then the reality dawned on him. Phillip pressed his fists into his eyes and sat on the top step. "No. Oh, *no.* Claude *cannot* be that moronic."

"I don't understand," Mrs. Brecken said.

"It wasn't Miss Hansen in the picture," Phillip said more to the ceiling than to his landlady, who looked strangely peaked at the base of the stairs. "That was Hannah's *cousin* kissing the man she's engaged to. And Claude destroyed my studio over it!"

Mrs. Brecken put a hand to her mouth and said, "So she was telling the truth all along. Poor girl." She shifted her feet uneasily and avoided his face. "She was here when it happened."

*Hannah was here? Did she see Claude destroy the studio? Did she see the photo? Had Marie told her about it?* The questions swirled in his mind. He hurried down the stairs back toward her. "Please, tell me everything."

She gave only the bare details about how Claude had destroyed the studio and had accused Hannah of being unfaithful—and more—in front of all the customers. How Hannah had run off after insisting on her innocence. How the town had begun talking about it since.

Phillip could hardly believe any of it. Why would Claude get so angry and suspicious over something so silly? It wasn't rational. *But then again, when has Claude ever been rational when it comes to his feelings?* Phillip put his hands to his head and groaned. As badly as he wanted to stay and salvage what he could of his studio, he felt a greater urgency to race home and clobber his brother for being such a numskull.

Why wouldn't Claude believe Hannah if he loved her? Phillip couldn't imagine assuming the worst of the woman you supposedly loved. Then again, Phillip couldn't imagine having such a suspicious, paranoid nature, either. Poor Hannah.

"I've got to see Claude," Phillip said, moving toward the door.

"Wait," Mrs. Brecken called.

"What?" Phillip asked, his hand on the knob.

"There's one other thing." She stared at the floor as if reluctant to say it.

"What is it?" Phillip demanded. By Mrs. Brecken's account, people in town already thought Hannah was carrying another man's child. What more *could* there be?

Mrs. Brecken fiddled with the edge of her apron and avoided looking at Phillip. "Miss Hansen left quite upset."

Phillip gripped the handle with impatience. He needed to leave. "I'm sure she did."

Mrs. Brecken rushed on, spitting out the rest as if to get it over with. "Word has it that she ran home blindly and stumbled into the family well."

Phillip froze. "She what?" He turned back, stomach dropping. With swift strides, he crossed to Mrs. Brecken and grabbed her by the shoulders. "Is she all right? Tell me she's all right." His mouth went dry as he waited for her answer.

Mrs. Brecken tried to pull back. "I—I don't know. Last I heard, people were saying they didn't know yet if she'd make it."

All thoughts of Claude and the studio vanished in the wake of his concern for Hannah. Phillip raced out of the store and didn't stop running. He sprinted through city streets, past shops and staring pedestrians until, breathless, he came to the Hansen place. He ran even faster down the lane and pounded on the side door, wishing he had the nerve to just barge in and find Hannah. He imagined walking inside and finding her working in the kitchen.

If only.

When no one answered his knock, he abandoned all pretense of good manners and blatantly pounded with his fist. "Bishop! Bethany! Are you in there?"

Eventually, he heard footsteps. "Ben, did you forget something?" Bethany asked as the door opened. "Oh. Hello, Phillip. I thought you were your brother. He just left." She had circles under her eyes, and her hair was disheveled in a loose bun. Her eyes were puffy with sleep—or lack of it. She looked ready to fall over at any moment.

"Ben?" Phillip asked. "Has he been here bothering you?"

Bethany looked confused. "Bothering me? Oh, no—no." She blinked wearily. "He's been helping out."

*Helping out?* Phillip's mind raced . . . *Oh* . . . He'd forgotten about the Cupid experiment. "How is Hannah? May I see her?"

Bethany rubbed her eyes and nodded. "Come in."

Phillip followed Bethany inside and closed the door behind him. She walked slowly through the hall and up the stairs. "She's awake now. Finally," she said over her shoulder. "But she had us worried when we couldn't wake her up." She paused outside the bedroom. "She's not quite herself yet. I thought I'd better prepare you before you go in."

"Will she—mind me seeing her in bed?" Phillip asked, suddenly feeling bashful at going into Hannah's room.

"I don't think so," Bethany said, moving like a specter in a dream. "Not at this point." She hesitated as if she were about to explain more, but instead opened the door.

Inside, Hannah lay in bed. Her eyes were open, but they seemed empty as she stared at the floral wallpaper on the far wall. Her left arm was in a sling, and a nasty bruise surrounded her left eye. Her left leg was elevated, the foot in a plaster cast.

Bethany crossed to the bed and sat at the edge. She reached over and gently brushed some hair from her sister's face. "It's me—Bethany. Can you hear me?" Hannah turned her head and stared with a vacant expression. She didn't speak at first. Bethany glanced over her shoulder at Phillip. "This morning the doctor told us to ask her some basic questions every few hours to see how she's doing." She sighed, betraying the fact that the results hadn't been encouraging.

Phillip pulled up a chair as Bethany began quizzing Hannah. "Do you remember your name?"

Hannah's brow furrowed as if she'd just been asked to solve a difficult sum. Finally she murmured, "Hannah?"

Bethany smiled and nodded. "That's right. Hannah." Phillip detected tears in the corners of Bethany's eyes as she held her sister's hands. "And where are you?"

Again her eyebrows knitted together. She stared past Bethany at a needlepoint on the wall, one hand picking at her sling. "Home?" she asked, her voice unsure.

"Yes," Bethany said. "We're home. In your bedroom. Do remember what happened?"

This time Hannah bit her lips together and gazed at the ceiling. She finally shook her head. "No." She winced. "I'm dizzy. It hurts."

Watching the exchange, Phillip sat horrified. The fact that Hannah struggled to answer such elementary questions was downright shocking. What *did* she still remember? What had she forgotten? Would her full memory ever return?

Bethany turned to Phillip and sighed. "She's talking now and knows her name. That's the kind of improvement the doctor said to look for."

"She didn't even know her name?" Phillip felt as if someone had knocked the floor out from under him. If only he could do something for her. But assuming there was something—anything—he could do, would she even recognize him? "What else did the doctor say? Will she get better?"

Bethany looked warily at Hannah, who had closed her eyes as if asleep. Bethany shrugged in answer to his question. She looked so haggard that Phillip almost felt guilty dredging up information that she had likely been grieving over. She stood and motioned to him to follow her onto the landing by the stairs. After closing the bedroom door, she whispered, "Dr. Wood says there could be any number of injuries, with ranging degrees of seriousness. If only there were a way to look inside her head for a moment, we'd know what's wrong. For now there's no way of knowing what her injuries are or what will happen."

*What will happen.* The phrase sent chills through Phillip. Could she end up as an invalid for the rest of her life? Would she be practically an infant? Was the old Hannah gone forever?

# CHAPTER 16

Bethany led Phillip back in to visit Hannah, but he felt utterly helpless. He wished he had an excuse to stay longer. No one had told him to go, but after less than an hour he felt uncomfortable, as if he were intruding on the family's privacy. He stepped away from the bed and made his way to the door, where Bishop Hansen suddenly stopped him, holding out a small bottle of oil.

"Brother Adams, would you assist in blessing my daughter?"

"Of course," Phillip said, turning around and going back inside. Finally—something he could do instead of standing by powerless.

The bishop paused by Hannah's bedside, his brow deeply lined. "I came home this morning to find my daughter hurt. I wish I could have been here earlier." He put one arm around Bethany, and she seemed to melt into her father's embrace, fatigue showing in every line of her face.

He looked at Phillip. "Would you anoint?"

"I'd be honored," Phillip said, taking the bottle. He hung his hat on the bedpost, then uncorked the bottle, his hand shaking slightly as he tipped it just enough for a drop of oil to fall onto Hannah's bandaged crown. He replaced the cork, put the bottle aside, and placed his palms on her head. He could feel his fingers trembling; he had never touched Hannah so intimately before. After swallowing hard, he pronounced the anointing, his hands lingering on her head for just a moment after he whispered "amen." He helped her father seal the anointing, and as he listened to the blessing, he wished it had been more specific, that it had promised her a full recovery. Instead her father had spoken in generalities about comfort and strength and growth through the experience.

"Thank you," Bishop Hansen said.

"You're welcome. Please let me know if there's anything else I can do." Phillip took his hat. "I can see myself out."

He walked home, hands clenching and unclenching, wishing he could do something about Claude's ludicrous—and tragic—reaction to the photograph. Phillip couldn't very well go home, set Claude straight, and expect him to crawl back to the Hansens with sorrow and sincere repentance.

Something wasn't right. Claude's behavior simply didn't make sense. Nothing about his brother did. Phillip looked up some clouds and sighed. Is there anything about Claude I can trust at face value? He thought back over their childhood, their mission, to his courtship with Hannah. Even back to Cybil. His confession. Somehow it all rang false.

Phillip shook his head and continued down the street, unsure of much except for one thing—if anyone could knock some sense into Claude's head, it was Ben, whom Claude at least respected and looked up to. It wouldn't be Phillip, the brother Claude had always seen as less than himself.

The powerless feeling returned, giving everything a dreamlike, unreal quality, as colorless as his photographs. He passed a cluster of young women talking with their heads close together. Thinking nothing of it, he kept going, but a single word from the trio stopped him.

"Hannah?" one girl said. Phillip's step came up short. "Are you sure?" She spoke again.

He braced himself against a brick-sided building and hesitated, hoping his listening wasn't obvious.

"Surely you don't mean Hannah *Hansen?*" another girl asked.

"Of course I do. Everybody's talking about her."

Phillip closed his eyes and gritted his teeth, wanting to confront the girls but wanting even more to know what people were saying. How big was the problem that had been created—that Claude needed to fix?

"I don't know," the first girl said with a shake of her head. She had dark hair like Hannah and looked familiar. Phillip tried to place her. Returning after years away made it hard to recognize young girls who had gone from sporting braids and bonnets to pulling their hair up and wearing full-length dresses and fancy hats.

"Rose, why is that so hard to believe?" The speaker was a girl with fair hair pulled back into a chignon. *Rose.* That was the brunette's name. Now he remembered. Of course—Rose Donaldson—one of Hannah's childhood friends.

Rose reached up and adjusted the flowers on her hat. "It just doesn't sound like something Hannah would do, Marilyn."

The blonde rolled her eyes. "Things aren't always what you expect. My mother was in the general store when Claude Adams found out about it. Ma says Hannah was obviously lying—you could tell by the look on her face, all red and puffy. And there was a photograph as proof, after all. How can you deny *that?*"

Phillip's fists clenched. He'd need to find the photo and post it on the window so everyone in town could see it for themselves.

"I don't know . . ." Rose shook her head back and forth. "It just doesn't make sense. Some people say she's actually in the family way. You can't tell *that* much from a photograph unless she's far enough along. What do you think, Bertha?"

The last girl—quiet and mousy-haired—hadn't spoken yet. She shrugged and quietly said, "I don't know what to think."

Marilyn shook her head, making her ringlets bounce. "Well, I think it's just shameful. Poor Claude. I'd give a great deal to be able to cheer him up. He deserves a real woman." She gave a light, pointed laugh.

Phillip had had enough. He walked right up to the girls and said, "You don't know what you're talking about. Hannah has done nothing wrong, and my brother is the one who should be hiding his head in shame. The girl in the picture was Hannah's cousin. I took the photo."

"Then you know better than anyone what is in the photo," Marilyn said.

"Exactly," Phillip said, smiling. Finally, someone with sense. "So you see, it's all a great misunderstanding. As soon as I can find the picture, it'll all be cleared up."

"You mean it's missing?" Marilyn laughed. "How convenient. You've 'lost' the picture so no one else can see what's in it. Oh, that's rich."

"You'll see," Phillip said, seething. "I'll prove her innocence."

"You do that," Marilyn said, tossing her head. "I'll believe it when I see it."

Without waiting for a response, Phillip strode away, not looking back. He now knew that the story about Hannah's supposed disloyalty and immorality had spread—and was being snatched up by a lot of people, by the sounds of it.

He went straight to the studio and searched for the one print he had made of the photo, looking under every scrap, every piece of glass, but it was nowhere to be found. Most of his pictures were stuck together, destroyed by chemicals. Only a handful of glass negatives remained, and none of them were of Marie with Ted. Maybe Marie herself could clear her cousin's name. He'd send her a letter asking for a statement. That might do it.

Resigned, Phillip returned home and found Ben sitting alone in the kitchen.

"You're home early," Ben said.

"They closed the quarry," Phillip answered. "So you're home early too. Sorry about that."

Ben offered a grim smile. "Oh, don't worry about me. I'll find more work somewhere. If nothing else, I can probably get enough work carving headstones when we're done with the stone that's left."

Phillip pulled out a chair and sat down heavily. "I heard about what happened to Hannah. I'd like to kill Claude myself and give you a headstone to carve." They laughed ruefully, painfully aware of how their lives all might change. "So where is he?"

"See for yourself," Ben said, sliding a piece of paper over the table. "He's gone. For now."

Curious, Phillip scanned the sharply slanting lines of his brother's penmanship. His head came up. "He's living at a hotel? Why?" The news sent a strange sense of loss through him; he and his brothers had always been together. Claude had never been the model brother, but the three of them were each other's only family, and they had stuck by one another no matter what came their way.

Suddenly looking a bit uncomfortable, Ben rubbed his stubble. "It's probably my fault. While you were gone, I told him my mind and—and hit him. A few times." His sheepish look turned defensive.

"But the blithering idiot was drunk and speaking crude things about women and blaming everything on everyone else and—"

"I get the idea," Phillip said, handing the note back. "But he can't stay at a hotel forever. He has no job."

"I thought the same thing," Ben said. "But to be honest, I'm glad he's not here right now. After the other night, I wouldn't know how to look him in the eye without spitting."

Phillip nodded, wondering what he'd do or say next time he saw Claude. Maybe he should write that letter to Marie now. "I think I'll go upstairs," he said with a sigh. Ben hardly glanced his way as Phillip scooted his chair back and left the room.

He went upstairs and wrote a quick note to Marie, explaining the situation—trying not to alarm her unduly but at the same time trying to make the urgency clear. He continued,

> *I hope your engagement has been announced by now so that there is no impediment to making an open statement about your identity in the photograph. I apologize for not mailing it to you immediately. Had I done so, none of this would have happened. In the meantime, Hannah desperately needs to have her good name restored. Only a handful of people know the truth of the picture—that it captures nothing but an innocent moment and that Hannah is not portrayed in it. You, Ted, and I are the only ones who were present. Claude of course has also seen the photograph. No one else knows the truth firsthand.*
>
> *I was surprised recently when my word as the photographer was not enough to convince a small group of busybodies of her innocence. I will continue to do what I can to clear her name, but I'm becoming doubtful that I will succeed without evidence. The photograph cannot be used, since I no longer have it or the negative in my possession. I've searched for the photograph in hopes of posting it in the shop window or publishing it in the paper, but it is*

*gone. Whether it's destroyed or simply missing, I do not know, but it can no longer serve our purpose. Claude hasn't been honest and has, in fact, perpetuated the falsehoods. I pray your word will help bring forth the truth.*

*Your response requires the utmost urgency.*

*Respectfully yours,*
*Phillip Adams*

He blew the ink dry, then folded and sealed the letter. Grateful he still had her address, he hurriedly scrawled it across the front, then hurried to the post office. After handing the letter over, he put his hands on his hips and watched the worker tuck it into a sack.

*Please hurry, Marie.*

* * *

For two days, Claude hardly slept. He hardly ate. He wandered the streets of the city, more than once ending up at the fence that bordered Hannah's home. He wanted to race to the door, pound his way up the stairs, and demand answers. The next moment, he had an urge to gently take Hannah into his arms and hold her tight. His feelings ebbed and flowed in a confusing rush of jealousy, rage, and sadness. A lump came to his throat, and he tried to think clearly, but for the thousandth time, he couldn't make sense of anything.

There, standing next to him, was the tree where the offending picture had been taken. It stood there, mocking him. A breeze picked up its branches, making the tips brush his arm. He pulled back as if they were sharp and let out a cry of frustration.

Who *was* in that picture that now lay crumpled under the mattress of his hotel bed? Was it Marie, or whatever her name was? It looked so much like Hannah—and it was *his* comb in her hair . . .

The pain that hit his gut when he first saw the picture returned, and he nearly doubled over. He pounded his fist on a fence post, wishing it were the face of the man in the picture. For the slightest moment he wished he could strike out at Hannah as well—let *her* feel the pain of betrayal—then was horrified at himself for letting such a thought even flit across his mind.

His gaze lowered to the well, now covered; the family would be sure to keep it that way from now on. *As they should have done before,* Claude thought. It was their own fault that Hannah had fallen down it; he'd had nothing to do with that.

He remembered the things he'd heard people whisper as he walked past: "Poor Claude. He looks terrible. And no wonder, after what Hannah's done. Carrying another man's child." Then he remembered what he'd done after hearing those things.

He had kept walking.

Claude turned back to the house, again wanting to race inside to see Hannah. But even if he trusted himself, he didn't dare face Bishop Hansen's wrath. Then again, he almost feared Bethany's ire even more. He rubbed a fist against one eye, then headed down the road toward the hotel. He felt faint. He needed to get some water and lie down.

* * *

Phillip didn't sleep well his first night home. He couldn't, not with his mind full of the images of Hannah lying helpless. It was strange to wake up and remember that Claude wasn't home. He and Ben went to the Hansens' and helped out a bit around the farm, doing odds and ends but feeling a bit useless. The next day, Ben had to work at the temple block, and Phillip knew he needed to get back to his studio.

Late Saturday morning he headed toward the store, deciding to clean things up and see if anything could be salvaged from the wreckage, but when he reached it, the door was locked and a sign was posted on the window.

*Closed for vacation. Will reopen Monday.*

Phillip had a suspicion that Mrs. Brecken wanted to hide out until the hubbub surrounding her store died down and people stopped going inside just to point to where Claude and Hannah stood when they fought. He hoped no one had managed to sneak upstairs out of morbid curiosity to look where the photo had been found. Somehow that would feel like an invasion of privacy, even though he had nothing to hide.

He walked away from the store, hands in his pockets, figuring that perhaps it was just as well that he couldn't go inside for a few days and dwell on the facts. His equipment was completely destroyed—all the money he'd invested was gone. Instead of being a place of refuge, his studio would probably just have mocked his dreams.

Might as well go to the Hansens' again and see if he could chop firewood or something. As he walked north, head down and thinking hard, he ran right into someone.

"Excuse me," the other man said. Both stopped short and stared at the other. It was Claude. "What—what are you doing here?" Claude backed away as if protecting himself. He held a hand to his face, not quite blocking a cut on his eyebrow and a swollen, discolored eye.

"Nice to see you, too," Phillip said dryly, eyeing what must have been Ben's handiwork. A knot formed in Phillip's middle as he thought of what people were saying about Hannah. "I hear you've been busy causing trouble."

"You don't know what you're talking about," Claude said, trying to push past him.

But Phillip blocked his way. "I could say the same of you."

"Oh really?" Claude snapped, obviously irritated. He tried stepping to the side, but Phillip moved into his path. "I'm going home, if you don't mind."

"You mean the hotel? Since when is that your home?"

"Since when is my business any of yours?"

"Since you destroyed my livelihood."

Claude's eyes widened. He took a step back and bit his lips together. "I—" He stared at the ground as if trying to find something to say, an apology, perhaps.

Phillip knew his brother had no words to explain what had happened or to compensate for it. "I know about the photograph. And I know what happened to Hannah."

Claude turned red and looked as if someone had physically struck him. He swallowed hard, his Adam's apple bobbing. "You know about that, too?" he asked, trying a bit too hard to sound casual. He ran a hand across his face—emphasizing a puffy, red nose, plus more discoloration circling his left eye. "Look, I didn't do anything. Everyone's blaming me for an accident. It's not like I pushed her into the well."

He took a step forward, but Phillip drew himself up taller, making his brother hesitate, and looked at him eye-to-eye.

"Word has it that you called her a bunch of horrid names and that now everyone believes she did a heap more than just kiss a man—which she didn't even do." Phillip made a move forward.

Claude backed up, glancing behind him as if trying to find an escape route. "You know as well as I do what happened, because you took the picture. You of all people can't blame me."

Phillip grabbed his brother by both lapels. "The girl in the picture was her cousin Marie, you dolt." He shoved Claude into a tree.

Stumbling against the trunk, Claude had to shake himself to gather his wits. His forehead crinkled with confusion as Phillip's words registered. "It—it *was* her cousin?" He walked in a circle, confused. "I don't understand."

"You met Marie. Didn't you recognize her? She and Hannah could practically be twins."

"I met her once, for about thirty seconds," he snapped. "It was the first time I saw Hannah after she got my letter. I was a bit preoccupied. So, no, I didn't recognize a different woman who happened to be in Hannah's dress, wearing the hair comb I gave her, standing in the Hansen yard, and *kissing* a strange man." He raked through his hair with both hands and then covered his mouth with his fist. "It *wasn't* Hannah." The words came out in a tone of shock.

"But you wouldn't believe her when she told you who it really was." Phillip's eyebrows drew tightly together, and he shook his head. *"Why?"*

"I thought—"

"You never really knew her or loved her," Phillip interrupted. It was only too true; how could Claude have deep feelings for Hannah when he hadn't so much as noticed her until the day they'd returned from back East?

Claude balled his fists and took a bold step forward. "How dare you say that? I love Hannah more than you'll ever know. That's the only reason I got so jealous. If I didn't care so much, I wouldn't have gotten so upset."

"There's more to this mess than that, isn't there?" Phillip said, stepping forward.

"Such as?" Claude said, challenging.

"Such as what really happened with Cybil," Phillip said, in a voice so calm it surprised even him. He didn't have to ask for Claude to admit it, because in his heart, he just knew. Claude's face fell.

A pained, long silence stretched out between them until Claude finally spoke.

"How—how did you know?"

Phillip's eyes smarted at the admission. "Listen, Claude. You don't really love Hannah. You just want her to yourself. Same thing with Cybil, I'm guessing. If you really loved Hannah, you'd rather see her happy without you than miserable at your side." Phillip knew that firsthand. It was why he had survived watching Hannah be with Claude as long as he had. "But you do need to make this right with both Hannah and her father. We're going to the Hansens' so you can apologize to the bishop."

Claude seemed ready to bolt, no longer quite so willing to race to the Hansen farm if it meant admitting guilt. Phillip took his arm and pulled him forward. "You're going to fix this. I'm not going to make you confess anything before you're ready, but you need to apologize for what you did to Hannah. First with the bishop, and then with the rest of the community. She deserves to have her reputation back, something you destroyed in a matter of hours. Everyone's talking about it, and you are the only person who can make it fully right."

Looking terrified, Claude nevertheless allowed Phillip to lead him toward the Hansen place. But as they walked he grew more tense, and Phillip had to push harder to keep him moving. As they reached the front porch, the door opened, and Bishop Hansen came out. He looked older somehow—his shoulders more stooped, his wrinkles more pronounced. He seemed to lean harder on his cane than he had before. Claude flinched when the bishop's gaze landed on him.

They stood staring at one another in silence for several moments. Phillip wanted to speak, but felt it wasn't his place. He wondered if Bishop Hansen would yell at Claude, but instead the man spoke with a voice full of pain. "My daughter may never be the same again, you know."

Claude began shaking his head. He stepped forward and pled, "Bishop, sir, I am so sorry. You have to believe that I would never intentionally harm your daughter—"

Bishop Hansen raised a trembling hand. "I know what you did. I've heard all about what you accused her of. The entire town is talking about her as if she's a soiled woman. If rumors are to be believed, she's not unlike the harlot Isabel." As soon as the words left his mouth, he grimaced as if the very idea were physically torturous. "You know my daughter would never do such things. Don't set foot on our property again." He closed his eyes, lips pursed tightly together. When he opened his eyes again, he took a deep breath and said, "Mr. Adams, if I were a different kind of man, I would seek vengeance, but I am trying to remember my office. Just go."

Behind them at the door, Bethany appeared, her eyes weepy. She pushed open the screen and wearily said, "Father?"

"What is it?" Bishop Hansen turned, increased concern on his face. "Is Hannah all right?"

"She's fine," Bethany began, her eyes darting to Claude. Her face flamed. "She—she heard Claude's voice through the window and is asking to see him."

Phillip's stomach clenched, and the bishop's face twisted in resigned disgust. But a smile slowly spread across Claude's face. "See? She's forgiven me. She knows it was all a misunderstanding. She knows that I love her."

The bishop lifted his cane and blocked the way. Claude's smile faded as the bishop said, "I'll ask you again. Leave my property."

But Bethany came to them, rubbing her forehead. "Father, remember that Dr. Wood insisted that we honor *all* her wishes. We can still spread word about what kind of man Claude really is."

Her father shook his head. "We'll do no such thing." The bishop eyed Claude sharply. "I trust he'll take it upon himself as an honorable gentleman to clear her name, because as bishop I cannot be seen taking sides in disputes, even with my own daughter—and it certainly wouldn't do for me to disparage a young man's name as I explained the situation. I trust *you* will do the right thing, Claude."

"I . . ." His knees seemed to go weak under the bishop's gaze. He shoved his hands into his pockets, and he looked like a scared squirrel, clearly terrified of answering. "May I see her now?"

"Her room is this way," Bethany said, sounding disgusted.

The bishop lowered his head sadly and blocked the doorway with his cane. "You may see her because of the doctor's orders. But I will expect more from you."

"I know, sir." Claude's voice was quiet.

Bethany grunted. It was clear what she thought of the doctor's orders and what she would do to Claude if she could avoid carrying them out. Phillip wondered suddenly if Bethany had ever skinned a squirrel.

A timid smile returned to Claude's face, this time with a touch of smug triumph. Phillip wanted to make Claude's right eye match his left. Reluctantly, the bishop lowered his cane, letting Claude pass. Bethany led the way upstairs. Phillip took up the rear with the bishop—there was no way he could leave Hannah now. The door had barely opened when Hannah's voice rang out clearly. Maybe the blessing had helped.

"Claude!" Hannah cried.

He rushed inside and knelt by the bed, then took her hand and held it to his lips. "Oh, Hannah darling, how are you feeling?"

She managed a nod. "My mind is fuzzy, and I'm still hurting quite a bit. I'm all right, but it's been horrible." She clung to his hand and smiled. "I feel better already with you beside me, but—"

"But what?" Claude prompted.

She shook her head slowly. "It's a bit frightening to not even remember what happened."

With a start, Claude turned to her family. "She doesn't remember?"

Phillip felt a sense of victory in that she hadn't simply forgiven him.

"She doesn't remember—*yet,*" Bethany said significantly. "The doctor said we should let her memory come back on its own."

*If it comes back,* Phillip added to himself. He had heard enough from Bethany and the doctor to know that it might not.

Claude nodded, obviously deep in thought. "Hannah, is there anything I can do for you? Anything at all? I'd do anything for you. You know that, don't you?"

"I know," she said, smiling and leaning her cheek against his hand. "And all I need to get well right now is to have you near me." She blinked sleepily, then focused her eyes on Phillip. "Oh, hello, Phillip. It's so nice to see you back from the quarry."

Phillip cleared his throat to keep it from going scratchy, but nothing came out. She didn't remember his visit from that morning. And as far as she recalled, Claude was still her hero. Where was justice when you needed it?

*I've never had justice in my entire life,* Phillip reminded himself. *Why should now be any different?*

*Because Hannah's future and happiness are on the line, that's why.*

Claude smoothed a piece of hair from her face. "I'll be with you as much as you need me."

"Thank you."

And there was the lovesick gaze into each other's eyes. Phillip turned away, unable to stomach it. If only he were still headed to the quarry. If only Claude hadn't been such an oaf. If only Hannah remembered what had happened, especially Claude's part in the mess.

Bethany approached Phillip. She too bristled at the moment between the two. "I'm sorry," she whispered so no one else could hear. "If it hadn't been for the doctor's orders . . ."

"I know," Phillip said. "And thanks." He let out a deep breath, threw one last look at his brother, and walked out the door.

He made his way home, wishing more than anything that Hannah would remember—and dreaming that someday she'd ask to see *him.*

# CHAPTER 17

A few days later, Ben headed again to the Hansens' to help out. Hannah seemed more coherent, but her memory hadn't returned. The bumps were going down, and the scrapes had scabs, but the bruises had turned nasty colors as they healed, so they actually looked worse. In spite of everyone's efforts to give Hannah whatever she asked for—just as Dr. Wood had said they should—her spirits were low and her energy weak.

So was Ben's. He had spent days now trying to find a chance to speak with Bethany alone. Plenty of times they had almost come to verbal blows as they had in the past, but somehow he had managed to end it. Or maybe she had—it was hard to tell. And there were moments when he caught her looking at him in ways that perhaps—maybe he hoped, confirmed—what he had overheard his brothers saying about her heart.

He turned onto the Hansen lane and found Bethany drawing well water. One basin was filled, and she was pouring water from the well bucket into a pail as he approached. When he stopped, she looked up. A lock of hair fell into her eye, and he had a mad desire to push it behind her ear. She blew it out of the way and smiled at him.

"Good afternoon."

"May I?" he asked, leaning down for the basin.

"Thank you." She picked up the pail, and together they went inside. He set the basin on the kitchen counter, and she did the same with the pail.

"Is there anything else I can help you with, anything at all?" Ben prayed she would look into his eyes and know what he really meant—that he wanted to do more than haul water and chop wood. That he would do anything, even if it meant climbing a mountain for a flower if it meant winning her over. They had spent days next to each other, virtually silent. At least when they fought they spoke. While he didn't want to hurt her anymore, the silence was driving him crazy.

"I'm sure there's plenty Father could find for you to do," Bethany said as she dampened a dishcloth and headed for the kitchen table.

Before she reached it, Ben took her by the arm. "Bethany, I—"

"Yes?" Her eyebrows went up, a question on her face, and as he looked into her eyes, he saw nothing in them but friendship and suddenly felt unsure about saying anything more. She lowered her head slightly and looked up at him. "Ben, are you all right?"

"I'm—I'm fine. But, Bethany . . . this has been a hard week for you."

She nodded and answered with a shrug. "It has, but—"

Ben interrupted. "I don't *ever* want to see you suffer again."

She looked at him in awe and shook her head. "You've been so wonderful this week. It's like you're a different person suddenly." Bethany lowered her head and began picking at the dishcloth. "I don't know what to make of it."

He smiled. "In a way, I guess I am a different person." He shook his head and took a deep breath, then pointed upward toward Hannah's bedroom. "This is crazy. Here we are in the middle of your family's crisis, and the one thought I have is that I . . ." He closed his mouth, unable to quite say the words. After all this time, could he really just *say* it?

Bethany looked up. Their eyes held. This time there was definitely something more in her gaze than friendship. "The one thought you have is . . . what?"

He felt sure she could see into his soul. He swallowed hard. "After all of these years, I suddenly can't stop thinking about you. Isn't that strange?"

Bethany dropped the dishcloth. She put a hand to her middle and turned away. Ben's stomach fell to his toes. She hated him, after all.

He shouldn't have said that. At least he hadn't said that he *loved* her, which had almost slipped out.

The silence in the room seemed to stretch into eternity. All Ben could hear was his own breathing, but he couldn't speak, just stare at the back of Bethany's head, where her red-gold locks fell down her back.

She finally spoke, but in a voice so quiet he had to strain to hear them. "I've imagined you saying those words for so long." Her head turned ever so slightly over her shoulder.

*What does that mean? Is that good or bad?* Ben screwed up his courage and took a step forward. He reached out and rested his hand on her shoulder. Her head tilted toward his fingers. "Bethany, if I'm being perfectly honest, I still care for you as much as I ever did. In fact, I—I—" He strengthened his resolve before saying the word. "I love you. Isn't that strange?"

*There. I said it.*

She didn't turn around, but he could tell she breathed in suddenly as she stared out the kitchen window. Her hand came up and touched his. "It's almost as strange as the fact that . . . that I could *almost* admit to feeling the same way." She ventured a quick glance at Ben, but then she quickly looked away and closed her eyes tightly.

He grinned as he watched her cheeks turn bright red. She had come close to saying it. He knew that they both had the same icy finger of fear keeping them from abandoning caution and embracing what could be—what *should* have been.

Ben gently took her by the shoulders and turned her to face him. He looked her squarely in the eyes. "Bethany, are you admitting that you love me?"

Flustered, she stumbled over her words and avoided his gaze. "Well, no, not exactly." She grimaced. "I'm not denying it, but . . . What I mean is . . . I'm going to fetch a glass of water for Hannah." She reached for a glass on the counter.

He snatched it first. "You *do* love me," he cried, celebration in his voice.

"*Don't* say that," Bethany said, her voice wavering.

He could hear fear in her voice, so he stepped closer. Facing her now, he put his arms around her. She didn't pull away. He was so near he could smell her hair—the same sweet scent of lavender he remembered from behind the barn all those years ago. "I *will* say it, Bethany, a thousand times, and I'll tromp on anyone who suggests you don't love me."

"Even if I'm the one suggesting it?" Bethany's voice was scarcely more than a whisper.

Ben reached down and lifted her chin to look into her eyes. Everything in his gaze said he cared for her, that he'd die for her. Live for her, too.

When he spoke, his voice was tender. "Never you, Bethany." He leaned in. She tilted her head and raised her heels just enough to let him kiss her. It was a short kiss, but enough to ignite a fire inside Ben and send his heart racing. A moment later he pulled back, wishing it had lasted longer, but not daring to make it so. He looked into her eyes, waiting for her reaction.

Her face was flushed as she took his hands in hers. "I—I *do* love you, Ben."

There. She had said it. He wanted to soar. Instead he looked into her eyes, grinning. "You can't take it back now."

Bethany leaned a few inches closer and whispered, "Why would I want to?"

* * *

"You're looking well, Sister Hansen," Dr. Wood said after listening to her heartbeat. He put his stethoscope around his neck and made a note on a piece of paper. "Can you believe it's already been two weeks since your accident? Just over two weeks, actually. I think you're well enough now that I can visit less often than daily."

Hannah leaned against her pillow and stared at the ceiling. Two weeks—was that all? It felt like two months or more. It was maddening to lie in bed day after day without knowing when she'd be able to get up and resume her life. Taking laudanum helped the pain, but it also made her mind so fuzzy that she didn't even remember the doctor coming every day. Some days melted into a blur, while others extended into vast stretches that felt endless.

"Can I get up soon?" she managed to ask, blinking slowly because her eyelids seemed to have a will of their own, wanting to close all the time.

"Not yet," Dr. Wood said with a light chuckle.

"That's what I keep telling her," Bethany said, drawing open the curtains so the sun could come in. "But she won't listen to me."

"Your sister is right," the doctor continued. "Bones mend slowly. And besides, you're too weak to stand right now. If you tried, you'd fall right over."

*The same with my mind,* Hannah figured. *It must mend slowly, too.* But Dr. Wood avoided discussing that part. *What I wouldn't give to be able to think clearly and remember.* Until Dr. Wood had confirmed that it had been two weeks since the accident, she hadn't had any idea how long she'd been in bed. She had looked out the window often and figured it couldn't have been too long, since the seasons hadn't changed, but to finally know was disconcerting.

She felt the doctor's touch on her wrist and pushed her eyelids open again, straining to see through the shifting, cloudy world around her. She had to stare at Dr. Wood's hands for a few seconds just to focus her eyes. Her mind always felt blurry, and as soon as she could wipe away the cobwebs from her thoughts, pain surfaced in her consciousness.

Pain from what? She had to keep reminding herself she had fallen down the well. That was as much as she could draw out of Bethany, her father, or even Dr. Wood. Father *had* warned them time and again that someone might fall in.

Dr. Wood nodded, jotted something on a notepad, and pulled up a chair. He lifted Hannah's left eyelid and peered into her eye and then did the same with her other eye.

"I would really like to get out of bed today. Please?"

"Heavens, no," Dr. Wood said, turning away to jot down another note. "I'm afraid your balance won't be what you're used to, and even if it were, that foot is a far cry from being able to bear weight." With his pencil, he indicated the big lump under the blanket which was her broken foot. "Be patient. These things take time. It's a miracle you've progressed this quickly."

Hannah nodded, knowing that she could have died in the fall and should be grateful that she had nothing more than a concussion and a few broken bones. Dr. Wood packed up his black bag and gave a satisfied nod. A knock sounded downstairs, and Bethany excused herself to answer it. A moment later, arguing voices were followed by the sound of a slamming door, and a few seconds after that, Bethany reappeared, pink cheeked and smoothing a displaced lock of hair behind her ear.

"Well, Sister Hansen," Dr. Wood was saying, "you stay in that bed and keep it up. I'll be back the day after next to check on your progress."

"Thank you, Doctor," Bethany said, seeing him out. She closed the door, then leaned against it with a troubled look in her eye.

"What's wrong?" Hannah's voice came out as little more than a whisper, although she felt more alert than she had a few moments ago.

Immediately Bethany shook off the look and replaced it with a smile. "Nothing's wrong, silly. A slight headache is all." She went to the side table and began cleaning up the breakfast tray.

Knowing better, Hannah leaned over her sling to touch her sister's arm. "What's wrong?" It was more a request than a question. "Tell me."

Bethany sighed and put the tray down. She sat on the chair Dr. Wood had abandoned, then took Hannah's hand in hers. "It's nothing you need to worry about. Your only job right now is to get yourself well."

"What happened downstairs? I heard angry voices and a door slamming."

Lowering her eyes, Bethany cleared her throat. "That? Oh, that was nothing."

"Just because I'm stuck in bed and unable to help around the house doesn't mean I can't lend a listening ear to my sister. Please tell me."

For a moment, Bethany's mouth opened, but then it closed again, and she shook her head. "I can't. I have orders from Dr. Wood not to discuss—well, let's just say I'll only be talking about happy things with you."

Now it was Hannah's turn to look disturbed. She lowered her eyes. "You've always been able to tell me anything." The moment the words left her mouth, she knew they weren't entirely true—one topic had always been off limits. *Ben.* Understanding dawned on Hannah.

"Is it about Ben?" she ventured.

Bethany's head came up quickly. "Ben? No. It's not about Ben." Her cheeks colored, and she cleared her throat awkwardly while trying to hide a smile. "I should bring your tray down."

Hannah smiled to herself. Bethany hadn't said so, but by the flush of her cheeks, Hannah hoped that their plan had worked. Perhaps Bethany and Ben were getting along. Thoughts of Ben and Bethany's possible romance made her think of Claude. Had she seen him when he first came back from the quarry—*before* her fall? He had visited a few times since she'd woken up—at least she *thought* she had seen him more than once. It was hard to remember, since everything in her mind blended together.

"Bethany?"

Her sister stopped at the doorway with the tray in her hands. She turned around. "Yes?"

"I miss Claude."

Bethany licked her lips, seeming reluctant to answer.

"Could you ask him to visit me?" Hannah pressed. "It would do so much for my spirits."

"I—" Bethany avoided Hannah's gaze. She adjusted the fork on the plate and stared out the door.

Worry twisted its way into Hannah's middle. "Is Claude all right? Has something happened to him?"

"No, no. Claude is—he's as he's always been." Bethany smiled flatly.

"Then will you send word for him to visit?"

Bethany raised her chin and looked at her sister. Their gaze held for a moment, and Hannah tried to read Bethany's face as she said, "I'll send word." She left, and Hannah lay back with a contented sigh.

Not half an hour later, someone rapped on the door. Since her father and sister generally knocked and came right in, Hannah knew this had to be a visitor. *Claude.* He must have come over the moment he'd heard she wanted him. She bit her lip at the thought. She drew her fingers through her hair and smoothed out the comforter, then called, "Come in."

The door squeaked open to reveal someone taller and darker than Claude. He had to step into the light of the room before Hannah recognized him. She knew him immediately, but her mind still worked slowly, and it took her a moment to form his name with her tongue.

"Phillip." She hoped he didn't detect her disappointment.

He stepped in awkwardly and held out a handful of flowers that were such a dark pink they were almost purple. "I brought these for you," he said with a crooked smile. "Figured you could use something pretty to look at while you're cooped up in here. I heard they're called 'shooting stars.'"

"Thank you," she said, taking the flowers with her good arm. She laid them on her lap and ran her thumb along their delicate petals and green stems, which were tied together with a length of twine. The uneven knot was obviously Phillip's own handiwork, as were the rough-cut ends of the flowers, but Hannah appreciated the effort.

They sat in awkward silence for a moment. Hannah tried to think of something to say, but her mind felt too cloudy.

"Nice weather for late summer, don't you think?" Phillip managed.

"It is," Hannah said, not mentioning that while being cooped up she really couldn't see more than a blue square of sky out of the window. "How was your trip to the quarry?"

"Good. Good," Phillip said, nodding. "They've closed it, though. Ben'll be out of a job soon."

"I'm sorry," Hannah said. "What about Claude?" She paused, trying to think if she knew of any job that Claude had.

"Claude? He's . . . he's not working right now," Phillip said. "I suppose he's still living off his share of the farm sale."

"Is . . . is he around?" she asked, flushing slightly as she wrapped the end of twine around her finger. She hoped her face didn't look as pink as the flowers, because her cheeks felt as if they were burning.

"Claude? Well . . . he's around."

Hannah managed a peek at Phillip, who seemed intent on examining the ceiling boards. "Is he all right? Bethany won't tell me where he is, but I just can't wait to see him."

"Is he all right." Phillip said it as a statement. He sat on a chair and fiddled with the brim of his hat.

Hannah flopped her hands on her quilt and groaned. "Why won't anyone be straightforward with me? I ask a simple question, and everyone dances around it like they're doing the polka."

"I'm sorry," Phillip said with a shake of his head. "Claude is fine, I think. I haven't seen him for a while. We've all kept to ourselves of late. I've been trying to figure out the cost of the damage to my studio, and—"

Hannah tilted her head in confusion. "Damage? What happened to it?"

Phillip sat back as if a realization had dawned on him. "I forgot you probably didn't know about that. Sorry I said anything."

"No. Please tell me. Everyone is so afraid of upsetting me with any unpleasant news, and I think not knowing things is more upsetting than knowing the truth. What happened to your studio?" Hannah sat up, grimaced at the pain in her collarbone, and leaned back again. Phillip had been so excited about his new photography supplies and skills. To think that something had tarnished those dreams . . .

Phillip's eyes seemed to skitter around the room. "There was a bit of an . . . accident. Some broken jars of chemicals and such. Nothing that can't be fixed over time . . . and with money."

"Oh, that's horrible," Hannah said, feeling bad that she didn't have any recollection of her friend's misfortune. What else didn't she remember? "How did it happen?"

He rubbed his hands together and breathed out heavily, but didn't answer right away. "It's nothing to worry about. What's done is done." He smiled and shrugged. "So, tell me what you've been up to." He immediately looked contrite and laughed. "Sorry. Silly question. How are you feeling? That's probably a more appropriate query."

"A bit better, I think." She studied his face. What was going on behind those eyes? What was he thinking about, and why did he insist on being so vague about his studio? Was it really because Dr. Wood didn't want anyone to upset her with bad news? The condition of the place was worse than he had let on—something in his eyes made her sure of it. Yet Phillip didn't say so. He refused to be selfish even when his own burden could be lightened.

She adjusted her blanket and leaned back. "How about you tell me what you've been up to. What's life like outside these walls? Why are they closing the quarry?"

"To build a railway so they can transport the stone to the temple a lot more quickly."

"I suppose that makes sense," Hannah said. "But it's a shame the progress is halting again. At this rate, I'll be an old lady by the time the temple's complete. When I was a little girl, I thought I'd be married there, but chances are it'll be in the Endowment House instead."

The thought was sad. She knew that the ordinance still counted as much as it would in a temple, but it would lack some of the glory and beauty that a temple wedding would surely have. When Phillip didn't answer, she looked up and saw him gazing out the window in the direction of the construction site, a faraway look in his eyes. She tried to coax him out of his reverie. "But I don't think things such as the location of a wedding matter to you men, do they?"

"No, I suppose they don't," Phillip said somberly. "I doubt *Claude* would care one way or the other." He pressed his lips together in thought, leaned toward her, and clasped his hands together. "Hannah?"

The look in his eyes was intense. For some strange reason, she seemed to feel all flushed. "Yes?"

"Hannah, I've wanted to tell you for a long time that—" Before he got another word out, they heard a knock, followed by the squeak of hinges.

Claude peeked his head into the room, grinning broadly. "I heard you wanted to see me."

"Claude!" Hannah reached toward him with her good arm as Phillip meekly stood and stepped to the side, making way for Claude. The two brothers stared at each other for a charged moment before

Claude walked to the bedside and knelt beside it. He kissed the back of Hannah's hand, then held it to his cheek.

"I've been so worried about you," he said.

A thought fluttered across her mind, curious why he hadn't come to see her more often, but she pushed it aside, figuring she had probably forgotten his other visits.

Phillip shifted his feet and coughed. "I—uh—I'll be going."

"Thank you for coming," Hannah said. "Having a friend around sure helps the time pass."

"You're welcome," he said softly, then headed for the door.

As he retreated, she felt a twinge of disappointment and wished he'd stay a little longer. Phillip had always been a man she felt comfortable around. She had never heard him speak a word against another person—she could rely on someone like him to be utterly loyal. She counted herself lucky to know him.

"Thanks again for the flowers." She wasn't sure if Phillip heard her before the door closed behind him.

"Hannah?" Claude's voice broke through her thoughts. She felt suddenly guilty for not paying attention to him, so she smiled broadly.

"What were you saying?" she asked, turning her attention back to him.

"That I've missed you." He brought her hand to his lips and kissed it again.

* * *

Phillip exited to the hallway, where Bethany was waiting for him. As soon as he came out, she immediately headed for the door to go in.

"Why is *he* here?" Phillip hissed, grabbing her arm.

She let the door close, came back into the hall, and shut her eyes. "Trust me—it's not *my* idea. I sent him away earlier. But Dr. Wood insists that we not upset her and that we grant her whatever she wishes, including letting him visit. And since she specifically asked for him, I had to let him come. But I'll be dag-blamed if I'll let him be in there more than every few days, and certainly not alone." Her eyes flashed as she gripped the doorknob. Phillip nodded gratefully.

"Thank you for that," he said. "I guess I'll see you tomorrow." He was headed for the stairs when Bethany spoke again.

"Phillip?"

He paused on the steps and raised his head but didn't answer.

"I'm so sorry. About everything."

Bethany's tone said much more than her words did. He could tell she understood his inner turmoil over Hannah and Claude, especially since Hannah had no recollection of what Claude had done. It wasn't fair, and both of them knew it.

"Thanks." He paused again, thinking there should be more to say, but instead he just shook his head and went down the stairs to let himself out.

* * *

"Surely when I visit, you can put other things aside in your mind," Claude said to Hannah after Phillip left. He leaned closer to her and smiled. His eyes crinkled at the edges. "You really are the most beautiful thing in the world, Hannah, my dearest," he said. "Your eyes are like pools of water—they refresh my soul."

Hannah flushed warm at his words and felt a wave of guilt. Why hadn't she given him her full attention? Dear Claude. Whenever he came, he seemed to notice nothing but her, complimenting her on the slightest thing. How could she be so inconsiderate?

"How have you been?" she asked, as Bethany returned to the room to be their chaperone.

"Not so good, but I'm glad to be home now. The canyon is such a miserable place." He launched into a diatribe about the misery of driving a three-yoke ox team and pulling a 2,500-pound block of granite. Hannah listened politely, trying not to fidget. When she scratched her leg, Claude paused and didn't speak again until she settled back into position.

"Go on," she said, smiling. "What was that about the axle grease?"

An hour into his story, Bethany interjected and shooed him away, insisting that it was time for Hannah to take a nap. Claude sighed, kissed her hand, and bowed himself out. Bethany closed the door behind him and groaned, then caught herself when she noticed Hannah looking at her. "Sorry."

"He's just uncomfortable up here," Hannah said. "It's hard to know how to act around someone who's ill." She lay back on her pillow and sighed, then reached over and touched the shooting stars Phillip had brought. If only everyone could just behave like a plain old friend.

# CHAPTER 18

"As if from heaven, an angel came from above. Unworthy am I; How pitifully I deserve her love."

Alone in the Hansen yard, Ben stopped reading aloud, groaned, and balled up the paper, then stubbed his toe on a tree root. "Pitiful is right," he said under his breath, hopping from the pain in his foot. "I can't even make a decent rhyme." He raised his arm and threw the offending verse into the bushes. Then he pictured someone finding the paper and reading his foolish attempt at poetry. Even if it was just Phillip who found it, Ben would rather die than have anyone see his lyric failure. And what if it were someone else altogether? *No.* At the base of the bushes, he got down on his knees, pushing prickly branches out of the way until he triumphantly secured the balled-up paper. After shoving it firmly into his jacket pocket, he stood, brushed off his pants, and began pacing.

All the old poets made it look so easy. Shakespeare's sonnets flowed smoothly along on an even road of blank verse, and Ben could name a dozen other writers whose words did the same—instead of bumbling and knocking along a jolting cobblestone road like Ben's did.

*I bet none of those poets felt as turned upside down with love as I do.*

He eyed the house, wishing he had something on paper to take inside with him for Bethany, something that would convince her that he loved her more profoundly than ever before. But he simply couldn't express his feelings in writing. And not for lack of trying. He had spent a good portion of the night—plus a candle and a half—trying to come up with something that even came close to reflecting his true feelings. He had left home this afternoon with what he thought was a good verse, only to read it now—one more time, just to be sure—and realize it was utter drivel.

Years back, he had sent Bethany love letters all the time, often with poems included. Now he cringed, realizing that his attempts then were almost certainly as sorry as his current ones. She had probably laughed at his old notes. Later on, she had probably burned them out of anger—that was a small comfort.

*I could use the gift of tongues about now.*

The sound of cracking sticks make Ben whirl around. Bethany stood there, smiling. His heart, instead of calming down, thudded heavily in his chest. "Bethany." His tone suggested more, something he couldn't yet verbalize. He wanted to called her "sweet Bethany," "dear Bethany," or "beautiful, angelic Bethany."

Instead, he checked to be sure the paper was still in his pocket and said, "What a lucky coincidence that you came out just now."

She raised her arms to the sides. "Here I am. You don't even have to call me, and I show up." She stepped closer.

"Let me get this straight," Ben said, easing toward her, "you'll come whenever I call and stay until I say so?"

"Sounds good to me," Bethany said, a laugh toying at the corners of her eyes.

Ben looked up at the leafy branches above them. "So . . ."

"'So?' You just said that's my cue to leave." She turned away, but Ben grabbed her hand, and she faced him again, laughing. He pulled her closer, wanting to kiss her but not knowing if she'd let him again so soon.

Bethany stood so close that Ben wondered if she could hear his heart. She smoothed his shirt with the flat of her hand and said, "Actually, I was watching for Dr. Wood and saw you from the window. I was hoping you'd come in for a bite. Sister Hunter brought over some tarts this morning. Fancy coming in for one?"

"I'd enjoy that very much," Ben said. He pushed a branch to the side as they walked down the lane arm in arm. "I know I haven't always been an angel to be around, so if I may ask, which of my bad parts was it that made you first realize you still loved me?"

"That's easy," Bethany said, her eyes dancing. "All of them together."

"Now, that's not fair!"

She laughed and stopped at the same spot he had first seen her at his homecoming, spilling that silly bushel of onions. The memory felt bittersweet—it had been exhilarating to see those flushed cheeks and flashing eyes, but now . . . now he felt shame for all the horrible things he had said to her that day. And all the days that followed.

"But now you tell me, Ben Adams," Bethany said quickly before he could speak again, "for which of my *good* qualities did you first suffer love for me?"

"*Suffer* love is about right," Ben said. "I'm afraid I love you against my will."

Bethany put a hand to her hip and raised an eyebrow. "Pardon me, *Mr.* Adams, but no one dragged you here today, and you're perfectly welcome to leave." She pointed to the road behind them.

"And since when do I obey any woman who yells at me? If I wish to stay, I will." Ben's voice had risen. "And I *do* wish to stay, because I love you, and there isn't a particle of chance you can get me to say otherwise." Their eyes caught one another's, and they both burst out laughing. Ben gently pushed a lock of her hair behind her ear. "We can't even love one another without fighting, can we?"

She shrugged and said, "We're just so good at it. Old habits are hard to break." She stood on her toes and kissed his cheek. "Truth be told, Ben Adams, I'd rather fight with you for the rest of my life, knowing I have your love, than spend my days in boring peace with anyone else."

Ben kissed her cheek in return, and as they pulled apart, they gazed into one another's eyes. Bethany suddenly grew shy and looked at the ground. Ben had a sudden urge to kiss her fanned-out lashes. "Let's go inside," Bethany said, taking his hand and leading him toward the house.

When they reached the side door, Ben nodded to the upper story. "How is your sister doing?"

Bethany sighed, and the sparkle in her eyes dimmed. "Poorly. She'll be fine, but her spirits are low, and it's getting harder to keep them up. And then last night she developed a fever. For a moment you helped me forget."

"And how are you?"

She raised her gaze to his, and the sadness in her eyes felt wrenching. "Poorly too. I'm so tired all the time."

"I'm not Dr. Wood," Ben said, running a thumb over her hand, "but here's what I think you should do—care for your sister. Love me. And forget about everything else."

"I like that prescription," Bethany said, leaning toward him.

He lowered his head, leaning in for a kiss, when a voice called from behind them. Dr. Wood was walking at a brisk pace up the lane, swinging his black bag. "Sister Hansen, any news about your sister?"

Bethany and Ben pulled apart and tried to look nonchalant. "He's in a hurry," Ben said quietly, clearing his throat. If only the doctor weren't quite so punctual.

Dr. Wood stopped beside them. "Any improvement?" he demanded of them both, giving no indication that he recognized what he'd interrupted. Ben was certain the man could figure it out if he took half a second to notice that the two of them were both flushed bright red. But the good doctor seemed more intent on finding out his patient's status.

"She developed a fever last night," Bethany said. "And she hasn't remembered anything new since your last visit."

"I see," Dr. Wood said, consulting his notebook and jotting something into it. "Anything else? Swelling? Rash?"

"No, nothing like that," Bethany said. "But her spirits are worse. And she keeps trying to get out of bed and use her arm, because she doesn't remember that she's injured. Father's with her now, if you'd like to go up."

*Yes, go up,* Ben thought, smiling broadly.

Dr. Wood hesitated at the door, expecting Bethany to lead the way, but she just motioned with her arm. "Feel free. I believe you know the way."

"All . . . right . . ." Dr. Wood looked quizzically at them, removed his hat, and stepped inside.

For a moment Ben thought she would follow after him, but when she let the door close, he nodded with satisfaction. *Good.* She needed a break from the stress and worry of nursing her sister around the clock.

"Come," he said, tugging her arm. "You need some fresh air. Let's go on a walk and find another place to argue."

Bethany gave him a crooked grin. "Only if you let me win."

"Oh now, that wouldn't be any fun."

"It would be for me." Bethany slipped her arm in his, and together they headed toward the street.

* * *

Phillip carried another bouquet of flowers as he followed Bethany up the stairs to Hannah's room. No word had come from Marie yet, but he expected something from her any day now, and the thought that Hannah's reputation would soon be fixed—before she ever knew it had been sullied—made him happy.

"I wrote to Marie asking her to clear Hannah's name," he told Bethany. "We should be hearing back from her soon."

Bethany smiled wanly. "But do you think that will make much difference? The rumors have gone hog wild. Since Hannah's stuck at home, people are saying that she's hiding out because she's in the family way. Without the photograph, we can't stop the rumors from circulating. You *took* the picture, and no one believes *you*."

Phillip shrugged. "Even so, I'm hoping Marie's word will help."

"You're right," Bethany said with a nod. "I shouldn't give up hope." Before opening the door, she stopped and smiled.

He raised his eyebrows and looked over. "Can—can I go in?"

"Those are for her, I assume," Bethany said, inclining her head toward the flowers.

"Of course." He looked at the three yellow irises clasped in his hand. "Is . . . that all right?"

"Claude never brings her flowers," Bethany said with a glint in her eye as she opened the door.

Phillip cleared his throat uneasily. As he walked into the room, he could feel her eyes boring into the back of his head. His brothers knew. Bethany knew. The only one among the five of them who didn't was Hannah herself. And if he wanted to maintain his comfortable friendship with her, he would have to keep it that way unless she indicated that she returned his feelings.

He took a deep breath and went inside.

# CHAPTER 19

One evening, three weeks after the accident, with Hannah fast asleep upstairs, the family retired to the kitchen with Dr. Wood, who had accepted their invitation to eat a bite with them. He and Ben sat at the table with the bishop, and Bethany served them bread with preserves, wishing she had a cake or pie. Any attempts at being a prepared hostess had fallen by the wayside since Hannah's accident. It was all Bethany could do to keep the family fed and their clothing clean.

"Bethany, you look so tired," her father said as she set a plate of sliced bread on the table. He patted her shoulder.

"I'm fine, Father," she said, returning to the counter where she ladled well water into metal cups. The lack of time had created a strain; she couldn't deny that. *Thank heavens for Ben.*

"You need some rest," her father declared as he spread apricot preserves across his bread. "Hannah's fine for now. You can leave her side for more than a few minutes at a time. A little diversion would be good for you."

Bethany stared at the wood grain in the counter and didn't answer right away. His words were only partly true—Hannah *wasn't* fine. Her condition had stabilized—and her bones seemed to be knitting—but otherwise she hadn't improved for several days. She still woke disoriented and struggled with her memory. She still needed help with almost everything. Her fever was gone now, but it might return.

It didn't help Bethany's nerves that Hannah kept asking for Claude.

"Father, I don't mind being with her. Truly, I don't," Bethany said, turning to face the men, holding a cup of water in each hand. She hoped her smile was convincing as she brought the water to the table, because in reality she felt enveloped by fatigue most of the time. In the few hours she did sleep she had two types of dreams—nightmares of Hannah's funeral or of Claude causing her even greater harm, or comforting dreams of walking in the sun, picking flowers, even of sleeping. Many of her dreams involved Ben, and she secretly wondered if the two of them would ever have much time to get to know each other's new selves. Such thoughts immediately made her feel selfish for wanting to do something besides nurse her sister back to health.

Dr. Wood popped the last of his bread into his mouth, chewed thoughtfully, then said, "I agree with your father, Sister Hansen. Caring for a loved one can be taxing. Even the most devoted family members need to take a break at times. There's no shame in that." He brushed his palms together, letting crumbs fall onto his plate.

Ben finally spoke up. "Bishop, how about I take Bethany to the theater on Friday?"

At first she clung to the idea, but she quickly shook her head, imagining something happening to Hannah in her absence. If that happened she'd never forgive herself. She still felt guilty for the long walk she and Ben had taken. "I couldn't. But thank you, Ben." She snatched a wet washcloth and began cleaning the table.

Her father put a hand on her arm. She stopped wiping and stared at the table as he spoke. "I think that's a marvelous idea."

"But Father, the tickets are probably sold out," Bethany tried to protest. She looked at Ben. "And I couldn't ask you to spend so much money on one night. Besides, I couldn't possibly consider leaving Hannah for that long."

Ben slipped his hand into the breast pocket of his jacket and withdrew two tickets. He waved them back and forth. "The deed is done, Miss Hansen. You wouldn't waste good money already spent, now would you?"

"Good for you," Dr. Wood said with a clap. "Sister Hansen, you'll end up ill yourself if you don't have some time away. Therefore you *will* go to the theater on Friday with this young man. Doctor's orders." He put on his jacket, picked up his bag, and headed for the door, then turned back to make a final point. "Even Brother Joseph knew he had to 'unstring' his bow now and again."

"Yes, Doctor," Bethany said a bit grudgingly as he left. But inside, she couldn't help feeling a flutter of excitement.

* * *

Friday evening Bethany spent a full hour after supper getting herself ready, deciding which of her two best dresses to wear, finally settling on the dark blue silk with the bell sleeves and laced back. It had stays in the bodice, which made it hard to move and breathe, but she wouldn't be dancing, and besides, she knew she looked pretty in it. Her father came into the kitchen as she painstakingly curled her hair with a heated rod.

"You look beautiful." He always said that when she went out. His words made Bethany realize how long it seemed since the dance when Ben first came home. It had been only a couple of months, yet remembering Hannah's energy and comparing it to how she fared today, the time since felt much longer.

She gave her father a grateful look but shook her head and pointed to the top of her head. "Just look at that," she said, lifting a small hand mirror to the part in her hair. "It's supposed to go straight down the middle, but it looks like an old river, weaving all over the place."

"It does not," her father said with a chuckle. Bethany didn't know whether his laughter stemmed from the truth—that her part really did weave—or from seeing her flustered.

She picked up the heated curling rod and struggled to produce one perfect curl. "These ringlets are supposed to pile nicely at the back and gently fall onto my shoulder. But *look* at them!" She slapped the curling rod onto the stove and groaned.

Her father stepped into the kitchen and tilted his head. He pressed his lips together as he considered her hair. "Your ringlets look wonderful."

"They're as lively as dead fish."

"Bethany." He took her hands in his, even though she still held a comb in one. She paused in her tirade, flushed from nerves and exertion. "Ben will think you're beautiful with or without perfect curls. Tonight will be delightful. Enjoy yourself."

She nodded and took a deep breath. "I'll try," she said, withdrawing her hands. She lifted the mirror and inspected her hair again, then tapped the comb on the edge of the table as she noted another misbehaving curl. She felt an urgency to be perfect for Ben in every way. "But—"

Her father shook his head and removed the curling rod from the stove before she could take it back. "Go into the parlor and wait for him. He'll be here any minute." He held the rod out of reach, grinning. There was no getting it back, and Bethany knew it.

"Very well then," she said, then laughed, grateful her father could stop her fretting. "Thank you." She leaned in and kissed his cheek. Walking toward the parlor, she paused and looked up the stairs, wondering if she should check on Hannah one last time.

"On you go," her father said, gently pushing her down the hallway. "I'll see to your sister."

"Yes, Father." Bethany smoothed her bodice and took as big a breath as the stays allowed. Then she went into the parlor and stood by the window, where she waited to see Ben come at the end of the lane. She stood at the wide window, gazing straight out toward the spot where the infamous picture of Marie had been taken. Her gaze quickly moved on when the memory returned of all that the picture had led to. She didn't want to think of such sad things tonight.

Ben would arrive at any moment. She couldn't help but wring her hands and pace the room, glancing frequently out the window and down the road for any sign of him, then looking up at the ceiling, hoping Hannah would be all right without her. Smoothing her hair, Bethany knew her face had flushed pink. She put her hands to her cheeks, feeling them hot against the nervous coolness of her fingers. She felt excited to see Ben again—to be with him for the entire evening—yet she was equally nervous to be seen with him in public. What would people say?

The next time she looked, Ben was strolling toward the house. He wore a freshly pressed suit with long tails and a gray cravat with a pearl in the center, his hair slicked back as it was that night so long ago when he'd first kissed her. The sight took her breath away, and she put a hand on the pianoforte and bit her lips together. When he knocked on the door, she felt paralyzed. Her father answered, and a moment later Ben walked into the room, smiled, and stopped next to the pianoforte. He put his hand over her trembling one. She hoped he didn't notice that it was shaking.

"You look stunning," he said. Hearing him speak so sincerely was still new to Bethany, and she felt sure such things would never get old.

"Thank you. So do you. Look *handsome,* I mean." Why was it easy to land barbs with precision, but so difficult to say something kind and honest and have it come across how you meant it?

Ben lifted her hand and drew her toward the door, where her father waited to see them off. At the porch, Ben brought her to the road and put his arm out. "Ready?"

"Ready." *I think.* "Good night, Father," she said over her shoulder. She slipped her arm through Ben's, and together they headed toward the theater on the corner of State and First South. It could have been her imagination, but as they walked, Bethany sensed Ben standing a little taller, prouder than usual with her at his side. It made her stand taller, too.

When they reached the theater—one of the largest and most beautiful buildings in the entire city—they had to wait in line to get in. While standing side by side, the couple got plenty of stares and quiet murmurs, no doubt from people shocked at seeing two former enemies behaving like friendly allies.

"Who knew we'd be paying for two shows tonight," someone behind them was saying. "With those two together, we're bound to be entertained by a fight."

A few feet ahead in line, a pair of young women kept glancing at them, twittering to each other, then looking again.

Ben leaned in and whispered, "Are they bothering you?"

"No," Bethany said, and was surprised that she meant it. Instead of feeling embarrassment as she'd feared, she just smiled to herself.

She didn't care if people talked; she was with Ben. Contrary to what some people apparently believed, she and Ben wouldn't be fighting tonight. They'd be enjoying one another's company like any other courting couple. *Courting.* The word felt strange, but she supposed it was the only one that fit.

Those with pre-purchased tickets went inside, where men checked their weapons, and one woman was threatened with a ten-dollar surcharge if she insisted on bringing her baby inside the theater. At the ticket office, a handful of people wore dusty, travel-worn clothing instead of the finery of the locals, and they paid for tickets with poultry and produce brought from their farms. Ben and Bethany were ushered to their seats, which were padded with red velvet cushions. They were near the center of the row about halfway back in the mezzanine.

As she waited for the play to begin, Bethany looked around the impressive room, marveling that the people of Utah had been able to build such a grand structure with limited means—having to bring everything west on wagons. The newspaper said that in a couple of years the transcontinental railroad would be complete. At that point, a similar construction wouldn't be nearly as big a feat.

Dozens—if not hundreds—of oil lamps lit the theater, with three big kerosene lamps on either side of the stage that provided light for the actors. Stoves edged the hall, surely lit during cooler months to keep the audience comfortable. With it being early fall, Bethany wondered if they'd be lighting any of the stoves tonight. The air had a bit of a nip in it already, although the number of people in the room might warm it up enough.

Several minutes later, a man slid through the curtain opening and raised his arms. The crowd quieted as he addressed them. "Thank you for coming to this evening's performance. We are honored to have acclaimed actor Edwin Booth with us tonight with his touring theater group. Mr. Booth will perform the title role in Shakespeare's *Hamlet.* Before we begin, we will have an opening prayer by President Franklin, former stake president of the Fourth Stake."

Another man appeared from behind the curtain. Stocky and balding, he had a red, shiny face. He looked like he had spent more time behind a plow than in the worn suit he wore. The lines around his eyes and mouth tugged downward, and Bethany couldn't imagine him ever smiling. "Before I offer the invocation," he said, "let me first say a few words."

At the unusual request, murmurs rippled over the audience. Ben and Bethany exchanged looks of impatience, both wanting the play to begin.

"A sad circumstance in our community has come to my attention, as I'm sure it has come to many of yours." The former President Franklin raised a folded newspaper, which Bethany hadn't noticed he carried under his arm. His voice was gravelly, as if he yelled often. "You may have read about it in my editorial in this week's paper." Bethany hadn't. President Franklin went on. "It's a sad, sad, time when we see a young woman caring so little for her virtue. Such immoral behavior is shocking."

Of all the thousands of people in Salt Lake City and the surrounding areas, what were the chances he meant the rumors about Hannah? Slim. Even so, Bethany's stomach knotted. *Please, don't be that. Not here in front of hundreds of people.*

"Since the photograph in question has not been seen—it has probably been destroyed—we may never know the extent of what occurred. But reliable eyewitnesses have stated that the girl's original beau knows that the girl has done more—*significantly* more—than kiss another young man. In fact, these witnesses attest that a child born out of wedlock may result from the young woman's actions, and that the photograph itself indicated as much." The crowd murmured in surprise.

Bethany's fists balled tightly. The mention of a photograph clinched it. The chances of there being another rumor so similar to the one about Hannah were nearly nonexistent. She still couldn't believe how far the story had evolved, twisting ridiculously out of proportion to what had actually happened. But to think that now it wasn't just being passed from person to person, but was published across the valley . . .

She wished that Marie had written back already—although it was unlikely that would have quelled the rumors. But why hadn't she responded to Phillip's letter?

"Our youth are clearly forgetting the values of their fathers. It's certainly a sign of the times when a young woman lets herself fall so far."

The murmuring in the audience had turned into a rumble. People spoke to one another, many obviously uncomfortable with the direction the man's story was taking things, true or not. He seemed to be nowhere near ending his commentary, but to Bethany's relief, the stage manager stepped through the curtain and whispered in his ear. Brother Franklin sighed and nodded, turning to the audience.

"Without further ado, I'll offer tonight's invocation. Please pray with me for this young woman's soul that she will have a change of heart, that she will see the need to repent of her sins—confess them and forsake them."

Unable to help herself, Bethany wrung her hands and shifted in her seat, knowing she was rumpling her dress but not caring. The wooden seat around the padded portions seemed particularly hard and uncomfortable. Many around her seemed to dismiss what Brother Franklin was saying, but a few clusters of people seemed shocked and abhorred, clearly believing every word as they covered their mouths and shook their heads sadly. Some leaned their heads together, whispering. If there had been any doubt about who President Franklin referred to, it was erased when two or three people pointed at Bethany and nodded ominously. If only she could break the dag-blamed stays in her dress so she could actually breathe—or scream. She covered her face with one hand, and Ben took the other between his own.

He leaned in and whispered, "It's all right."

"No, it's not," Bethany said, trying not to cry.

Ben paused, then squeezed her hand. "I know."

Brother Franklin bowed his head. The rest of the room did the same. Mid-prayer, he launched into a sermon about virtuous women. Bethany ground her teeth to keep herself from protesting.

"Please bless the woman at the center of the problem. She is within our midst, Lord, and must repent. So bless Sister Han—I mean, bless the young woman in question."

Bethany's eyes shot wide open. Had he intended to say Hannah's name, or was it an accident? She didn't know or care if anyone there assumed "Sister Hansen" to be herself. All she cared about was that Hannah's reputation was permanently marred. Bethany's blood seemed to boil. Prayer or no prayer, she could take no more. She bolted to her feet and stumbled past theatergoers toward the aisle. They opened their eyes, surprised, and moved their legs so she could pass. Ben followed close behind, but she escaped well before he did. As soon as she reached the side aisle, she ran blindly down the steps and into the foyer, covering her face with both hands.

"Bethany!" Ben called after her, running. When he reached her in the lobby, he said more quietly, "Bethany."

She stopped by some elegant carved doors and caught her breath. "It's vicious lies, all of it!"

"I know," Ben said, reaching out to touch her shoulder.

Bethany turned and crumpled into his arms. "How can they say such things? How can he spread rumors in front of hundreds of people? How can my sister ever show her face again?"

He held her close as she cried into his shoulder. "I don't know. I wish Claude would fix it."

Pulling away, Bethany shook her head and scrubbed her cheeks with her hands. "But he *can't* fix this. Don't you see? This goes far beyond our street and our ward now. Thanks to that man's editorial, the lies are already spread throughout the valley and beyond. By dawn they could reach California." She covered her face with her hands again, hating how her voice sounded like a whimper. "From now on, my sister will be looked at with suspicion and pity no matter where she goes."

Through the doors they could hear the audience applauding. They could hear the witches from *Hamlet* begin their dialogue. Bethany gestured toward the auditorium. "The play is starting." Her voice was listless. She didn't want to go back in. How could she face the throng of people? They all knew who she was—the sister of the "tarnished" girl.

"We don't have to go back in there." Ben gestured toward the outer doors as if confirming his words.

"Really?"

"Really." He held the door open for her, but she paused before stepping outside.

"I'm sorry, Ben. The tickets must have cost a bundle, what with the touring group performing, and—"

"It was nothing. We can come to the theater another time, and I don't care a hoot for Edwin Booth anyway. It was worth the expense just to be with you tonight. I'm glad I was the one with you when this happened."

*Dear Ben.* She searched his eyes and found pure sincerity. He really didn't mind that the money he had spent on tickets had been wasted. Since the quarry closure, Ben had been out of work, and he had no new source of income. He truly was a gentleman. "Thank you."

He leaned in and brushed his lips against her cheek. "Anything for you."

# CHAPTER 20

Hannah was sitting in bed, miserable, when a knock sounded on her bedroom door. She wiped away a tear and called, "Come in."

Phillip walked in, bearing a bouquet of pink roses.

"Oh, hello, Phillip," she said brightly, hoping he wouldn't notice her sadness. "It's good to see you again."

He came in smiling and holding out the flowers. "I figured the irises would be nearly limp by now. So I brought some roses from our garden to replace them."

"Thank you so much," Hannah said, clasping her hands together. "They're beautiful. I'm glad you picked ones that are already open. That's when roses are at their prettiest."

"I agree." Phillip hesitated, almost putting the bouquet in Hannah's hands. "I'll leave them on the table so Bethany can take out the irises and replace the water. The thorns might prick you." He set the flowers down gently, almost reverently. "I cut them from my mother's bushes." They were beautiful, wide blossoms, and bright pink. She could already smell the fragrance wafting about the room. The other flowers he had brought had all been pretty, but these were by far the most pleasant smelling.

"How are you feeling?" he asked after putting the flowers on the table.

Hannah laughed and wiped away another tear. "Honestly? As if I'll wilt like a flower if I don't get out of this room." She shifted her covers. "I never thought that lying around and resting would be something I would tire of. But I would give almost anything to be able to *work.* If I have to do nothing but sleep, eat, crochet this ugly brown scarf and read book after book for much longer, I'll go completely mad."

"I can imagine," Phillip said with a wan smile and a chuckle.

"Dr. Wood came again this morning. He let me stand up for just a moment and walk to the rocking chair. And he let me spend a whole hour sitting up in it."

"That's good," Phillip said. "It was probably a relief to get out of bed."

"You'd think," Hannah said with a laugh. "But after a bit of freedom, lying back on this tick felt like even more of a prison than before." She leaned back on her pillow and looked at him. "Phillip, I'm glad I can tell you the truth. For everyone else I try to put on a happy face and pretend I'm just fine, that I don't mind lying here day in and day out, or that it doesn't bother me to have lost some of my memory. But it does bother me, tremendously." Her eyes watered.

She ventured a look at him, grateful that she didn't have to pretend to smile for him. He nodded sadly and didn't try to placate her. Instead, he merely said, "I know. I'm sorry."

She smiled at him. "You're such a great friend, Phillip," she said, taking his hand and letting several tears tumble down her cheeks. She looked out the window at the puffy clouds that drifted by. "I've needed that."

She sniffed and dabbed at the corner of one eye with part of her sheet, then tried to look cheerful. "Enough of dwelling on what can't be changed. How about we play a game to pass the time?"

"Very well," Phillip said, clapping his hands together and looking about the room. "How about checkers?"

Hannah shook her head. "Too hard to reach a table from the bed, and my lap isn't flat. How about a parlor game, like Twenty Questions?"

"Sounds fun." Phillip settled back in his chair. "You first."

Squinting in thought, Hannah came up with her secret item. "I'm ready," she said, tilting her head at him.

"Is it an animal, vegetable, or mineral?"

"Animal."

Phillip stared at the beams in the ceiling and thought.

Hannah raised her eyebrows. "Not even one question? Does that mean I win?"

"It's an animal, is it? Then I'm going to have to ask if it's a bird."

Hannah laughed in surprise. "How did you guess?"

"Because you'd love fly away from this room about now," Phillip answered, nodding toward the window.

She smiled in disbelief and folded her arms over the blanket. "Very well, yes, it's a bird. But you don't know what kind." She would stump him, she was sure of it.

Smiling, he ventured another guess. "An eagle?"

With wonder in her voice, she said, "How could you possibly know that?"

"I've seen you watching eagles. Friends notice these things."

"Only the ones who really care," Hannah said.

Phillip raised his eyes, lifted one shoulder into a shrug, and said, "Of course I care."

He didn't stay long after their game, but Hannah didn't stop thinking about it for hours. She didn't read or crochet or anything else for some time. Instead she lay back and stared at the ceiling, trying to sort out the strange thoughts and feelings that kept unsettling her.

Eagles. How could Phillip possibly know she loved eagles? She shook her head and sank into her pillow as she pictured his face.

*Dear Phillip.*

Claude visited every so often, and she enjoyed his visits. Naturally. But somehow she always felt more excited when she saw Phillip arriving, and she felt happier after being in his company.

When she considered these feelings, she felt guilty. Shouldn't she be happier after seeing Claude? Shouldn't he be the one who cheered her up more?

Every time she asked herself such questions, more would come.

Shouldn't Claude be the one bringing her flowers? Shouldn't he be the one who knew she loved eagles? Shouldn't he be the one asking about how she felt, instead of talking about himself?

She sighed, not understanding why she felt so unsettled. Phillip had always been a dear. They had been friends for ages. That was all—

right? Her gaze landed on the wilting irises, the same color as her ball gown. The sight sent her dreaming of dancing again. Wouldn't it be wonderful to float across the dance floor? She imagined holding a man's hand as she made the formations of a cotillion—then jolted with a start when she realized she had pictured Phillip at her side instead of Claude.

She shook her head and covered her face with her hand, guilt washing over her.

*This mustn't be! It mustn't!*

Determined to shake such thoughts from her mind, she picked up her worn volume of *The Pilgrim's Progress* and opened to the bookmark. She read page after page, not comprehending any of the words, because her mind still pictured dresses swirling across a dance floor.

# CHAPTER 21

Straight from visiting Hannah, Phillip went to his studio. He hadn't dealt with cleaning up the mess yet—he didn't want to face the end of his dreams. Fixing everything would take a far cry more than what he had told Hannah when she first asked about it.

Originally he had put off the task because Mrs. Brecken had closed up shop. Then he spent days helping out at the Hansen farm. Then he just couldn't face seeing his studio. Had Mrs. Brecken been willing to return part of his rent for clearing out sooner, he would have done so, but she wouldn't budge. So what was the point of cleaning up a broken dream until he had to? At some point he'd have to pay back his creditors, but he had no idea how. Maybe he'd look for work with the railroad when it got started in a few weeks. Until then, he had no way to earn money.

He spent some time taking in the damage, looking around for anything that wasn't destroyed. He didn't find much that wasn't destined for the garbage heap. As he stood in the middle of the disheveled attic, a measure of sorrow spilled over him in spite of his determination to remain optimistic. He squatted down and tried to peel photographs away from each other. The first one came off, but the edge of the next one stuck and ripped, leaving behind it the image of a leafy tree on top of the pile of other photographs and photo paper. Warped and stuck together from moisture and chemicals, they were all that remained of the time, money, and energy spent on a dream that hadn't even managed to take its first baby steps. At least, it was all that remained if he didn't count the heap of debt he still had hanging over his head.

He silently cursed himself for ever snapping that picture of Marie. If he hadn't, none of this would ever have happened. Grimly he thought back to the last time he'd been here, so sure that the things in his studio would change his future.

They had changed it. Oh boy, had they ever. They had affected his future and the futures of several other people to boot.

Resting his arms on his thighs, he looked at what was left of a photo—his favorite landscape picture from that afternoon in Parley's Canyon. He thought back to that day, its perfect conditions, the time spent with Hannah . . . Poor Hannah. How would she face the gossip going around when she finally heard it—as she must at some point?

He smacked the photo against his hand and looked over what was left of his studio. As he stood, his boot heels crunched glass from one of the many shattered plates meant for capturing photos. He stepped to one of the three windows overlooking South Temple and gazed out, remembering how dirty the glass had been when he'd first asked Mrs. Brecken to let him the space—and how much work it had taken to make the place shine. He'd only been able to rent the room in the first place because of Claude's intervention, yet the destruction was equally attributable to Claude. It was ironic that Mrs. Brecken had been so concerned about Phillip, but it had ended up being Claude who brought the trouble.

The thought made Phillip want to punch something. He had spent the last of his money—and piled up a heap of credit—learning the trade and getting supplies, which were difficult to get in the West. He had hauled them home and worked tediously to make sure every detail was right. For what?

A creak on the stairs behind him made Phillip look over his shoulder. Claude's tawny head appeared, pausing when their eyes met. "What are *you* doing here?" Phillip demanded.

"I saw you from my hotel window," Claude said. "I want to help."

"Go away," Phillip said, turning back to the window. "You've done enough here."

Claude clomped up the stairs anyway, and a moment later there was the sound of papers shuffling together and glass crunching. "What do you think you're doing?" Phillip asked, this time facing

Claude full on with his arms folded. "You finished off the place pretty thoroughly last time. Nothing is salvageable."

"Nothing?" Claude looked up, the papers clasped to his chest sticking out every which way. "What about the tripod?"

Phillip shrugged one shoulder. What good would a tripod be without any collodion, hypo solution, or glass? "The legs might be fixable. Make yourself a stool out of it."

Standing, Claude still clung to the stained papers and destroyed photos. He searched the attic room, turned in a circle, then said, "Do you have a garbage can? I want to help clean up the mess."

*Hah,* Phillip thought. *As if that would solve anything or win my trust back.* Even though the pages were impossible to separate from one another, the idea of tossing the photos into the rubbish heap made Phillip's stomach twist. Those were the photos he had practiced his skills on, had learned with, invested both time and money into. Some of them had turned out as good as anything he had seen in New York, and he was proud of them. Others had sentimental value, like the ones from Parley's Canyon. Somewhere in that stack were probably the shots he had taken by the old craggy tree.

But what was the point of keeping them now when they were stuck together? Angry, he raked his fingers through his hair, then pointed to the stairs. "The garbage is out back."

Claude hopped into action, hurrying toward the stairs like a small child trying to please a parent. Halfway down, right before his head disappeared below the floorboards, he paused and grinned. "I'll help you get this place as good as new in no time. You'll see."

He scratched his cheek with his little finger, revealing a cut on his arm with a streak of red through it—a cut from some glass, probably. He hefted his load and raced down the stairs and out the back door before Phillip could say anything else.

Phillip walked to the other window and looked down to the backyard, where Claude marched to the trash pile beneath the birch and dumped his load. He studied his palm, picked something from it, then wiped both hands on his pants and winced. He probably had other small cuts from the glass. The nasty scratch on his forearm was visible from the window. Claude wiped the blood off, then hurried back inside. Phillip stepped away before Claude reached the attic room again.

Phillip couldn't quite believe his brother's motives were altruistic. There was something more to his sudden helpfulness, he was sure. *If he thinks this will make everything all right, he's out of his mind. What's he really up to? Is he trying to make me think he's changed? Why?*

Without a word, Claude made four more trips to the trash heap. Phillip stood at the window over the street and ignored him, letting him work. It wasn't until Claude began sweeping glass shards from the floor that Phillip spoke, still gazing over the southern side of the city. "Why are you here? Are you doing this so I'll think you're great and won't say anything to Hannah about Cybil?"

Claude's head snapped up. His grip tightened on the broom. Phillip didn't say another word, but he watched Claude's Adam's apple bob as his brother swallowed hard. "*Have* you said anything?"

Phillip shook his head. "Not yet."

His brother nearly collapsed with relief against the broom. "You won't, will you?"

"Why shouldn't I?" Phillip said, turning on him. "What assurance do I have that Hannah isn't in any danger of being hurt like Cybil was?"

"She *isn't* in any danger," Claude said curtly. "You can be sure of that. For starters, we're never left alone. For another, I respect and love Hannah too much to do something like that to her. I've promised myself I'll never, ever do that again. *Ever*." He looked at Phillip and glared, then started sweeping in stiff, quick strokes.

"But Hannah has already been hurt by you, and I don't just mean physically. Her reputation around town is destroyed. Meanwhile, I've searched this entire attic for any scrap of that photo, but even the negative was shattered. I wrote to Marie asking for her help, but I haven't heard back. I'm doing everything I can to vindicate her, but it's like swimming uphill—and I'm not the one who did anything wrong. And your idea of fixing a problem is sweeping up?"

The broom hesitated. Claude pushed it, and it dropped to the floor. "It's a start, isn't it? I ruined your studio, so I'm trying to help clean it up. I wasn't thinking about Hannah when I came over here. I was thinking about what I did to my brother. I was trying to make it up to you."

Phillip shook his head. "You *can't* make this right. Cleaning it up is like putting a bandage on a wound. The only way to fix it is to replace all the equipment, all the photographs."

"But—but that's impossible." Claude's eyebrows drew together. "I can't replace the photographs. And the equipment costs so much . . . The only money I have is from the sale of the farm, and that's supposed to get me started on my own place when I get married, and—"

"Exactly." If Claude were to genuinely try making amends, replacing even some of the equipment would be enough. But he wouldn't want to go even that far, and Phillip knew it. Significant sacrifice—discomfort and inconvenience—weren't part of Claude's understanding. Phillip eyed Claude, who had picked up the broom again. He was slowly sweeping a pile into the metal dustpan, looking far less cheerful than he had only moments ago.

Phillip sighed aloud as Claude filled the dustpan. Destroying the studio was bad enough, but Hannah mattered much more. Phillip took the broom away. Claude opened his mouth to protest, but closed it when Phillip held the broom out of reach. "Tell you what. I know how you can make this up to me, and it doesn't entail a lot of time or money."

For a moment, Claude's countenance lightened, but just as quickly they clouded again. "What's the catch?"

"Clear Hannah's name."

Claude didn't react at first, as if the cogs in his mind were trying to sort out exactly what that meant. Phillip rested the broom against a window. The idea that had sparked in his mind a moment ago was growing, and the more he thought about it, the more he liked it. "Everyone in town must be informed of the situation—the *truth. Everyone.* And as many people as possible throughout the rest of the valley."

With a step backward toward the wall, Claude shook his head. "First off, that's impossible. Second, there's no reason for that. It would be enough to speak with some neighbors and a few ward members. Even that's more than is needed—and plenty to humiliate me for life." He moved toward the broom, but Phillip put his arm out and stopped him.

"Haven't you heard what people are talking about on the street?"

Claude's guilty face showed that he certainly had. Phillip knew the stories made Claude out to be a victim and a hero, which would make countering the stories and facing a bruised ego that much harder to do. "It's not as bad as all that . . ."

"It's *worse* than that. You heard from Bishop Hansen what people are saying. Ben and Bethany heard the same at the theater. You know full well about the editorial. The story is everywhere. Have you heard the names they're calling Hannah? I think I'm being generous in keeping the job within the confines of the city."

Claude scoffed. "Oh, please. What do you expect me to do? Stand on a crate at every street corner and read a statement about it at the top of my lungs? Knock on every door in the city and explain?"

"If that's what it takes," Phillip said. "Provided I get to read the statement beforehand and make sure it's perfectly clear that *you* behaved like a fool and that Hannah is completely and utterly innocent. But I was thinking something more along the lines of an advertisement in the paper plus a declaration at the theater."

"This is nothing but crazy," Claude said, heading for the stairs and waving his hands as if swatting the idea away like an annoying mosquito. "I'm not making myself into a laughingstock. In a few weeks, all of this nonsense will be forgotten. We'll go on with our lives. When Hannah's well, I'll ask her to marry me, and if there's still any question in people's eyes of her worthiness, that will show them the truth better than anything I could do now."

Could Claude really be so dense? "First off, things *won't* just go away, and even if they did, you're the one who started the rumors, so you should stop them."

"I didn't mean to!" Claude yelled. "Those people assumed things that aren't true. I didn't say those things."

"But it's as if you did say them, because people think you did and you haven't refuted them," Phillip said coolly. "And do you really think Hannah would marry you after all of this? One of these days, she'll find out what you did—or she'll remember on her own. Don't you think she'll hate you for it?"

Claude closed his eyes. "I doubt she'll ever remember, but when she hears about it, she'll understand. Hannah's one of the most forgiving people in the world." He moved toward the stairs.

"You owe her and her family a clean name." The tension and urgency in Phillip's voice made his brother pause.

Gazing toward the bottom of the stairs, Claude gripped the banister hard with one hand. "At the expense of my own?"

"If that's what it takes."

Claude turned his head, eyes glassy as he looked straight at Phillip for the first time since coming in. "I don't know if I can."

A hint of a smile tugged at the corners of Phillip's mouth. "That's the most honest thing I've heard you say in a long time."

* * *

The sun hung just below the horizon as Bethany came downstairs with a basket of dirty laundry under one arm. In the full day since the incident at the theater she had almost come to the point of not raging within anymore—although she dreaded going to church tomorrow. Surely everyone would know about the editorial and the theater—and would give her expressions of pity, whether because of her own rushed escape or because of her sister's supposed immoral behavior. Until now, the rumors had been circulating, but now with the worst of them published for everyone to read . . .

She would have to find a way to tell her father tonight. He couldn't go to church without knowing.

Entering the kitchen, she blew a piece of hair from her face, then reached over to pick up the used washcloths from the kitchen counter to add to the pile in the basket. Her hand stopped midair when she noticed her father sitting at the table. Pale, with bloodshot eyes, he sat still as tears slid down his cheeks.

"Father!" She dropped the basket and rushed to his side. "What's wrong?" Her heart pounded with dread. Only once had she ever seen her father cry—the night her mother died.

Elbows on the table, he wearily took off his spectacles and combed both hands through his hair, then pointed at the newspaper clipping sitting on the table in front of him. Bethany didn't want to look at it; a heavy feeling in her middle told her what it was, and a glance confirmed it. The ragged edges suggested that someone—perhaps a "well-meaning" neighbor—had torn it from the paper and passed it on to the bishop. She had burned their copy, hoping her father would never read the atrocious lies. She berated herself for not telling him about the fiasco sooner.

Bethany scooted a chair over and sat in it. "Father, I'm sorry I didn't tell you. I meant to, but—" Her voice cut off. The paper had been out nearly a week, but she had harbored a slim hope that perhaps her father would never see it. Now, she had no idea what she could say to comfort him. She could imagine what he felt—something close to what she had felt in the theater.

"What would Sarah think if she could see how her daughter has been so maligned?" Bethany's father spoke listlessly to himself. He gestured with disdain toward the paper. He turned it over so the masthead, *Deseret News,* couldn't be seen.

"I'm sure Mother would be saddened by it, too," Bethany offered.

He went on as if he hadn't heard her. "When she left us, I vowed to do my best to raise our daughters as she would have, had she been allowed to stay. I tried to instill values into our daughters, to teach them the correct paths."

A prick of fear shot through Bethany. Surely her father didn't believe the article. "You have done all of those things, Father. You know Hannah is innocent, don't you?"

"Yes," he conceded, his voice wavering. "But what good is the truth when one's reputation is soiled to this degree? Your mother and I were determined to see you and your sister wed to good men. No good man will look past this."

"Claude still seems interested in her," Bethany said quietly, hating her own words.

"You call him a good man?" He shook his head. "Now, both of your chances might be ruined."

The look on his face convinced her that even though it wasn't her secret to share, she had to say it anyway. "I think Phillip might want to court her, too."

The slightest glimpse of hope seemed to jump into his eyes. "Do you think so?"

"I think so," she repeated.

"If only she might have such a husband."

"Oh, Father." Bethany put her hand on his arm, and he virtually crumpled at her touch and cried again, his shoulders shaking with emotion. She didn't dare comfort him by declaring that she had a good prospect in marrying Ben Adams. She could scarcely acknowledge the possibility in her own mind. And besides, that didn't solve the problem of Hannah's reputation. She frantically tried to find something to say. "Remember what you've always said, Father, 'This too shall pass.'" Immediately she bit her lip, hating how trite the phrase sounded. An idea flashed before her mind, and with it, a spark of hope. "Father, maybe we can send a rebuttal to the paper, a letter refuting everything in the article. We could clear Hannah's name, and—"

"No." The single word stopped her speech. He put a hand on her arm, and Bethany looked at him in surprise.

"Why not? It would be the simplest way—fight fire with fire."

"An eye for an eye? Is that it?"

"That's not what I meant," Bethany began.

"What would such a thing accomplish, really?" her father said wearily. "We have no proof of her innocence. No argument beyond our faith in our own flesh and blood."

"But Hannah is innocent!"

"I know that," he said, tapping his chest with his fingertips. "And *you* know that." He shook his head. "But a letter in the paper with only our names will not convince anyone else. And I'm afraid that as a bishop I shouldn't tangle myself in matters of local gossip." His face crumpled with pain. He looked up at Bethany. "Don't send anything to the paper. Please. It won't do any good coming from either of us. Our hands are tied." After a long sigh, he added, "If only your mother were here. She'd know what to do." He balled up the article and tossed it to the floor. He wiped his palms together as if they were dirty, then lowered his head into his hands again.

Bethany stared at the piece of paper on the floor, hating the fact that her father was right. There wasn't much they could do to fight the rumors. A letter to the editor would come across as so much blustering wind.

"Let's go upstairs." She eased him out of his chair.

"I have no strength left. A thread could lead me." At her urging, he followed, leaning against her, his body frail. Bethany looked for his cane but couldn't find it, so she supported his weight as they made their way step by step. She had never seen her father like this, so broken.

First Hannah, now her father. She prayed a good night's sleep would make all the difference—but what if it didn't? As they climbed slowly, her breath became short and rapid, as if panic were about to overtake her. *I can't be the only strong one in the house.* Anxiety rose like a wave inside her, and Bethany had to force her lungs to take in air and slowly let it out. She had to be able to think, to manage the situation. Losing her head would help nothing.

"Let's get you to bed, Father," she said, leading him to his bedroom.

His eyes no longer focused on anything. He sat on the bed, staring dully at the wall. She took off his shoes and slid his suspenders off his shoulders. Ignoring the nightshirt on its peg, he slowly leaned to the side until his head met the pillow. Bethany gently drew the quilt over him. A slow blink seemed to be his thanks. She stood back and looked over his figure, which looked disturbingly similar to that of a frightened child. Bethany's hand went to her chest, trying to calm her emotions.

*I'm the child. He should be comforting me.*

After taking a deep breath, she leaned down and kissed his cheek. "Father, would you like something to eat? I picked some peaches this afternoon."

In answer he closed his eyes and almost imperceptibly shook his head no. "I'll bring up some water then." A couple of steps from the door, she paused. "Let me know if I can do anything else." She left, closing the door behind her and knowing there wasn't a thing in the world she could do to make the situation better for her father.

*A good night's sleep—that's all Father needs. Then he'll be good as new.*

But as she glanced at Hannah's door and went down to the kitchen to fetch her father's drink, she wasn't so sure.

# CHAPTER 22

Hannah couldn't sleep. She lay in bed, the heavy comforter feeling like dead weight against her legs. Lying in bed day after day had grown so old; she ached to get up and move around. Shifting positions no longer sent pain shooting through her body, unless she lifted her left arm too high, bringing a shocking reminder of the break in her collarbone.

Today Dr. Wood allowed her to get out of bed again to sit in the rocking chair. After weeks of disuse, Hannah's limbs felt as weak as jelly, and Bethany had held her tight so she wouldn't fall as she hobbled the few feet to the chair. A crutch under Hannah's right arm helped somewhat. Once in the rocking chair, Hannah had a blissful hour with her cast propped on a footstool, enjoying every minute of being upright again.

When Dr. Wood insisted that it was time to return to the confinement of her bed, her muscles needed to be reminded of their duty. But now she lay awake in the darkness, unable to sleep and desperately wanting to get out of bed again. When Phillip had left, she had fantasized about abandoning her cast and going on a walk with him, but would have settled for Phillip staying a little longer. His visits, though not all that frequent, were the highlights of her recovery.

*What about Claude?*

Deliberately, she shoved the thought from her mind. Claude was Claude; Phillip was Phillip. She didn't have a dear brother like Phillip to dote on her the way he did. Was it wrong to enjoy his presence so much? He knew her well, and they talked so easily together.

Once again, she had to halt her thoughts, because if she wasn't careful, a stray image or two would sneak into her mind. The thoughts were inevitably of Phillip—his smile, his touch as he handed her another bouquet of flowers, his voice. Other times she'd think back to their childhood and remember quiet moments after his mother had passed away. Like the day she had followed him to the temple foundation and they had shared that quiet moment of friendship. In the days following that, she had purposely gone to work beside him in the fields. At the time she thought she had done it just to be nice. But every hour he had stopped to bring her a drink of water, and as their hands touched, her stomach flipped over itself. Now, as she lay in bed, she remembered the feeling and placed a hand over her middle, having the same sensations.

Every inch of her body felt restless. She had been cooped up for far too long—nearly four weeks now. Her right foot wiggled back and forth restlessly. She punched her pillow and tried to get more comfortable. Nothing worked. She wouldn't be able to sleep unless she got out of bed and satisfied her need to move.

She tossed the comforter off and gently lifted her left leg off the bed. Balancing on her right leg, she reached for the crutch. For the time being, it was supposed to be used solely for making her way from bed to rocking chair and back again—under supervision. Tonight it would help her get around a little more than that. She hobbled step by step, circling her room twice. She felt stronger now than she had that afternoon, although the short walk sent her breathing hard.

She noticed her door standing ajar, and she bit her lip. Earlier that day, Bethany had made fresh bread; Hannah had smelled it baking all morning. Perhaps she could get downstairs to the kitchen and eat a slice with butter. Now that she had experienced a bit of sweet freedom, the temptation to keep moving was too much to resist.

Carefully and quietly, she hobbled her way out of her room and to the stairs, grateful that Bethany no longer insisted on sleeping in the same room with her. Hannah sat at the top of the stairs and gently eased herself down one step at a time, sliding her crutch alongside her. At the bottom, she stood, feeling an odd sense of triumph at sneaking out of her room alone. She put the crutch under her arm and made her way to the kitchen.

Four loaves of fresh bread were lined up on the counter, wrapped in cloths. Hannah leaned the crutch against the wall and lightly jumped her way to the counter. First she lit the small kerosene lamp, sending a warm glow throughout the room. Then she sliced a thick piece of bread, slathered it with butter, and made her way to the table. As she crossed to a chair, she noticed a shadow on the floor and leaned down to push whatever it was out of her way so she wouldn't trip. The object proved lighter than expected—a crumpled piece of paper. Strange. Bethany was notorious for being an immaculate housekeeper—she'd never allow trash to be thrown about the kitchen.

Curious, Hannah picked it up and tossed it onto the table. She pulled out a chair, then dropped onto it, feeling weak. The bite of bread tasted divine—better than it ever had. As she chewed in pure bliss, she absently opened the paper and realized it was a torn section from the weekly *Deseret News.*

*Odd.* The family always read the paper, then used the newsprint for wrapping or kindling. She had never seen an article balled up and tossed aside. A small kerosene lamp sat on the table, and Hannah lit it, then held up the paper so she could read.

Her eyes scanned the words, a sad story about an unnamed young woman, a "Miss H" who had committed immoral acts with a secret beau. "So sad," she murmured to herself, taking another bite. The story felt vaguely familiar, she thought as she paused, and wondered if she had heard it before. Maybe it resembled something from one of the dozens of books she had read while in bed. Perhaps. She read on, whispering the words aloud.

"'Instead of acknowledging her guilt and wrongdoing, the young woman in question continues to insist upon her innocence, concocting a story to clear her name in spite of photographic evidence proving her guilt.'"

Hannah let the paper fall to the table. She leaned against the chair as something about the story niggled the back of her brain, just out of reach. Did she know this woman? Was she a friend? No, she couldn't imagine any of her friends doing such a thing.

*Wouldn't it be sad if the girl were really innocent?*

The idea came without much thought, but once it crossed her mind, it held tight and wouldn't let go. Her finger traced the headline at the top of the article, then smoothed out some of the wrinkles with her palm. She scanned the words again. A single phrase jumped out at her:

*Photographic evidence.*

Would Phillip know about this? Perhaps a colleague had taken the photo or seen it, or . . . Her eyes flitted to an earlier line where the young woman was identified: *Miss H.*

Hannah felt as if the lamp had suddenly illuminated the dark corners of her mind. In an instant, every memory she had forgotten rushed to her mind in perfect clarity. She gasped, dropping the paper like a hot coal. Astonished, she followed the memories as they raced past her mind's eye, one after the other.

The photo of Marie. Waiting downstairs in the store while Claude smashed Phillip's studio to bits. Claude accusing her of being unfaithful. Her begging him to believe that it was Marie in the picture. Racing home blindly, wanting to be alone. Bethany and Ben trying to ask what was wrong. Moving backward toward the house as she cried, refusing to be comforted. Tripping. Falling into the well . . .

Her eyes squeezed shut as it all came back. Every image, every sound. The look in Claude's eyes. The tone of his voice.

"No," she whispered. *"No."*

She pushed her chair away from the table as if the newsprint held some contagious disease. But the truth could not be ignored, and she knew what had happened. She thought of the past weeks, of Claude visiting her and holding her hand, comforting her. Worrying about her. Suddenly her hand felt dirty, and she hardly noticed herself picking up a dishrag from the table and wiping her hand with it again and again. She wanted to remove any trace of Claude's touch. She no longer knew him, a man who would blindly accuse her of something so terrible and refuse to listen to reason. And now it was in the paper. Everyone had read it. Everyone in Salt Lake City thought she had not only kissed another man, but thought she had . . .

Her eyes grew wide at the thought.

It was as if a dear friend had been revealed as a criminal. Who was Claude Adams anyway? Was anything he had ever said to her the truth? Did he always suspect her of unfaithfulness? Had he ever really loved her?

Tears streaming down her face, Hannah hugged herself with her free arm and rocked back and forth. The fingers of one hand wrapped themselves in her hair then clenched tight. "Oh, Claude. How could you?" Unaware of her surroundings, Hannah sobbed uncontrollably. She had trusted Claude with her heart, yet he was the one who had put her in this position to begin with. How could she even start to comprehend what that meant?

Upstairs a door slammed shut, and a moment later Bethany ran down the stairs in her nightgown, a shawl around her shoulders. "Hannah!"

She raced to her sister's side and knelt on the ground. Hannah glanced up, but looked away as Bethany put her hands on her sister's arms. "I heard you crying, and when you weren't in your room . . . What's wrong? Did you fall?"

Hannah shook her head and silently pointed at the paper. Bethany looked at it only long enough to recognize what it was. Her forehead wrinkled. "You—you read that?"

Closing her eyes, Hannah nodded. "Oh, Bethany, I remember now. Everything. It all came back." She leaned forward and collapsed in her sister's arms.

Bethany rose enough to sit on a chair and hold her sister, stroking her hair. "I'm so sorry."

"How could he do this and then pretend nothing ever happened?" Hannah pulled away. "And why didn't you *tell* me?"

Tears slipped from the corners of Bethany's eyes. "I wanted to. Oh, how I wanted to. But Dr. Wood said you probably wouldn't believe me if I did. And if you did believe, bringing up the trauma would hurt your chances of getting better."

Hannah searched Bethany's eyes and was finally convinced that her sister hadn't withheld the information willingly. She lowered her head. "I might not have believed you," she admitted, hating the fact. She wouldn't have believed it, because she thought she knew Claude

Adams. "I still have a hard time believing it now, even though I remember it happening—even though it's in the newspaper." She looked away from the page and wiped her cheeks. When she spoke again, she stammered, a bit afraid of what the answer would be. "Do—do a lot of people know who *Miss H* is?"

After a deep breath, Bethany answered slowly. "If Dr. Wood knew you had read that, he'd tell me to hold my tongue about this, but—"

"Please tell me everything. I can't bear not knowing the whole story."

Bethany nodded in agreement. "You need to know. The answer is yes—everyone knows it refers to you. And some believe the lies."

If she could have, Hannah would have raced outside into the night, screaming at the sky. Instead she was powerless against the feeling of the world closing in on her, crushing her entire body. She shook her head, imagining what life would be like going to stores or church functions with everyone whispering and pointing fingers. If Claude hadn't believed her, why would anyone else—especially after of the so-called "photographic evidence"? She would wager no one but Claude had seen the picture since that fateful day.

"How can I ever show my face in this city again?" Her tears had begun to dry, replaced by a painful ache in her chest. She stared out the window, suddenly knowing why Dr. Wood didn't want her to know the truth.

"I want to go to bed now," she said quietly. *And stay there for the rest of my life.*

Bethany nodded and helped Hannah to her feet, then carried the crutch while she supported Hannah up the stairs step by step and eventually to her bed. Bethany drew the covers over Hannah's thin form—thinner than usual now after eating so little and exercising less. "Do you need anything?"

"No." *Except a new heart.*

"Would you like me to stay in here tonight?" Bethany drew her shawl tighter around her shoulders and pulled up the chair.

"No. I'd rather be alone." Hannah's eyes stung with dried tears, and she had an aching, empty feeling in her center, like an old hollow tree. She wondered if she would ever feel whole again. She rolled to her right side, away from Bethany, and stared at the wall. "Good night. Thanks for helping me to bed."

Bethany hesitated as if wanting to do more, but she took the hint. "Good night. Call out if you need anything. I'll leave my door open."

Hannah could only manage a nod. *Call out if I need anything. What could I possibly ask her for? I need more than anyone can give me right now. Why, Claude? Why?*

* * *

Hannah stayed awake for hours, watching the shadows of clouds and branches shift as the moon crossed the sky. All she could do was relive every moment she had spent with Claude and wonder if any of it had been real, if she had ever known the true Claude Adams.

The memories were all bittersweet: Seeing his face light up at the sight of her when he first came home. His letter—the sweet, heartfelt letter with language and emotion that bordered on poetry. Their walks through the city together. The time he kissed her in the parlor after giving her the comb. Their first real kiss, when they had met under one of the family's dwarf apple trees. She had sat on a low branch, and he had leaned down, oh so slowly. Her heart had beat harder with each inch of his approach until finally their lips had touched—softly, just long enough for her entire body to tingle before he pulled away.

Such memories were more bitter than sweet now. When they had first happened, she was sure the two of them would be together forever. Yet a single event had changed all of that. For a moment she hoped that Claude really did trust her now, that everything could go back to the way it had been. But within moments she grew so angry at his false accusation that she swore to never speak to him again. Why would she *want* to win such a man back? All she had lost with Claude was something not worth having in the first place. But that didn't make the pain of loss any less.

She pressed her fist against her closed eyes, willing away the headache behind them. *What does it say about me that I was drawn to a man like that?* She thought back to Claude's visits, realizing that he generally talked more about himself and her appearance than anything else. *I want to be more than an accessory. But will anyone consider marriage with me now?* The thought stopped her short.

A few times during the night Hannah heard shuffling in the hall, and more than once she wiped her cheeks dry and held her breath, assuming her sister was coming in. It would be such a relief to cry on Bethany's shoulder. But each time the sound continued past the door. The stairs creaked a few times with Bethany going up and down.

*Maybe she can't sleep, either. I won't trouble her with my heavy heart tonight,* Hannah thought, eventually drifting off to sleep.

It wasn't until an hour or two after the sun had risen that Bethany came in, much later than usual. She looked pale and drawn, but she tried to smile anyway. "How are you this morning?" She arranged Hannah's covers and brushed her hair out of her face.

"How are *you?*" Hannah asked.

Bethany's smile didn't reach her eyes. "I had a long night. Did you get back to sleep?"

"I did, eventually." So like Bethany to be more concerned about Hannah than herself. But the weight of worry pulling on Bethany's shoulders was obvious. *Something is bothering her. If it's not fatigue, what is it?* A sudden possibility dawned on Hannah. "Is something wrong between you and Ben?"

"No, Ben's fine," Bethany said. Then, when Hannah raised her eyebrows, she added, "Really. I haven't seen him for a few days since they asked him to come back and finish up some work so they can shut down the temple block." She smoothed back the worry lines on her forehead and sighed. "Would you like some eggs this morning? I haven't been cooking much lately, so the eggs are piling up. I can make you some before I leave for church."

"I'd like a fried egg. Thank you. I bet Father would love a couple."

At the mention of their father, Bethany flinched. Only then did Hannah realize she hadn't heard any of the normal noises from him—heavy boots down the stairs, gathering firewood outside, his low voice as he read scriptures aloud to himself. She suddenly noticed the cow lowing in the stable—she hadn't been milked yet today. Father never milked the cow so late that she moaned in discomfort.

Taking care not to put pressure on her left arm, Hannah leaned forward. "What's wrong with Father?"

"He's—" Bethany began in her same overly casual voice, but then stopped. "He became a bit ill last night. He's resting. But don't worry. I've notified his counselors that he won't be at church. And after breakfast, I'll milk Margo and bring in the wood. Did you say one egg or two?"

Hannah's least concerns were the cow, the wood, or the number of eggs she'd get for breakfast. "Is he feverish? I want to see him." She flipped the comforter off her legs and sat up.

With one hand, Bethany gently pushed her back down. "I've sent for Dr. Wood, but I'm sure it's nothing. Just a little fatigue and his rheumatism acting up. You know how much travel and church work he's been doing. He felt a little warm last night, so I don't want you checking on him and getting yourself a fever."

Fatigue. Nerves. Worry. Hannah leaned against her pillow and nodded absently. She was sure her father's condition had more to do with *her* than church work. As Bethany left, she lifted her head and asked, "Was it Father who crumpled up the article?"

Bethany hesitated at the doorway, her eyes trained on the floor. That was all the evidence Hannah needed. She sighed in resignation. "Two eggs, please," she said. After a nod, Bethany left. Hannah lay back and closed her eyes, wishing she could reverse time and undo the last several weeks.

*Poor Bethany. Poor Father. Poor me.*

# CHAPTER 23

Claude walked confidently as he made his way to visit Hannah before church. Life seemed to be looking up. After getting chastised by Phillip, he had spent his time at the hotel doing a lot of soul searching, and while he wasn't quite ready to confess his past, he was trying to find the courage to clear Hannah's name—at some point. He still thought the best way would be to marry her and show the world that he loved her. He visited Hannah as often as he dared. While he didn't want to face the bishop more than he had to, it was Bethany's ire he feared more than anything, so he had limited his visits to once a week—or less—on that account alone. But Hannah seemed happy to see him, even if she still didn't remember anything about the day of the accident.

That had him worried, but he figured she would understand if she ever did remember. Hannah would forgive almost anything—and she loved him. And if he knew Bethany, she would keep the editorial as far away from her sister as possible. With any luck, Hannah would never know about the rumors until was after she became Mrs. Adams.

The only thing that really had him worried was that Phillip kept bringing flowers. That made him look better than Claude in Hannah's eyes. But since Phillip was nothing more than a brother to her, Claude wasn't overly concerned, even if Phillip told her about his feelings—which was about as likely as Claude ever going back to New York. It would never happen, not in this lifetime.

If Claude ever felt a little guilty for taking Hannah away, well, at least he was trying in small ways to make amends. He had helped

Phillip clean up his studio, after all. And someday when he started earning some money, maybe he'd help Phillip start replacing his equipment here and there.

He still hated that he'd let himself get so down that he'd turned to drink on the night of the accident. Touching his nose where Ben had punched him, Claude wished he remembered more of what had happened that night. It had been enough to make Ben angrier than Claude had ever known him to be, that's for sure.

But that was all in the past. Never again would Claude use alcohol that way. He was back to proving his devotion to Hannah. He'd never let his temper get the better of him again. He had done well ever since leaving home—it was being in that house full of men that got him all riled up. Leaving was the best thing he'd ever done.

Now, he needed to find some kind of employment. He figured Bishop Hansen wouldn't look too kindly on him as a prospective son-in-law unless he had at least some way to support his daughter after everything that had happened.

As he walked to the Hansens' house before church, his boots were polished, his hair neatly combed, and his scriptures held in one hand, swaying back and forth with each step. Turning into the lane, he began whistling a tune and stopped only after Bethany opened the door. When he saw her haggard face, his final note turned sour.

*Please let me in to see her,* he thought.

"Morning, Bethany. Anything wrong?"

Bethany glared at him. "As if I would share my problems with you."

She still blamed him for everything, but he was used to it. She treated him this way—or worse—whenever he visited, only letting him inside because of Dr. Wood's orders. Just as he raised his foot to come in, she spoke. "Today might not be the best day for you to visit."

"Why? Has Hannah's health taken a turn for the worse?"

"No, she's mending as well as ever . . . physically."

"Then I'll lift her spirits," he said, stepping inside.

"I don't think so." Bethany spread her arms and blocked the doorway.

Claude laughed and stepped back. "Hannah's mending, she's happier than ever, and suddenly you won't let me in? Hmm. What *will* Dr. Wood say?" He peered over her shoulder, gauging whether he dared just barge in, when he saw Hannah sitting at the kitchen table. Relieved, he smiled and waved.

"Hannah. Good morning. Will you tell your sister to let me in?"

"Bethany, let him in," she said quietly.

Her words were exactly what he expected, but her tone sounded like ice. His brow furrowed, and he hesitated. "May I come in then?"

"If you wish." Bethany's flat tone didn't ease his worry. Something wasn't right.

Grudgingly, Bethany stepped aside, her arms folded across her chest. Claude put on his best smile and stepped inside. "Good morning, Hannah."

"Morning." She looked at the tablecloth and avoided his eyes. She still wore the sling, but she was upright and out of bed. He almost commented on the improvement, but she didn't look happy, so he bit his tongue. Her eyebrows were raised, and she seemed intent on picking at some stitching on the linen.

Claude pulled out a chair and sat down across from her. Still she said nothing. He glanced over his shoulder at Bethany, who looked at him viciously. She kept her arms crossed as if that were the only thing keeping her from pummeling him. He wasn't so sure it wasn't. He ventured, "Hannah, is—is something wrong?"

With deliberate movement, she lifted her head. "How *could* you, Claude?"

The words sent Claude reeling. "How could I . . . what?"

Her eyes narrowed. "I remember now. Everything."

"What?" Claude couldn't think fast enough to comprehend what this meant. She remembered? He thought back. *She remembered.* She was referring to their fight in the store. Did she know about the rumors? "Hannah, you have to understand. I was jealous. I was confused. I didn't know what to think. It was all because I love you so much—you have to understand that. It was all because I love you. I went completely out of my head when I saw the picture, but you have to believe that everything I did, everything I said was because I . . . because I *love* you." His words raced one on top of the other. He tried taking her hand, but she jerked it away.

"No! We never loved each other. It was nothing more than an infatuation. *Love* doesn't mean accusations. It isn't making the world think something horrible of the other person. It means trusting them. Believing them. And . . . and . . ." She covered her face with her good hand and burst into tears.

Horrified, Claude sat there, unable to do anything. Hannah was slipping farther away from him by the second. "I'm . . . so sorry," he finally managed. If only she knew how sorry he was that he had said anything of the sort. If only he had learned to control his temper years ago. If only he wasn't so possessive. *If only . . .* "*Truly,* if you knew how sorry . . ."

She lowered her hand and glared at him as tears streaked down her cheeks. "Have you read the paper? Do you know what people think I've done?"

"You—you saw that?" He could feel his face draining of color. As if she were fading away, Hannah was slipping out of his reach. The prize he had longed for, had planned for. He had spent weeks imagining what it would be like to have her on his arm as his wife. Gone.

"You are nothing but a cad," Hannah said. "A useless, spineless, lying cad."

"Hannah, please. If you'd just listen to me and let me explain—"

"In the same way you listened and let *me* explain?" Her face crumpled and she shook her head. "I want nothing to do with you."

Panic welled in his chest, but he wasn't about to let her go so easily. He put on a sweet, calm voice, leaned toward her, and tried again. "Hannah, please. Let's discuss this rationally. You know I love you."

Behind him, Bethany snorted. He ignored her and leaned forward, hoping against hope that Hannah would bend.

She leaned in as well, and for a moment hope returned with full force. Then she spoke. "No. You don't love me. And I *certainly* don't love you." With one arm, she shoved him away. "Leave now," she said, adjusting her silverware as if nothing untoward had happened.

Claude stood, but he didn't want to leave. Walking out of the house meant certain defeat. "Please, Hannah. Let me prove myself to you. I'll do anything—"

"You already proved yourself by showing your true colors. So *good-bye.*"

"But—"

"I said good-bye in words, but I'll say it differently if I have to." She reached for a glass of water, lifting it into the air as if ready to throw it at him. "Go."

He flinched as if the glass had already flown through the air, then he raised his hands in surrender. "I'm going, I'm going." He had to walk past Bethany, who wore a triumphant smirk on her face. Claude glanced down to make sure she wasn't holding a glass as well. He pushed open the screen door and paused. "Hannah?"

In answer, she hurled the glass through the air, and it shattered beside his head on the wall, splattering water on him. He jumped in surprise, looked at the mess on the floor, then nodded. "Very well then. If that's how you want it. But you'll regret this someday, and when you do, remember that you brought it upon yourself."

Bethany took a threatening step toward him, so he hurried out the door, letting it slam behind him.

*Someday she'll be begging me to take her back,* he thought as he strode toward the chapel. *Just wait and see.*

* * *

After Claude left, Bethany tentatively sat at the table across from Hannah. "Are you all right?" She expected to see Hannah crying, but although her eyes were red-rimmed and seemed to water, her cheeks were dry. "Are you all right?" she asked again, this time touching her sister's arm.

Hannah's gaze left the table and fell on Bethany. "It's over. I told him to leave."

"I know." Bethany couldn't find anything else to say that wouldn't sound trite. "I'm sorry."

Closing her eyes, Hannah said, "I just wish I understood why he did this to me. I'll never understand him."

Bethany didn't have an answer to that, but she had to pause before speaking so that her emotions wouldn't run away with her.

"Perhaps it's best to know someone's true character early, before it's too late."

"You're right," Hannah said with a sigh. "I suppose I'm most sad for what I thought I had, not for what I've actually lost with him." She put her hand over Bethany's. "Would you mind giving me some time alone?"

"Of course not," Bethany said. "I'll just clean up the glass so you don't have to see it. Why don't you go back upstairs and rest for a spell?

"Thank you." Hannah gave a pained half-smile.

Bethany helped her upstairs and settled her into bed. On her way out, Hannah called, "Please shut my door." Hannah's voice sounded strained, as if she were holding back tears.

"Of course," Bethany said, smiling grimly as she left. "Call if you need anything." Heading for the stairs, she paused by her father's door, which was still shut. He wasn't up, yet sacrament meeting was about to start. Was he even aware that it was the Sabbath?

She had sent notes to his counselors asking them to take care of any church business for the time being. She wondered how long her father would be in bed—and how long she would be able to keep her father's emotional collapse a secret if it went on for long.

She went back down and swept the shattered glass, then sopped up the water that had splattered onto the floor and the wall. That done, she lowered herself to the top stair and rubbed her temples as she thought of everything she needed to do that day. She had already fed and watered the animals, although their stalls needed to be mucked out. She had milked and fed the cow. The wood pile was completely empty, so while chopping wood wasn't the best of Sabbath activities, it needed to be done—at least enough to get through the day. Maybe Ben would come by tomorrow and chop enough for the rest of the week.

Tuesday would mark four weeks since the accident. Four weeks without Hannah to help out around the house—double the work and half the time to do it in, since Bethany also had to care for Hannah. Her regular laundry day had come and gone without any clothes getting clean. The orchard needed tending; if she didn't start putting up peaches, they'd rot. The garden was nearly overgrown. The mending pile now resembled a small mountain. It seemed that every day, no matter how hard she worked, more and more built up. Soon she'd be crushed under the weight of it all.

A knock suddenly sounded on the side door, followed by a cheery, "Hello?"

*Ben.* Bethany stood, straightened her dress, and smoothed her hair, grateful she hadn't cried—yet. She went to the kitchen and opened the side door. "Ben! It's so good to see you!"

He was dressed in his Sunday best, carrying his scriptures in one hand and a canvas bag in the other. "I was on my way to church and thought I'd stop in. Any chance you can come this week?"

Glancing over her shoulder, Bethany said, "I thought I would, but no."

"Why? Is Hannah worse?" Ben stepped inside, concern on his face.

"No, actually. Her memory returned."

His eyes widened. "It did? That's terrific!"

She smiled wanly. "Yes, but now she's facing everything that Claude did." Bethany sighed. "She's heartbroken. He came by a few minutes ago."

Ben grunted under his breath. "And what happened?"

"She sent him packing." Bethany chuckled. "And hurled a glass of water at his head."

"Good for her," Ben said with a laugh. "So she needs you to stay with her today."

Bethany nodded. "But I'll try to come to church next week." Hannah needed her, so did her father, and she had a hundred chores that needed doing today. But she wouldn't complain about any of it. This was her cross to bear. And truly, she reminded herself, she wasn't the one with the tarnished reputation, knitting bones, or newly returned painful memories. She gestured toward the table. "Do you want to come in for a minute?"

They sat at the table, and only then did Bethany realize how messy the kitchen had become. She hadn't swept the floor yet today—other than the glass—and there were still dirty dishes from yesterday.

With any luck, a bachelor like Ben wouldn't notice such things—or care if he did. But she cringed anyway.

Ben plopped the canvas bag onto the table. "I thought I'd bring by one of my sad baking attempts from yesterday," he said as he opened it up. He pulled out four small cinnamon cakes with brown sugar sprinkled over the tops. "They taste pretty good, and they didn't burn or anything," he added with a grin. "Have one."

A single bite melted with sugary sweetness in her mouth. It tasted like heaven. "You made these?" Bethany asked, amazed.

"Had some extra syrup lying around," Ben said with a shrug, but then grinned. They both knew that he had gone to special effort to make her a treat. And it *was* delicious.

They ate their cakes, talking with one another until nothing but a few crumbs remained. By then it was time for him to leave—he would probably be a little late to sacrament meeting as it was.

"Thank you for coming by," Bethany said, "and for the cakes. Maybe you can teach me how to make them sometime."

Ben laughed. "You can out-bake me any day, and you know it." He squeezed her hand and kissed her cheek. "I'll see you later."

She watched him walk away, wishing she could call him back and say that she was miserable, that the wood pile was empty, that she felt ready to collapse in tears, that her father lay in bed. At the end of the lane, Ben turned and waved. She waved back, then closed the door, leaned against it, and wiped her eyes.

* * *

Ben and Phillip met up at church and sat together in a pew near the back. They searched for Claude but didn't find him. They hadn't seen him but a moment or two since he'd moved into the hotel—once at Phillip's studio, and the few times he had returned home to retrieve something he needed. It wouldn't be his first week missing sacrament meeting.

When Brother Marks, one of the counselors, stood up to begin the meeting, Ben's eyebrows came together. Where was the bishop?

"We have to excuse Bishop Hansen today because of illness," Brother Marks said from the podium. He went on to announce the opening hymn, but the counselor's words stuck in Ben's mind. Illness? Did he mean Hannah's? It had sounded like the bishop was the one who was ill. Why hadn't Bethany said anything?

Throughout the meeting, Ben debated whether to go back to the Hansens' after church and find out. If Bethany's father were ill, she could use all the support she could get. On the other hand, she might skin him alive if she'd kept the information from him for a reason—such as pride. And if the bishop weren't ill, she might get upset anyway for him thinking she *would* hide something like that. He couldn't win.

The postlude music finally began, and the brothers stood to go. Members filed out in front of them, several shaking their hands. As they headed toward the doors, Phillip looked back. He paused and pointed. "Is that Claude?"

Ben turned around. Sure enough, there making his way through the crowd, was Claude, polished and combed and at church for once. Ben moved toward the doors, but Phillip put a hand on Ben's arm.

"Let's wait for him."

The two stood aside to let the ward members pass. The building was nearly empty by the time Claude reached them. He greeted them with little more than a nod.

"I've missed you at home," Phillip said.

Ben highly doubted the truth of *that.* By the look of disbelief in Claude's eyes, he did too. It said something about Phillip's character that he was so willing to reach out to the one who had hurt him most.

"I'm sorry for what you're going through," Phillip tried again.

Claude glowered at him, then looked away. "You don't have any idea what I'm *going through.* Hannah threw me out. My life might as well be over."

"Look," Ben snapped. "We're your family. We can't excuse the way you've treated Hannah and allowed the rumors to spread, but we're still family. Your own brother—who's future you've likely ruined—is trying to reach out. But because you're miserable, you think it's all right to act like a melodramatic half-wit and make everyone around you miserable, too?"

"You don't know what it's like," Claude said, raking his fingers through his hair, making it stand on end. "You don't understand the pain of losing the love of your life."

*For heaven's sake.* Ben had to resist smacking his brother upside the head. Claude wasn't the only man in the world to ever be lovesick. Ben himself had felt his heart break before, as had thousands of others through time. It didn't make Claude unique.

Phillip touched his arm and said quietly, "*I* understand."

Claude laughed—a high, piercing sound that echoed through the chapel, now empty save for Brother Marks, who stood back, looking uncomfortable. "Oh sure, you pined after her with your pathetic little heart, but you never *had* her heart to lose." Claude tapped his chest. "I did."

No longer able to stand his brother's callousness, Ben headed for the door, but at the threshold, he turned around. "Claude, you think we can't understand? Maybe it's you who can't. Do you have any idea how painful it must have been for Phillip to watch you and Hannah cooing like lovebirds? Do *you* understand *that?*"

For a second, Claude's mouth opened, but he quickly closed it again, as if he knew he had no defense against the argument. Encouraged, Ben went on. "Need I remind you that Phillip, in spite of his own feelings, helped you write the letter that won Hannah over in the first place?"

Lifting his chin, Claude said, "At first. But then she learned to love me without anyone's help. And now I'm worse off than any of you."

Gritting his teeth, Ben strode toward Claude, his hand clenched in a fist.

Phillip stopped him. "Don't, Ben. It's not worth it."

Claude must have decided to take his chance at escape, because he hurriedly stomped out. Ben watched him go.

"He's hurting," Phillip said.

"I know," Ben said, shaking his head. He let out a groan of frustration. "I just wish it were a different kind. It's the pain of anger, not the pain of guilt or sorrow. Like those people in the Book of Mormon."

"What do you mean?" Phillip asked.

"You know, 'the sorrow of the damned.' Claude doesn't care so much that he's done something wrong as he hates the consequences of what he's done and wishes he could avoid them." Ben headed for the door. "Good day, Brother Marks. Sorry for the ruckus." Brother Marks gave them a hesitant wave as they left.

When they got outside, they could still see Claude striding down the road in the distance. Ben leaned in and clapped Phillip on the shoulder as he said, "I wonder if he's really worried that *you'll* win Hannah over now."

Phillip stopped in mid-step. "You—you think?"

"Yeah, I think," Ben said, still walking. He looked back at Phillip and gave a crooked smile. "And frankly, I hope he's right to worry."

Phillip hurried to catch up. "I don't know," he said. "Hannah certainly enjoys my visits; I can tell that much with my own eyes. But she treats me as nothing more than a friend."

"Could that be because you treat her as a friend?" Ben said, tilting his head in thought.

"Well, what else can I do?" Phillip said, throwing his hands up in frustration. "I almost told her once, but the more time I spend with her, the more I'm just a great friend—and the more grateful I am that I've never said anything. If she doesn't feel the same—and chances are she doesn't—she would just feel cornered. And she would pity me." He sighed heavily and hung his thumbs in his belt loops. "I couldn't bear to have her pity."

* * *

Bethany dried dishes, glanced up, and saw a group of women trotting down the lane toward the house. Curious—and a little defensive for Hannah's sake—she put down the crock she had been washing and picked up a dish towel to dry her hands. She pushed open the porch door to see ornery Sister Shipley striding toward the house in front of a group of women—some of her older daughters and a few Relief Society sisters from the ward. With Sister Shipley at the head and the rest of them trailing behind, they looked like a mother duck and her ducklings. They carried trays of food as they waddled up to the house and stopped at the porch before Bethany.

"We're here to see Hannah," Sister Shipley announced, her hooked nose in the air.

Bethany tilted her head. "I'm not sure if she's up to visitors." *Especially a dozen of them.* But she quavered a bit. The elderly woman had always seemed a bit intimidating. She might be small in stature, but she had a fire in her belly and could get anything she wanted. And apparently, she wanted to see Hannah.

"We *must* see her," Sister Shipley said, wagging a finger as she held a plate of tortes in the other. "We *must.*" And without waiting for Bethany's approval, she pushed the screen door aside and marched into the house. Her ducklings followed behind, leaving Bethany stunned at the door.

"But . . ."

The women placed their baked goods on the kitchen counter before following Sister Shipley up the stairs. Bethany, horrified, followed. She braced herself, praying with her entire soul that Sister Shipley wouldn't call Hannah to repentance, not after everything the family had been through over the weekend. With horror, Bethany noticed a newspaper tucked under Sister Shipley's arm.

*No, oh please, no!*

Bethany reached the bedroom last and saw Sister Shipley sitting in a chair pulled up next to Hannah's bedside. The other sisters stood close by. Bethany expected to see Hannah looking upset, but instead, she was smiling.

Sister Shipley held Hannah's hand, and her usual grouchy-looking face was puckered with intense emotion. "My dear Hannah," she was saying, "We just had to come and tell you that we *love* you."

At those words, Bethany was taken aback. Sister Shipley came to say she loved Hannah?

"And that we support you. We know all the silly things going around right now are ridiculous lies, all of it. As soon as I read that ridiculous thing in the paper, I wrote a rebuttal. It won't come out until this week. Rather punchy, if I say so myself." She unfolded a paper from her pocket and handed it to Hannah, who read it over, laughing a couple of times at Sister Shipley's acerbic wit.

"Thank you, Sister Shipley. But you didn't need to do this," she said.

"I know I didn't. And I know it doesn't fix your problem—everyone knows I'm just a busybody." Sister Shipley's face grew more solemn. "But you need to know that people care about you and that not everyone believes what they read. Everyone in this room loves you."

Hannah bowed her head, overcome with emotion, but Sister Shipley lifted it. "Now, don't you hang your head, young lady. Lift it up and be a woman of God. That's better. Listen now. You need to know that you have sisters in the gospel who love you, no matter what. That's all of us." She leaned in and spoke with conviction. "But even if there was not a soul in the entire world who believed in you, remember that there is only one person's opinion that matters. And He knows the truth. *He* believes in you."

By now, Sister Shipley's wrinkled face had tears streaking down it. She held Hannah's chin cupped in her hand. "Do you understand what I'm saying?"

Hannah nodded tearfully. "I do. Thank you."

Sister Shipley leaned in and kissed Hannah's forehead, then patted her cheek.

"Well then, we're off." She turned to Bethany. "You should have plenty of food downstairs to last you for a spell. Call us if you need anything."

Without so much as a good-bye, Sister Shipley walked out of the room as if at the head of an army. The other women fell behind her and left as well. Bethany hugged herself with one arm and wiped away tears with the other, amazed at the simple kindness. She and Hannah smiled at one another.

*Thank you, Sister Shipley. Hannah needed you today. And so did I.*

# CHAPTER 24

Several days passed, and on Friday Hannah sat on a kitchen chair under the branches of a young oak tree, free of her cast, several thin quilts pulled up to her waist and a book closed on her lap. Above her, green acorns clung to the tree, swaying in the wind. She took a deep breath and let it out, relishing the cool air now that it was September and the summer's heat had abated.

*Thank heavens for Dr. Wood,* she thought, absently running a finger along the spine of the book. If it hadn't been for his insistence that she needed fresh air, she'd still be cooped up in that miserable bedroom where she had spent over a month already. As it was, she didn't even want to go back into the house by way of the kitchen. Just a whiff of the smells that always lingered there—yeast, cinnamon, baked beans—was enough to remind her that the kitchen was a painful room now, a room that brought back the night she had sat at the table, reading the newspaper article, and everything had come crashing back into her mind like a tidal wave.

*So cruel the way the mind works,* she thought. If only she could have remembered bits and pieces at a time. Perhaps then she would have been prepared for the full truth, and she wouldn't have gone through the misery of the last week.

A tall figure walked along the road, his hand brushing the top of the fence as he went. Immediately Hannah's middle tensed, as it did every time she saw someone who might be coming to visit. Her visitors always fell into one of two groups: either they were so sympathetic that Hannah felt she couldn't breathe, or they wanted to call her to repentance—or possibly find out every detail of what she had "really" done. While the well-wishers were numerous and the condemners were few, having any visitors soon grew tiresome and upsetting. Unless it was someone like Sister Shipley, Hannah didn't want to see them. Fortunately, Bethany was usually close by and sent them on their way.

And if this visitor turned out to be Claude . . . She pulled the blanket closer and swallowed as she tried to make the person out. On closer inspection, the person looked much darker than Claude.

*Phillip.*

Hannah sat back with a relieved sigh. Too much time had passed since his last visit. She wished he'd come more often. She could have used a friend like him in the days since she'd read the editorial. She still wished she could tell her mind to Dr. Wood about his ridiculous order not to upset her by telling her the truth. She couldn't be angry with Bethany for following his instructions, but she almost wished she could.

She smoothed out the blanket, hating how each time she saw or heard anything that reminded her of Claude, she grew nauseated and wanted to run away. Running was not exactly an option when she still limped and used a cane to get around. Her foot no longer hurt much, but it was still weak. Technically she wasn't supposed to be walking yet.

"Hannah!" Phillip called with a wave as he turned into the lane. Arms swinging as he walked, he held another bouquet of flowers in one hand, this time blue globes of hydrangea.

She smiled as he drew near, feeling the smile reach her eyes and enjoying the sensation. Of late, she hadn't known much to be happy about. Her heart still fluttered over the brief scare of thinking it was Claude coming again. At least, that's how she explained the beating in her chest as he offered the bouquet and gave a slight bow. She loved how Phillip always replaced her flowers just as the last ones began to wilt.

"For you," he said.

She took them, feeling his strong but gentle fingers brush against her skin, and for a wild moment she wondered what it would be like for his hand to enclose hers. The thought suddenly tightened her throat, and she half worried he could read her mind. *What am I thinking?* She chided herself for a brief moment and had a sudden fear that a gossip would be watching, ready to tell the world that Hannah Hansen was indeed of low moral fiber—something the touch of a hand would never have caused her to fear in the past.

"Thank you," she managed. "They're beautiful."

"You're welcome," Phillip said. "I figured the roses would be brown by now and that you could use some color to liven your room."

"I could. Thank you. It's been a difficult week." She gazed at the flowers. "Did you hear that my memory has returned?"

He nodded. "I did. I wanted to visit sooner, but I thought you needed some peace after that. I imagine it has been hard." He looked up, then back at the ground. "Do you . . . remember everything now?"

She nodded but didn't speak for a second. If she did, she'd cry.

He glanced around at the trees, the grass, and swiped at a fly buzzing nearby. "I didn't know you were spending time outside now."

"Bethany's beside herself over it. She's sure I'll get a cold and catch my death—or worse." Hannah laughed and adjusted her blankets. "I asked her what could be worse than death, but she answered by tucking three blankets around me."

Phillip laughed, then glanced away shyly, seeming unable to come up with something to say. He gestured to the book. "Did I interrupt your reading? Maybe I should let you be alone . . ."

She reached for his arm, sending the bouquet tumbling to the ground from her lap. "No. Please don't go." The force in Hannah's voice surprised even her. She sat back and tried to look more relaxed than she felt. "I mean, I'd enjoy some company."

"All right then." A slight spark brightened Phillip's eyes. He reached down and picked up the blue flowers, set them in her lap again, then looked around for something to sit on. He spied a rusty old milk pail beside the house. After retrieving the bucket, he turned it over and sat on the makeshift stool, so short he had to look up just to see Hannah's shoulder.

She laughed and shook her head. "There must be something better than that. Your knees are practically in your ears."

They both looked around a second time, seeing nothing in the yard that would work for sitting, when Hannah said, "Just fetch one of the kitchen chairs."

Half standing, Phillip paused. "Are you sure Bethany won't have my hide for bringing one outside?"

She waved away the thought. "Heavens no. That's what I'm sitting on." She paused. "But try it with a parlor chair and she'll whip you good."

"Then I'll be right back."

Hannah watched as he went in the side door. She tried to analyze the confusing emotions within her. The fluttering started by the earlier fright hadn't stopped—in fact, it had increased since Phillip had joined her. She could hardly blame it on thoughts of Claude anymore—especially, she admitted to herself, since this sensation was far more pleasant than the anxiety-riddled one usually connected to him. She bit her lip, wanting Phillip to come back quickly so she could feel it again.

*What's happening to me? If I didn't know better, I'd think . . . No. He's never expressed a desire to court me.*

She shook the thought away and took a big breath. Phillip might as well be the dear brother she'd never had. Much like Ben.

*But Ben has never made my heart speed up.*

*Stop!* Such thoughts would never do. Not when her feelings still needed mending over Claude. Not when the chances of Phillip seeing her as anything more than a little girl—a little sister—were about as likely as Hannah herself sprouting wings. Besides, how could she even begin to toy with the idea of caring for a man when she was still trying to put her shattered heart back together? Could she dare trust another man after Claude? At one point she had thought she knew him. She thought she loved him. And she had been proven horribly wrong on both counts.

The side door swung open, and Phillip appeared with the chair. Instead of carrying it with two hands like she would have, he easily hefted it with one arm as he strode toward her. A breeze kicked up, ruffling his hair as he approached, and Hannah had a tender desire to smooth it out. Suddenly she couldn't look him in the eye.

He set the chair down and sat at an angle so they were nearly side by side but could still look at one another. She studied her cuticles intently, feeling awkward and wondering if it was a good idea after all that she'd asked him to stay.

"Are you . . . all right?" Phillip asked, seeming to sense a shift in her mood.

"I'm fine," Hannah said, lifting her head and smiling, but avoiding his eyes. She searched for something to say, then realized she had never asked about his photographic equipment now that she remembered Claude destroying it. "How's your studio?"

One of his shoulders lifted and then fell. "Not so good." She was grateful that he was no longer shielding her from negative information.

"Mrs. Brecken has given me a week to clear out. I can't make the rent, and someone else wants to lease the space for more than I was paying for it anyway. On top of that, I have creditors to pay for the supplies—which I no longer have, of course. I was supposed to use them to make enough money to cover their cost."

"Oh, Phillip, I'm so sorry," Hannah said, all awkwardness gone and replaced with sincere concern. "What are you going to do now?"

Another shrug. "Earn some money somehow, I guess. We have enough for our basic expenses, but I don't have enough to cover my debt, rent studio space, and resupply everything." His mouth curved into a grim version of a smile.

"This can't be the end," Hannah insisted. "You're so talented, and the city needs more photographers. There are so few of you, yet so many people, and so many historic events happening all the time. You can't stop."

"Thanks, Hannah." Phillip seemed to really appreciate her sentiment. "You know, I partly blame myself for this whole mess. If I hadn't taken that photo of Marie in the first place, none of this would have happened. At the very least, I could have mentioned it to my brothers—if only I hadn't promised Marie I'd keep it a secret."

Hannah shook her head and touched his forearm. "This wasn't your fault, Phillip. You're a man of your word. You couldn't have predicted any of this." She looked at her fingers touching his arm and awkwardly pulled back, once more feeling her stomach flip. She clutched her book to her chest and said, "You have to find a way to continue your work."

With a shrug, Phillip said, "If you have an idea of how I can keep going, I'd love to hear it. I need to find another job first of all, and if I do, it'll still take me months if not years to earn enough to get started again. But finding new employment might be tricky. There are a few old-timers like Mrs. Brecken who won't trust me to work for them."

"What? Why?" Hannah asked, turning in her chair to face him. That made no sense. The Adams brothers were hard workers. What could possibly prevent Phillip from finding a job? "There should be plenty of farm work right now with the harvest coming in. Have you tried talking to Brother Johansen?"

"Yes. He's one of those old-timers who first settled the valley. The newer folks who don't know the story don't care. But they're also struggling to pay their own way and can't hire someone else. Any extra money goes to the temple fund, not toward a hired hand."

"What *story?*"

Phillip rubbed his hands together and leaned his arms against his thighs. "You don't know?" Now, he was the one avoiding eye contact, and she had no idea why.

"Truthfully, I don't know what you're talking about." But she wanted to. Whatever it was, it clearly went deep, and she wanted to know everything about Phillip. The thought made her a little dizzy.

He smiled. "You probably don't know about it because your father is one man who doesn't hold it against me. The story is about my father."

Hannah adjusted her position, suddenly feeling uncomfortable. "You grew up without him. Is there something else? Let me guess—he robbed a bank," she added, trying to lighten the dark cast that had come over Phillip's eyes.

He looked up, and their eyes caught. They both laughed, but Phillip smiled wanly. "For all I know, he might have."

Hannah's lips pursed, confused. "I don't understand. I'm quite sure your father did no such thing, but even if he had, what does that have to do with you? Why, you came back from an honorable mission, for goodness sake!"

"I'm amazed you haven't heard the story from someone." He told her the basics of his parentage, including how he found out by overhearing his mother talk with a friend and calculating the years.

She stared at the grass and thought hard. "You know, now that I know the story, I remember hearing something similar at a quilting bee once. It was two older women talking, and they didn't use names, but they all seemed to know exactly who was being talked about. They predicted dire things to come from the boy. I was disgusted that they'd place any blame on an innocent child. Some other women got upset and refused to let them keep talking such nonsense, and I never did hear the story again." She looked up at him and shrugged. "It was always 'her son,' so I assumed it was a recent thing. I didn't know they meant you—or that 'her son' was a grown man." She shook her head. "Your poor mother. But it still makes no sense. None of that has anything to do with you being an unfit worker."

With a shake of his head, Phillip said, "I wish all women were like you." His eyes turned down, and Hannah wanted so badly for them to light up with their previous spark.

"People really hold that against you?" Hannah tried to comprehend it but couldn't.

"A handful do. Most recently, it was Mrs. Brecken. She didn't want to rent me the space because of it, but Claude vouched for me, and she agreed because of him."

Hannah sat there perplexed and disturbed. One's birth had nothing to do with his worth or potential for righteousness. If a bad father were an indication of a child's evil nature, Abraham himself should have been shunned. And if the reverse were true—that a righteous father yielded righteous sons—there would have been no Lamanites. And before her was the same kind of evidence. From all she had heard of the elder Brother Adams, he had been a good, righteous man. Yet Claude hadn't exactly turned out to be the most honorable person.

"It's not pleasant living under such a shadow," Phillip said. "The worst is that the story is true. There's no denying my 'real' father was an utter scoundrel."

A glimmer of understanding dawned on Hannah. "You know firsthand—far better than I do—about people seeing you differently due to no fault of your own."

Phillip nodded, his lips pushed together. "I'm sorry you have to go through anything like that. It's one thing for a man—I can ignore it most of the time, and I do. And as time has gone on, the rumors have faded more and more. Fewer people care now than used to. Fewer know about it. Life was easiest during my mission, when no one but my brothers knew." He glanced over at Hannah's worried expression. "Oh, don't worry about me. I'll find a way to make some money. The stigma of my parentage won't last forever, and if it continues to be a problem, maybe I'll just move away." He gave a light chuckle at the last idea, then sobered when he saw Hannah's face. "I'm sorry. I didn't mean that you would need to do the same."

"I know." She sighed sadly. "I hope I won't end up with two choices—either staying home all the time or moving away to escape the rumors."

Phillip laughed and said lightheartedly, "You know, we could always leave this place together. Then no one could bother either of us." His laugh suddenly turned into a cough, and he avoided her gaze. Hannah flushed, thinking how nice it would be to flee with Phillip. But immediately she looked away and hoped her thoughts weren't transparent on her face. If Phillip suspected she felt anything along those lines, she'd feel uncomfortable and start acting strange around him. What if he stopped his visits and their friendship fell apart?

She cleared her throat, hearing the beating of her heart. If it grew any louder, Phillip would be able to hear it, too. They sat in silence for an awkward minute, and then Phillip finally spoke.

"It would be fun to travel with a friend, though," he said, "even if we couldn't ever really do such a thing."

*Friend.* Hannah smiled and agreed, then sighed with relief.

# CHAPTER 25

One Monday night, Dr. Wood came over for one of his visits, which were now much less frequent. "Hannah's mending quite well, I'm happy to say," he told her father and sister as if she weren't in the room. "It's been six weeks now, so the next step is getting her strong again. She's lain in bed so long that her muscles are weak. And putting weight on that foot will take some getting used to. I want her out of bed every morning, walking up and down stairs, and getting some strength to her muscles. No more lounging around."

Bethany had to hide a smirk forming at the corners of her mouth. She knew that Hannah would be angry at the implication that she had been lazy rather than following doctor's orders.

Hannah needed to get out of the house to prove her innocence. Even before showing Dr. Wood out the door, Bethany knew what Hannah's first outing would be: the upcoming community dance on Friday night. The timing couldn't have been better. Hannah wouldn't be able to dance, but she would be out in public, looking beautiful and unashamed.

Bethany pursed her lips and smiled to herself. *That will show those pesky gossips.*

* * *

Friday night Hannah sat in the buggy, wearing her yellow silk dress. The doctor had said she'd lost weight, and he was right. Her dress was loose, and being all dolled up after spending weeks in nothing nicer than muslin and calico felt odd. So did having her hair swept up and wearing gloves again. She sat beside Bethany as Ben drove them to the dance. A nervous warmth tingled all over, and even with her gloves on, her hands felt cold and clammy. She still wasn't used to having the sling removed, so her arm felt loose and wobbly. She held it close to her waist, where her ribs stuck out.

"I didn't realize I had grown so thin," she said, smoothing the fabric and then twisting her torso side to side in the loose bodice. "I look a sight."

"You're beautiful as always," Bethany said, putting her hand over her sister's.

Hannah knew that Bethany hadn't entirely meant what she said. Earlier that evening Hannah had taken a hard look at herself in the mirror. She knew her cheeks were pale—well beyond the classic "alabaster" white from books, and beyond what any amount of pinching could help. Beneath her eyes were clear rings of blue. They stemmed from stress and fatigue, Dr. Wood had said, and would fade in time. Regardless of their cause, they were unsightly, and Hannah had no desire to walk into public appearing unwell. If tonight was supposed to make people believe she was not guilty of wrongdoing, she wasn't so sure her appearance would help. Instead it might spur rumors about how guilty she supposedly felt—that "you could tell by looking at her."

Ben stopped the carriage in front of the ward building. "You're sure you want to do this?"

Hannah was not even close to sure.

"We'll be fine," Bethany said, her hand already around Hannah's arm, leading her out of the buggy.

"Can we leave after a couple of hours?" Hannah said. "I don't think I'll have the strength for more than that."

"Of course," Ben said. "You two go enjoy yourselves. I'll take the buggy around back and be inside in a few minutes."

Bethany gently but urgently led Hannah toward the doors. Hannah suddenly wanted to call out to Ben and beg him to take her home, where she could burrow underneath her quilt and hide. But that was the last thing that would help her face people again—Bethany was right about that. So she went inside.

When they first walked in, Hannah limped on her foot and stayed close to Bethany. No one seemed to pay her any notice. She kept her hands clenched together and tried to stay calm, preparing for the first person to speak to her. The pews used for Sunday meetings had been pushed to the sides of the walls. Fiddles, a banjo, and a trumpet played in the background as several couples on the floor went through the formations of a quadrille. The sisters watched a dance or two and were clapping in time to the rhythm when Ben snaked his way through the crowd and greeted them.

"How are we doing so far?" he asked as he took Bethany's arm.

"Nervous," Hannah said with a laugh, then hurriedly followed up with, "but well. Better than I expected."

The three of them stood around for a while, and Hannah felt more and more comfortable—and slightly guilty for being the cause of the two of them staying close by. "Ben, take Bethany out for the next dance," she said. "I'll wait for you by the refreshment table."

Ben and Bethany eyed one another. Hannah could tell they liked the idea but were hesitant to leave her alone. "Really. I'll enjoy myself more knowing you've had at least one dance together. I'll be right by the table when you get back, and then you can be my shadows the rest of the evening." Even as she said the words, she knew they were only partially true. She would feel better knowing they had danced once, but she'd also be horribly uneasy until they returned to her side.

"Are you—are you sure?" Bethany asked.

"I'm sure," Hannah said with a grin as she held back her nerves. "Go," she added with a wave of her hand.

"All right—but just one," Bethany said.

Ben winked, then led Bethany to the formation. As the dance began, Hannah tried to hide behind a pillar. She watched the couples moving in and out. One of the men danced near her, clapping with his back to her. He turned around, and their eyes caught. He grinned. *Phillip.* She returned the smile, relief washing over her at seeing another friendly face.

He mouthed, "I'm on your card tonight," before turning and dancing the other direction. She hugged herself with delight.

She knew she couldn't dance on her foot. Dr. Wood had been quite clear about that. But as the music drew Phillip to the other side of the room, Hannah no longer felt quite so alone. With any luck, he would chat with her after the song ended. She leaned against the pillar and watched him dance.

Near the end of the song, Jared Foley came by. She swallowed hard, wondering if he was intending to talk to her. Jared was one of the most handsome men in the city, a boy most girls had dreamed of at some point. His dark hair and eyes were something out of a book, and even though Hannah didn't view him romantically, having him stop two feet away sent stabs of excitement through her.

"Good evening, Jared," she managed, surprised it didn't come out as a squeak.

He wore the best suit in the room. His shirt and collar were starched stiff, and Hannah could see the reflection of the candles on the tops of his shoes.

"Hello, Hannah," he said. "I haven't seen you in a while." She was surprised that he even remembered her name. Then again—she groaned inwardly—who in the entire city *hadn't* heard stories about the infamous "Miss H"? Maybe he was mocking her.

She flushed slightly—and wondered if it helped her appearance. "Yes, well, the doctor only recently gave me leave to go out."

"That's nice," Jared said, his tone suggesting a hidden motive. He held out a hand and tipped his head in a bow. He looked over, eyeing her dress up and down. She smiled awkwardly.

"Enjoying the dance?" she ventured.

"Quite," he said and looked away, then looked over again curiously with one arched eyebrow. "Have you . . . had many partners tonight?"

"Me?" Hannah said, gesturing to herself. Jared's question seemed to have a hidden meaning, and she wasn't sure what to make of it. "No. I . . . I mean, we just arrived, but . . ." Her voice trailed off, and she looked around uncomfortably. Should she explain further? "You see," she began, sticking the toe of her boot out from her hem, "I broke my foot not long ago and it's not quite strong enough to bear much weight. I'm afraid I'm here as a spectator only."

Jared put on a gallant smile and edged closer. "But what if *I* were to ask nicely for a turn about the floor?"

She backed a step away. "I'm sorry, Jared, I can't dance even with you." She shrugged.

He matched her step. "But Hannah, tell me. I've heard a few . . . *things* . . . recently, and I'm eager to hear the truth of the matter from the horse's mouth as it were." He put out an arm as if expecting her to take it and go walk with him.

Hannah looked at it and swallowed hard. Was he sincerely asking to know what had happened to her, friend to friend? Or did he have some ulterior motive?

Before Hannah could answer, Marilyn suddenly appeared and said, "Oh, Jared, don't tell me that you're seriously thinking about dancing with *her.*"

Hannah's eyes flashed as Eleanor appeared at Marilyn's side, followed by Rose and Bertha. Hannah had known them all since girlhood, even if they hadn't ever been exactly on friendly terms—and now the four looked like cats that had caught a mouse.

Marilyn spoke above the music. "Why did you come today, Hannah? You had enough sense before now to stay home and not shame your family."

Hannah stared at Marilyn, dumbfounded at her rudeness. She could hardly believe that anyone would be so vicious—so publicly. "Marilyn, this is a private conversation."

"Is it?" Marilyn looked around the crowded room. "This is a public affair." She leaned toward Jared and said rather loudly, "I assume you've heard about it all."

"I've heard," Jared said, nodding. "I was hoping to hear her side of the story. I presume it would be a . . . *colorful* version." He smiled sardonically.

"I have friends who were in the store when Claude found out about it. It's all true, you know," Marilyn said.

"No, it's *not,*" Hannah said, looking between Marilyn and Jared.

"So there wasn't a photograph?" Marilyn said innocently, walking toward her, hips swaying.

"Well, yes, there was, but—"

"You see?" Marilyn said to Jared. He nodded in agreement. Hannah wanted cry out to Jared, to remind him of all the times in school that Marilyn had been the one to gossip and lie. Didn't he remember the time she stole his lunch pail and blamed it on Barbara, in hopes that he'd have eyes for Marilyn instead? It was as if Marilyn hadn't aged a day since the fourth grade.

Since it was useless to appeal to her, Hannah said, "Jared, I've done nothing to be ashamed of. The rumors are false. It was just a misunderstanding." She smiled and stepped toward him. He took a small step back.

Hannah put out a hand, pleading. "Truly, you have no need to worry about being seen with me. It just so happens that I'm not able to dance." She poked the toe of her boot from under her hem again and nodded to it. "My foot isn't quite strong enough. But when I am able to dance again, I'd be honored to be your partner. I'd be happy to walk about the room right now and tell you everything." She walked toward him, arm outstretched.

But Marilyn sidled up to him and took his arm.

By this point, a few conversations around them had hushed, and some people were staring. If Jared wouldn't believe her, would anyone in the room? Hannah took a step backward, wishing she could hide. As if sensing her sudden anxiety, Jared moved forward, as did Marilyn and the girls with her. Hannah felt trapped.

"After all you've done to shame yourself, Hannah," Marilyn said, cozying up to Jared. "I am amazed at the nerve you have to show up and pretend that nothing has happened."

Hannah's eyes began to sting, and a few more groups of people stopped talking to watch the encounter. The dancers on the floor twirled, blissfully unaware of what was happening. Hannah wished she could catch the eyes of Ben or Bethany so they'd stop dancing and come to her aid. How could one dance last so long? "None of it is true. I've done nothing wrong." No one responded. Hannah tried again. "Rose, Bertha," she pled. "You've known me all my life. Why do you believe I would do any of this?"

"She's right, Marilyn," Rose ventured. "There's no proof of any of it."

"What about the photograph?" Jared asked. Apparently his opinion could be swayed if it meant getting a pretty girl like Marilyn on his arm.

"Yes, there was a photograph, but it proved nothing. It wasn't me." Their questions felt like arrows. Hannah's eyes stung with tears. "It was my cousin and her fiancé."

"Then why have you been hiding at home?" Marilyn demanded. "One would think that someone who is innocent would have nothing to hide."

A female voice from the crowd joined in, saying, "Yes, *Miss H,* explain why you've been hiding."

"Stop bothering her," someone else said. "She hasn't done anything wrong."

Hannah turned around—trying to see who had spoken and wanting to cry, *Thank you!* to whoever had defended her—and was summarily ignored. She raised her voice and turned to the sides, facing her accusers, which now numbered around ten, gaining courage. She wished she could free herself from their trap and reach the dance floor, where the rest of the crowd was still enjoying their evening. "I haven't been hiding. I fell down a well and hurt myself. I finally came tonight to show that I have nothing to hide."

Jared snorted and leaned against a column. "So this is all a ploy. You're trying to manipulate us."

"No. Not at all!" Hannah's breath caught, and she searched for another friendly face or voice. Surely beyond this small pocket of angry peers were dozens of people who were rational. She thought of Sister Shipley. Were her daughters here? If she could spy one of them . . .

*Stay calm,* she scolded herself. She wanted to disappear, to go back to the safety of her room. At the back of the group, Claude appeared. She looked at him with hopeful eyes. If he were really sorry, he'd vindicate her. "Claude! Claude, *tell* them."

Everyone turned to face him. His jaw clenched, and he noticed people staring at him. His expression was unreadable as he looked at her. Their eyes locked for just a moment, hers pleading for him to say something. Instead he backed away into the crowd and disappeared. Her stomach dropped as Jared, Marilyn, and everyone else laughed. Nothing she said had helped. Her lungs tightened; she couldn't breathe as she searched the group for a friendly face.

"Claude," she shouted again, panic surging through her chest. "Claude knows the truth—just ask him," she said to the crowd in another feeble attempt.

Marilyn glanced over her shoulder at Claude's retreating form. "Is that why he left?" she asked, her voice derisive. Next to her, Jared smirked.

Hannah's breath came in shallow gasps. Nothing she could say would help now. *Ben, Bethany, where are you?*

"You said you'd be honored to walk about the room with me," Jared said. He paused for effect before saying, "But I withdraw my offer. I wouldn't tarnish my reputation by spending a moment of my evening with the likes of you."

Even though most of the group had egged Marilyn and Jared on, several still gasped at this, as if he had gone too far. Hannah felt the color drain from her face. Her knees weakened, and she wasn't sure if her foot would hold her up much longer.

The crowd parted, and a set of heavy footfalls crossed the wood floor. Jared's expression changed from disdain to curiosity as he looked up to see where the sound came from. A fist that seemed to come out of nowhere punched his face. He spun, stumbled, and fell to the ground, sprawled on the floor. Hannah gasped, and the band squeaked to a stop. The entire room grew quiet.

"Don't *ever* speak to a lady in such a way again!" Phillip stood over him, shaking his fist out from the force of the punch.

Hannah didn't know whether to laugh or cry . . . or to throw her arms around Phillip's neck. He stood over Jared, as if daring him to get up and fight. No one else made a move or a sound; the throng was paralyzed. Jared brought his hand to his face and groaned. Hannah saw with mixed horror and satisfaction that his nose was bleeding. He rose up on an elbow, glared at Phillip, then collapsed.

Taking the action for surrender, Phillip turned to Hannah, who cowered several feet away. He swooped over to her and put his arms around her protectively. "Let's get you out of here."

She could only manage a nod as he led her out of the silent, stifling room. It was a relief to reach the doors and breathe in the crisp night air. Phillip didn't stop walking when they got to the sidewalk outside. "Let's go farther so no one bothers you."

She merely nodded and went with him, deeply grateful for a bodyguard. She glanced over her shoulder to see if anyone followed. The cool air felt shockingly refreshing. Phillip took off his coat and put it around her shoulders to keep her warm. By the light of the chapel door she could make out the silhouettes of several people, but none of them seemed inclined to follow. Phillip kept his arm around her as they walked, making Hannah feel safe. She wished she could lean her head against his shoulder and that he'd pull her even closer.

"They probably think we need a chaperone," she said quietly. "Are you sure you want to be seen with a tarnished woman like me?"

"In their eyes I'm as much of a miscreant as you are." Phillip laughed, breaking the tension of the night air, which was crisp with the oncoming autumn. Hannah laughed too. It felt good as her strained muscles began to relax. He paused and looked over his shoulder. "We're quite a pair here, aren't we? A man and a woman, both with questionable characters, strolling down a dark street alone. The only thing we could do to spark even more gossip would be to—" He broke off so suddenly that Hannah looked up in surprise. He had a silly smile on his face, as if he were embarrassed and trying not to show it.

"What?" she asked, pulling his coat around her tighter and breathing in the scent of it. "I can't imagine what could make for worse talk. After all, neither of us has a reputation to worry about."

Phillip just shook his head and laughed again. "Never mind."

*Neither of us has a reputation to worry about.* The words stung even as she thought them. But at the same time, the admission was a relief. That anyone would treat her in such a way hurt tremendously, but in the end, if Marilyn and the others had opinions that changed as regularly as bedsheets—and were based on something equally flimsy—they weren't friends to begin with. *Do I have any friends outside of my family?* She looked up into Phillip's face. *One at least.*

And in the long run, it mattered more to her what Phillip and the likes of him thought than what Marilyn and Jared thought anyway.

They turned a corner and were out of view of the chapel completely. "Can we rest a moment?" Her foot had started to throb, and she was hobbling on it now; she hadn't walked on it this much, let alone this fast, since the accident.

"Of course," Phillip said, gently leading her to a step in front of a store. He sat beside her. "Is it your foot?"

She nodded. "It aches a little." She paused and licked her lips. "Phillip . . ." Her voice trailed off as she searched for a way to express her emotions. Having Phillip sitting so near made her feel much more than safe—it made her feel alive. But she couldn't admit that to him.

She tried again, this time raising her face to his. "Phillip, thank you for being there for me through all of this."

"You're welcome."

"I mean more than just tonight. Tonight too, of course, but . . . visiting me and bringing flowers and talking with me, and . . ." She covered her face with one hand, hating how awkward she sounded. "You know what I mean, don't you?"

"I think so."

"Aside from Bethany, you've been my one friend through everything. I don't think you can have any idea what that means to me." And then she realized he probably did know—and had always wanted the kind of friend he had been to her.

After a moment of silence, Phillip lowered his head. "Hannah, I have a confession to make." He raised his eyes to hers and cleared his throat awkwardly.

"What is it?" As Hannah searched his face, a thrill shot from her head to the tip of her toes and back again.

"Being your friend was largely a selfish act on my part."

She smiled. "We can both use a friend. I'm glad to be yours."

"Yes, but—" He paused and nodded. "Yes." He smiled, took a breath, and gazed at the starry sky. "Ready to go home?"

She wanted to say no, to insist he finish what he had begun to say. But he had already stood up, so she did too. She slipped her hand through his arm, and they headed for home.

# CHAPTER 26

"I'll be right back," Ben said in Bethany's ear. He kept an eye on Claude as his brother slipped out the door. Spitting mad with his pulse pounding between his ears, Ben pushed through the crowd and raced out after his idiot of a brother, who had stalked behind the chapel.

The night was chilly, and as he ran, his breath came out in white puffs. At the sound of footsteps, Claude looked back at Ben, started, and raced off. Ben gritted his teeth and ran faster, quickly gaining on his brother. Hands out, he gripped Claude by the shoulders and tackled him, pushing him to the ground.

They rolled into a heap, Claude punching and kicking. Ben managed to hold him down. He dodged a punch and pinned Claude down harder. They glared at one another, panting heavily.

"What was *that* for?" Claude said between gasps as he struggled to move.

Ben grabbed Claude by the lapels and pulled him to his feet. "Do you have any idea what you just did in there? You had a chance to fix everything. *Everything.*" Ben shoved Claude away as if his brother disgusted him. He shook his head. "And you threw it away like so much dross."

"What? Just because I didn't say anything? Do you have any idea how hard it would have been to stand in front of a crowd and admit to the world that—"

Ben jumped in. "And do *you* have any idea how hard it was for Hannah to stand in the middle of that same crowd? You just don't get it, do you? You say you're sorry for what you've done to her reputation. Very well. *Show* it."

"What was I supposed to do?"

"Anything," Ben said. "Defend her. Admit that the photograph wasn't of her. Maybe even fight for her like Phillip did."

Claude's eyes narrowed. "*What* did Phillip do?"

"He knocked Jared Foley to the ground for talking down to Hannah."

Claude shook his head, obviously impressed.

"Would you have been able to do that?" Ben already knew the answer; they both did. "Don't you have a shred of decency left in you? You say you're sorry, but you won't face the music like a man." Ben just stared at Claude, trying to make him understand. "For a split second, you had the world in your hand. Hannah looked to you to save her. You could have won her back, fixed her reputation, and had everything you ever wanted."

At that, Claude looked up.

"That's right, Claude. But instead, you threw it all away. What were you thinking?"

"I . . . I . . ." Claude turned red and shifted his feet.

Ben shook his head. "She can't stand the sight of you, and neither can I." He headed back into the chapel, leaving Claude alone.

* * *

*They're right to despise me. I'm the monster they say I am.*

Claude stood outside, watching his brother leave. He touched his shoulder, which was bruised from Ben landing on him. *I suppose I deserved that.*

He lowered his head and walked the streets, finally thinking about his actions from everyone else's point of view.

Eventually, he found himself at the temple block. He sat on a granite stone and stared at the packed dirt ground, hating himself. Why *hadn't* he stepped in to defend Hannah? Because it would draw attention to himself and his own error in the situation. People would look down on him.

*Am I so shallow then?* He hated the answer.

No one else was at the temple site this late in the evening. He could see where workers had laid their tools in boxes and piles before stretching their backs and heading off for their suppers at home—homes that were likely filled with loved ones waiting for them.

A couple of years ago such thoughts wouldn't have had any impact on Claude. He and his brothers had been young, eager to see the world and experience new things. His mission had been an adventure. Now, he had seen enough of the world to satisfy that hunger. Now, as he sat on the cold stone, he knew he wanted something more.

He smiled wryly at how the thought of home and hearth had become his heart's desire, when before it would have seemed too mundane to actually wish for. Even yesterday he would have laughed at such a dream. Walking through the streets with a handsome woman on his arm seemed like the better prize. Yet today he would give almost anything to have the mundane dream—now that he had destroyed his own chances of finding happiness with a sweet, kind woman. Not just a woman who was beautiful to look upon, but a woman who was beautiful inside, as well.

Someone like Hannah.

Was there any way he could rectify his mistake and still win the prize? He recalled vividly the moment she'd sent him away after her memory returned—the bitterness in her voice and the hard expression on her face. The image tore at his mind, and he winced.

He pictured the look on her face at the dance—begging, pleading. What had he done?

He had walked away. He couldn't imagine anything he could do now to compensate. After tonight, seeing him around town would cause her pain. And if Phillip were to pursue his feelings with Hannah, Claude's presence would only complicate that and make life miserable for them.

He sighed, hating his dismal life. Instead of anyone who cared about his whereabouts, he had two brothers who surely despised him by now, plus a woman he loved who also despised him—not to mention her family.

More and more of late he had wanted to move back home. He missed eating burned dinners with his brothers. But now he felt even more like a stranger.

*Can I at least make things right at home? If so, how?* He looked up at the dark sky, posing the question to the heavens. The stars gave no answer. Claude pushed himself up off the stone, hardly noticing the rough surface scraping his palms. He paced around the rising walls, stopping on the east side, in front of what he thought was Ben's Earth stone. Now put in place, it stood taller than Claude. He ran his hand across the orb carved into the front, smooth and perfect. He sighed, then walked along the edge of the temple and turned to the south side, where the walls weren't as tall. Here, only a couple of Earth stones were in place, with the rest of the wall shorter between them. He hoisted himself up between two Earth stones where the rock was only about four feet high, then slid across the nine-foot-deep wall. Once inside the temple proper, he looked at the stones from the back. Sure enough, there was the *J* scrawled on the back of a stone. It was the block they had hauled from the quarry.

He ran his hand over the letter, then walked along the course of the other stones, his fingers brushing the letters of the alphabet running in order along the row. Each block represented the work of possibly dozens of men—drilling, cutting, blasting, and forming the rock to just the right shape and size, then loading it onto wagons, transporting it, doing final adjustments, fitting it in place, securing it with mortar. He turned and looked around at the gray walls that grew so slowly. Abandoned tools and a myriad of footprints testified of the work done each day. Now, he saw no one else save the occasional passerby on the street.

He was alone. So alone.

It wasn't that long ago—and yet it seemed a lifetime—since he and Phillip had come here to mark history by taking photographs of the rising walls. Now, Phillip's dreams of running a photography business were in ruins, thanks to Claude's actions.

*First Cybil. Then Hannah. Then Phillip. Then Bishop Hansen. How many lives have I personally ruined?*

He shook his head, hating how the temple walls made him feel. Instead of joy and anticipation—which everyone else in town seemed to be experiencing at the thought of the temple—he felt only self-reproach and loathing. And a complete lack of worthiness. Someday years hence, the temple would be complete. And then what? Would he feel worthy to enter?

*No. I don't belong anywhere near these walls.*

As if he was doing wrong just by being there and needed to escape sacred ground, Claude hurried toward the eastern side. One day doors would be there, and he could already see a gap marking the space. He scrambled down the new granite steps. As his feet hit the dirt on the other side, his breathing grew ragged. Anxiety growing inside him, he wanted nothing more than to escape the growing symbol of his unworthiness.

*I have to get away.* Hands deep inside his coat pockets, he strode down the street toward the hotel. An urgency built inside him, one that didn't dissipate even when the temple grounds were well behind him.

Moonlight spilled weakly onto the road as he picked up his feet and ran faster, trying to leave the oppressive feeling behind. He ignored the burning in his lungs and the cold sweat breaking on his forehead as he rounded corners and eventually reached the hotel. His legs pumped, taking the steps two at a time. He practically ripped his door off its hinges.

The dark, heavy guilt still covered him like a cloak, making him anxious and restless. He had to do something, anything to rid himself of this feeling. Back and forth, back and forth, he paced his small room.

*Away. Leave the city.*

But the thought immediately brought others on its heels—Phillip and his studio, Hannah at the dance.

*I have to make things right. I can't just run like a coward,* he thought, wishing he could do exactly that.

But cowardice and fear were exactly what had led him to this point. If he hadn't been so afraid of losing Hannah, he would never have exploded like he did. He would have listened. He would have believed her. And he wouldn't have destroyed the studio or accused Phillip of betraying him.

*I'm not just unworthy. I'm yellow-bellied.*

He exhaled heavily, then glanced at the corked ink bottle on the table. His stomach sank, and the more he thought about what needed to be done, the heavier it felt. If it dropped much farther, it would reach his toes.

He eyed the table as if it were an opponent in a game or a wild beast he had to fight. With another deep breath, he strode to the desk, pulled the chair out, and sat down. When he placed his arms against the top, he noticed they were shaking. He wiped his palms on the sides of his pants and opened the drawer. Gingerly, as if reaching for a flame, he lifted one sheet of paper, a second, and a third. He'd start with Phillip. That letter would be the easiest.

With an unsteady hand, Claude uncorked the bottle and dipped the nib of his pen into the ink. The note was short and to the point.

> *Phillip,*
>
> *Except for a few dollars to cover expenses on the road, I'm leaving behind my share of the farm sale. It belongs to you now. I hope it's enough to pay off your creditors and give you a new start on your studio.*

The pen hovered over the page for a moment as Claude debated whether to add more.

Should he add an apology—I'm sorry? I'll miss you? I know I'm a pathetic example of a brother? Good-bye?

Nothing felt right, so he just signed his name and set the paper aside to let it dry while he wrote the next letter. This one would be harder, but he already had a good idea of what it needed to say, so he went ahead and began writing. He prayed it would be enough.

> *Dear Editor,*
>
> *Please print the following announcement, using the enclosed payment.*

Then he sighed hard and wrote the difficult part.

> *Be it known throughout Salt Lake City and its environs that the young woman known in the recent editorial and around the Salt Lake City area as "Miss H" is completely and utterly innocent of any wrongdoing. The situation that resulted in the recent scandal was nothing more than an unfortunate misunderstanding.*
>
> *The photograph in question was actually of a relative of Miss H in a private moment with her betrothed. I refused to accept Miss H's explanation and reacted unfairly. The resulting escalation of rumor is completely unjust. There is nothing in this young woman's character to support such accusations. I apologize to the family of this young woman and hope that one day they can forgive me for not being the man I ought to have been in this situation.*
>
> *I, Claude Adams, declare that I am the only person at fault, and that Miss H should be exonerated and her reputation restored.*

He shook his head and set the letter aside, hoping that it would be enough. The third sheet of paper lay on the desk, waiting for him to write his final message. He stared at that one a long time before beginning, and when he did, he moved slowly, dipping the pen into the ink, wiping the nib on the edge of the bottle, holding the tip over the page for a long moment before making a single stroke.

After writing *Dearest Hannah* he stopped. What could he say that she would actually read, that she wouldn't hate him for? He took a deep breath and launched into the letter, acknowledging his responsibility and hoping that one day she could forgive him.

He went on to explain his attempts at restitution in the newspaper and with Phillip, then poured out his soul and his hopes for her future happiness. He stared at the end, wishing after he had written it that he hadn't closed with *love* before adding his signature, but knowing that it was still true. Now, he saw more to Hannah than her raven-black hair and her deep brown eyes. He saw her inner goodness, her heart, her humor, her worth as a daughter of God. He truly loved her more now than he ever knew he could love another human being. But he needed to let her go.

The hardest part was done.

Claude pulled on his jacket and checked the other two letters to be sure the ink had dried. He blew slightly on the last one, then folded them up and slipped them all into envelopes. Into the one for the newspaper, he included some coins—what he hoped would be plenty to cover the cost of the announcement.

He packed his belongings, checked out of the hotel, then went back home for the last time. Quietly, he went inside and stole up to his room. He quickly packed his remaining clothing then dug the last of his money from under his mattress. He counted out a few dollars for travel and put them into his pocket, but the rest he left in a sack.

He quietly went down the stairs and into the kitchen, where he left the sack of money on the table with the letter to Phillip. He paused and added one more thing to the sack, then went to the front door. He opened it and stepped out, but turned around to look into the house a final time—only shadowy shapes in the darkness.

"Good-bye," he whispered, then stepped out.

He made his way first to the *Deseret News* office, where he slipped the envelope into a mail slot. The letter wouldn't be published until Monday, but it was the best he could do. Before he lost his nerve completely, he hurried to the Hansen home and tucked Hannah's letter into the screen door.

Then he walked down the lane and paused at the end, his hand on the gate.

"Good-bye, Hannah," he said. "Have a good life."

Claude hitched his duffel bag onto his shoulder, hefted his valise in the other hand, and trudged toward the rail station. He'd spend the night there and catch the first train heading back East. He realized now that he had one more person he needed to make amends with—quite possibly the one he had hurt the most. Cybil.

For her, a letter most certainly wouldn't be enough to make things right. He wondered if he would marry her, if he'd arrive to discover that he'd soon be a father. He gulped at the thought but knew he'd do what was necessary. He had made her a promise and would make it right.

And what if he didn't need to marry Cybil? Then where would he go? It didn't matter, and he didn't care, so long as he left Salt Lake City and Zion behind—everything that reminded him of his shame.

* * *

The morning after the dance, Hannah sat at the kitchen table with her head against the wall, staring blankly ahead. After last night's fiasco, she hadn't wanted to get out of bed. Sitting in the kitchen, it was too easy to let her mind go back to the tone of Jared's voice, the look on Marilyn's face, the actions of the crowd—and the total humiliation of being surrounded by people who thought she was riffraff.

Under her quilt she could burrow into the folds and keep the world out of her personal reality. In the near darkness of her room, she didn't have to think or talk or face anyone. Visitors alone would do her in. So she sat at the table, facing the door in case she needed to bolt—or hobble—up the stairs.

Between Bethany, her father, and the doctor all insisting that she get up and get dressed each morning, she didn't have much say in the matter.

This morning, Bethany had thrown the covers aside and pulled her off the bed. Without the strength to fight, Hannah figured it would be simplest to obey orders—but no one could expect her to do so cheerfully. What did strengthening her legs and arms matter when she couldn't venture into public without being mocked and ridiculed?

"Are you going to eat your toast?" her father asked as he stood from his breakfast.

She shook her head slowly. Her toast was cold and hard. The fried egg beside it, intended as a treat for her, was cold, too. She didn't care. Her father left the room, sadly shaking his head.

Bethany lifted a pail of dirty water from the counter and carried it to the back door. Holding it open with one leg, she swung the pail out, sending the water into an arc over some shrubs. On her way back inside, she paused as her eye caught something. She bent down and picked it up—an envelope.

After looking at the handwriting, Bethany's face screwed up in anger. With one hand, she balled up the envelope and marched to the oven. She snatched a dishcloth, used it to open the oven door, then paused and looked at Hannah.

"What?" Hannah asked, bewildered.

Bethany slammed the metal door closed and folded her arms with the crunched-up envelope still in one fist. After a deep sigh, she said, "Do you want to read it? It has Claude's name on it."

She shuddered. "No. Burn it."

With a nod, Bethany turned back to the oven. "That's what I thought."

But as soon as the oven door had opened, revealing the orange ribbons ready to consume the paper, a strange urge came over Hannah. If the words were burned before she read them, she'd always wonder what Claude had to say for himself.

"Wait."

Bethany already held the paper so close that the edges were singed, but she pulled back and stood straight. "You want to read it?"

"May I?"

"If you wish," Bethany said in a tone that made it all too clear that she disapproved. She blew on one corner of the envelope where smoke rose in a white spiral, then dropped it onto the table and stalked out. Hannah was grateful to be alone, even if that meant Bethany was angry.

Hannah smoothed the envelope onto the table, trying to make the wrinkles flat. She pulled out a single sheet of paper. Without opening it at first, she smoothed it against the table, too.

Finally she lifted the first fold, and then the second. Reading the words was painful at first, especially since, as she read them, Claude's voice spoke them in her mind.

*Dearest Hannah,*

*I did not fully understand what I had done to you, your family, and your future until I witnessed the events at the dance last night. I see now that I am indeed the foul villain your sister has painted me to be. I turned away, a coward, and as I left the room, Phillip did the right thing.*

*I wouldn't blame you at all for hating me for the rest of your life. But I certainly hope that one day you will be able to forgive me, as I do not think I will ever be able to forgive myself.*

*Tonight I try to make restitution. As soon as I finish writing this letter, I will deliver an announcement to the newspaper declaring your innocence.*

Relief washed over her. A recantation might not travel as quickly as scandalous news, but perhaps people would now read—and believe—the truth. She imagined what it might be like to resume a normal life, without any taint.

*I am giving my share of the farm money to Phillip so he can restore his studio.*

Such a sacrifice couldn't be easy for Claude.

*And then I will leave town so that you may begin a new life without ever seeing me and being reminded of what I have done to you.*

To think of Claude no longer living in town was a relief, albeit a bittersweet one. She felt guilty for being glad she wouldn't be facing him anytime soon. For his sake, though, she was sad. Where would he go and what would he do? How would his brothers take the news?

> *I hope my efforts are enough. If nothing else, I know you will be in better hands now than if I had stayed and somehow managed to win back your love. Phillip is much more worthy of such a prize than I ever was or could hope to be. His love for you is purer than mine. The letter I wrote when I first declared my feelings for you was really written by Phillip. He poured out his true feelings to you, but he let me sign my name at the bottom. I wish you happiness together. If I never see you again, know that I am deeply sorry and regret everything I did.*

In shock, Hannah didn't even register his signature at the bottom. Instead, she stared at a paragraph above for several seconds. Not until she gasped for breath did she realize she had been holding it.

*Phillip is in love with me?*

Like the sun outshining a candle, that one revelation overshadowed everything else in the letter. She could hardly comprehend it.

Could it be true? Did Phillip really love her? Claude wouldn't lie about such a thing, would he? Certainly not if he were being repentant.

Phillip had taken such time to care for her of late. She thought about the flowers and the times he'd started to tell her something, only to stop himself. She remembered Claude's first love letter, and the tender words came back to her.

*It was written by Phillip? By Phillip!*

Her heart pounded so fast and so hard that it felt ready to leap out of her chest.

*What do I do?*

Suddenly having more energy than she'd had in weeks, she stood and paced the room, still favoring one foot as she clasped the letter in her hands as if it were a love note from Phillip himself.

Claude clearly assumed Phillip had said something. *Does Phillip really care for me,* she wondered, *or is Claude assuming that Phillip wrote the love letter so poignantly because he must have felt the same way? Did Phillip actually* say *he felt the same way toward me as Claude did?*

Phillip had never done or said anything to indicate such feelings. *Neither have I, and yet . . . I do feel that way toward him.*

It was the first time she had admitted as much to herself, the first time she had entertained such thoughts without squelching them. But now what? Someday soon Phillip would arrive with another bouquet of flowers, and she couldn't behave as if she knew nothing.

Yet how could she do otherwise?

She tucked the letter into her pocket, then plopped onto the chair and dropped her head into her hands. *What am I to do the next time I see him?*

# CHAPTER 27

Phillip balanced this week's flowers in their earthenware pot, hating that he was bringing only petunias. He didn't want to repeat the same flowers, and he was running out of options. Yet he never did like petunias. Why the kind of flower he brought her bothered him so much, he wasn't sure—unless it was because his last visit with Hannah had been different, special, and petunias were so ordinary.

As he turned into her lane, he wondered if he had been right to remain silent last night. Hannah had given him a look that gave him hope of her affections. It was that look, plus her ease with his touch as they had walked with his arm protectively around her shoulders, that made him think maybe, just maybe, he could have shared his true feelings with her.

*But I let fear get the better of me,* he thought as he raised his hand to knock. Had it really been too soon to mention anything, or had he wasted a romantic, moonlit evening, which—as Ben had said once—was the most conducive atmosphere for romance? "Trust me on this one," Ben had said, grinning. "I know."

"Phillip!" Hannah peered at him from the other side of the door, looking flustered. He hoped his visit wasn't an unpleasant surprise.

It was good to see her answering the door. He smiled and held out the flowers. "Purple petunias." He almost mentioned how he wanted to find another yellow flower to match her dance gown. But she might not want a reminder of the dance. On the other hand, it might make her recall their private moment, which could be a good thing. Either way, he wasn't sure, so he bit his tongue.

She leaned against the doorjamb and held the flower pot. "Thank you, Phillip." Her cheeks had much more color than they'd had the night before, but she seemed to be avoiding his eye. She picked at a leaf. "And thank you for—for helping me last night."

"You're welcome." Phillip flushed, wondering how much of last night she was thinking about. Punching Jared wasn't the part his thoughts kept wandering back to. "When Claude left the dance, I couldn't help myself and—" His voice cut off, and he silently berated himself for bringing up his brother.

Hannah lowered her eyes. "Have you heard from Claude? Because I . . ."

Phillip frowned. His brother was not a subject he wanted to think about. Of course, Phillip was the one who had brought him up—right when he was dreaming about confessing his heart. Brilliant. His brow knit together, and he stammered, "Claude? No, I . . . uh . . . have you?"

Hannah fumbled with her skirt pocket, seemingly distracted. "Actually, yes. This morning Bethany found a letter from him by our door."

A knot formed in Phillip's throat. What did it say? Had Claude tried to undo his actions from the night before? Had Hannah decided to give him a second chance? Hannah took a moment to say more. It felt like an eternity.

"You don't know then?" she asked. "Claude's gone."

"What do you mean?" Claude hadn't lived at home for weeks now. That wasn't news.

"He's left the city," Hannah said, rushing on. "He said he was sorry and that he would try to make things right. Apparently he sent a letter to the paper explaining the rumors and clearing my name, and then he said that . . ." Her voice trailed off as if she were about to say something more, but instead she shook her head. "Then he left town. He didn't say where he was going."

"Strange," Phillip said. "I wonder if he left us a letter. If he did, I didn't notice it." After being with Hannah last night, he had hardly slept, and this morning he had no stomach for food, so he hadn't gone into the kitchen.

She finally lifted her chin and met his gaze. Phillip searched her face for what it all meant to her. "Did he say anything else?" He hoped his brother hadn't planted one more love letter to woo and confuse her.

He was surprised to see a smile slowly steal across her face. She blushed, and, instead of answering, lowered her head and shyly asked, "Would you like to go for a walk?"

Her response made no sense, and he felt as if there were something big he was missing. But she seemed eager to be with him, so there was no reason to turn down a stroll. "Sure. I'd like that."

She nodded toward the flowers. "I'll put these inside first and be right out." Backing into the house, she seemed to have a glow about her, making her even more beautiful. His heart skipped a beat as he said, "I'll wait for you by the fence."

She nodded silently and watched him go. He looked over his shoulder and caught her staring at him. Starting, she quickly went inside, letting the screen door bang shut.

* * *

Hannah stood at the kitchen window, clutching the pot of flowers in her hands. She could see Phillip standing outside, his back to her. What she wouldn't give to be able to see his face—and read his thoughts. A bit of dirt fell from the pot, bringing her back to the present. Fumbling with shaky hands, she watered the flowers and set them in the center of the table, then stood back and admired their color. She felt the shape of Claude's letter in her pocket, glanced out the window at Phillip, and stepped outside.

As she approached Phillip, she felt a queer excitement in her middle and put a hand on her stomach to calm it. Of late she had come to admire how truly handsome Phillip was. She still couldn't understand how she hadn't noticed until recently, with his dark hair and deep brown eyes, so different from Claude's blond hair and blue eyes. But when she thought of Phillip, it wasn't so much his appearance she pictured, but rather the feel of his arm pulling her close as they walked the dark streets of the city, protecting her from those trying to do her harm.

She walked closer, having a wild urge to come up from behind and put her arms around him. Maybe he'd turn around and hold her in return, and then . . .

She shook off the notion and tried to breathe deeply. Claude might have been horribly wrong about Phillip's feelings, after all. Men rarely discussed such things with one another—at least, so she'd heard. What were the chances of Phillip sharing such an intimate emotion with a brother who felt the same way about her?

*What are the chances of having two suitors from the same family?* Instead of being flattered, she felt divided in what she could believe.

She joined Phillip by the fence. At the sound of her footfall, he turned around. His face was unreadable as he held out his arm and she slipped her hand through it. With her other hand, she felt the envelope in her pocket. They walked for a block or two before she broke the silence.

"I—I hope Claude is all right," she said, trying to find some way to broach the topic that was burning into her soul. Instead, all she could think of was the stunning news of Claude's disappearance. "He didn't say where he was going, just that he didn't plan on coming back."

Phillip sighed, his shoulders sagging slightly. "It's a bit of a shock, and I still can't quite believe it. He's just . . . gone?"

Hannah nodded.

"Claude's a smart one," Phillip said. "He has a good head on his shoulders, so he'll be fine. We'll miss him, that's for sure. I hope he writes to let us know where he is. But it's sad that he decided that was the only solution."

"But he was trying to *find* a solution," Hannah offered. "That's saying something."

"Yes, it is." Phillip hesitated in his step, as if he wanted to stop and question her.

*You simpleton!* Hannah berated herself. *Stop talking about his brother! He probably thinks I want Claude back in my life.* Why had she brought him up? In a sense, he led to the point she wanted to get to, but surely there was a better way of arriving there. But what else could they talk about? Certainly not the other piece of information in the letter. If it was accurate—if Phillip really did care—how could she take a step to cross the divide between them so he'd know that she felt the same way? She couldn't confess anything unless she was certain the sentiment would be requited.

Phillip didn't say anything for a while. The longer he remained silent, the worse Hannah's stomach squirmed—and the more intensely she knew something must be said to break the silence.

They approached the Adams home, and Ben came down the porch, walking with determination. With his eyes on the ground as he strode, he didn't notice the pair until he nearly ran into them.

Ben stopped short when he saw them. "You," he said, "are just the person I'm looking for." He carried a sack in one hand and waved an envelope in the other—an envelope exactly like the one hiding in Hannah's pocket. She stifled a gasp.

"Seems to be a day of letters," Phillip said dryly. "I assume that's from Claude. What does he say?"

"That he has up and left, the half-wit," Ben said, pushing the envelope and the sack into Phillip's chest. "These are for you. He left them in the kitchen. I didn't realize what the letter was until I read it."

"What did it say?" Phillip asked, taking the envelope so he could open it.

"Just read it," Ben said, still holding the bag.

Phillip unfolded the letter, which was brief. He held it to the side, letting Hannah read along. She held her breath, wondering if Claude had hinted at anything between her and Phillip in the letter. He hadn't. This note was short, explaining what she already knew—that Claude had left his money to pay for the studio.

Phillip slowly folded the letter and walked to the house porch, then sat on a stair. "I can't believe it."

"Believe it," Ben said, tossing the money sack to Phillip. "This is all yours. I never would have thought he was capable of doing something like this." He sighed and looked around the street. His eyes looked shiny. "Wish I knew where he was, though. Ma would have a fit if she knew one of us was on our own." He stared at the ground, jaw working. "I kind of blame myself. Last I saw him, I said I couldn't stand the sight of him. Apparently he took me at my word."

"You can't blame yourself for this," Phillip said, rising.

But Ben waved his brother's words away. He rubbed the back of his neck with his hand and sniffed, avoiding their eyes. After clearing his throat, he said thickly, "I—uh, I think I'll go inside for a bit."

As he strode up the stairs, Hannah felt a twinge of guilt because she was glad he had gone—she needed to be alone with Phillip for a minute. She joined him on the porch but didn't say anything. Phillip seemed lost in thought.

He hefted the sack, noting it held something besides coins. After untying the cord on top, he looked inside and pulled out a heavy, folded paper that had obviously been crumpled. He opened it and smiled wryly. Marie's photo, or what was left of it. Hannah chuckled. "So he had it this whole time. The image is almost gone now."

Phillip quietly folded it again and put it back into the sack, wondering if he'd eventually burn the picture that had cost them all so much. He tied the cord again and sighed. Where was Claude now? What would become of him now that he had no more money? He had never been a worker. How would he support himself? Phillip lapsed into worried silence.

"Are you all right?" Hannah murmured a few minutes later.

"I'm fine," Phillip said absently, staring at his hands, which were clasped together. "It's just so strange. I haven't seen Claude much in the past several weeks anyway, what with him moving out, but his leaving has created a sudden hole, you know?"

She nodded, not knowing what else to say. He turned toward her. "Would you mind if we went back to your place and read the letter he wrote you? Mine is so short, it doesn't say much of anything. Maybe if I understood why . . ." His voice trailed off because of the panicked look on her face. Her fingers went to her pocket, feeling the letter inside. Phillip raised a hand and apologized. "Never mind. I'm sorry. I shouldn't invade your privacy."

"No, it's not that," Hannah said quickly. Thoughts flew past her mind in a whirlwind. What should she do? He didn't know that the letter was in her pocket. On one hand, giving it to him would be an easy way to open a conversation about their relationship. On the other, if Claude were wrong, sharing the letter was an easy way to damage their budding friendship.

And yet . . .

She inhaled deeply, steeling herself, then withdrew the letter. "My letter does say a bit more," she said weakly. "And I brought it with me." She held it out for him to take and noticed it trembling.

"Are you sure?" Phillip raised his eyebrows and tilted his head. "You don't mind?"

Everything from the anticipation of joy to utter terror shot through Hannah. Her throat constricted with emotion. She couldn't speak and instead just nodded her head to encourage him. As he opened the letter, she turned slightly away and squeezed her eyes closed as if waiting for a verdict. Silence unfolded behind her like a long stretch of never-ending road, and the torment was almost more than she could bear. She could feel her neck and ears heating up and thought the letter must have grown in length for all the time it was taking Phillip to read.

Why, oh *why* had she let him read it?

"So . . ." Phillip said quietly as he replaced the letter in the envelope.

Hannah could do nothing but nod. She rotated a couple of inches away. "Is it—is it true?"

Again, silence. Hannah's chest was ready to burst with anticipation as she waited. When he didn't answer, her expectations crumbled. She swallowed, then turned her face a few inches over her shoulder as he spoke.

"Do you *want* it to be?" he asked.

Sudden tears welled up in her eyes. Risking everything, she nodded and slowly turned back to face him. A blink sent tears spilling down her cheeks. "Very much." Phillip let out a stuttered breath and closed his eyes. He faced her straight on.

"Last night, I almost made a confession." He reached forward, his fingers smoothing through her hair and urging her head forward. If her heart had been thudding before, it was now an entire drum section. She swallowed hard, unsure of anything but leaning into his hand and closing her eyes at his touch. She had a fleeting thought—*What's happening?*—before she felt him move forward quickly and press his lips against hers.

For a second she couldn't breathe. Then she relaxed and kissed him back, thrilling at the feel of his lips. She reached her hands around his head and ran her fingers through his hair, unable to believe what was happening, yet wanting nothing else. Here she sat kissing a man in public, and she didn't care. Let anyone see her. Nothing mattered; she was safe in Phillip's arms.

A moment later they drew apart, and Hannah turned and rested her head on his shoulder the way she had wanted to after the dance. She could hear his heart thudding wildly in his chest, a twin to her own.

Neither spoke for several minutes, instead relishing the moment so it wouldn't end. "That's my confession," Phillip finally said.

Hannah closed her eyes and smiled, unable to imagine being any happier for the rest of her life. "Mine too."

* * *

"Father?" Bethany spoke quietly as she pushed the door open with her arm and brought in a supper tray, the newspaper tucked under her arm. He didn't say anything in reply, just rolled slightly and looked over to acknowledge her presence. Bethany crossed to his bed and sat at the foot. "I brought you some corn and fried potatoes. I left the skins on just the way you like them."

He nodded and slowly sat up. He had managed to get up and take care of his basic church duties recently, but he still didn't quite have his strength back yet. Yesterday's Sabbath meetings had sapped much of his energy, so Bethany insisted he get a lot of rest today. She placed the tray on his lap, then pulled the *Deseret News* from under her arm. "Here, Father. I thought you might like to read today's paper."

Wearily, he shook his head, then spoke. "I don't think I'll ever want to read a newspaper again as long as I live."

"You don't mean that, Papa," Bethany said, slipping into the name she used to call him as a little girl. "Besides, there's an interesting notice you'll want to see." She flipped through the pages then folded the paper and pointed. "Right there."

Her father rubbed at his forehead and squinted at the page. Bethany reached for his spectacles on the end table. "Here," she said. "These might help." Caring for him in this way still made Bethany feel as if she were the parent, an unsettling sensation at best, since her father had always been the strong one.

He leaned closer and read aloud. "'Take Notice: Left his home at Centreville Davis county, Utah Territory, on the 4th of September, THOMAS LYON, about 12 years old. He had on light blue pants, blue denim shirt, and a grey woolen cap.'" Looking up, he let the paper fall as he said, "Well, now, that's sad. He's been missing for a while now. I don't know the boy or his family. Why did you want me to read that?"

"Wrong notice," Bethany said. "I do hope they find the boy, but that's not the one I meant. Look at the one below that."

Again he squinted, brought the paper higher, and read. "'Be it known throughout Salt Lake City and its environs that the young woman known in the recent editorial and around the Salt Lake City area as 'Miss H'—" He stopped and looked up sharply at Bethany.

She nodded encouragingly. "Go on. Trust me. You want to read this."

He cleared his throat and went back to silently reading the page, but he looked wary, as if he were unsure whether this notice would be a good thing or one more catastrophe. Toward the end he spoke aloud again. "'. . . I, Claude Adams, declare that I am the only person at fault, and that Miss H should be exonerated and her reputation restored.'" He finished the notice with a trace of wonder in his voice. Leaning back against his pillows, he said, "I'm shocked and amazed. I didn't know the boy had it in him. Where is he? I'd like a word with him."

Bethany took the paper from his hands and said, "No one knows. He left town Friday night, leaving nothing behind except for this notice and a letter of apology for Hannah." She stared in alarm at his face. "Father, are you well?" She leaned forward in concern as he covered his face and began to shake.

"My sweet girl," he said as he cried. "My dear Hannah. Exonerated at last."

Through the window came the sound of wheels bumping over the road at a jarring pace. "What in the world?" Bethany said, dropping the newspaper to the bed and moving to the window. She pulled the curtain to the side and peeked out. "Why, it can't be!"

"Who is it?" her father asked, sitting up.

"It—it looks like Uncle Raymond and Marie," Bethany said, looking at her father, then back out the window to confirm. "And they're turning into the lane at a terrible pace. If he goes much faster"—she cringed—"the wagon just might tip. Why, it *is* Uncle Raymond."

She lifted her skirts and raced out of the room, down the stairs, and through the kitchen to meet them outside. Hannah beat her there, and the two of them waited, stunned, to see their relatives pulling into their lane for a second time this year. Before the wagon had a chance to stop, Marie jumped down, nearly catching her dress in the wheel. Her face was drawn, and she nearly threw her arms around Hannah, held her tight, then pulled back and began talking faster than a hen.

"Oh, Hannah, just look at you! Phillip's letter made it sound like you might not even be alive anymore, but you look like you could run circles around me! What about all the horrid rumors? What can I do to make them better now? Say the word, and I'll stand on the roof and yell to the world anything you say. I just wish I would have gotten his letter weeks and weeks ago when he first sent it, but when I got home from my summer visit, my Aunt Ruthanne was horribly ill in Nephi, and I had to go right away to help with her children. I was gone for ever so long. My parents just held the letter until I returned, not thinking it was anything urgent. But the moment I read it, I told Father that I had to come back to Salt Lake right away, and here we are. Is there anything I can do, anything at all?"

When she finally stopped for air, Bethany and Hannah laughed. "Everything is fine now," Hannah said. "But you certainly missed a lot. Come inside and we'll tell you everything."

# CHAPTER 28

FRIDAY, NOVEMBER 15, 1867

The leaves had changed to orange and red when the Hansens and two of the Adams brothers gathered at the Endowment House.

Grinning, Ben brushed aside a lock of hair from Bethany's eyes and whispered in her ear, "Do you suppose we should really do this?" With a nod of his head, he indicated Phillip and Hannah standing a few feet away, also dressed in wedding finery. They all waited just outside a sealing room in the Endowment House. Their father stood at the door, leaning on his cane and looking proud and happy prior to his daughters' double marriage.

Bethany took the bait. She leaned in to Ben and whispered back, "You think we shouldn't? Do you think we'll make everyone jealous at how happy we are together? That might be cruel." She smoothed his cravat and probed the baby's breath behind her ear, grateful she had dried some flowers before the first frost. They almost looked fresh. Her fingertips went to her breastbone, where her mother's pendant lay. Having her mother here was the only way this day could have been any better, but perhaps she was watching from on high.

"That's a better answer than mine," Ben said with a laugh. "I was just thinking that having two couples suddenly becoming Brother and Sister Adams—made up of a pair of brothers and a pair of sisters—could be a bit confusing." He tilted his head to the side in consideration. The gesture was one that endeared Ben to her. He looked more handsome now than she could ever remember. "On the other hand, it could provide some amusement. We could have fun doing things and blaming them on my brother and your dear sister." He played, "'Oh, heavens, *we* would never do such a thing. It must be the *other* Brother and Sister Adams.'"

Bethany laughed, then added, "Or to avoid the confusion, you could take my name instead, and the two of us could be Brother and Sister Hansen." Bethany grinned, knowing how ridiculous that would be—and what kind of talk such an arrangement would generate. The family had learned all too well of late what gossip could do.

Before Ben responded, Bethany continued. "You know, to avoid the whole problem, we could just move away." As soon as she said the words, she bit her lip, regretting them. Her words brought Claude's sudden flight back into raw focus. "I'm sorry—I shouldn't have said that. I wasn't thinking."

"It's all right. I know you said it in jest," Ben said, looking deeply into her eyes. "I love you, Bethany."

"And don't you forget it," she said, poking his chest with her finger. She rose to her toes and kissed his cheek. They turned to face Hannah and Phillip, who seemed lost in one another's eyes. For the briefest of moments, Bethany thought they looked like silly, puppy-eyed children. After all, she and Ben shared a deeper, more mature love after having gone through years of trials. But no, that wasn't fair. Phillip and Hannah might not have years to claim, but they most certainly had endured just as many trials.

"If you don't mind the interruption, may I hug your bride?" Marie asked, smiling.

"Well, I suppose," Ben said rolling his eyes as if it were an imposition, then laughing.

Marie and Bethany embraced. "I'm so glad you were able to make it."

"And be your maid of honor? Of course. Nothing would prevent me from going to my dearest cousins' weddings. You're beautiful. And I just had to come to say I told you so—although I never would have predicted such a tangled way of getting to the altar as the four of you managed. I'm still so sad I wasn't able to help clear Hannah's name."

"That wasn't your fault," Hannah said.

"I know," Marie said with a shrug. "But I still feel responsible for the whole mess."

"So when do we get to come to *your* wedding?" Bethany broke in.

Marie grinned. "In April. You will be there, won't you?"

"We wouldn't miss it for anything," Hannah said.

A man came up the stairs and approached them, carrying a paper. He looked around paused, suddenly perplexed. He consulted the paper again and looked up at the two couples ready to be married. "Brother Adams? Sister Hansen?"

They couldn't restrain chuckles as all four raised their hands.

The man raised his white eyebrows. "Oh, goodness. This could be confusing. Will you all make sure I seal the correct man to the correct woman?"

Hannah and Phillip sidled close to one another, and Ben and Bethany instinctively did the same. They all smiled, with looks that said there was no chance any of them would allow themselves to ever be separated from their beloved.

"Shall we?" Ben said, gesturing toward the open door where the sealer had entered.

Phillip held out an arm. "Elder brothers first," he said with a nod toward the sealing room.

"And elder sisters," Hannah added, her face glowing.

"If you insist." Ben patted Phillip on the shoulder as he led Bethany inside toward the altar.

Phillip and Hannah came in behind them, followed by the bishop, Marie, and Uncle Raymond. With the door closed, they all took their seats. Bishop Hansen sat at the head as one of the witnesses, and Uncle Raymond was the other. At the same moment, both brothers noted the chair of the second witness, and Bethany felt her throat grow tight when Ben and Phillip exchanged sad glances.

That witness seat should have belonged to Claude.

Bethany took Ben's hand across the altar. He still had his eyes trained on the chair. "He's fine," Bethany whispered, noting the furrow in Ben's brow. "And he'll be back. You'll see."

Looking emotional, Ben nodded. He squeezed her hand, looked at the sealer, and said, "We're ready, Brother. Let's make this woman my wife before she can argue her way out of here."

# EPILOGUE

APRIL 6, 1892

"We'll be able to see better over there," a young man of about twenty years said. He waved his parents closer to him, and the three wove their way through the heavy crowd. Not even in New York had he ever seen such a huge group of people in one place. If he had to wager a guess, he'd say there were a good fifty thousand gathered. "Pa, I had no idea there were so many people in Salt Lake City," he called over his shoulder.

"There *weren't* this many back then, Phil," his father said, gazing up at the huge temple and its towering spires. "Isn't it a sight?" he said with an awed shake of his head. Phil took his mother's gloved hand and led her forward, with his father following close behind.

"Almost there," Phil called over his shoulder. He glanced at his father, who was looking around as though he couldn't believe the throng either. How did Pa feel right now, coming back after all these years? Did he recognize anyone? Did he feel as if he'd come home, or did he feel like an outsider? By the look on his face, his return was more nerve-racking than happy. Phil wasn't surprised; they wouldn't have come at all if his mother hadn't insisted on it.

"Claude, you'll regret it for the rest of your life," Phil had heard her say a dozen times if once. "It's been a quarter of a century already. Go home for the celebration."

Pa hadn't agreed to the trip until just last week—*after* Mother had purchased the rail tickets. Phil led the way toward a platform built in front of several businesses, hoping they'd be able to stand on a step there.

If they couldn't get onto the platform, they might miss out on seeing the speakers and the choir, but even so, there really wasn't a bad spot. No matter where a person stood on the south side of the grand temple, he couldn't help but see the giant United States flag draped across the side of the enormous building, and he certainly couldn't miss seeing the object that was the center of the event—the big round capstone at the top of the tallest spire. Near it was a golden statue of an angel blowing a trumpet, which the newspaper said would be placed on top later that evening.

With the spire a good two hundred feet or more above the ground, everyone could see the capstone ready to be set into place—by electricity, no less. When they had first arrived at the temple block, the news that an electrical switch would release the capstone had buzzed through the crowd. Phil smiled to himself. Living in New York City, Phil no longer found electricity to be quite the novelty that folks in the West apparently did. He stopped at the crowded platform and helped his mother squeeze onto it.

"Thank you, son," she said quietly, leaning in and pecking his cheek. She stepped up, the soft, brown feather in her hat brushing Phil's hair as she went. Not finding enough room on the platform for themselves, Phil and his father stood in front of her. Phil looked over at his pa, wondering what he'd looked like when here a quarter century ago. People back home in New York often commented that Phil was clearly his father's son, that they resembled one another in a most startling way, except for the hair. Phil's was a few shades darker than his father's pale blond, which had in recent years turned almost white as he'd neared his fiftieth birthday—although Pa frequently reminded Phil that the five-decade landmark hadn't arrived quite yet.

Phil breathed in the early spring air, still crisp with a hint of winter, and looked around. The huge gray building before them was stunning in its beauty and majesty. It sparkled slightly in the springtime sunlight. To think that it had been built by rugged pioneers in the middle of a desert was almost incomprehensible. He almost wondered why it hadn't taken *more* than thirty-nine years to finish the exterior. They had a goal to finish the interior in one more year. He wondered if they'd reach it. That thousands of people had gathered here today in celebration of the capstone—and that hundreds more Mormons continued to come to the area—made him shake his head. Try as he might, he couldn't understand it. What made these people come here in the first place—and then *stay?*

So many stayed—but not his father, who had come to Utah as a toddler. That's all Phil knew. He turned his head, and from the corner of his eye he studied his pa—a man who had insisted that Phil treat women with the utmost respect, who valued honesty and integrity almost to a fault. From what Phil had heard about Mormons recently with all the newspaper coverage about the new temple and the people who built it, his father would fit right in. Not that his father was any less tight-lipped about the Mormons. If anything, he was more quiet about his past than ever. Phil's brow furrowed slightly. So what was it that had sent his father away from this place, from his family? He never spoke of whatever those events were—he refused to—but it didn't stop Phil from wondering about what had happened and whether Phil had any family in Utah. The ceremony began with the choir singing and the band playing grandly, their music so loud it surely carried for blocks. Phil couldn't hear the speakers all that well—and could only see their heads—but even so he felt impressed by one speaker, a man with a shock of white hair who seemed to captivate the audience. His father's eyes suddenly looked watery as he gazed at the temple.

"That's Wilford Woodruff," Phil's father said, his voice shaky. "I think he's the prophet now." He swallowed hard as if willing away emotion. On seeing such a swell of emotion, a similar wave came over Phil, and his eyes too began to water, even though he didn't know the import of what his father said.

Someone spoke loudly, and although Phil couldn't make out the words, he knew what it meant by watching those around him. A movement from the front of the crowd to the back sent everyone's heads tilting upward, and all eyes were on the capstone. Several men surrounded the scaffolding at the top, and only now did Phil realize that one of them hovered around what must be a camera.

"We're ready to drop the capstone!" a man yelled from the top of the spire.

With that, Wilford Woodruff nodded and, with great ceremony, flipped a large electrical switch. The stone was lowered slowly into place. After quickly assessing to be certain it was in proper position, a man on the scaffolding waved to the crowd below, and everyone cheered.

Behind him, Phil heard a young mother whisper to her daughter, "It's time for the Hosannah Shout, dear. Get out your handkerchief."

Led by the speaker with white hair, the crowd began waving white handkerchiefs, and in a powerful, loud voice, as one, they cried out what sounded like a sacred prayer of celebration to their God. The power and volume startled Phil. He looked around him as they shouted the words three times in succession. People around him had tears coursing down their faces. A sensation went through Phil that he did not understand. It made his very bones tremble.

Trying to shake off tears, Phil looked around and studied groups of people perched on roofs for a better view, mostly men and boys. On a handful of roofs, cameras on tripods snapped photographs of the event—the people, the enormous flag, the choir, the statue, and the scaffolding. But one cameraman wasn't focused on his work. Instead, he seemed to be staring directly at Phil. With so many people in the crowd, surely the man wasn't looking at *him*. Phil searched for someone else the man was studying, then looked back at the roof. Still the man gazed right in Phil's direction. The choir finished another number, and the group was dismissed. The man was climbing down his ladder.

Mother put her hand on Pa's shoulder, and his hand covered hers. His lips were pressed against each other as if he were fighting back emotion. She leaned down and said, "Are you glad we came? Isn't it all wonderful?"

Pa nodded, apparently too moved to say much beyond a husky, "Yes."

"The temple is beautiful," she said. "Magnificent. Just as you said it would be."

Pa just nodded and coughed, then turned his head and rubbed his hand down his face.

With a handkerchief, Mother dabbed her eyes. A sudden breeze caught the cloth and carried it away. "Oh!" she said, lifting her hand as if to call it back. "My handkerchief."

"Don't worry, I'll get it," Phil said, starting out to chase down the white square. It was his mother's favorite, with her initials embroidered on one corner.

When he was merely a step behind the handkerchief, someone else picked it up. Phil stepped forward, his hand out. "Thank you. That's mine," he said. Looking up, he was suddenly taken aback. The person holding the cloth was the man who'd been staring at him from the rooftop. Suddenly uncomfortable, Phil said, "It's—it's my mother's."

The man traced his finger along the embroidered letters *AA* as if they were meaningful to him.

Still with his hand extended for the handkerchief, Phil said, "Do I . . . know you?" He asked the question knowing full well he didn't know the man and couldn't have ever laid eyes on him unless he had been in New York City recently.

The man ran his open hand down his face as if in wonder. After another glance at the handkerchief, he shook his head. "I'm not sure . . . You look so much like someone I once knew. Last name Adams." He held out the cloth, letters forward.

Phil's head popped up. *A. Adams.*

Shock must have registered on Phil's face, because the man reacted to it and said, "You're an Adams, aren't you?"

Phil snatched the handkerchief away and tucked it protectively into his pocket. "Who wants to know?" he asked with all the brass of a boy raised in New York City.

The man shook his head and kept talking. "The resemblance is uncanny." He leaned in with a look of sudden understanding on his face. "Is Claude here? He's your father, isn't he?"

Phil's eyes widened, and he found himself nodding. "That's right," he said cautiously. He inadvertently looked over his shoulder toward his parents. The man followed his gaze but clearly didn't know exactly where Phil had been looking and couldn't spot his father.

The man extended a hand and said, smiling broadly, "I believe I'm your Uncle Phillip."

Stunned speechless, Phil took the outstretched hand and shook it. *Phillip?*

"I take it your father's over there?" he asked, inclining his head in the right direction.

Phil nodded and, with his jaw hanging slightly open in wonder, watched his newfound uncle walk toward his parents.

*I was named after an uncle?* Until this moment he hadn't known he *had* an uncle. He trotted after the man, trying to keep up as he wound his way through the thick river of dispersing people. Uncle Phillip—since that's how Phil had to think of the salt-and-pepper-haired man—glanced back as if making sure his nephew followed. He nodded with satisfaction when he saw Phil coming up from behind. Phil pointed toward his parents just a few yards to the right.

"Over there," he said, having finally gotten use of his voice.

Uncle Phillip paused in his step and searched the sea of faces that moved as people left the area and headed to their homes. When Phil reached his side, he said, "In the gray coat. My mother has a brown feather in her hat."

"Oh. There." Pointing, Uncle Phillip said it as a statement, not a question, his voice low. He no longer looked so eager to keep moving.

"Shall I introduce you?"

Without taking his eyes off his brother, Uncle Phillip shook his head. "No need. But thank you." With that he stepped forward deliberately, one foot at a time, until he reached Claude Adams. Phil stayed close, feeling as unsure as he was curious at what was about to transpire.

"*Claude?* Claude, is it really you?"

Pa, who had been openly enjoying the morning, suddenly froze. Phil held his breath as his father turned his head slowly toward the voice that had called his name. Almost imperceptibly his mouth opened, then closed. For the first time in his life, Phil couldn't read his father's face. Was he angry? Afraid?

After a moment of silence, Uncle Phillip closed the gap and threw his arms around his brother. Pa's arms hesitated only an instant before closing around Uncle Phillip. They clung roughly to one another. Pa's eyes closed tight, and his hands clenched his brother's coat as if he'd never let go. Phil watched, amazed, as the two men suddenly broke down and began sobbing onto one another's shoulders.

"You're back! I can hardly believe it!" Uncle Phillip cried out the words, pulled away and looked at Pa's face, then embraced him again as if the moment were all a vision liable to vanish with the morning dew. "Where have you been? Why did you never write to us? So much time . . ."

Phil had never seen his father shed a tear before, let alone sob like a child. It was almost as if Uncle Phillip were the father comforting a son. Pa pulled back and searched his brother's face. "Can I ever earn your forgiveness?"

"Oh, Claude," Uncle Phillip's face contorted with emotion. "You had it years ago."

Pa nodded, pressing his lips together with emotion as tears welled up again and spilled over. He lowered his head, rubbed his fist against his eyes, and quietly said, "Thank you." He stepped to the side and introduced his wife. "This is Annabelle, my wife."

Mother held out her hand. "I've heard so many good things about you, Phillip," she said. "It's good to finally meet you."

Stunned speechless, Phil could hardly believe his mother's words. She had known about Pa's brother? For how long? No wonder she had wanted Pa to go home. How much of Pa's past had she known, and why hadn't Pa ever told *him* about it?

A minute later, three women—one a good twenty or more years older than the other two—pushed through the crowd. They stopped several yards away, near the shop where Uncle Phillip's camera was still perched on the roof. They each held a music booklet; they had likely come from the choir platform. They looked inside, then backed up to search the roof. Not seeing who or what they were looking for, they put their hands on their hips and conferred amongst themselves.

Another woman joined them a moment later, this one with strawberry blonde hair swept up in a twist. She peered at the roof, shrugged, and gestured to a man a few steps behind her.

"I think some people are looking for you," Phil said, touching his uncle's arm and pointing.

Uncle Phillip grinned. He waved broadly and called to the group. “Hannah! Ben! Bethany!”

They all came over, including the two young women, who both had dark hair. Phil assumed they were sisters. The woman answering to “Hannah” looked to be about the same age as his mother. She was pretty, also with dark hair, but with a hint of gray in spots and with slight crow’s-feet at her eyes.

When she drew near, her hands flew to her mouth. “Claude? Oh my heavens, Claude!” She too threw her arms around him and hugged him hard, and as she pulled back, a stream of questions tumbled out. “We’ve wondered about you for so long! We never stopped praying for you. Have you been well? Where did you go?”

He laughed at her reaction and nodded, extricating himself enough to wipe his cheeks again and introduce his wife to the rest of the group. “To New York. I had to make things right there. Shortly after that, I met Annabelle, and she was willing to be patient and find the good in a man like me.”

Annabelle swatted his sleeve and shook her head. “You *are* a good man, Claude.”

“So, everyone, this is my wife, Annabelle. Annabelle, this is Hannah, my brother Phillip’s wife—correct?” Hannah and Phillip nodded, and he went on. “And this is my other brother, Ben.” His voice choked up at that point. “He gave me a whipping I certainly deserved not long before I left.”

Ben looked a bit sheepish and shrugged. “Probably shouldn’t have whipped you quite so well. I’ve regretted it many times, if it’s any consolation.”

The strawberry-haired woman stepped forward, smiling. “And I’m Bethany. Hannah’s sister, Ben’s wife, and the talkative—”

“Opinionated,” Ben interjected.

“—one of the group,” Bethany continued with a grin. “A pleasure to meet you.” She held out a hand to Annabelle.

“Likewise,” Annabelle said with a nod. She looked shy, but she smiled the entire time and kept leaning in to Claude and patting his arm, her eyes wet. “It’s so wonderful to meet you all. Claude has told me so much about you, and I’ve wanted to meet you for ever so long.”

Phil turned on his mother. "You *knew* all this time. Why didn't you tell me?" He had uncles and aunts and cousins—family—and never knew it. He yearned to know his father's past. He thought about the city streets he had walked through over the last day or so and wondered what his father had done in them as a small boy, as a youth—he wanted to know it all.

His mother put a hand on his cheek. "It was your father's place to tell his past, not mine. And he wasn't ready until now."

Claude gestured toward the two young women and then glanced from Hannah to Phillip. "Are these your . . . ?" His voice trailed off, making it a question.

"This here is one of our daughters, Rebecca," Phillip said, gently bringing her forward. Rebecca curtsied, then turned to the other girl, who Phil thought was quite pretty, with ringlets around her face and a pink flush to her cheeks. She shyly tossed a glance toward him, and his stomach turned over on itself. "And this," Uncle Phillip said, "is Hannah's niece—I think. Or maybe it's a second cousin once removed. I'm still confused at the relation. You remember Marie, Claude? This is her eldest daughter, Theresa."

Introductions made, Phil was secretly glad that this pretty girl wasn't a direct relation.

"We need to catch up. We bought the Hansen place. Come eat with us," Ben said. "Bethany's made one of her famous feasts. We'll have plenty to last us into next week as it is."

"Do come," Bethany said. "We have so much to talk about. And I need to get to know my sister-in-law."

Looking around the circle, Claude couldn't stop moving his head side to side in disbelief. "I can hardly believe I'm here with you all. It feels as if I never left, and yet—I can't believe you want me to stay."

Hannah stepped forward. "But you're family."

Annabelle leaned her head on her husband's shoulder. "I told you, Claude. I knew it."

He nodded, his eyes welling with tears, but was unable to speak for several seconds. Finally he said, "Thank you."

Phil didn't know what had just happened, but he could feel his heart swelling in his chest. He could sense a powerful love between these people and knew that his father was loved by them, even though Pa hadn't been sure he would be accepted, for whatever reason. These were people Phil himself would feel right at home with.

"The past is past, big brother," Phillip said, putting an arm around Claude's shoulders and leading him toward the street. Everyone else followed behind. "Forget about everything but today."

Claude nodded, put his arm out for his wife to take, and headed down the road without looking to check whether his son followed.

Phil came up behind. His mind swirled with everything that had just happened. He understood almost none of it—only that something had been fixed from his father's past.

He also knew that he now had an entirely new family, and the idea of having uncles, aunts, and cousins sent a joy through him that he hadn't known he was missing. He couldn't wait to get to know them all and feel even more connected to his roots than he did right now.

Theresa stepped up by his side. "Do you have any idea what all this is about?" she asked, nodding toward Phil's parents, aunts, and uncles.

"None whatsoever," Phil said with a laugh. He put his arm out for her to take, and together they headed for a delicious meal the likes of which Phil had never eaten.

That evening, after warming up leftovers, the family went back to Temple Square. The huge golden statue—which Phil learned was named Moroni—had already been put into place. They purchased tickets, then climbed the scaffolding high into the air, up to the highest tower, and looked over the city.

Block after block of businesses and houses extended across the valley. To the east were rugged, beautiful mountains, with more in the distance. The early spring breeze was chilly, more so from the top of the temple, and everyone hunkered farther into their coats.

The moment was like water on a parched throat, and Claude seemed eager to take it all in. "I never thought I'd feel right coming to see the temple—let alone stand on top of it."

His brothers moved instinctively to either side of him. Phillip spoke up first. "And now?"

"Now . . ." Claude looked down, cleared his throat, and raised his head. "Now, I feel like I'm finally home. Everything's *right* now."

Ben and Phillip both clapped their arms onto Claude's shoulders. "It *is* right," Ben said, "Now that you're home with us."

As they stood at the top of the temple, young Phil scanned the group gathered together. Here were his parents, plus more family than he had ever dreamed of having, including fourteen cousins between the two families. Wind or no, Phil couldn't imagine wanting to be anywhere else than right here, right now, with his expanded family—and a pretty girl just a few feet away.

Phil looked over at Theresa, whose nose was tipped with red in the cold. She smiled at him, warming him despite the chill.

Uncle Phillip's earlier words echoed in young Phil's mind.

*The past is past. Forget about everything but today.*

For the moment, that sounded pretty good.

# HISTORICAL NOTES

The fact that the Salt Lake Temple took forty years to complete is common knowledge, but some of the reasons are not. Roughly the last fifteen years of construction progressed at a good pace, but it was the first quarter of a century that was painstakingly slow.

The groundbreaking for the temple took place in 1853, and progress on the foundation went along until 1857, when the Utah War forced Saints to leave Salt Lake City. It was then that they buried the foundation of the temple—made of sandstone—to hide it from the U.S. Army. Upon unearthing the foundation, they found cracks all over it.

Due to a number of factors, including the Utah War and crop failures, the original sandstone foundation wasn't taken out until about 1862. Obviously, having to redo the foundation hindered progress considerably. But no one wanted another cracked foundation, so debate began as to what to use to make the new temple. Granite became the new choice. According to Wallace Alan Raynor's thesis about the Salt Lake Temple, although most of the foundation was replaced, not all of it was, and a handful of sandstone pieces remain today.

Granite, while stronger than sandstone, created another big factor in slowing construction. The original sandstone—a relatively lightweight rock—came from the Red Butte Quarry, only a few miles from the temple lot. The road from that quarry back to the site was mostly downhill, making for an easy haul. As a result, a team of horses could bring in two loads a day.

However, the gray granite was cut from the Little Cottonwood Quarry, nearly *twenty* miles from the temple block. Granite is much heavier than sandstone, and much too heavy for horses to pull. Only a three-yoke ox team could manage the weight of the blocks, which were about 2,500 pounds each. In addition, the teams didn't have the luxury of a gentle downhill slope, because the road from Little Cottonwood went up and down hills to navigate the canyon. The result of all of these elements was that one round-trip took *four days* to complete.

For this story, I assumed that one day was spent getting to the quarry, since traveling twenty miles without a load would be a relatively simple matter, and that the other three days were spent hauling the granite back to the temple site.

Finding enough oxen and wagons for the job became a significant challenge for Church leaders. This was due to a couple of factors. In both the spring and fall, most ox teams and wagons were needed for farm work. Then during the summer, animals and wagons still proved elusive because of another Church effort—helping Latter-day Saint immigrants make it across the plains to the Salt Lake Valley.

As indicated in the book, in the fall of 1867, the wards in and around Salt Lake were asked to bring in 1,500 loads of granite, and specific assignments were divided among the wards as to how many loads they were expected to haul from the quarry. Raynor observed that the load assignments appeared to be given largely based on a ward's geography and size, so the farther away and the smaller the ward, the fewer loads assigned.

Church leaders asked workers to bring their own wagons when possible because repairing Church-owned ones was proving so costly. I imagine that using their own wagons would make workers more careful as well. They were also required to bring food and supplies for both their animals and themselves.

Several solutions for the transportation problem were attempted, including a wooden railroad and a canal to float the stones to the temple block. All failed. The quarry was temporarily shut down in 1867 to await the completion of a standard railroad, which was finished in 1873, several years after the main story of this book. With the railroad in place, the progress on the temple increased dramatically: two dozen blocks of stone could be delivered in a single day.

The layers of granite (called *courses*) were fourteen inches high, and the walls of the temple at their thickest are nine feet deep. The stones are extremely large. For example, according to Raynor's thesis, the dimensions of the Earth stones Ben would have worked on were four and a half feet wide and twenty inches deep. The round globe of the stone was cut to be three feet, eleven inches in diameter. Each Earth stone weighed an enormous 5,600 pounds. Some have figured that each Earth stone, from start to finish, may have cost as much as $300 to complete (which today would be equal to about $4,000).

The shop where Ben first learned the stonecutter's trade, Parry Brothers', really existed, and the Parry brothers were instrumental as workers and even master masons for many early temples.

The pace of construction increased further in 1876 when the temple effort received an engine that could lift heavy stones. When the Logan Temple was completed in 1884, the engine that had been used there was brought to Salt Lake. With two engines running, stone could be laid twice as quickly, and the Salt Lake Temple rose relatively rapidly.

One thing to remember regarding Claude's drinking is that in 1867 the Word of Wisdom was considered a guideline rather than a measuring stick for Church membership and/or worthiness. It became binding at a 1908 general conference. The vast majority of Latter-day Saints still drank alcohol and used tobacco in 1867, many even growing tobacco on their farms. Once such example can be found in the Cotton Mission, which extended through much of Southern Utah, including the cities of Washington and St. George, which had tobacco fields and wine vineyards. Mission leaders reported about two-thirds of the Saints in the area abiding fully by the Word of Wisdom during the 1870s, which was considered high for Church membership, and they were rather proud of that percentage. Decreasing the use of those substances was a gradual effort—one that took decades. It is likely that missionaries in the field and returned missionaries alike would have had alcohol periodically, although getting drop-dead drunk like Claude did would probably have been highly unusual.

The Salt Lake Theater, the first in Utah—and at the time, the largest west of the Mississippi—was built at Brigham Young's request on the northeast corner of State Street and 100 South. The theater thrived for many years, finally losing ground to motion pictures, vaudeville, and people using automobiles to go longer distances for their entertainment. In 1928 it was sold to Mountain State Telephone and Telegraph, which razed the building.

Edwin Booth was a famed Shakespearean actor known for his signature role of Hamlet. He was the brother of John Wilkes Booth, who assassinated Abraham Lincoln, and the son of Junius (June) Booth, who was also an actor, known for playing Macbeth. Edwin was active in theater in New York and elsewhere for many years. While he did perform at the Salt Lake Theater, I do not know whether it was during the timeframe of this book. Edwin managed the Winter Garden Theater until 1867, when it burned down, so I thought it possible that without a theater keeping him back East, he could have been in Salt Lake late that summer. However, his trip to Utah might have been when he toured in the mid-1870s. Other famous people who performed on the Salt Lake Theater stage include Maude Adams, Ethyl Barrymore, Billie Burke, Buffalo Bill Cody, and P. T. Barnum. Much of the information about the theater, including the description of the interior, came from the book *Through Our Eyes* (published by the *Deseret News* on their 150th anniversary to commemorate the years of Utah history they'd reported on).

The Fourth Stake is fictional. A stake with that name probably existed, but any reference to it is fabricated and not intended to portray anyone who really lived there or served in leadership positions. As mentioned in the acknowledgments, Brother Franklin, the former stake president portrayed, and his adopted son Abe, the young Indian boy who helped Bethany, were added to the book briefly as a "hello" of sorts to my previous readers. Those who do not know these characters but who would like to learn about Abe as an adult can read my previous historical novel, *House on the Hill,* and its sequel, *At the Journey's End.*

In Phillip's time, a photography studio would have been referred to as a *gallery.* Since that term has a different connotation to modern readers, I avoided using it even though it would be correct in context. The so-called "wet plate" technique was used in photography during this time.

The worker at the temple lot who informs Phillip of the quarry closure is a nod to my husband's great-great-grandfather, Charles Lyon. Records indicate that he worked on the Salt Lake Temple, but we don't know exactly when or in what capacity. He moved to Hyde Park, Utah, in April of 1867, just four months before this book opens, so he wouldn't have really been in Salt Lake City during the time of the story.

The notice about twelve-year-old Thomas Lyon being missing was actually published in the *Deseret Evening News,* although it appeared three years earlier than in the story, on July 4, 1864. At the time of this story, the paper was weekly, and it came out on Mondays. The version of the notice here is slightly abbreviated from the original. There is a chance that Thomas Lyon could be a relative, since we had family living in Salt Lake City during that period, but we have no documentation to clarify any relationship.

As a side note, November 15, 1867, really was a Friday, and I picked the date for the double wedding not only because it fits well with the timeline of the story, but also because it's my father's birthday.

The temple capstone ceremony was held during the week of general conference on Wednesday, April 6, 1892, following a conference session in the Tabernacle. It boasted the largest crowd ever assembled in Utah—some 50,000 people—a record that remained unbroken for many years. People crowded into the area south of the temple, and many climbed onto rooftops to see better. Following the conference session, the congregation joined the rest of the crowd outside to witness the placing of the capstone. The events of that day portrayed in the book are accurate, including the Hosanna Shout, the angel Moroni being put in place later that evening, and people getting tickets that allowed them to go up onto the scaffolding and view the city from the temple towers. This opportunity began a few weeks before the capstone celebration.

The decades of work had been spent mostly on the exterior of the temple. As a result, finishing the interior in time for the dedication was a monumental feat that required long hours of labor and many pleas for donations to fund the effort over the course of that last year. Tens of thousands of dollars were raised to help complete the temple by the forty-year mark. During that time, art missionaries who had been sent to Europe to enhance their skills were called home to paint murals on the interior temple walls. Some of the murals weren't completed for a couple of months after the temple dedication, but most of the building was finished in time.

The Salt Lake Temple was finally dedicated one year to the day following the placing of the capstone, on April 6, 1893—exactly forty years after the cornerstone dedication marking the beginning of construction.

The month before the dedication, President Wilford Woodruff sent out a letter to Church members asking them to let go of grievances, forgive one another, and repent of any past offenses so that they would all be ready to be partake of the blessings of the temple. Many testimony meetings were held throughout the Church during that month to help heal some of these rifts between Saints. President Woodruff indicated that he felt the Lord would accept the temple, but he wasn't sure that the Lord would accept the people unless they repented.

While the dedication happened a full year after this story ends, I found it fitting to have Claude returning to Salt Lake City and receiving forgiveness from his family at such a significant temple event.

# ABOUT THE AUTHOR

Annette Luthy Lyon, Utah's 2007 Best of State fiction medalist, has been writing for most of her life. While she's been successful in magazine, newspaper, and business writing, her true passion is fiction. She graduated cum laude from BYU with a BA in English, and served on the Utah Valley chapter board for the League of Utah Writers for three years, including one year as president. She has received several awards from the League, including a Quill award and two Diamond awards. Annette and her husband Rob live in American Fork, Utah, with their four children. She figures she must have read *Anne of Green Gables* one too many times as a teen, because all three of her daughters are redheads. Her son didn't get the red hair, but since brains seem to come with all colors, he doesn't mind.

Annette loves corresponding with her readers. She can be reached through her website at www.annettelyon.com or through Covenant email at info@covenant-lds.com or snail-mail at Covenant Communications, Inc., Box 416, American Fork, UT 84003-0416.